Ed said, "I need to hear it from them."

The captain took his earphone out and handed it to him, but kept hold of the transmitter. The first thing Ed heard was the slosh of water, the men wading. Then an urgent whisper. "Did you hear that, Kovac?"

"Yeah. Someone yelling help. Where's it coming from?"

"That tunnel there. What was the colonel's name again?"

"Sheffield."

"COLONEL SHEFFIELD!"

Ed ground the earphone against his head, but could hear no answer. His heart hammered, wild with hope.

"That's him," whispered the voice in the earphone. "He heard us. COLONEL, HANG ON, WE'RE COMING."

"Reggie, did you see that?"

"Where?"

"Three o'clock."

"I don't see it."

"The water moved over there, about twenty feet."

The sloshing sound stopped, followed by silence. Ed pushed the earpiece so hard that pain spiked his eardrum. Nothing.

"Oh, God . . . Kovac, KOVAC!"

A scream blared, distorted, in the earphone, then gargled away to silence . . .

SLEEPER

STEVEN HARRIMAN

BERKLEY BOOKS, NEW YORK

SLEEPER

A Berkley Book / published by arrangement with the author

PRINTING HISTORY
Berkley edition / February 2003

Copyright © 2003 by Steven Spruill.
Cover illustration by Ben Perini.
Cover design by Jill Boltin.
Interior text design by Julie Rogers.

For information address: The Berkley Publishing Group,
a division of Penguin Putnam Inc.,
375 Hudson Street, New York, New York 10014.

ISBN: 0-425-18881-7

BERKLEY®
Berkley Books are published by the Berkley Publishing Group,
a division of Penguin Putnam Inc.,
375 Hudson Street, New York, New York 10014.
BERKLEY and the "B" design
are trademarks belonging to Penguin Putnam Inc.

PRINTED IN THE UNITED STATES OF AMERICA

10 9 8 7 6 5 4 3 2 1

To the Honorable David R. Oliver, Jr., submarine admiral and then Pentagon "bureaucrat"—always a leader and, in all ways, at all times, a dedicated public servant.

In the interests of security, the author has altered certain details of layout and construction inside the Pentagon. All possible accuracy has been preserved in portraying the hallways, offices, and inhabitants of this remarkable building we will never again take for granted.

PROLOGUE

←————————————————●————————————————

U-36, the North Sea
June 8, 1940

"I don't know what you're so nervous about, Lieutenant," the Gestapo major said.

Lieutenant Erich Hartmann kept his eyes to the periscope and his mouth shut. No point crossing swords with one of the Geheime Staatspolizei, even if the man was a waste of the boat's air.

Ja, I'm nervous, and you, Herr Major, are terrified.

Hartmann could smell Reinhard Grau's fear through the stink of diesel fuel and the gamey stench of the forty-four other souls bottled up in the U-boat. Five showerless days in the same clothes had overwhelmed the crew's fragrant lotions, but the major's soured adrenaline stood out—the reek of a man wrestling with dread.

Hartmann cupped his hands around the periscope's eyepiece to screen out the glow of the control room. Surface chop had forced the U-boat into an erratic corkscrew motion exaggerated at the tip of the scope, giving Hartmann a jerking image of a rugged cliff cut by an occasional glimpse of tan that might be the narrow target beach. The Abwehr briefing had promised a ladder bolted to the cliff but Hartmann couldn't make it out, even in sunlight far too bright for ten P.M. He longed for a steadier view through his 7x50 Zeiss binoculars, but that would mean surfacing, which he dared not do until dark, when binoculars would be useless. He risked enough as it was. The sun was painting the sea a bright green, in which the U-36 at periscope depth would make a dark, wavering streak, as eye-catching to an RAF pilot as the dartboard in his favorite pub.

"Maybe we should've given this mission to Prien," Grau said.

Hartmann felt his mouth twisting. Golden boy Günther, toast of the Fatherland for slipping his U-47 right into Scapa Flow and attacking the British fleet in its base. Sank the battleship *Royal Oak* at its moorings, winning himself the Knight's Cross from the Führer's own hand.

And sharpening the risk for all future North Sea missions.

The English would not be taken by surprise a second time. The U-36 prowled just eighty-odd nautical miles from where Prien had dished gall to the Home Fleet—waters now crisscrossed by RAF spotter aircraft from the nearby coast of northern Scotland, not to mention a Royal Navy hungry for revenge. The Abwehr's last intelligence report before the U-36 had assumed radio silence had put the destroyer HMS *Ivanhoe* on patrol somewhere in the North Sea, as well as two frigates and a number of corvettes, all capable of sending a U-boat to the eternal bottom. If that wasn't bad enough, just last November, Otto Kretschmer, sneaking his U-23 along this same undersea route, had laid mines in the broad mouth of the Moray Firth, there off the port bow, uncomfortably close to where they must launch the shore boat. That such mines tended to break loose and drift did nothing to improve Hartmann's mood.

"You can see the beach?" the major said.

"I think so."

"This is no time for 'think so,' Lieutenant. You'll need to get us in close. The way the sea is bouncing around, we require the shortest possible run, unless you're a better rower than I think. Are you listening? I'm speaking to you, Lieutenant."

"Captain," corrected a mild voice behind Grau. "The skipper of a warship is addressed as Captain regardless of rank."

"Thank you, Herr Doktor," Grau snapped.

Hartmann turned from the scope at last, his face carefully neutral, taking a mental snapshot of his two passengers to smile over later—the muscular, red-faced major with the now-filthy blond hair, his neck bulging over the collar of his black uniform, glaring at the skinny fellow who had squeezed himself against the dials and gauges of the curving bulkhead to keep out of the way. Dr. Johannes Witte, man of mystery, the only soul on board who wasn't sweating in the heat from the batteries now cooking away belowdecks. Cool in his undershirt and khakis, his mop of dark hair and outsized hands and feet making him look too adolescent for a baccalaureate degree, much less a doctorate.

A kid who makes my peach-fuzz torpedomen look grizzled, Hartmann thought, and yet Grau defers to him.

Witte returned Grau's stare; the major blinked and cleared his throat, rounding on Hartmann again. "So. You can get us in close?"

"I'll do what's necessary, Major."

"I hope being kept in the dark about this mission hasn't prevented you from grasping its importance. Success will be getting the package and slipping the doctor and me back to Kiel without anyone knowing we were here. No parades or medals like Prien got. Maybe your efforts will be recognized someday, but even if all goes well tonight, the work of years lies ahead, and for all that time you must say nothing. We are not here now. We were never here. This mission does not exist."

"You've made that quite clear, Herr Major."

"Your men, too. You're the only one going ashore, and if word of what you may see tonight gets out later, you'll be as fucked as whoever talks." Grau glared around at First Officer Heinrich Jodl and the crewmen stationed at the rudder, the diving planes, and the navigational plotting desk, as if they all stood a dozen feet away instead of inches. No one acknowledged him, remaining still as mannequins, their gaze riveted on their stations.

Bastard, Hartmann thought, browbeating me in front of my crew. He wished the major would get hold of himself. If Grau were most men, he could sympathize. Few were cut out for life in a U-boat. The vessel looked big enough at the dock, but that was the outer hull. The inner held less than half the volume, a tube barely ten feet wide and six high at its roomiest. If crawling over other men like a tunneling ant didn't clamp your chest, if you were at peace with tons of water squeezing in from every direction in a tireless effort to drown you, you were one of the few.

Grau was not.

From the moment the U-36 slipped out of Kiel in the dead of night on June 3, his belligerence had worsened by the hour, killing any impulse for sympathy. Anger's his crutch, Hartmann thought, to keep him from collapsing in panic.

He slapped the handles up and the periscope sank back

into its well with a groaning whine. Squeezing around the chief engineer, he leaned through the bulkhead into the sonar room. "We still over the trough, Ulrich?"

The plump, pimple-faced kid in the earphones nodded. "Fifty fathoms, Captain. Good and wide right here, but just aport we've got a steep rise to only four fathoms."

"Right."

Swinging back into the control room, Hartmann touched the shoulder of his chief engineer. "Take her down."

"Aye, Captain. Planesmen, fore hard down, after down five."

The U-36 trembled and began to cant toward the bow, the pitch of the electric motors rising as the depth-gauge needle began its clockwise pirouette. "Boat descending," the chief said. "A hundred feet. A hundred twenty feet."

"Fifty fathoms," the major muttered.

"Three hundred feet," Dr. Witte said, "if that makes you feel any better. Relax, Reinhard. The boat is good to seven hundred."

"I'm aware of that, Doctor. I am relaxed. Perfectly relaxed."

Hartmann made a mental note to laugh later at the tremor in Grau's voice. Of the half dozen men in the control room, only Witte was permitting himself a smile.

An important man back in Berlin, yes.

"How long until full dark?" the major asked.

"Hour and a quarter," Hartmann said. The rest he kept to himself—that trying to get ashore and back under cover of night less than two weeks from the summer solstice at nearly fifty-eight degrees north latitude was lunacy. Stretching it to include late twilight and the cusp of dawn, they'd still have little more than four hours of dark— enough only if all went well. It told him two things about this package the major and doctor were after: It had become available only recently and it couldn't wait.

"Two hundred feet," the chief engineer said.

Dr. Witte eased away from the bulkhead, careful not to bump his head on the skirt of the conning tower. "Captain, you still haven't shown me the motor room."

Hartmann saw Grau's brow knit. The electric motors were in the sternmost compartment. Throughout the voyage, the major had kept as close as possible to the center of the U-boat. Hartmann had seen it before—an obsession with escape that magnetized the area around the conning tower for those afflicted. Quite irrational now that the boat was sinking to the bottom; no one could swim up through fifty fathoms, even if the water weren't a frigid fifty-six degrees. But that wouldn't break the conn's hold on Grau. Suspicious or not, he'd be unlikely to follow them to the stern.

Hartmann turned to his first officer. "Number one, put her on the bottom for me, then all stop. Spread the word— nonessential systems shut down, everyone to their bunks, you know the drill."

"Aye, Captain."

"Doctor, follow me."

Hartmann felt Grau staring at their retreating backs as they bent through the bulkhead and ascended the sloping deck into compartment 4. On either side of them, junior petty officers climbed into their bunks as the lights in the narrow passage dimmed. He led Witte past the tiny galley, ducking under mesh nets sagging with sausages and black bread as he passed through another bulkhead. The 1,160-horsepower engines stood eerily silent on either side, like mammoth armored beasts who'd hunkered down to rest. Behind him, Witte coughed and cleared his throat, even though the fumes of diesel fuel and grease had faded after hours submerged on battery power. If I can make it out of the Kriegsmarine alive, Hartmann thought, will I ever be able to smell anything again?

Inside the final bulkhead, two crewmen squeezed aside to let them through into the aft torpedo room. Hartmann waved them out and pulled the watertight door shut, and he and Witte were as alone as you could be on a U-boat.

Witte gazed with interest at the motor generators on either side of the compartment. "How many horses?"

"Three hundred seventy-five each."

"Fairly quiet."

"Sweet as a sonata. The driveshafts from the diesels go right through their cores. While submerged, we clutch the electric motors to the driveshafts and they take over powering the screws, a tidy piece of engineering. But you didn't really come back here to praise my motors, did you, Herr Doktor?"

Witte grimaced, his face ghostly in the emergency lighting. "I hope it wasn't so obvious to the major."

"I doubt it. He's preoccupied with all that cold water out there."

"He'll be braver on land."

"You know the man well?"

Witte shrugged. "Beginning to."

"I haven't seen many Gestapo," Hartmann said. "Until Grau, my impression was of a runty lot, on the whole."

"The major just missed making our Olympic weight-lifting team in '36. You'll see why it's important when we get ashore."

"If he thinks I'm doing all the rowing, he can think again."

Witte spread his feet to brace himself against the steepening angle of the deck. "Do you wonder, Captain, why you, the skipper, would be ordered on a shore mission?"

"Whoever planned this assumed the crew won't strand their captain, no matter what comes."

Witte smiled. "The files on you were right. You're wise for twenty-eight."

"And you'd be what, twenty-four?"

"Two."

Hartmann blinked. "You're really a doctor?"

"I skipped a few grades."

"A doctor of what?"

Witte hesitated. "Easy enough for you to find out, I suppose. Genetics."

"Ah, Gregor Mendel. The inheritance of garden peas."

"We've come a fair ways since Mendel. Erich von Ischermak-Seysenegg, Carl Correns—these names mean anything to you?"

"Sorry."

"Just as well, Herr Kapitän, just as well."

The deck began to level out. When it was almost flat again, a solid impact rang the gratings underfoot. The motors went still and, in the abrupt quiet, bottom debris displaced by the landing rattled and pinged on the hull. In seconds, this died out, too, and the air thickened with silence. A pressurized pipe overhead began to drip onto Hartmann's shoulder, sizzling cold against his skin until he shifted away.

"So, Herr Doktor," he murmured, "I'm to risk my life with you and Major Musclegruppen without knowing why."

"There shouldn't be much risk. Our contact ashore will meet us near the top of the ladder with the package. Then back to the U-boat and on our way."

Hartmann's turn to smile. "Just how many grades did you skip, Doctor Witte?"

"I suppose things could always go wrong."

"This contact is German?"

"A Scot. But we can trust him. He's a retired professor of ancient languages and an ardent nationalist, which is starting to come back in the Highlands. His son took it to extremes. Went with a small delegation down to London in 1938 to demand that the crown restore some lands taken by the English way back when. A police plainclothesman provoked a fight with him in a pub. The bobbies rushed in with their sticks and cracked his skull. Whether they meant to kill him hardly matters to his father."

Hartmann nodded.

"Major Grau was out of line, goading you about being afraid."

"Out of line," Hartmann said, "but not wrong."

Witte gave a disbelieving smile.

"Herr Doktor, it is said that somewhere in his late twenties a man begins to realize he can die. We in the Kriegsmarine reach that point earlier."

"Captain, I may be only twenty-two, but I know I will die. If I'm aware when that moment comes, everything that went before will seem too brief, whether my death comes in seventy years or tonight. Dying old will feel as unacceptable as dying young, so it really makes no difference when I die, and why worry about something that makes no difference?"

"Are you trying to convince me or yourself?"

Witte smiled. "Myself, of course."

"What is the package, Doctor?"

"You wouldn't believe me if I told you."

"Try me."

Witte's eyes seemed to take on a light of their own in the reddish glow of the motor room. "I can tell you that tonight might give the war effort a huge boost."

"You overwhelm me, Doctor."

Witte leaned toward him. "When your brave colleague, Günther Prien, managed to slip into the Scapa Flow, he risked an expensive U-boat and the lives of forty-four men. When Prien had to surface to slide over the sunken block

ships, cars on the land swept the U-47 with their head-
lights, and by some miracle no one comprehended what
they had glimpsed. If a single British warship had been
manning its sonar, he'd have been trapped, dead. For all
this, he sank just one battleship."

Prien again, Hartmann thought with annoyance. And
now I'm obliged to shine his medal. "I would give up a
year of my life to sink a British battleship."

"An accomplishment, certainly, but if tonight pans out,
the day will come when the British fleet will be at our
mercy. We could sink all their ships, with little or no risk
to a select few of our own . . . men."

Witte's gaze went distant. "This mission is a very long
shot, Captain Hartmann. It may come to nothing, but you
are playing a vital role in a heroic cause—one I hope will
outlive any need to destroy. For now, you are best off if I
say no more. Whether or not we win this war, if you and I
survive, I swear on my honor I'll seek you out wherever
you are and answer all your questions."

Hartmann was impressed, despite himself. He considered himself immune to the grandiose exhortations of the
new German leaders. He'd joined the Kriegsmarine for no
cause save that, God help him, he loved U-boats, loved
slipping along deep and quiet under tons of water, crowded
in with other men like himself, who craved risk and understood and preferred that in themselves and each other.
But this young pup had just made him believe without
even telling him in what. If Dr. Witte commanded a U-
boat, Hartmann thought, his crew would follow him to the
last fathom.

Witte said, "Tell me, Captain, how do you plan to get
the major to row?"

"You're joking, right? When we get that little boat into
the water, and he sees dry land, he'll be able to think of
nothing else but rowing."

Witte laughed.

"Shhh."

"Sorry—"

"Quiet!" Hartmann hissed, holding up a hand. The sound was barely perceptible, but he'd have heard it in his sleep—the distant thrumming of screws. A merchant? Straightening, he pressed an ear to the overhead. The soft thrum bounced between the two hulls, growing louder, not a merchant, no—not at that speed. It was the muscular beat of a warship, a destroyer, possibly. The *Ivanhoe*? The sound grew steadily closer, raising the hackles on Hartmann's neck. The whole crew would be hearing it now, stiffening in their bunks or at their stations.

Putting a finger to his lips, Hartmann motioned the doctor to follow. He worked his way back through the compartments, slipping along through the darkened sub, conscious of frightened eyes peering at him from the bunks. In the control room, Heinrich Jodl gazed up the skirt of the conning tower, his face pale. Major Grau stood, frozen, against a bulkhead. Hartmann squeezed past him to the sonar room, where Ulrich bent over the console, pimples glowing against chalky skin. "Asdic, Captain," he whispered, and a second later Hartmann heard the faint pings.

Hell and damnation. A fucking plane must have flown over and spotted the U-36 at periscope depth. Were they going to die down here in the dark?

Hartmann was too aware, suddenly, of the chill in the U-boat. With its motors shut down and the batteries cooling, the hull at this depth was absorbing a water temperature near freezing. Water trickled from pipes overhead as the condensation grew too thick to cling. A smell of mildew had supplanted the odor of the diesels.

The pings grew louder, the screws thrashing closer, and, chill or no, Hartmann could only thank providence he'd

put the U-36 on the bottom when he had. As long as no one
made a sound loud enough to register on the destroyer's
hydrophones, they might be all right. The asdic would not
pick them out from the solid bottom unless the operator
was a witch.

It might not matter, though. If a plane had spotted them,
the destroyer would not go away, and they could not stay
down here forever with a warship searching back and forth
above. The batteries were already low. They'd have to surface, and the moment they lifted from the bottom, they'd
be fucked, and Doctor Witte would have a chance to prove
his indifference to when he died.

"Captain—"

Grau's voice cut off as Dr. Witte's hand smothered his
mouth. Hartmann glared at the major, teeth on edge.
Christ, the destroyer was right above. Had its hydrophone
picked up the Gestapo man's panicky bleat?

The screws passed over, the pings constant now, a
steady lash across the hull, and also from the sea floor all
around the U-36. Hartmann held his breath, waiting for
any change in the sound of the screws.

They continued overhead, receding, dying away.

Thank you, Jesus.

A plane had not spotted them earlier, or the destroyer
would have come to this spot and worked back and forth
above it, come what may. They were all right. The destroyer was probably on routine patrol. Hartmann blessed
its timing. If it had come along half an hour earlier or later,
it would have caught the U-boat on the surface.

Grau had covered his eyes with a trembling hand. Hartmann wanted to cuff him. Instead, he said, "It's almost
time, Herr Major. Dark in fifteen minutes. You'd better get
out of that uniform. Lieutenant Jodl, let's take her up, nice
and slow."

•   •   •

The world had gone dark at last, the only radiance a pale glow from the sliver of new moon. Climbing from the conning tower, Hartmann drew deep lungfuls of blessed fresh air, fizzed with salt spray. The shore cliffs loomed dark and indistinct, his eyes only partially adapted from ten minutes in the red glimmer of the control room. Two crewmen hurried ahead of him, releasing from its davits the rowboat the Abwehr had provided back in Kiel, flipping it upright and lowering it on two lines over the sloping flank of the U-boat.

The swell had calmed some, Hartmann was glad to see. Turning, he helped Grau down from the conning tower to the deck. The major hiked his shoulders up around his ears and darted across the slippery deck with surprising agility. Sliding down the side of the U-boat into the dinghy, he beckoned with an urgent wave. Doctor Witte staggered and wove across the heaving deck like a drunken stork, finally toppling safely into the boat. Hartmann joined them, reaching for the oars, but Major Grau already had them, and in seconds the U-boat's conning tower dwindled to a dull shadow against the shimmer of black water. Grau, heaving frantically on the oars, looked absurd in his dark cardigan and watch cap. Witte was more convincing as a spindly Scottish lad in a baggy sweater.

"Where did you learn to row?" Hartmann asked, amused at the fierce dedication on Grau's face, but also impressed by the steady headway they were making over the swells.

Grau grunted, his mind clearly on only one thing.

"A suggestion, if I may—I believe our beach is that way." Hartmann pointed over the major's shoulder. At once the dinghy veered onto the right course.

Grau settled in, drawing deep but disciplined breaths, propelling the dinghy over the waves with a single-minded purpose. At his side, Witte grinned, a maniacal glitter of

teeth. What did he think this was, a picnic on the Rhine?
At least Grau had enough soldier in him to be scared. I'll
have to watch Witte when we get ashore, Hartmann
thought, make sure he doesn't do anything foolhardy—
Christ!

The sea lit up with sudden brilliance, as if a huge klieg
light had switched on, and for a second Hartmann feared
the destroyer had somehow slipped back and they were
running right up against it, then he realized it was the sky
itself, rippling with light—blue and red, with brilliant
bands of yellow.

"The aurora borealis," Witte said with wonder. "I've always wanted to see it."

"Shut your hole," Grau said, "you silly fucking college
boy." His wide eyes looked poleaxed with fear. Hartmann
turned in the dinghy, terrified the U-boat might still be surfaced, but he could see nothing, not even the periscope
Jodl no doubt had trained on them.

God bless you, Heinrich. "We're all right."

Grau shook his head. "If someone's up on that cliff—"

"We're just a trio of Scottish fishermen who stayed out
too late, right?"

Witte grappled in the bottom of the dinghy and came up
with the fishing pole, waving it in front of Grau's nose.
The major was pulling with all he had now, the narrow spit
of beach seeming to rush at them. "I apologize for what I
said, Herr Doktor," Grau mumbled.

"Quite all right," Witte said gaily.

Hartmann felt hideously exposed, the lights rippling
across the water, painting the faces of Witte and Grau in
shifting colors. Sand grated under the prow and Witte leapt
out, foundering in the surf as he struggled to haul the boat
up. Dropping the oars, Grau jumped out behind him,
jerked the boat up onto the beach as easily as if it were
made of balsa wood, then dragged it to the base of the cliff.

Another boat was already there, and Hartmann's spine tingled, but then he saw a hole in the keel; nothing more than a rotting relic of some past misadventure.

Trotting along the beach toward the jetty of rock at the far end, Hartmann searched the cliffside for the ladder.

There!

Grau pushed past him and hauled himself upward with the alacrity of a panicked ape.

"After you, Doctor," Hartmann said.

Witte grinned and lifted himself up the first few rungs, then began to slow. Behind him, Hartmann gripped the wet steel rungs hard, hoping Witte had the sense to do the same. If the kid fell on him, it would be worse than a headache. Why is he along? Hartmann wondered. A geneticist should be off in his laboratory, wearing a white coat, fiddling with test tubes. He's the sort to think this is a lark, but the people back in Berlin know better. They should have forbidden it—

Damn!

Hartmann swallowed, sorry he'd glanced down. Squeezing his eyes shut failed to erase a dizzying afterimage of surf swirling below him, reddish white in the radiance of the aurora. The vertigo passed and he wrenched his gaze up again. He hated heights. The space under them was too thin. You didn't sink gently through air, you plummeted.

As he neared the top, arms aching, his mind achieved a sort of clarity and he realized that Witte, despite his youth, might be along to keep an eye on the major. The two were as different as night and day, more antagonists than allies. Maybe the Gestapo wasn't the only group back in Berlin with a stake in this mysterious package. Witte isn't the Gestapo's boy scientist, Hartmann realized, he's someone else's. They sent him along to watch after their interests.

And I get to baby-sit him.

Grit rained down on him, startling him so badly he almost lost his grip. Looking up, he saw that Witte and Grau had gained the top. Grau reached down, grasped his wrist, and pulled him up onto the bluff. As his feet found purchase, Hartmann scurried away from the edge, hoping the others hadn't noticed the spastic burst of effort.

Grau pointed away from the cliff, and Hartmann saw a trail through the scrub and heather, all too clear under the northern lights. Not twenty feet away stood a big fellow in a wool coat and watch cap. Grau wasn't looking at the man but beyond to another, an old man judging from his slow gait and hunched frame.

"Scheisse!" Grau exclaimed.

"English, Angus, English," Witte prompted, his gaiety fading.

"Shit, then. Who is that?"

"Our friend Simon. As for the other . . . I guess we'll find out."

Simon had turned now, and was watching the old man draw closer. "Let's go," Grau whispered, again in German. He led the way up the path, reaching Simon just as the old man did, a duffer in shapeless corduroy slacks and woolen coat. He had huge ears and a snarled head of white hair. His eyes were pinched with suspicion. Spitting phlegm, he said, "Who would these fellows be, then?"

"My cousins from the south paying us a visit, Wallace," Simon answered, "come up to Dornoch for the salmon. Meet Angus Grant, wi' young Ian Tavish and Mr. Neil, there behind. Wallace McCamly, boys."

Hartmann noticed an armband on the old man's coat and his heart sank. Home Guard. *Wunderbar.*

"Your cousins, eh?" McCamly's voice was sharp with doubt. "Whyn't I ever hear you mention them before, Professor? I saw you three from yonder cliff when the aurora flared up. You, there, Angus, you seemed in an awful hurry, pulling that boat to shore, like the furies was after ye—"

Grau reached out with both hands, grasped the old man by his mammoth ears, and twisted, snapping his neck with a loud crack. Wallace McCamly fell to the ground and flopped for a second, then was still.

Hartmann stared in shock.

"Jesus, Reinhard," Witte gasped. "You didn't have to do that."

Simon's eyes had taken on a cold glitter. He gave McCamly's leg a kick, as if unconvinced he was dead. "Nosy old bastard. More English than the English. I'm not the only one around here won't miss him. I'll say I saw him fall."

Witte was still staring at Grau, as if the major had just popped into existence from some fiery pit in hell.

What did you think? Hartmann wondered. That he's a weight lifter in a uniform? He's fucking Gestapo.

"Do you have it?" Grau asked Simon.

"It's over there in that clump of heather, in the knap-sack, just as you asked."

Grau knelt and fished through the scrub, lifting away a canvas sack with a grunt of effort. Witte's paralysis broke and he scrambled to Grau's side, falling to his knees. Forgotten, Hartmann moved up behind them. Witte lifted the flap of the sack, revealing the upper end of a large slab of stone. The aurora pulsed above them, illuminating rows of characters carved into the stone—a language Hartmann could not remember ever seeing.

"There's something more you should know," Simon said. "I went back to the cave where I found the stone, and deeper in I found bones." He swallowed. "It resembles a human skeleton, but a fair sight bigger. Half crumbled away to dust."

Witte sprang up. "What do you mean 'resembles'?"

Simon looked uncomfortable.

"Out with it, man."

"In English," Grau said, staring at Hartmann.

The other two looked at him as well, and he felt himself flushing. In his U-boat he lived three feet from drowning for the Fatherland, but these *Landratten* didn't trust him.

Witte turned back to Simon and asked him a question in English.

The Scot nodded.

"Take me to it," Witte said. "You two can wait here."

"No," Grau said. "There isn't time. We have to get back to the boat."

Witte turned on him. "I have to see it."

"The major is right," Hartmann said. "If we don't get out of here now, we might not make it."

Simon nodded agreement. "Yon dead bastard there has a nephew will come looking for him. And dawn's in an hour. The cave is too far."

Witte looked agonized.

"It's all right, Herr Doktor," Grau said softly, as if soothing a child. "This proves it is possible. Now we have to get back." Turning to Simon, he said, "Photograph the bones, then destroy them. Do it right away."

"I'll bury them."

"No. Burn them. Make sure nothing's left. And as for the photos, don't even take the film from the camera. One of our people will pick it up from you as soon as possible."

Witte groaned, a man in agony, but let Grau prod him back toward the cliff's edge. Grau hoisted the knapsack onto his shoulders, his knees buckling, then bearing up. "Let's go."

Hartmann went down the ladder last, feeling naked under the dazzling northern lights. An eerie snatch of music floated on the damp air, then trailed away.

In the boat, Grau kept the knapsack on his back. Row-

ing, Hartmann imagined the boat capsizing, the stone taking Grau straight to the bottom. Witte stared at the sky,
then pressed his face into his hands. Once, he reached over
Grau's shoulder to touch the knapsack.

Ahead of them, water streamed away from the conning
tower of the U-36, rising from the waves. They reached the
U-boat just as the deck eased above the surface. Two crewmen caught the line and helped them on board. As Grau
staggered to mount the rope ladder thrown down the sloping side, Hartmann thought, Slip, you murderous shit, and
go to the bottom with your stone. But Grau did not slip.

When they were back on the U-36, safely underway at
a depth of a hundred feet, Hartmann went to his cabin aft
of the control room and pulled the curtain to seal away the
rest of the ship. Sitting at his small, drop-down table he
examined his hands to see if they were shaking. Strangely,
they were not.

That he knew English was not in his file. He didn't,
actually—or not very well. But that amazing summer of
1936, when the American sprinter Jesse Owens had won
four gold medals outrunning the finest of the Fatherland,
Hartmann had decided it might be well to know English.
He'd not gotten all that far with it, but far enough. He
thought about the question Witte had asked Simon in English: *Did the skeleton have a tail?*

He thought about the fear in Simon's eyes as he'd
nodded.

CHAPTER I

◀ —————————

Washington, D.C., the Pentagon
Monday, September 23

Herb Bodine was alone in the outermost ring of the basement when he heard the sound. Sitting at the bottom of the world's biggest office building, thirty feet beneath the floodplain of the Potomac, resting his aching back against the wall he'd fought all morning—a real bastard, twenty inches of concrete and rebar. Arms already twitchy from the jackhammer, and now this thump from down the hall, jerking his head around and almost making him drop his bologna on rye. What the hell? Shouldn't be anyone else down here, not with the rest of the crew gone off to lunch.

"Hey!"

The corridor swallowed his shout, like yelling into a mattress, part of the weirdness of the place. He yelled a couple more times, no answer.

Staring down the wall to the bend in the corridor two
football fields away, he had an attack of dizziness, everything tilting, like he was lying on his back, his feet propped
on the wall, not the floor. Too many hours on the hammer,
what it was, a whole morning of shake-rattle-and-roll
messing up his balance. He'd had trouble looking down
this hall ever since they'd cleared out the dividers that used
to cut the distance into lengths your eye could handle. The
proportions made it worse, somehow—overly square, the
walls, floor, and ceiling all roughly the same width—

Everything tilted again, and for a second he was staring
down a mine shaft six hundred feet deep. His stomach flipping, he focused on the electrical conduits dangling from
the ceiling a hundred feet down the hall until he had himself oriented again.

The jackhammer, and all that Jack Daniel's Matt Gerakis had so sneakily served up at poker last night. If his
straight had held up, and that full house early on in the
game, he'd be buying at the hot dog stand in the Pentagon's center courtyard, the sun on his face, joking with the
crew about what a nice target the striped awning must have
made for the Russki missiles all those years of the Cold
War, instead of down here alone in this spooky half-light.
Damn money—couldn't hang on to it. Why his wife had
left him, same reason he had to live in a shack way out in
Loudon County and drive his '85 Ford pickup an hour and
a half to the job because he couldn't afford an efficiency
closer in. And down here now instead of up with the guys,
eating the last of the bologna from the freezer part of his
fridge, the only part could keep anything cool anymore.

Herb listened, not chewing or breathing, but the subbasement stayed silent, the concrete tunnel stretching away
on both sides. His eyes began to burn, making his vision
jitter around the edges. Just plain hard to see down here,
the hall so damn long, like no hallway you'd ever seen be-

fore, so your brain had no practice looking at it. Light down here sucked, too. You could never bring in enough of it, and whatever you did string up just increased the weird, rusty glow of the place. A reflection thing, probably, the light bouncing around that square made by the walls, floor, and ceiling and not finding any place to pool. Long time ago, someone had painted the walls moss green, which had faded back into the concrete, leaving patches the color of pond scum. . . .

Yeah, okay—stop freaking and suck it up. The sub-basement might get on a man's nerves, but he was damn lucky to work in this place, the honor of a lifetime, helping put right what those al-Qaeda fucks on the airplanes had done. Cowards, sucker-punching unarmed civilians, not caring about the women, children, and old people who couldn't fight back or escape, giving the innocent no chance. So pumped up on their hate they couldn't see they weren't brave at all. Didn't even have the courage most people would need to kill themselves, having it figured they weren't really going to die. How brave was it to blow yourself up in a split second so God could make you im-mortal and surround you with beautiful women?

Let them look up from hell and see how long their filthy deed at the Pentagon had lasted. The damaged section of wall, spewing smoke and flames on that dark day, had been back up well before September rolled around again, look-ing good as before the attack. Herb felt a tingle of pride, re-membering the ceremony, all the praise heaped on guys in jeans and hard hats, who no one had much noticed before 9/11. Now his crew was back to work on the renovation that had started before the sneak attack, a huge job, redo-ing the entire insides of the giant building. All five "wedges" to be worked on, one at a time—a twelve-year job, total, probably end up more like fifteen before all the crews were through. Probably the biggest renovation pro-

ject of all time, something to tell your grandkids about
even if the plane had never hit.

Herb's spine twitched with a sudden sense of the awe-
some weight of the building above him. After the smashed
and burned section was rebuilt and they'd let him stay on
for renovation work, he'd decided to find out more about
the place. A book he'd found in the library said 680,000
tons of sand and gravel had been dredged from the Potomac back in '41 and '42 to make the cement for this
monster. The Pentagon was so big you could put the Great
Pyramid of Egypt inside it and have room left over for the
Sphinx. But it was even bigger than you could see, almost
a fifth of it hiding underground. The first level down
they'd called the mezzanine so the one below it could be
just a basement.

Whatever you called it, you'd have to run up a lot of
steps to book out of here.

Herb set his sandwich on top of his lunch pail and used
the paper towel he'd brought for a napkin to mop the sweat
from his face, strangely hot down here, for how far underground it was—

Damn! There it was again, a clatter of rubble from that
pile of smashed concrete he'd shoveled up after he'd
punched through the wall. Herb blinked half a dozen
times, then saw it—a rat, sitting on the pile he'd broken
out, staring at him.

He shook the tension from his shoulders and laughed at
himself. At the sound, the rat didn't even flinch, just kept
peering at him.

"Hey, big guy, what are you looking at? My sandwich?
You lose at poker last night too, hey, buddy? Aren't either
one of us thin, say that for us." He shoved himself up, gri-
macing at the pain in his forearms. A serious muscle burn
ramping up there and in his thighs and calves, better pick

up another bottle of aspirin on the way home—should have enough loose change for that.

The rat let him get to within ten feet before it took off, diving back through the hole. He could hear it a minute longer, skittering away inside the wall. There was a three-foot utility space in there between the wall and the outside foundation—which doubled as a sunken retaining wall, built thick with extra rebar to keep groundwater from the Potomac River out of the basement. Through that space between it and the inside wall ran heating ducts, plumbing mains, and electrical wires. The ducts looked pretty much all right, but the pipes were rusting through after nearly sixty years, and insulation had been chewed off the wiring in a lot of places by Mr. Rat and his ancestors going back to when the place was built.

Which is where I come in, Herb thought with satisfaction. Six or seven years to go, regular paychecks until I'm forty-five and too broken-down to hoist a jackhammer anymore.

Herb inspected the hole he'd made. Not bad. Plenty wide enough for a man to step through, and nicely rounded off if he did say so himself. Not that the foreman or any of his plumbers would notice—just another hole in the wall to Gerakis and his boys.

Leaning in, Herb stared into the dark crease between the wall and foundation but couldn't see the rat. Stale air cooped up behind the wall since '42 was still oozing out, smelling of mildew, rust, and an animal odor like hamster. Except a hamster wouldn't last five seconds in there with Boss Rat and his gang.

"Gonna be some noise and confusion for a while," Herb said into the blackness, "but hang in there and everything will settle down."

I'm talking to a rat, he thought.

Why not? People talked to their dogs and cats. Everybody thought squirrels were cute, and a rat was just a squirrel without fur on his tail. Smart animals, rats, living off the land, making it on scraps. Like me, Herb thought.

The light flared behind him, one of those power surges that came along every few hours down here, and a glint inside the wall caught his eye. Right down there under the rubble he'd knocked in, what the hell was that? Herb stared at it, feeling a ripple of nerve up his backbone.

Kind of like an old coffee urn, like those ones made fifty cups.

Ducking inside the wall, Herb knelt and cleared away the chunks of concrete with his hands until the upper curve of the cylinder was exposed. Bigger than any coffee urn. Follow that curve into the dirt and you'd have something the size of a big garbage can but a lot smoother and shinier. Herb went and got his flashlight and the shovel he'd used to tidy up the debris. Laying the light on the ground, he used the shovel to dig out the sides of the can, going at it hard as his mind worked the angles. This space in here probably hadn't been accessible since they'd finished off the building during what Dad always called the big war. Maybe this was a metal barrel of secret papers somebody had decided to hide back then.

Or Nazi gold, there you go, long as he was dreaming. Those G.I.s coming back from Europe, telling stories about gold and jewelry that some of the guys had found while they were mopping up Hitler's goons. Not Dad, of course—money had never come his way either; like father like son.

Maybe the son's finally gonna get lucky, Herb thought.

He got the dirt down far enough to expose most of the cylinder, then sat back on his haunches, sweating like a bottle of Bud on a ball field. He shined the flashlight along the smooth side of the thing, wondering that the metal could stay so clean walled up in here with leaking pipes for so long. Not a fleck of rust on it. Aluminum, or titanium, maybe.

What was that along the side there, stamped into the metal? Brushing off dirt, he shined the light on it.

ABWEHR

His heart started to thump. That wasn't an American word. Not Japanese or Italian, either, which left German. German secrets buried in this big can? Maybe maps to where gold was hidden, or the gold itself?

Herb swallowed, his throat dry, hands starting to tremble, and he realized he needed a salt pill, with all the sweating.

How long before the guys got back? No more than ten minutes.

Better know what he was dealing with before then.

The bottom of the can was recessed slightly, like the butt end of a metal garbage can. Grabbing the edge, he set his heels and tugged back. At first the can wouldn't budge, but he put his legs into it, and the can broke free of the dirt and lurched upright, then tore away from the ground, dumping him onto his back inside the wall.

Damn, that hurt, sharp hunks of cement gouging him. He scrambled up, rubbing his spine, and then the smell hit him, a musk so sharp it made him gasp and cough. Picking up the light, he saw that the ground still held the top lid—that he'd torn the can away from it when he'd levered it up, and then the fluid inside—some kind of chemical—had gushed out into the dirt.

He backed off, scared. What if this was Nazi poison?

But no, he was still breathing, the smell fading a little. What did it remind him of? That wet smell at the zoo that came off the glass in the reptile house.

He realized he was still holding the big can, propping it

up with one hand, and that, even drained, it still had con-
siderable weight in it. Easing it down on its side, he shined
the light inside, and went cold all over.

Was that a foot?

A foot and ankle, yeah, trailing out of the end of the can.
Naked, a sickly green color, the size of a kid's foot, maybe
a boy ten or eleven. Something weird about the toes. Herb
shook his head, baffled. A body, sealed up in embalming
fluid all these years, buried down here inside the walls. . . .

But what was that other thing trailing out the end of the
big can, beside the other foot that had slipped out? Looked
like the tail of an alligator. They'd put a gator in here with
a kid?

Herb's mind churned and spun, trying to get a grip on
what he was seeing. A body, a preserved body in a can with
German writing on it. He couldn't make sense of it. Maybe
there would be money in this somehow, him being the one
to find it, but he was damned if he knew how to play it.

First, get a better look at the body, form an idea who it
might be and why he'd been sealed away with a gator.

Herb pulled on his work gloves, then made himself
grasp the ankle, hoping the foot didn't come off in his
hand. Grunting, he pulled the wet leg from the big can and
kept pulling until the body slid out and lay in the dirt, lit
along one side by the flashlight.

Herb blinked and blinked again, his heart stuttering inside him.

Lord, look at that. Not a kid, no way. Its hands—and
that was a tail, not like a gator's, smoother, like the dinosaur tails in *Jurassic Park*—the small, fast, killer ones.

Herb scrambled backward out of the hole, leaned
against the wall, breathing hard. We're talking *X Files*,
here, he thought.

Except he didn't believe in Martians—or aliens from
any other planet, for that matter. But maybe there had been

something to the UFO and Roswell stories after all. If you let up on your biases, this could square with Roswell being real, the officials involved deciding to bury one of the aliens inside the Pentagon walls, where it would take a whole damn morning with a jackhammer to break through.

Herb felt a sweet conviction pumping through him. If I'm lying, I'm dying, he thought, but if I'm right, I'm rich. He envisioned himself on *Larry King Live,* explaining to the famous man with the gravelly voice how he'd broken through a wall in the Pentagon and discovered the alien from Roswell, proving that the government cover-up all these years had been real. Giving his impressions of that first sighting, describing the creature in detail, while a hundred million people watched him on TV.

What would going on *Larry King Live* be worth?

I'll need an agent. . . .

Herb remembered the writing on the can. *Abwehr.* Why German writing on a can the U.S. Air Force had brought here from Roswell to hide inside the wall of the Pentagon's subbasement?

Maybe it's not German, he thought. Maybe it's one of those made-up words they're always using in this place. What did you call them?—acronyms. Everywhere you went in the halls, BMDO, ATL, PAE, DEPSEC—like that. Abbreviations, and not German at all.

Herb checked his watch. Two or three minutes left until the guys got back, and then things would happen fast. The foreman would get some Pentagon brass down from the renovation office.

I've got to see all I can before the authorities try to put the lid back on.

He scrambled back into the hole in the wall. The body lay there on its side in the dirt, about four feet long—double that if you counted the tail. The forehead slanted back, no hair there or anywhere else. Playing the flashlight along it, he could see the rib cage, bony ridges under the green-ish skin. He picked up the wrist, expecting it to be stiff, but it was limp, rubbery almost—

A sobering thought struck him: This was a setup. The crew had put this in here for him to find—sneaked in after he'd broken through the wall, and buried the can. The body was made of rubber, a rubber alien, supposed to spin him up, get him to make a fool of himself, so they'd have something to rag him about the next five years. They were good guys basically, for plumbers, but if you were a common laborer it was a rare skilled tradesman who'd give you credit for any brains.

But, man, did it look real. If this was plastic or rubber, whoever made it was as good as those F/X guys in Holly-wood, with their special effects. You couldn't go out just anywhere and buy something this realistic—

Hey!

It did not move, Herb told himself. I imagined it.

The leg twitched again, shooting cold through his veins. *It's not dead.*

Within the cone from his light, he saw the ribbed chest expand, swelling out like a balloon. The body shuddered and then rolled half toward him, gushing fluid from its mouth. Herb stared, frozen, watching its arms and legs shake in spasms. Another huge breath, and then a lid peeled back from an eye red as a ruby. It stared right at him, the pupil narrowing to a slit in the beam of light.

Herb stared back, awed. Not only was the body not a hoax, it was alive, and he had discovered it.

Both eyes open now, shiny red, the lids rolled almost shut, but the slit pupils staying focused on him. The thing lay there breathing, staring at him, until the spasms in its legs and arms stopped. It tried to get up, shaky at first, making him think of a newborn fawn.

Serious muscles bunching in those legs and arms, though.

The skin tightened across Herb's shoulder blades, but he nerved himself, thinking of Larry King, the money. Standing up, the thing was bigger than he'd thought, but not as big as him. Its waist was thin enough he could probably get his hands around it. In another minute, it would be steady enough to run off inside the wall. Better grab it quick.

Herb lunged.

CHAPTER 2

←——————————

Pentagon
Tuesday

Ed Jeffers tried to focus on the renovation progress report, but the words kept sliding apart into fuzzy clones of themselves. Waiting in line was a stack Dixie had dumped on his desk an hour ago, layout plans for partitioning the huge bays now being cleared in Wedge 2 into *Dilbert*-style office cubicles. He'd be more interested if the bays were anywhere near cleared instead of weeks behind schedule. Contractors hadn't even finished the flooring yet, and the old windows—over fifteen hundred of them in that fifth of the building—hadn't been touched. On the other hand, Ed thought, they worked like maniacs repairing the 9/11 damage well ahead of schedule. That buys them a lot of grace.

Pulling a breath, he glanced up at the round government-issue clock over his door. Half past three, and he'd be here until seven if it went like most days. Then, after microwave meatloaf and tonight's tape of *The Jim Lehrer NewsHour,* he'd log on to his home computer and slog on until eleven, e-mailing tomorrow's top priorities to his department heads.

"Coffee?" Dixie, leaning in from her desk outside his door.

"You are an angel."

She brought the pot in and poured as he savored the expanding aroma of primo Colombian. As always, she left a two-inch cushion of air. He waited for her to go so he could pick the mug up, but she lingered, the pot in one slender hand, the other planted on his desk. Not beautiful, Dixie, but super fit from all that working out in the sweaty warrens of the Pentagon Athletic Center. He liked her face, round and freckled, with that big smile she flashed. Natural honey blonde, ten years younger than he, and a skilled flirt, but she had a boyfriend over in Force Management and Personnel, *and she works for you, so just keep right on putting that idea out of your mind.*

"Got a call from Security just now," she said.

"You park in the Secretary's space again?"

"Why not? I'm a secretary, aren't I?"

"As always, your logic can't be pecked."

"Seems like one of your workers disappeared yesterday."

Realizing he was gazing with longing at the mug, Ed made himself look at Dixie instead. "Disappeared, how?"

"I believe into thin air is the usual way. How do I know? Captains in the Defense Protective Service don't confide in people who answer phones for other people."

"Hardison?"

"That's him. He wanted to talk to you, but you told me no calls, you had to catch up on the reports, so I lied you were out, and he gave up that a worker was missing so dumb little me would know it was important and remember to have you return his call."

"Hardison's got all the authority he needs in security matters, what's he want with me?"

"Cover, I'd guess. Plus you sign all the workers' checks."

"My machine does that."

"Shall I have it call Captain Hardison?"

"Good idea."

She raised an eyebrow. "Aren't you going to drink your coffee?"

"When it cools."

"You need to speed yourself up to talk to this man, believe me."

So he had to pick the mug up, and of course she'd set it by his right arm. He moved the new prosthesis carefully, still unsure after three weeks, thinking about just how to move the child-sized arm inside, watching the manly hand at the end of the fake adult arm express each little movement of his stunted true hand. Easy does it, thumb and forefinger on the handle of the mug, that's it. Pinching his stubs together inside the prosthesis, he watched the handsome hand at the end of the arm do the same, mimicking the point-to-point surface mapping of the VR glove. Bending the new arm was trickier, since the meat one inside it barely came to the elbow of the prosthesis, but the engineers at Bell Labs had programmed the artificial arm to translate and magnify the cramped movements it detected in his real elbow. The servomotors made no sound as the arm bent and raised the cup to his lips. With care, he tipped and sipped.

"I'm impressed," Dixie said.

Nothing to say except thank you, but the coffee turned bitter in his throat. Why couldn't she just pretend to ignore the damned arm? Trying to make him think it was no big deal to her? Best way to do that was just forget about it.

"This one looks so much more real than the last. That your own hair they put into the back of the hand?"

"Dixie, go see if you can get Hardison on the phone for me, would you?"

"Grump."

As soon as she was out, he shifted the mug to his left hand and drained it.

"Mr. Jeffers," the intercom said, "I have Captain Hardison for you." Her cryogenic voice, or maybe just being proper in front of Pat, his other secretary, and whoever else was milling around out there.

He picked up. "Josh, what gives?"

"Hate to bother you with this," said the crisp voice on the other end of the line, "and it may turn out to be nothing, but a laborer, name of Bodine, disappeared at lunchtime yesterday, down in the E-ring basement, river side."

Ed felt a moment's confusion, then reminded himself he had okayed an advance inspection down there, even though it was Wedge 5, where office renovation proper wouldn't start for years. The plumbing contractor had wanted a quick read on whether the river-side pipes would last until the renovation crews got there. The shock of the airliner hitting the building had broken or unmoored hundreds of pipes. While the river exposure was on the opposite side, a sample inspection was the only way to be sure that vibration from the huge jolt hadn't pushed aging pipes on this side to the brink of failure.

Ed said, "Are you telling me the workman disappeared inside the building? How do you know he didn't just decide to blow off the job?"

"His foreman is sure this guy wouldn't do that. The man is pretty concerned. You want to talk to him, I could meet you down there."

Ed looked at the stack of papers. The coffee was starting to boogie in his veins, giving him that treacherous feeling he had time to burn, could go all night if he needed to.
"Fine. Ten minutes?"

"Good."

Hanging up, Ed felt the back of his meat hand cool as
the office darkened around him. He turned to the tall windows behind his desk, pressing a cheek to the glass to look
up through the light court that separated the D ring from
the outermost, E ring of the Pentagon. Down here on the
third floor, you couldn't see as much sky as on four and
five, but plenty of good outside light made it down. In the
slice of sky he could see, a dark bank of cumulus clouds
had edged across the sun. Looked like Washington was
headed for more rain tonight. The good news was he
wouldn't have to water the flowers in the morning, with
the mosquitoes waiting to suck him dry. The bad was more
puddles for them to breed in, a real plague, with all the rain
in July and August. What had possessed him, anyway, to
plant so many impatiens in June, when he hardly ever got
to see them in the light?

As Ed stepped into the outer office, his deputy, Bart
Sinderman, closed in from the side, big shoulders hunched,
basset-hound face creased with the usual worry. "Ed, got a
minute?"

He stopped. "One."

"I just got a call from an assistant secretary of defense,
upset because his wife can't pick him up at the River Entrance. The M.P.s won't let her wait at the guard gate, either, but make her loop down to visitors' parking, which is
another thirty or forty yards away. He wants you to issue a
special pass for her, so she can drive up to the entrance."

Ed made himself refocus. The particular assistant secretary of defense Bart was talking about had a numbered
parking space right up against the wall of the Pentagon

near the steps of the River Entrance. No doubt he had a second car he could, in theory, drive to work, but he also had two teenage daughters he doted on, which meant four cars might not be enough.

"What did you tell the assistant secretary?"

"I asked for his patience and stressed the security benefits of strictly limiting the number of people allowed to drive close to the building. I reminded him that, while his wife was using the car during the day, someone could— God forbid—put a bomb in his trunk that would blow a hole in the side of the building. It didn't faze him, Ed. He's demanding clearance for his wife." Bart shook his head. "Amazing."

Ed felt vaguely depressed. "Want to hear something else amazing? The man you're talking about took a ninety percent pay cut from a job with TRW, gave up a chauffered limousine and a list of other perks as long as your arm, and got rid of millions of bucks' worth of his best stocks in order to come and work for the people of the United States."

Bart's mournful eyes underwent a spasm of blinking. "I guess when you put it like that."

"Call him back and tell him you'll do everything in your power to get his wife that pass."

"Right."

Ed headed out, resisting the urge to shake his head, in case Bart might see. The man was smart, likable, and hardworking, but if he couldn't master the Zen of VIP relations, he'd never make director. Nine-tenths of the job was revving people up or calming them down. Take Captain Hardison, uptight about this "disappearance." With over a thousand men now working on the renovation crews, they must come and go every day. Chances were, this worker had just gotten fed up and taken off.

What the hell—a walk was just what he needed right now.

Ed hung a left out of his office, his brain already mapping the shortest course from the D ring, concourse side, to E ring, river: With his office just past the center of D, four hundred feet would take him to Corridor 9, penultimate of the ten broad halls that connected the Pentagon's perimeter to its center courtyard like the spokes of a wheel. Fifty feet of 9 would take him out to the E ring and he'd follow that down to the center stairway just this side of the Secretary's office. That staircase went all the way down and would bring him in just past the cleared-out offices that used to be Navy Ship Acquisition. Seven minutes of peace, the longest walk you need ever take in the Pentagon if you knew what you were doing. People's jaws usually dropped when they were told the twenty-nine-acre building had over seventeen miles of corridor, but it was that very mileage that ensured a relatively short walk between any two points.

Ed shifted right and left down D, weaving between men and women in uniform, evading a motorized cart and a cleaning crew. Ahead of him, a knot of civilians had started an impromptu meeting in the hall. The woman in the group caught his eye—tall, snappy dresser, a director in the Office of the Secretary. She was always friendly to him, and the few times they'd talked, he'd gotten the impression of a first-rate mind. She'd be good company, someone who understood the job.

She was also happily married.

Ed felt a momentary emptiness, then told himself what he always did: that friendship with women wasn't a bad substitute for marriage. How many husbands and wives were really friends, anyway? Time to ask Marianne out to dinner. Or Candace. Dinner, some good conversation.

Catch up on things, have a few laughs, and whatever might come after, if they'd both relaxed enough.

As he passed the director, she turned from her four companions to say hello. He gave it back with a smile, thinking how unusual she was, a pure extrovert in a civil service neck deep in introverts—most of them pleasant enough, but rarely outgoing. He must have some extrovert in him, too, because he felt at least a glimmer of recognition for most people he saw in the halls. His renovation duties took him all over the building, and the broad halls and cross corridors guaranteed lots of human contact. Twenty-five thousand civilians and military poured in here every weekday, more people than a lot of towns had; if the Pentagon had been built high instead of wide, you'd never see more than a fraction of them. The ill-fated World Trade Center had held more workers—if you counted both towers—but each 110-story behemoth had been smaller by 250,000 square feet of floor space. On average, 225 people had occupied a single floor of the WTC, compared to five thousand in here. For all its hugeness, the Pentagon's design fostered contact. Your office couldn't be more than three floors away from the mammoth central cafeteria, which sold more pizzas, salads, and fried chicken every day than any hundred restaurants. If you stopped by every few days for breakfast or lunch, within a few weeks you'd have been in the same room with a majority of your twenty-five thousand coworkers.

As Ed turned left into the E ring, bare tiles and unadorned plaster gave way to the red carpet and dark oak wainscoting of the Eisenhower Corridor. On either side, paintings of Ike glowed in gilt frames. Approaching the Secretary's office, Ed recalled how a military guard at the door had once meant that the Pentagon's top man was in. That was back before terrorist threats began to mount.

Now, if the Secretary was in his office, the guard would be hidden away behind that dark oak door.

Wherever Secretary Hastings was today, on Friday, only three days from now, he'd be in the Pentagon to escort the visiting president of Russia and his defense minister on a goodwill tour of the building. Of course, Hastings would not actually be leading the tour. That would fall to one Ed Jeffers, head of the Washington Headquarters Service, "mayor" of the Pentagon. The thought of walking dignitaries around made him wince. He wouldn't get a thing done that day.

Ed hung a left into the broad stairwell guarded by a bronze bust of Ike. As he descended, polished oak banisters gave way to the more typical iron rail. The granite steps from the third floor to the second and first had been worn into foot-shaped gullies by sixty years of daily beatings from thousands of shoes, but as he reached the mezzanine, the gullies disappeared. This first basement level and the one below had seen far less traffic over the years.

When he stepped into the lower of the two basement levels, Ed saw a knot of men about a hundred yards off— Captain Hardison in his uniform and half a dozen workers in T-shirts and jeans. The air, hot and still, pressed his face, and he felt his customary aversion to the bottom level, with its odd light, the incongruous heat, the creepy sense you got of looking the wrong way through a telescope. He found himself speeding up, ducking under dangling cables, wanting to get with other men. As he passed one of the basement's labyrinth of narrow side halls, the concrete flickered with a cold light from the sputtering torch of a welder.

Hardison turned to him, slim and dapper in the understated blue uniform, expression masked by his full mustache and deadpan eyes. Ed could feel the workers sizing him up with that mixture of interest and suspicion men in jeans reserve for men in suits.

"Thanks for coming down, Mr. Jeffers." Hardison skipped the handshake many men found obligatory—an enduring point in his favor.

"No problem."

"This is Matt Gerakis." Hardison nodded at a big-bellied guy with salt-and-pepper hair and grime on his face. "He's foreman of the plumbing crew. The missing man is one of his laborers. Matt?"

"Yeah," Gerakis said, "Herb Bodine, one of my best laborers, very reliable. Last we saw him was yesterday. He demoed the wall, there, in the morning, and everyone but him went off to lunch and when we got back he wasn't here."

Demoed . . . demoed—demolished. Looking where Gerakis pointed, Ed saw a hole in the wall, four feet high by three wide. A jackhammer lay beside a pile of rubble from the wall. He got an image of a big man with bulging forearms; for a second, the baby arm inside his prosthesis ached. "Maybe the jackhammer gave him a headache and he decided to leave early."

"Herb's not the type to take off without a word."

"First time for everything."

The foreman frowned, probably not liking to be pushed by a suit. Sorry, Ed thought, but I have to know if this is real.

Gerakis said, "Look, mister, after work yesterday, I saw Herb's pickup over there by Route 110, where we all park. That got me to worrying maybe he'd been feeling too poorly to drive and hitched a ride home, so I tried to call him but his phone was disconnected. Herb lives kind of hand to mouth, can't keep two quarters in his pocket, which is why it ain't like him to give up even half a day's pay. Anyways, I drove on out there and got the landlord to let me in. Everything looked normal, his stuff there and all, but no Herb."

Ed turned to Hardison. "Emergency rooms and hospitals?"

"For Herb Bodine and John Doe," the captain said, "in case he was confused. No hits."

Ed looked at the hole in the wall, black and uninviting. It must have taken a hell of an effort to break through a wall so thick. No ordinary man could hold a jackhammer in a horizontal position for long. Hot as it was down here, Bodine must have sweat buckets, screwing up his electrolytes, which in extreme cases could cause temporary dementia. He might well have wandered inside the wall and collapsed. "Did you take a look inside the hole, there?"

"Went in myself," Gerakis said, "and I didn't see any sign of him. . . ."

The man looked uncomfortable, his mouth half open as if he wanted to say more but was afraid to. Ed raised a prompting eyebrow.

"It's pretty dark, and it narrows down to a tight squeeze when you get twenty yards or so. I don't think Herb could get past that part, and why would he want to?"

"But you did go in."

"Twenty yards, like I said. I shined my light back in there beyond. Didn't see anything."

Gerakis wasn't meeting his eyes now and Ed realized he was afraid. A plumber, scared of tight places?

"Any of the rest of you go in?"

Gerakis's crew shifted on their feet, looking everywhere but at him. Absurd. Bunch of big, tough construction guys, afraid to make a proper search of a tight place inside a wall.

Captain Hardison said, "I sent one of my people in this morning. He didn't find anything either."

"Does someone have a good flashlight?" Ed said.

"Sure," Gerakis said. "We've got a couple of those Scorpions. Little things run on six-volt flash batteries, put out more light than the big ones."

"Want to get one for me?"

Gerakis looked at him as if he'd sprouted a second head.

"You're not going in there?" Captain Hardison said.

"Why not?" Careful to keep all truculence from his voice.

Hardison's gaze dropped. "You'll get that suit filthy."

Using the right arm, Ed peeled the suit's jacket from his left shoulder, no fumbling, thank you, God, then finished with his real hand, draping the coat over a hand truck. He loosened his tie, confident in the dim light that none of the crew could see through his white shirt to the harness of the prosthesis. Hardison had to know about the arm, but these others didn't, they just thought he was a suit, and he'd show them, but it was more than that, too, and he knew it.

"Mr. Jeffers—"

"The light, please."

Gerakis handed him a small black flashlight that looked like it wouldn't reach six feet, but when he found the button in the butt end and pushed it, he was amazed at the headlight beam that shone out. He ducked through the hole into the wall and squatted in the dirt, coughing at the smell—a powerful musk, part chemical, part . . . animal?

"Why is the floor dirt in here?" he asked Gerakis through the hole in the wall. "Shouldn't they have run the floor out to the outside retaining wall?"

The foreman shrugged. "It probably does go out, most of the way around the building. From what I've heard, they built this place in a hell of a hurry. Maybe the mixers ran short that day for the guys pouring and finishing along here. This is the bottom level, and they were pouring on top of solid fill dirt—at least it was solid back then. The outer wall goes on down to form its own continuous footing, so supporting the wall above wasn't an issue. They were being pushed hard, they could get away with it without harm, so they did."

Ed shined the light around his haunches. The dirt was almost too level, as if someone had dug through it, then raked it smooth. Hard to tell in the brilliance of the flashlight, but it seemed darker than the surrounding dirt. Touching it with his left palm, he found it damp. As he panned the light, the brilliant beam picked up a wink of moisture. He crab-hunched over to it, a puddle a few inches round. Shining the light up, he studied the plumbing line that ran overhead. Filthy, covered with rust, but no sign of moisture there that might have dripped down.

Kneeling gingerly, he lowered his nose to the puddle and sniffed. The odor of musk and chemical sharpened, nearly gagging him.

As he rose to a crouch beneath the pipes and electrical conduits, his light beam caught an odd-shaped pebble at his feet, maybe a broken arrowhead—four centuries ago, this same ground had been an Indian village called Namoraughquend.

Slipping the hard, pointed object into his pocket, he panned the light farther down the inside of the wall. The cement looked rough, spiked here and there with tips of rusted rebar. On his right, the backside of the Pentagon's outside wall was smoother. The bright beam sank back between the two walls into a slot of deepening blackness.

Imitating the posture Hawkeye Pierce had used to duck under the chopper blades in *M*A*S*H*, Ed crept deeper down the wall until he came to the narrows Gerakis had described. A tight squeeze, all right, but he should be able to get past.

He realized he was breathing fast. The hairs on his left arm were standing up stiff. He studied the obstruction. It was the upper terminus of a support piling, one of the thousands of concrete monoliths sunk through the fill dirt down to bedrock to support the building. It pinched the space between the walls down to about a foot and a half, the pipes crammed together to bend around it.

Leaning his back against the inside wall, Ed snaked his left leg through the gap and rode the wall into the tight spot, sucking in his gut and pushing with his right foot. The wall narrowed further, damn, he was stuck in here—no, don't yell!

Ed controlled an overpowering impulse to gasp, instead forcing air from his lungs as he pushed with his right leg and pulled with his left arm around the piling. With a lurch, he came unstuck and tumbled through, landing on his side.

"You all right in there, mister?" Gerakis, his voice muffled.

Ed pushed up and sat, catching his breath. "Fine. I'm past the piling. Going to take a quick look."

He shined the light on the dirt. At first he saw nothing, then a wet slick against the wall. Tracing a finger through it, he sniffed. The same chemical/animal scent, and suddenly he knew what it reminded him of—that time at the National Zoo with Candace. She'd wanted to see some snakes, weird woman that she was, and he'd gone in with her, into the dim building that housed the zoo's reptiles and amphibians, pretending he didn't have an aversion to the creatures. The air inside the exhibit had been close and damp, with a sickly sweet smell—just like this.

Swallowing, Ed shined the light ahead along the ground and moved deeper along the wall. All at once, at his feet, the light beam seemed to sink right into the ground. It took him a shocked second to realize he was staring down into a hole. He could see no sides going down.

Groping up a pebble, he tossed it into the hole.

After a second, a faint splash came back to him.

A cold sweat sprang up on his face. He was standing on the shelf edge of a sinkhole, on dirt that might be only a few feet thick, liable to collapse at any second. He held himself still, crouched over, afraid to move, to cause any extra pressure that might collapse the ground under him. His breathing sounded harsh in his ears.

He heard another splash from below, then two more, the sound a fish makes when it breaks the surface—or a man or animal running through a stream. The splashes echoed, signaling a large space.

Call out?

No. If Herb Bodine was down there and fit enough to move, he'd have been the one to yell, the moment he saw the light coming down into the hole. What I need to do, Ed thought, is get out of here as fast as I can without causing a cave-in.

He started to turn, freezing as the ground dropped an inch under his feet. Dirt pattered down into water, the sound reaching up to him from the hole.

Lie down flat, he thought. Spread your weight over as much ground as possible.

He eased himself onto his belly, wincing as more dirt pattered down beneath him. Stretched out on his stomach, he realized he'd need both hands to crawl. Reluctantly, he shut off the flashlight. A suffocating darkness pressed down on him, and he resisted the urge to scramble along the ground. Just take a deep breath, that's it, now another. After a few seconds, his eyes adjusted and he picked up the faint illumination from the hole where he'd entered the wall.

Okay, just crawl back to that, slow and easy.

Slipping the light into his pocket, he started back, worming on his belly over the dirt, his left arm out ahead, pulling at the ground. He placed the artificial hand on the wall, forcing himself to control the movements of his real arm, the stunted thing inside the prosthesis. Freak out now and he might well knock the ground right out from under him.

It took him nearly five minutes to work his way back to the piling.

"Mr. Jeffers? Mr. Jeffers, are you all right in there?"

He swallowed his answer, afraid the vibration of his voice might be enough to break the sinkhole's back.

"I'm coming in," Gerakis shouted.

"No! Hang on. I'm coming out."

"What?"

He said it again louder, wincing, but the ground under him held. Rolling onto his side, he reached past the piling with his left arm, finding nothing to grab on the smooth surface. If the ground collapsed now, he'd slide right down the side of the concrete pier into . . . what?

For a moment, he froze, unable to move. The air in the dark slot pressed in on his eardrums and he could hear his heartbeat, like feet thumping over sand.

And then another sound, in the hole behind him, a soft grunt, like a man might make, but somehow different. A frenzied burst of effort carried him past the piling; unable to help himself, he lunged to his knees and scrambled back toward the light, grabbing the sides of the hole and lunging out into the hallway. With an effort, he kept his footing and straightened.

Hardison, Gerakis, and the laborers stared at him.

He cleared his throat, conscious that his suit pants were filthy, his white shirt ripped, exposing the harness of the prosthesis. His face felt like a mask frozen over the bone. "We'll need dogs," he said.

At the bottom of the stairway, just outside the steel door to the basement level, the dog handler squatting beside his rottweiler held up a hand. Ed put Herb Bodine's shirt into

it—a spare the foreman had found in Herb's abandoned
truck. Bunching the red plaid flannel, the handler, Deputy
Sheriff Roy Strasborg, held it under the rottweiler's square
jaw.

The big dog sniffed and made a sound deep in its throat,
like table legs rattling on a wooden floor.

"Okay, he's got it," Roy said. "Good boy, Major."

Ed nodded at Captain Hardison, who held the door
open. Inside the basement hall, Roy stopped and squinted
at the work site a couple hundred feet away. "Damn, what
do you folks do down here, Mr. Jeffers, mine coal?"

Ed forced a smile. Unfortunately, the German shep-
herds on the Pentagon's SWAT teams were trained for
sniffing out bombs, not people, so here was Deputy Strasborg from out Loudon way, three Virginia counties west of
Washington—distant in more than miles. A good old boy
in jeans and a wide-brimmed hat, the bourbon nose, cheek
full of Red Man, trying to be funny, but Ed didn't feel like
laughing.

Major sniffed the floor, pulling on his leash. Roy let it
play and the dog surged ahead, nose to the floor, keeping to
one side of the corridor, where Herb had probably walked
on his way in yesterday. Fortunately, there wouldn't have
been many other people aside from Herb and the crew
along here since. Gerakis gave them a wave; his crew
fanned out behind him near the hole in the wall.

As they headed for the hole, Ed realized from Roy's
silence that he might be feeling snubbed. "That's a fine-
looking animal, Deputy Strasborg. I didn't realize rottweilers were used in search and rescue."

"Trackers come from a number of different breeds, Mr.
Jeffers. The individual dog matters more than pedigree.
Rottweilers been around since the Romans, good strong
dogs with a lot of intelligence and courage, won't shrink
from new situations. Major, here, has never been in the

Pentagon, but with that name I guess he'll fit right in. He's what we call a two-talent dog—a first-rate air tracker, plus a good surface tracker. Pretty rare to find both skills in one dog, so y'all are in luck today."

"I hope so."

Thinking about the wet grunting sound he'd heard, or might have heard, inside the wall, Ed was glad for the big, chesty dog with the head like a lion. If there was something larger than a rat in there, this animal should be able to handle it.

"Captain Hardison," Roy said, "we'll wait here if y'all would be kind enough to clear those men back a hundred feet from the hole, give Major some clear air to work with." He pulled up on the leash and Major stopped, seeming to freeze into stone as he glared ahead down the long hall. His nose quivered, winnowing the warm air. Suddenly, his muzzle lifted away from his teeth, and a soft growl rumbled in his throat.

"Think he has the scent?" Ed asked.

"I don't rightly know, Mr. Jeffers." Roy studied his dog with a frown.

"Looks like Captain Hardison has them cleared away."

"Track, Major."

The dog did not move, and Roy repeated his command.

Major gave a low whine and looked back at his handler.

"Track," Roy repeated in a stern voice.

Major began a stiff-legged walk, his nose no longer on the ground, but air-tracking now, sniffing, his steps slowing and becoming more rigid as he neared the hole in the wall. His teeth had bared and he was growling deep in his throat, the hair on the back of his neck spiking up.

Ed felt his own hackles rising. There *is* something in there, he thought.

"Track," Roy commanded.

The dog did not move.

He repeated the order and Major backed up a step. "I never seen him like this." Roy put Herb's shirt under the dog's nose again. Major ignored it, staring at the dark inside the wall, whimpering now.

"Major!" Roy snapped.

The dog lurched into Ed, knocking his legs out from under him. Falling on his side, Ed rolled to see the dog dash up the hall. The leash held, but Major strained on, dragging Roy several steps after him. The deputy sheriff looked over his shoulder, his face red with the effort of holding the big dog. "You okay, Mr. Jeffers?"

"Fine," he said, scrambling up. The urge to run flooded his legs, the dog's fear infecting him. With an effort, he held himself in place.

"I got to get him out of here," Roy said, "or he may never be any good to me again. I'm sorry."

"That's all right, go."

A spot of pain stung in Ed's thigh. He remembered the arrowhead he'd found inside the wall. He'd stuffed it in his pocket and it must have gouged him when he fell. He fished it out, and in the light saw that it was not an arrowhead. It was a tooth, a big one, curved . . .

A fang.

Hearing footsteps, he looked up to see Gerakis and his men hurrying toward him. He stuffed the fang back in his pocket—the work crew was spooked enough.

Ed recalled the scent from inside the wall, the alien perfume of the reptile house.

A spot of cold spread between his shoulder blades. Time to give the zoo a call.

CHAPTER 3

National Zoo, Amazonia Exhibit

"Is it true, Dr. Deluca, that humans have gills, too, when we're in the embryo stage?"

Andrea hid her delight at the question, knowing a smile would make the girl with the solemn, piping voice and thick glasses feel patronized. Precocious, clearly, standing there off to one side of her fourth grade class, as if afraid to be taken for one of them.

A tubby boy in the front of the pack groaned and rolled his eyes. "Suzie Salamander." A few kids laughed; their teacher, a young woman with a pleasant, sunburned face and the sinewy forearms of a rock climber, leaned over a couple of rows to give the boy a warning prod. Andrea thought: You just asked me if frogs give you warts, and you think Suzie's question is dumb? Can you spell post-cocious?

On the brighter side, a dozen or so of the twenty-five kids had been captured by the girl's question, their attentive faces glistening in the tropical heat of the Amazonia exhibit.

"You're right, Susan," Andrea said. "We humans do go through a stage, before we're born, in which gill-like slits start forming right here." Touching the sides of her throat, she found them reassuringly smooth.

"Why?"

"No one's sure. A hundred and forty years ago, shortly after Darwin published his theories on evolution, a scientist named Ernst Haeckel proposed that gill folds and other primitive structures appear briefly because the embryo is zooming through man's earlier stages as it develops into our present, more advanced form. This was a very big jump of reasoning, and there was no way to prove it, then or now. When it came out that Haeckel had fudged some of his evidence, his theory pretty much faded away. Today, some scientists are starting to think that, although old Ernst went too far, he wasn't entirely wrong."

She hesitated, knowing *she* was about to go too far. "How many of you know what genes are?"

A dozen hands eased up, others faltering along behind.

"Good. Genes are passed on to us by our parents. They are tiny structures inside us arranged in patterns which form a code. This code translates into instructions for producing the proteins of life, which our bodies are made of. So the code determines our eye and hair color, the shape of our nose and head, the makeup of all our bones and organs and so on. The Human Genome Project, completed a couple of years ago, was done to identify the specific 'code' on each of these many different genes. And there really are a lot of genes—the project found nearly thirty thousand. So far, we've only discovered what a very few of them actually do to help make us what we are. The main theory right now is that a lot of our genes are 'junk'—that they don't really do anything. Maybe this is true. Or maybe we simply don't know what role they play yet. We might someday be able to specifically identify many of them as holdovers from man's distant, nonhuman ancestors, and show that they aren't totally inactive after all."

"I've never heard that theory," Susan said.

Because I haven't yet won a grant to try and prove it, Andrea thought.

And probably won't.

"It makes sense, though," Susan said. "I heard that we have ninety-eight percent the same genes as chimpanzees."

"Maybe *you* do," the plump boy cracked.

"That's e-*nough*, Sean," said his teacher.

"Actually," Andrea said, "Susan is right. Most of our genes are the same as those in chimps."

"But chimps look so different from us," Susan said.

The teacher was standing right behind Sean now, a hand on his shoulder, so the boy said nothing, but his face reddened and his lips stretched tight, until finally, a snorting laugh exploded through his nose, and the rest of the class, except for his target, broke down in giggles.

When the teacher had restored order and taken Sean off to scold him, Andrea said, "Chimps *are* quite different from us, in brain and body size, head shape, bone structure, even the diseases we can catch. If all those differences can result from just the two percent of our genes that are different, why do we have all that other ninety-eight percent that we share with chimps? Maybe all those genes *are* just junk. Or maybe they used to do something way back before chimps and humans existed. Suppose we carry some of the genes of ancient amphibians, long before humans evolved. Suppose those genes started to work in the fetus, and then newer, more evolved genes turned them off. It could explain why we humans go through a brief 'gill' stage. Maybe some of our genes go all the way back to the beginnings of life in the prehistoric seas many millions of years ago."

Susan nodded, but the other kids were starting to look stupefied. These were not grad students, these were nine-year-olds, and it was time to get back on their wavelength. "Speaking of prehistoric times, how many are interested in dinosaurs?"

Every hand shot up.

"Good. The amphibians that survive today—frogs and toads, salamanders and newts, and the caecilians—are mostly quite small, but did you know that, back in the Triassic period about two hundred twenty million years ago, there lived an amphibian called the mastodonsaurus? We know this because its bones have been found in Germany and other modern-day countries. It belonged to an order of animals called labyrinthodontia. It grew up to sixteen feet long, lived mostly in the water, and was a fierce predator with a muscular tail, a huge head, and very sharp teeth."

"Cool," said several voices.

"If you'll follow me, I'll show you a picture of a mastodonsaurus and a full-sized replica of its skeleton." Skirting the class, she led them down the trail past the spreading roots of a mammoth kapok, the exhibit's biggest tree. Part of her savored the happy chatter behind her, but another part wished she were back in a real rain forest, doing field work among the elephant-eared philodendrons, smelling the rich earth, her arms glittering with winks of sunlight that managed to break through the canopy. At thirteen, Teddy was old enough to be a real help on a field trip, and he loved backpacking through the jungle. Last summer, his father had invoked visitation rights only once. *I could tell the judge Mark basically isn't coming to see his son anymore,* Andrea thought. *She'd probably let me take Teddy for the whole summer—*

She felt a tap on her hip, the little girl with the glasses catching up to her. "How did you know I like to be called Susan?"

"Lucky guess."

"I wish you taught at our school."

"I wish you were in grad school, so I could hire you as a research assistant."

"That would be so neat."

"Look me up in fifteen years."

Susan made an indignant sound. "Sooner than that. I'm going to skip to sixth grade next year, and I plan to take high school in three."

Andrea thought of her own self-abbreviated childhood. Lose the glasses and this kid could be me, she thought. Did I have a daughter I didn't know about?

She wanted to warn Susan not to go too fast, to pay attention not just to the kingdoms and the phyla, but to the life going on right around her—to study not just books but boys like Sean and boys not like Sean, so that when the boys got older and the rubber started trying to meet the road, she'd know which Trojaned horse to let in. I was a social nitwit, Andrea thought. Twenty when I fell for Mark, old enough to know better, but I didn't. Dad could at least have told me guys might want only the part of me they could see, and that I'd better watch out, but he's so unlike most guys himself it probably never dawned on him. Does a low romantic IQ run in our family—something in our genes?

"Don't go too fast," she advised Susan.

"You're kidding, right?"

She gave the child's shoulder a squeeze, knowing there was no way in the next few minutes to persuade her to skip a little rope while she was skipping grades. She could only hope Susan's parents were as wise as their daughter was smart, and that Susan would listen to them.

The class was waiting at the mastodonsaurus skeleton, gathered in a tight circle around it. Sean—who else—had a death grip on one of the big anklebones. Andrea told them of the skeleton's owner and its big, toothy pal, the trematosaurus; of the lush Triassic lakes and swamps the giant amphibians had roamed; and the mysterious extinction at the end of the late Triassic period that sealed the doom of these great beasts. All so long ago, the tragedy so far removed that it only made the tale grander, but she knew she ought also to be telling these children about the mass extinction underway among current-day amphibians that appeared to have started a decade and a half ago. The dwindling numbers of leopard frogs in the Colorado Rockies, the tubbily charming gold and brown Yosemite toad, once so abundant in the Sierra Nevadas and now hard to find. Tell the kids of toad and frog populations dwindling or disappearing all over the world, and what it might mean. That was part of her job as a Smithsonian curator, to get these young minds on board in the fight against development, habitat destruction, and pollution, which were destroying these beautiful and useful creatures she loved.

Looking at the happy faces in front of her, Andrea hadn't the heart to bring them down. She could give it a rest, just this once. You couldn't watch a show on animals anymore without having your heart clobbered by dire warnings of some poor creature's impending extinction. Maybe it galvanized some watchers to action, but how many others hit the remotes in their hands and hearts, bailing out of any emotional involvement at all to avoid the pain they knew had become an inevitable part of TV's nature show packages?

So she said, "And now, if you'll go next door to the lab, Maggie Lugenbeal, who is a graduate student in herpetology, will show you the amazing blue frog."

She watched them troop through the public entrance to

the frog lab. Susan, trailing the pack, turned to give her a last look of longing. Andrea waved, thinking, Hold on, girl, and in ten years I'll marry you off to Teddy.

Following the ramp down below water level of the exhibit's "river," she watched through the thick glass as an electric eel kept pace, nosing myopically along the reedy bottom. The beeper at her belt went off. The readout gave the number of her lab, back up across the zoo. Using the staff phone at the bottom of the ramp, she dialed.

"Herpetology." Tom, her assistant curator.

"Andrea. What's up?"

"Just got a call from your housekeeper. Your dad has given her the slip again."

"Damn."

"She wanted to know whether she should notify the police. I told her to wait and I'd have you call her."

"Thanks, Tom." Hanging up, Andrea dialed home.

"Deluca residence." The accent strong, a sure sign Heidi was stressed.

"This is Andrea. How long has Dad been gone?"

"Only about twenty minutes. I'm so sorry, Doctor. He asked me to go out back and put more safflower seed in the bird feeder. When I returned, he was gone. I think that means he is not lost but that on purpose he left. I should have expected a trick. I feel like such a dumb head."

"That's all right. You can't watch him every second. Look, don't call the police. He can't have gone far. What was he wearing?"

"His gray cardigan and those old brown corduroys he loves."

"Okay. Just stay in the house in case he comes back. If I haven't called by the time Teddy gets home from school, send him around the neighborhood. If Dad comes back, or Teddy finds him, just call the lab and they'll beep me. Meanwhile, I'll get my pickup and hunt for him."

"Thank you, Doctor, thank you."

Fortunately, she'd put on her running shoes to do the tour, but by the time she'd jogged the zoo path past the seals and bear pens and taken the switchback up to the great apes she was sweating. She sprinted past the reptile center to the parking lot. Though it was only in the seventies today, the sun had turned her '95 Ford pickup into an oven. She cranked the windows down and stepped on the gas, almost tipping onto two wheels as she made the sharp turn onto the Rock Creek Parkway.

She worked at calming herself. If Dad had tricked Heidi, he couldn't be that far gone. But the periods of confusion were starting to come more frequently now, and if he hadn't been addled when he started out, he might become so at any moment.

She took the parkway down to P Street, and P into the shaded high ground of Georgetown, with its narrow old houses and stately oaks. That little park off 36th—or would he head downtown?

She swung downhill; if Dad was in the park, he'd be all right, but if he got down to M Street and ran into a crowd of skinheads or some mutant in a Nazi motorcycle helmet, he might get himself into real trouble, confused or not.

Andrea worked her way over to Wisconsin Avenue and down, the traffic jamming up, slowing her enough for a thorough scan of the foot traffic streaming past the galleries, shops, and restaurants on either side.

No sign of him.

Turning left on M, she continued her search, looking for a thin, straight-backed man with an elegant step and baggy, pre-bum clothes. She slowed past a gaggle of Goths in dark jeans and Clockwork Orange derbies, ignoring the blare of a horn behind her, working her way down M, then hanging a U to work back up the street.

No Dad.

The canal, she thought. He'd go to the water.

Turning left off M, she scooted the pickup into a miraculous parking place behind a vacating SUV. Hopping out, she jogged the half block down to the canal bridge, and there he was, sitting on the bank below, feet together, arms hugging his knees. Scrambling down the bank, she sorted through hot words, but by the time she settled beside him, relief had won out.

"Andrea, dear," he said. "I thought you were at work."

"Oh, you're a card, you are."

"Heidi ratted me out?"

"You frightened her."

"And you. I'm sorry." He touched her hand. "But it's such a beautiful day. The leaves are starting to turn, did you notice? The bees still buzzing, and the cicadas, but fall is coming."

"Heidi will walk with you, you know that."

"Heidi is a dear, but a poor conversationalist."

She looked at her father, pleased at the flow of his talk, so like him in the old days. Why couldn't he have been twenty-five or thirty when she was born, like other people's parents? A pointless question, but it had rankled more and more as he'd aged before her eyes. Fifty when she was born, sixty-two when she entered high school, older than all her friends' parents, but it had really begun to hit her lately. Here she was, only thirty-four, and before long her father would either be dead or, worse, his brilliant mind would be eclipsed in shadow, and she still needed him.

"Have you started that grant application yet?" he asked.

"No. I can't decide if I want to do a comparative study of amphibian and human DNA or go hunt for golden toads. . . ." Too late, she caught herself. *Damn!*

He frowned. "Monteverde—the cloud forest? What would be the point? Not one toad has been sighted there in over ten years."

She thought about the preserve in Costa Rica, one of the most beautiful places she'd ever been, with its towering trees and morning mists, its brilliant, exotic birds. Dad was right about the toads—as far as it went. Professor Crump of the University of Florida was the last to see one, back in 1989. Just the year before, they'd been plentiful. Neither Crump nor anyone else had found bodies. Not surprising, since the golden toad hibernated in the ground all year except for their brief breeding season.

But shouldn't a mass extinction have left a bad smell at the least?

There'd been no mention of any odor, not by Crump or the caretakers who kept constant watch over the preserve. For once, man wasn't the obvious and immediate suspect in the disappearance—the cloud forest had been kept pristine by any standard measure. A new theory suggested that a warming trend at the forest's higher levels might have caused the extinction, but another idea kept nagging at her: What if the toads were not dead but extending their hibernation for some mysterious reason?

If I could find just one in the ground, alive, Andrea thought, it would be stunning. No one has documented suspended animation lasting longer than three years.

"Andrea?"

She suppressed a sigh. She'd let it slip and now she had to explain herself. She hadn't wanted to, knowing he'd insist she was wrong, or worse, stumble over her reasoning. But he seemed all right now, and how many more moments like this would they have, the old light in his eyes?

When she was finished, he said, "What makes you think an amphibian could survive a decade of dormancy?"

"Okay, the limit is supposed to be around three years, but 'supposed' is the key word. We don't *know.*"

"I hope you have the sense not to talk like this around your colleagues."

"You're the one who taught me to think outside the box. Haven't you always tried to drum into me that the most important advances in science come from people challenging what is 'known'? Our limits on amphibian hibernation come from anecdotal field observations. Why not do a controlled experiment?"

He started to say something, then stopped, his face oddly troubled.

She said, "We have the technology now to tag animals so unobtrusively they wouldn't even know they were carrying a little nonallergenic broadcasting chip around under their skin. We could trace frogs into their holes, monitor their metabolism during hibernation, keep track of individuals for years. But no one has done it. Which means we can't be sure the golden toads in Monteverde are dead."

"What are they living on?"

"Their own body fat."

"For so long? Impossible."

"Not if they can slow their metabolism down more than we think."

He shook his head, gazing at the canal again, the brown water lazing along the flank of Georgetown, unconscious of its mother Potomac half a mile south. A yellow maple leaf swirled in an eddy and passed into the well of shadow under the bridge.

"I think you should compare the DNA," he said.

"I'll never get that grant," she said, "and you know it."

"Not if you don't try. If you take a field trip next summer, you'll be running from what you should be doing—comparing human and amphibian DNA to check out your theory about 'junk' DNA."

"Dad, no one's going to fund me to run a salamander genome. We're talking big bucks, and the people who dole out foundation money prefer species closer to man because the data generalize better. Chimps will be next to have their genes charted, you know they will. Slimy swamp things would be very far down the list."

"You're right. What do I know? I'm just a senile old man."

"Stop it, Dad." She took his hand, panged by its bony thinness, recalling when it had a lithe strength. "You're not senile. I do value your advice, you know that. I always have and I always will. Without you, I wouldn't be what I am."

Some of the tension left him. "Remember that time in the Sierra Nevadas," he said, "when we camped out for a week and counted over a thousand Yosemite toads? You were what, five?"

"We had fun. I adored it."

He sighed. "I should have found another woman and re-married so you could at least have a nice stepmother. All you had was me, and I filled your head with my own obsessions. Frogs, always frogs. You should have been free to find your own way."

She leaned into him, kissed his seamed, sagging cheek. "Don't be ridiculous. You did great being Mom and Dad, nobody could have done it better. And I love what I'm doing. I wouldn't be anything else for all the money in the world."

"Good." He turned to her, returning her grip on his hands with some of the old strength. "Andrea, dear, take my advice and do the DNA study. The golden toads are dead. Nothing can survive suspended animation that long in the wild." He hesitated. "It's a dangerous idea."

His emphasis chilled her. "Come on, Dad, *dangerous*?"

"To your career. Promise me you'll forget it, just put it out of your mind."

Such conviction in his voice.

And why not? Before his mind started slipping, no one in the world knew more about frogs.

"All right," she said. "I promise."

Her beeper went off—her lab again, probably Tom relaying worries from Heidi on whether she'd found her father.

"I need to get to a phone." She held her hand out to help him up.

"You go. I'll stay here and wait for you."

She hesitated. What if he wandered off, fell in the canal?

In his eyes, she saw that if she did not grant him this small wish, it would cut him. He had never once stifled her independence when it could be granted, had always treated her with respect.

"Fine," she said, "I'll be back in a few minutes."

Up the hill and back on M Street, she turned in at Henry's, the first place on her right. At five o'clock, the long oak bar was packed with a noisy happy-hour crowd. A sign halfway down the wall behind the bar promised phones and rest rooms.

She squeezed down past the bar and found the pay phone.

Tom picked up at once.

"This is Andrea. What's up?"

He started talking, and she strained to get the sense of it—too noisy in here, she must be hearing him wrong. Pressing the phone against her ear, she asked him to repeat.

"There's a man from the Department of Defense here," he said in a louder voice, separating each word. "He's wondering if you can come to your lab and look at a tooth he found in the basement of the Pentagon."

CHAPTER 4

Entering her lab, Andrea caught the Pentagon man gazing out the window at the gorilla habitat next door. Mandera and her tykes must be romping, putting on one of their evening shows. Fur is fundable, Andrea thought grumpily.

On the other hand, it did free her to size the man up as she passed between the petri-dish colonies of frog eggs on her two lab benches. Not what she'd expected, the image she'd formed on her way here of a balding bureaucrat in his fifties, nerdy, no flair. This man had to be six-four, strong neck and shoulders, like alligator wrestlers she'd known, except guys who wrestled gators rarely dressed in expensive blue suits with understated pinstripes. Thick, dark hair, great haircut, full on top and tapered around the ears. As he turned toward her, his eye color surprised her, a deep, cornflower blue. Early forties, sexy creases on either side of his mouth—

Slow down, girl.

"Andrea Deluca." Offering her hand, she hid her surprise when he responded with his left, giving her fingers a quick clasp over the top.

Sprained wrist?

She denied herself even a glance at his right hand, but from the corner of her eye it seemed normal, no swelling or bandage.

"Ed Jeffers," he said. "I appreciate you coming back in, Dr. Deluca."

"No problem, I'm often here in the evening." She winced inwardly—why not just tell him she had no life? "Coffee? My assistant shuts off the burner when he leaves, but it should still be warm."

"Sounds good."

Conscious of his gaze, she went to the Braun, filled her mug, and found him a paper cup. "Black all right?"

"Fine." He took it with his left, the right now planted with apparent ease on the radiator beneath the window, all the angles natural, back of the hand looking so real a glance could not resolve it.

"I don't get many calls from the Pentagon," she said. "I mean from someone in the Pentagon."

He smiled. "The building *does* talk—ask any reporter. Just last night on *Jim Lehrer* 'the Pentagon said more money would be needed for force modernization.' "

She thought: He watches the *Lehrer NewsHour*, too. No wedding ring, why wouldn't a guy like him be taken? Shall I just ask him if he's gay and get it over with?

Forget it. Mark is handsome, and look where that got me. "Tom mentioned a tooth."

Ed Jeffers took a quick, preparatory breath. "Yes. I have it right here." Setting the cup down, he rummaged in his left pants pocket. The fang he placed on her lab bench was too white but otherwise convincing, just over an inch long, curving down to a point. A malformed shark's tooth, possibly, broken off just above the roots.

Picking it up, she examined the sheared-off base.

Her heart skipped a beat.

She took the tooth to the lab bench and put it under the magnifier, switching on the viewer light and bending down to the twinned eyepieces.

What she saw raised goose bumps on her arms.

"Where did you get this?"

"Found it in the dirt inside a basement wall of the Pentagon. It was dark in there and I put it in my pocket, thinking arrowhead. Later, I realized what it was."

She stared at the tooth. The real thing? But how?

Maybe this was a joke—Tom or one of her other assistants. Yeah, retaliation for that time she'd slipped caviar into one of the petri dishes, or when she'd instructed them to assemble the mastodonsaurus replica, neglecting to tell them she'd slipped in a bone from a velociraptor model.

"Mr. Jeffers, I forgot to ask for your ID."

He reached with his left inside his suit coat and pulled out a wallet, switched it to his right hand so he could use his left to snap open a photo section. The fingers of the right hand held the wallet in a natural, loose grip, but the hand was artificial, no longer any question, the skin poreless, good color, but not quite a match for the other hand, and the nails were too perfect. An incredible piece of technology—such lifelike movements. What could be controlling it?

How had he lost the hand?

She made herself focus on the photo ID he'd held out: Ed Jeffers, DoD—Department of Defense, yes. The upper left corner of the card said *SES-6,* and in a second, the meaning perked up from memory: When she'd wanted clearance for field work on the Navajo reservation, the Interior Department official who'd signed off had been an

SES-1—"SES" for Senior Executive Service, the government's elite managers. An SES-6 topped the civil service, as high as you could go.

"I'm curious, Mr. Jeffers. What would a senior Pentagon official be doing down in the dirt inside a basement wall?"

"I manage the physical plant of the Pentagon, the building, its offices and all their furnishings and equipment. We're going through a renovation—maybe you've read about it in the paper?"

She nodded—that article in the *Post*'s "Style" section a few weeks ago about the incredibly speedy repair of the 9/11 damage and the continued remodeling of the aging building. What a huge job!

"My work takes me all around the building. A plumbing crew has been down in the basement—the subbasement, actually—breaking through a wall to inspect some pipes. Along that stretch, the floor inside the wall is dirt, and I found the tooth there."

Okay, maybe she *could* see this guy down on his knees, getting his hands—his hand—dirty, but he still hadn't really told her why. What was he trying to hide?

He said, "It *is* a tooth, right? I mean, it's real."

"Mr. Jeffers, why did you call me, a herpetologist?"

"I thought this might be from a snake, a huge boa constrictor, maybe."

"You have boa constrictors in the Pentagon?"

"Yesterday, I'd have said no. What we do have is rats, lots of rats, some very big ones, who live inside the walls all through the building. At night, they sneak into the offices where they can and dine like kings on pizza crusts and chicken bones the cleaning crews haven't got to yet. The renovation crews are made up of construction workers from all around the area. I wouldn't be surprised if some of the workers read Shakespeare and listen to opera. Others

hunt deer and buy those cute white rats at the pet store to
feed to their boa constrictors. I can imagine one of them
working the basement, catching sight of some rats, and
thinking it might be a good place to bring his snake. Then
maybe the snake gets away and the guy decides it's better
not to tell anyone and get himself fired."

Ed Jeffers seemed to be trying to convince himself.

"I assume you check workers at the gate before they get
into the building?"

"Sure, and since 9/11 the security is really tight, but
nothing is foolproof. Workers have to wheel in big drums
of spackle, paint, and the like. The guards scan and hand
search often enough that no sensible person would try to
slip contraband through, but a guy who'd think of setting
his pet snake loose in the Pentagon basement can't be
called sensible. Dr. Deluca, *is* the tooth from a snake?"

"No." She turned back to the viewer. The tooth, the impossible tooth, had not changed. She could feel her heart
pounding. Dear God, what was she supposed to think
about this?

Stepping back, she offered him a look. As he bent over
the viewer, she caught a whiff of his cologne, a clean hint
of juniper, causing a lift in the sensitized nerves of her
stomach. A spectacular sunset had begun, flooding the lab
with a red glow that flamed off every edge. She battled a
dizzying sense of unreality. "What you're seeing," she
said, "is the tooth from the order labyrinthodontia. By its
size you'd expect a trematosaurus or maybe a mastodonsaurus—two of the largest labyrinthodonts. At the base of
the tooth, you see in cross section the outer layer, which is
ivory, working its way into the inner dentine. Notice the
interlaced pattern of ivory and dentine. It looks like a
labyrinth, hence the name." She stopped, realizing she'd
fallen into her professor persona. The real point about this
tooth was that it damn well could not exist—not like this.

"What are we talking, here?" he asked. "You're not going to tell me this is one of those mythical crocodiles big cities supposedly have in their sewer systems."

"Not a croc, but you're getting warm. Labyrinthodonts were amphibians."

"Were?"

"They're extinct. No member of the labyrinthodont order has walked the face of the earth for over two hundred million years."

He straightened from the scope with a relieved expression. "Then the tooth is just a fossil. It can't have anything to do with it."

"With what?"

He hesitated.

"Come on, Mr. Jeffers, you ask my help, but you don't want to tell me why?"

"I've got some worries that could turn worse in a hurry if they reached the press. Can I trust you to say nothing?"

"As long as it isn't something people should know."

"If it comes to that, I'll do everything necessary to keep my people safe."

"Your people?"

He winced. "That sounded like Moses, didn't it. Whoever holds my job is traditionally known as the 'mayor' of the Pentagon. Sometimes that goes to my head."

Andrea decided she liked more than Ed Jeffers's looks. "I take it one of your renovation workers ran into trouble inside the wall."

"Disappeared, yes. Whether inside the wall, we're not sure. We arranged for a tracking dog. It refused to go in. Big, tough-looking rottweiler, and I've never seen an animal so scared."

Andrea felt a chill along the back of her neck. Slipping a hand under her hair, she rubbed at it. "But how could a man just disappear inside a wall?"

"First, it's a very big wall. Second, when I went in there, I discovered the opening to a sinkhole. Plenty large enough for a man to fall in—"

"Wait. A sinkhole?"

"The Pentagon was built on some of the lowest ground in Washington. The basement levels are well below the floodplain of the Potomac River. To protect the building against erosion and settling from groundwater, the builders supported it on thousands of concrete pilings sunk down to bedrock. Some had to go pretty far down to hit rock—if the pilings were placed end to end, they'd stretch over two hundred miles. In addition to the extra support, an outer retaining wall was built down into the ground on the river exposure of the Pentagon to hold water back. But the earth moves constantly, even in Washington, and in sixty years the walls apparently have cracked in places, allowing groundwater through to ebb and flow under the building, possibly scooping out caverns and tunnels. We've suspected for some time there might be hollow areas under the subflooring of the basement. Not much of a worry, since the pilings are so massive, plus the floors were built at double strength to support thousands of loaded filing cabinets so the Pentagon could be turned into a records depot after the war."

"Swords into plowshares, huh?"

He eyed her. "You sound skeptical."

"It hardly squares with your image as a government behemoth, spending ever more money."

"Believe it or not, Doctor, if our jobs became obsolete tomorrow, I would (a) panic about getting another job, yes, and (b) feel relieved—me and most of the rest of us in the building. The idea that we in the Pentagon like war is, forgive my bluntness, asinine. What we do in there is *worry* about war, twenty-four hours a day, seven days a week. What we *like* is when there's no war or terrorist attacks, and we can feel we had something to do with that. When the Pentagon was built, America was fighting the war to end all wars. We didn't anticipate how fast our pals the Russians would turn into our enemy or that G.I.s would soon be fighting a war in Korea. . . ."

Something in her face must have cued him because he stopped, made a toss-away gesture with the right hand. "Sorry, I'm getting off point, which is the sinkhole. There's enough water down inside to make a lake-type splash when I tossed in a rock. Talk about labyrinths, there could be endless channels under there. If the worker *is* beneath the building, he could have been swept far from the hole by an underground surge. Rescuing him or finding his body would be a job for Superman."

"But why would a construction worker, presumably experienced, fall into a hole?"

"He probably wouldn't—unless he had 'help' from someone or something. Two days ago I wouldn't have imagined anything like a boa constrictor in the Pentagon, but a man *has* vanished, and I did find that tooth. I wasn't eager to put all that together for you because if it got out that a huge snake was loose in the building, carrying people off, half or more of the workforce might run for the exits and not come back until we dragged the thing out."

"Could you blame them?"

"I'd lead the pack myself if a mass exodus from the Pentagon weren't more dangerous than any snake."

"Really."

He rubbed his forehead. "What can I compare it to? Cops coast to coast fleeing their precincts? Or maybe air traffic controllers taking a powder. My point is that defending the nation is an around-the-clock job. . . . What?"

"What 'what?' "

"You're giving me that skeptical look again."

"No. I'm sure you're right."

"I hate to sound self-important, but you did ask. . . ." He cocked his head. "Or are you tweaking me, Doctor?" His voice mild, not accusing, as if he were amused at himself for falling for it.

"Sorry. I guess I'm a little weird about the Pentagon. When I was a kid, one of Dad's buddies was an army officer who worked there—my godfather, in fact. But Uncle Luther never wanted to talk about what he did, so I decided it wasn't anything good. And Dad, despite being buddies with Luther, was phobic about the military in general. When my eighth grade class took the Pentagon tour, he refused to come along, though normally he loved helping out with our field trips."

"Vietnam vet?"

I wish, she thought. "No, older. . . ."

Andrea hesitated. This guy was easy to talk to—a little too easy. She wasn't ashamed of what Dad had done in World War II. But it wasn't any of Ed Jeffers's business.

"Anyway," she said, "Dad is very antiwar. I guess some of that rubbed off on me. And since the main job of the Pentagon is to make war . . ."

"We prefer to think of it as keeping peace. To do that, we've made ourselves the world's experts on war, just like doctors study disease. We try to stay ready to fight one. . . ." He stopped, gave her a weary smile. "You're good, Doc."

"Sorry," she said again.

"You're not just tweaking me, though. Part of you means it, and you're not alone. Even the outpouring of sympathy after we lost people on 9/11 hasn't eliminated all public skepticism about us—nor should it. Many Americans think we're too big, we spend too much money, or we don't hate war as much as they do. We haven't done well at explaining what we do. Too busy doing it, I guess. When the Cold War ended, the nation demanded a 'peace dividend' from President Clinton, and they got it. Ninety-five percent of cuts in the government workforce came out of Defense, nearly three hundred thousand jobs eliminated. The Pentagon, as the headquarters of the Defense Department, took its full share of these job cuts, mostly at mid and upper levels, and as a result, few senior executives can manage their workload in forty hours a week. Sixty to seventy is more like it."

Andrea winced. "That's tough on the family."

"If I were married, i'd be in some other line of work by now—especially if I had kids." He hesitated.

She felt herself blushing. She hadn't meant to pump him—or had she?

He cleared his throat. "Don't get me wrong, despite the cuts, we've still got some shirkers and drones, same as General Motors, your local supermarket, and everywhere else. But most people in the Pentagon work their butts off." He rubbed at an eyebrow, still looking distracted. "What I'm trying to say, a panic is the last thing we need. Fortunately, on 9/12, enough critical personnel were back inside, even though the building was still burning, to hold things together. This may sound strange to you, but most of us have a serious aversion to big predatory snakes. The plane hit and it was over. News of a killer snake loose in the building could empty it for a week. Even a few days could be hazardous to all our health."

"Couldn't they do their jobs in temporary work quarters somewhere else?"

"Not really. We're talking twenty-five thousand people—more than most small towns. Even if you could empty out the next biggest building in Washington at a moment's notice, it wouldn't hold a fourth of them. They depend on fast, face-to-face access to each other at all times so they can stay up-to-date on developments they can't risk discussing over phone lines. Electronic snooping

has become so effective that anything secret or sensitive
can be discussed only in shielded rooms built like bank
vaults—not something you can take with you if you evacuate the building."

"You're telling me if Pentagon workers can't have their
meetings we're all in trouble?" Too late, she realized how
it sounded. She liked Ed Jeffers—so far—and she didn't
really want to bait him, but he was so damn grim about
this, and maybe he was scaring her a little. "I'm serious, I
really want to know."

"Dr. Deluca, some of those meetings could ultimately
make the difference between life and more death than any
of us want to think about. The Pentagon is under a constant
avalanche of information, like fleets of trucks backing up
to the doors to dump loads of puzzle pieces. Hundreds of
different offices examine the pieces that fall into their subject areas, then work together to assemble them into a big
picture. Budgets, planning, terrorist and other threat levels
now and in the future, the question of which weapons and
forces to fund and develop to defend against those threats,
and a lot of other critical factors join to form an overall
picture that morphs continually. To keep putting that puzzle together, you have to *be* together.

"Beyond that, the Pentagon has come to depend more
and more on snazzy hardware—computer and other electronic systems for everything from our own heavily fire-
walled intranet, to threat assessment, to high-tech
code-breaking. To protect these systems, certain areas of
the Pentagon have become virtual fortresses. Military and
civilian experts staff command centers in the building
around the clock, poring over satellite photos of suspected
terrorist hideouts, the nuclear labs of emerging powers, the
movements of Saddam Hussein's troops, vapors from factories in the Sudan where biological and chemical
weapons are brewing. A lot of people fear our country's

power, Dr. Deluca, and what you fear, you hate. The collapse of the Soviet Union not only didn't douse that fire, it
threw gas on the flames. Nations who'd built alliances
with the Soviets got a scare that never ends, because in sid-
ing with the loser, they put themselves on the outs with us,
and now there's no one left to hold us in check. In Russia,
itself, you now have a lot of bitterly frustrated generals and
thousands of badass weapons. How long before one of
those generals sells a matching set of nuclear suitcase
bombs to an al-Qaeda operative with the face of a prophet
and the bankroll of a sheik? Blink and you might miss it.
Hell, keep your eyes and ears open twenty-four hours a
day, plan for every disaster, and you could still miss the
one that could kill hundreds to millions of Americans. We
rarely even have fire drills at the Pentagon—not because
we don't take fire seriously but because of all the threats
we must take even more seriously." He squared his shoulders, then rolled his head around, as if his neck were hurting him.

He's tired, she realized. Seven-thirty in the evening, and
he is flat beat.

"So now," he continued, "a worker has vanished, and if
I find out something got him, I'll have to warn people and
deal with the consequences. In the meantime, I'm very
glad to hear this tooth is a fossil."

"I'm sorry, Mr. Jeffers, but I didn't say that."

He stared at her.

"The ivory is much too white. Ivory is porous. Fossils
are preserved, in part, by being packed away in earth or
some other medium that keeps the sun and other wearing
elements off them. If this were a fossil tooth, it would be
dark brown and you'd be able to pick up a layer of im-
pregnation of the ivory under the scope."

"But you said there haven't been any labyrinthodonts
on earth for two hundred million years."

"There haven't."

"Could someone make up a tooth like this?"

"A hoax? I don't see how. Look at that interleaving. No one in my profession would miss it, and I don't see how such a pattern could be produced artificially. That's ivory and dentine, I'd stake my reputation on it. The tooth looks fresh, like it just broke loose from the animal's mouth."

Ed Jeffers looked grim. "I've been calling it a tooth, but we mean fang, don't we."

"Yes."

"These labyrinthodonts, they ate meat?"

"They were pure predators, Mr. Jeffers, like their more famous distant cousin, *T. rex.* But look, there is no chance any species from the order could have survived in secret to this day and age."

Ed Jeffers held a hand out for the tooth. Andrea handed it to him, feeling a pang of loss as he slipped it back into his pocket.

He said, "I do hope you're right, Doctor. Because the next thing I have to do is find someone brave enough to go where a rottweiler won't."

Andrea had that feeling she always got when she was about to do something rash—that sudden awareness of her stomach, like a balloon was inflating in there. It has to be me, she thought. He has to let me go after it. I have to know what animal that tooth came from.

But her having to know wouldn't be enough for Mr. Responsible, here.

Following him to the door, she tried to come up with something to keep her in the game. More talk about a long-extinct species wouldn't do it—the tooth had to be from something else, and if she couldn't say what, he didn't need her.

She had a vague sense of Ed Jeffers thanking her and saying good-bye.

Of herself saying good-bye back.

Of standing at the door, staring at the word *Herpetology* backward through the frosted glass, thinking she could still catch up to him, her mind in the zone now, that swirling mist where the answer might step clear in five seconds or never.

Come on, Deluca, she thought. There has to be an explanation for that tooth. A logical, scientific explanation . . .

CHAPTER 5

Amazon Basin
July 9, 1940

Lieutenant Erich Hartmann bent down and wormed a finger into his boot, trying to get at an inflamed mosquito bite on his ankle—ah, there! Scratching, he assessed the ragged line ahead of him—the whole sorry-assed expedition except for Dr. Witte, who kept dawdling behind him, apparently unable to grasp the concept of rear guard. In the jungle's watery, greenish light, the line made Hartmann think of phantoms from a fever dream, ghosts in filthy uniforms stumbling ahead with numb persistence. Two days slogging through the relentless, suffocating heat had sapped them, this damnable air so heavy with water that your sweat had nowhere to evaporate and your lungs bubbled with each breath.

Could he really have been glad only two days ago for a

chance to get off the U-boat? Pleased that Major Grau had ordered him to bring a dozen of his best men along in case they ran into Indians? Sorry only that the whole crew couldn't escape the U-36 for some fresh air, sunshine, and an adventure guaranteed not to include being blown up or drowned?

To hell with adventure. His boat was adventure enough, and he longed to be back aboard her. His bunk might be little bigger than a child's crib, and the air might stink of diesel and worse, but at least he could fall asleep at night knowing he'd wake up without dozens of these damned bites to drive him mad with itching.

If Major Grau was to be believed, it could get worse fast: malaria from the mosquitoes, headhunting tribesmen, blood-sucking leeches, vampire bats, and snakes whose bite would kill within minutes.

Hartmann grimaced, then covered it with a cough. Fucking snakes, the worst thing he could imagine.

In fact, that's about all he'd done—imagine one lying in ambush at every step. He had yet to actually see one, though the major had assured him they were everywhere.

Maybe Grau was just trying to scare me, Hartmann thought. Revenge for how terrified he gets every time I dive the boat. Bastard's probably laughing at me for ordering the men to walk with their heads down. But it's not funny. What if, while they're watching for his damn snakes, a spear or arrow thuds into them? I should tell them to keep their eyes up. Or half of them to look up and half down . . .

No. They were scared enough as it was, clutching the Krupp carbines he'd issued them from the ship's armory instead of slinging them over their shoulders, the ensign and petty officers walking with their Lugers drawn. Wind them any tighter and they'd be shooting at anything that moved, including one another.

A hand clapped Hartmann's shoulder from behind. "Truly, my friend, doesn't this beat being cooped up in your U-boat?"

Hartmann gritted his teeth. He liked Johannes Witte, preferred him for all seasons over the Gestapo man whacking away with his machete up there at the head of the line, but if Witte didn't stop trying to cheer him up, he would strangle the doctor with a creeper and face a firing squad back in Berlin, asking only that they let him live until winter, so he could feel cool once more.

Hartmann said, "If you'd tell us what's the point of all this, maybe my men and I could be more help."

"But I did tell you. Here, would you like another look?"

Deliberately pretending to misunderstand, as if there weren't already enough vexations to wear you down in this hellhole. Hartmann leaned against the trunk of a mammoth tree choked with vines. Tipping his head back to force his airway open as wide as possible, he felt a head-spinning moment of vertigo at the way the tree seemed to sway above him, its tip circling against distant haloes of light. A rustle of paper told him Dr. Witte had gotten his precious drawing out, and was holding it up for him to see. A flower, right, with those peculiar spatulate petals Witte had colored in with a lavender pencil. Thick, straight stalk, a star pattern of five leaves circling the bloom.

"Doctor, I've memorized your drawing, believe me, though I'm starting to wonder if this flower really exists. What I want to know is why we are looking for it."

"You want to know too much, Herr Kapitän," Witte said, keeping his voice low, though Major Grau was far ahead, and the jungle rang with the chattering calls of monkeys, the cries of a multitude of birds, not to mention the constant *whack* of machetes, the *crunch* of booted feet through the tangled undergrowth—the noise of creatures who did not belong.

"You drew this flower based on the stone inscription, *ja?*"

Witte gave him a warning frown, but Hartmann wasn't to be put off this time. "Look, Doctor, my men and I have done everything you've asked. Isn't it time you started to trust us? Only if I were a *Schwachsinnige* could I fail to guess that this expedition is the result of that rock we took off Scotland—the writing on it."

"It might be better for you if you were an imbecile, Erich, but even Major Grau can't believe that."

"Johannes."

"Yes, all right, it has to do with the rock inscription."

"I only got a glimpse. I didn't think I'd ever seen the language before, but then it came to me. Runes, am I right?"

Witte's hesitation said it all and, as if realizing it, he gave a grudging nod.

He does want to talk about this, Hartmann thought. He's full of what he's doing, and it's killing him not to be able to tell me. "All right, runes, which means the inscription is druidic?"

Witte's mouth twitched.

"So what I'm wondering is how ancient druids, way up in the northern hemisphere, could possibly have had anything to do with the Amazon."

"Phoenicians," Witte murmured, as if it were a dangerous secret. "There was evidence, even before the stone was discovered, that Phoenician traders, in their heyday, got as far south as Brazil, maybe farther. They kept to coastlines, going ashore to collect whatever their customers might want, in return for a fat price."

"You are telling me that the druids bought flowers from Phoenician traders?"

"At least one of them did."

Hartmann's sense of unreality deepened. Was he really

leaning against a giant tree in the Amazon jungle, exposing his men to heat and malaria, the threat of snakes, head-
hunters, and cannibals, for the sake of a druid florist?

"Cheer up," Witte said. "We'll find it soon, I'm sure.
Nothing has happened in two thousand years to change
this jungle. . . ."

"The stone is that old?"

Witte sighed. "Yes, Herr Kapitän. Now will you please
stop? No more questions."

Hartmann gave a low whistle. "It goes back to Roman
times, to Christ himself. I didn't realize there were druids
in Scotland that far back."

For a moment Witte said nothing, but Hartmann knew
all he had to do was wait.

"More than a hundred years after Christ, actually, during the emperor Hadrian's rule. These particular druids had
probably looted some Roman villages in Britain, then re-
treated up to Scotland to escape legionaries sent to punish
them."

Hartmann struggled to put it together. The old Scot had
spoken of a skeleton he'd found in a cave—like a man but
larger, and with a tail. He'd had enough English to catch
that part and, ultimately, that's what this had to be about,
but he mustn't let on that he knew. Good a man as Witte
seemed, he might let slip to the major, and Grau had already proven he would kill to protect this project. What
was it Witte had said back in the U-boat that first trip, before they'd taken the stone? *If tonight pans out, the day
will come when the British fleet will be at our mercy. We
could sink all their ships, with little or no risk to a select
few of our own . . . men.*

That slight pause before "men"—Hartmann kept remembering it.

A thing with a tail was not a man. But what could a
flower have to do with any of it? Hartmann was no scien-

tist, but he knew enough to be sure that eating a flower, even from this alien place, could not make a man grow bigger or spring a tail.

Dr. Witte was staring ahead with a worried expression. Following his gaze, Hartmann saw that the line of sailors had frozen in their tracks behind Major Grau's upraised hand. He became aware of the silence. The birdcalls had stopped, no monkey chattered, no sound at all except for the ceaseless idiot whine of insects.

Alarmed, Hartmann eased away from the tree trunk and scanned the jungle. Impossible to see far in the ghostly light, with dense undergrowth all around them and the army of tree trunks rising above that. Grau remained frozen, the sailors rigid behind him. Then a monkey called out and the bird chorus swelled again and Hartmann felt the knot between his shoulder blades ease. Grau motioned everyone forward.

"A jaguar probably," Witte said. "No match for our guns, but big enough to scare the other animals and birds into silence."

"You're an eternal optimist, aren't you, Doctor."

"Why not? The world is what we make of it."

"Then why are we at war?"

"No one said all men are wise. And you must admit, Herr Kapitän, the British, French, and Americans had their feet solidly on our national neck until Hitler came along. They passed up no opportunity to humiliate us. Our economy was ruined, our veterans forced to beg in the streets. Some equilibrium must be restored. We gave the world Bach and Beethoven, after all, and more recently, Sigmund Freud—"

"The Jew."

"So what?"

Hartmann shook his head. How could he, a submariner who spent weeks at a time under the ocean, thousands of miles from home, know more about what was going on in German society than this brilliant man who lived there? I come home for R and R, he reminded himself, and when I'm home, I'm on the streets. A couple of weeks on patrol, then a couple in the Fatherland, going from tavern to shop to whorehouse. Of course I know more about what's going on than this academic who probably hides away with his books and chases after a flower because it is described on a stone—

"Look, there, Erich. Did you ever see a spider so large?"

Witte was pointing up in the air. It took Hartmann a moment to see the web, gleaming in a shaft of sunlight, dear God, it must be forty feet in diameter. And there, near its center, he saw the spider, a hideous giant with a belly bigger than a man's heel. His stomach clenched. The sooner he could get his men out of this nightmare place, the better.

"Here!" one of the sailors shouted. "I see it. Come!"

In a flash, Witte had churned past him, up the line to where the sailor pointed between two trees. Hartmann felt no excitement whatsoever. They had all suffered through too many false alarms, too many flowers with four leaves or six, or bifurcating stalks instead of the straight one in the drawing.

Then Witte started a clumsy jig, catching his foot on something and tumbling onto his behind, springing up, laughing.

"Quiet!" Grau cautioned, but even his pug face had lit up.

Suddenly, the heavy air sweetened in Hartmann's lungs. He hurried to Witte, looked where he and the sailor were pointing, saw nothing.

"No," Witte said impatiently. "There, on that mound, see it?"

And there it was, a lavender flower with a straight stalk and five leaves radiating from the base of the bloom. As soon as he recognized it, Hartmann saw others, growing all over the mound. Witte unslung the canvas sack he'd been carrying on his back and scrambled forward to the mound, scampering to its top—

And falling through to his hips.

For a second he looked shocked, and then he smiled. But as he glanced down, the blood drained from his face, and he went still as a statue.

Hartmann started toward him.

"Stop!" Witte hissed. "A snake—a fer-de-lance. Don't anyone move or I'm dead."

Grau said, "Remain calm, Herr Doktor. Don't move. I'll shoot it."

"No!"

Hartmann had never heard anyone put a wail into a whisper before. The doctor's fear invaded him in a cold wave. He motioned Grau to stop, but the major ignored him, creeping back to the sailor behind him and holding his hand out for the man's carbine. The sailor looked to Hartmann, who nodded permission, knowing if he did not, the major would try to wrest the rifle away.

Hartmann could see the snake's head now, emerging from the top of the mound nearly to Dr. Witte's hips. The snake continued to rise across Witte's groin and up to the pocket of his breeches, pausing there. No way could Grau shoot it without blowing a hole in Dr. Witte.

Hartmann felt his hand, of its own will, drawing his Luger. He had a better angle, could see the snake's head apart from Witte's body, but it would be a terribly risky shot.

Witte pleaded with his eyes, afraid even to whisper now, or shake his head.

Grau aimed the carbine at the snake; Hartmann could

see his finger closing on the trigger. The snake began moving again, around Witte's side and up. The shot shattered the air, loud as a cannon. The snake's head disappeared in a spray of blood.

Witte leapt out of the hole with a scream, charging at Major Grau. Hartmann intercepted him, pinning his arms, ignoring the feet hammering away at his ankles until, finally, Witte sagged.

"I'm all right. Let me go."

Hartmann released him.

Witte glared at the Gestapo major. "It would have gone away."

Grau shrugged. "Possibly. Or maybe you'd be twitching on the ground now, frothing at the mouth. It takes only minutes for the bite of one of those to kill you."

"Shall we pick the flowers," Hartmann suggested, "and get the hell back to my boat?"

Witte blinked, then brightened, his terror forgotten. He turned toward the mound, and at that instant, a sailor behind him gasped and toppled back, an arrow sticking out from his chest.

"Down!" Grau roared.

Hartmann tackled Dr. Witte from behind, pulling his skinny frame down into the scrub as the other men hit the ground. More arrows rained around them, but Hartmann still could not see anyone in the trees. Flattening himself in the scrub, he held his Luger out in front and cursed this mission. This was insane. Christ, he'd joined the navy so he wouldn't have to dodge bullets with no place to escape, no way to burrow under the surface—

He saw a blur of motion, a brown body leaning from behind the bole of a tree to loose an arrow. It whizzed over his head and he heard it thump behind him. Suddenly, he was furious. He took the Luger in a two-handed grip, arms outstretched through the weeds, and watched the trunk. In seconds, the Indian reappeared, a ferocious round face with a bone through the nose. He squeezed the trigger. Red bloomed in the Indian's forehead and he pitched down. A savage thrill went through Hartmann.

Carbines started firing all around him, a deafening roar that filled the air with acrid smoke.

Where was Witte?

Christ—there, crawling toward the mound, the canvas sack gripped in one hand. "Doctor, come back!"

Witte gave no sign of hearing.

A savage cry rose from many throats at once, and suddenly the jungle was full of red-and-brown-painted bodies hurtling toward them through the trees. The guns blazed again, volley after volley, and some of the Indians fell, but more kept coming, several dozen of them, swinging immense clubs above their heads.

Hartmann scrambled up. The Luger coughed in his hand as the Indians swarmed around them, and then he found himself locked in an embrace with a short, grunting man whose body was slippery with grease. Hartmann could not hold on to him. The Indian shoved him away and he stumbled over a root and slammed down on his back. He tried to squeeze the trigger again, but the Luger was no longer in his hand.

The Indian stood over him, swinging his club back, and then a surprised expression erased the fury on his face and he dropped the club and pitched over onto his side. Behind him, Hartmann saw Witte, holding his Luger with a look of horror.

Springing up, Hartmann grabbed the gun from Witte's unresisting hand and waded among his men, who screamed in pain as they warded off blows of the massive clubs with their forearms, the fighting too close for carbines now. Driven by a mad fury, Hartmann raced around among his sailors, firing the Luger into greased backs, jamming the barrel against skulls buried in thick, black hair, pulling the trigger over and over.

One of the Indians gave an undulating call, and the rest broke off the attack to dash away into the jungle. The carbines started barking again, and half a dozen of the warriors toppled down. The remaining few vanished into the forest.

Hartmann looked for Witte again. He was at the mound, stuffing the flowers into his bag.

The man was a maniac.

With a tight throat, Hartmann took a count of his men. Eight were up. Four bodies lay in the scrub, only two showing any life. The sailor who'd taken the first arrow was dead, and another of the men also, his skull crushed. The other two had broken forearms, their faces gray with pain.

Major Grau's face and hands were smeared with blood. A strange light filled his eyes, and Hartmann realized Grau was sorry the fight was over, this man who'd been such a coward on the U-boat. Seven Indians lay at or around the major's feet. He marched through the other bodies, firing his Luger, stiff-armed, into the heads of helpless, fallen warriors.

I should stop him, Hartmann thought, sickened, but he could not find the will to move. For the first time since he had entered the jungle, he was cold.

"I've got them," Witte cried. "A dozen, at least. More than enough. Let's go, before they come back."

"My men," Hartmann said. "We bring the dead with us."

"No," Grau said. "They'll slow us down too much."

Hartmann raised the Luger, aimed it at the major's forehead. Grau raised his own Luger.

"Stop it, both of you."

Witte's voice had a steel Hartmann had never heard before.

"Major Grau, these Indians are cannibals. If we abandon our dead, they will be eaten—good German lads who died for the Fatherland. I'd rather die myself than let that happen, and so, I am sure, would you."

Grau blinked, then lowered his Luger.

Hartmann found he could breathe again. Holstering his own Luger, he picked up one of his soldiers, a boy from Dresden named Holtz. The adrenaline still coursing through him made the body seem light. Grau slung the other body across his shoulders like a deer carcass. Hartmann turned back the way they had come, to the narrow trail the machetes had hacked through the forest. As he plodded forward the body grew heavier, but he would not put it down.

For a flower, he thought. All for a goddamned flower.

Herr Doktor, you said it would save many lives. You had better be right.

CHAPTER 6

Ed sat in his silver '00 Chrysler PT Cruiser, the puppet hand looking handy on the gearshift, but failing, somehow, to ease the idling car into drive.

Sitting there in parking lot C, his back to Dr. Andrea Deluca's reptile house, seeing the moon-creamed tarmac through a lingering image of her face. She could be Sandra Bullock's sister. Wonderful black hair like the actress, the same scrubbed freshness and girl-next-door appeal, that radiant smile, though she flashed it less. Tanned by the sun, not a salon, summer being field-trip time if you're a herpetologist.

Did people call her Dr. D?

Smart woman—the best kind of sexy. That direct gaze, no engagement or wedding ring. Been a while since anyone had made him pay so much attention to how he framed his end of a conversation. Her end had fascinated him, Dr. D and the labyrinthodont, beauty and the beast.

Ed found himself fantasizing an expedition with Andrea, just the two of them in some steamy jungle, talking and joking as they hacked their way along with machetes, her legs looking great coming down long and muscled from cuffed khaki shorts, her face glistening, dark eyes hot with the hunt.

While I sweat in a long-sleeved shirt to keep the arm hidden, even though by then she knows all about it—

The abrupt wrong turn in the fantasy startled him—letting the arm intrude when he'd only just met Andrea. If he could put it from his mind with Candace and Marianne and his other friends and lovers over the years, surely, too, with Andrea.

Or was she, somehow, another Jill?

The memory smoldered up like a cinder in a sudden draft, making his throat burn. Would it ever lose its sting? Jillian, years ago in college, who'd gotten him through French class and talked him out of hooking himself on Camel cigarettes. Studying together, they had traded fantasies about where next after college. He'd loved the offbeat workings of her mind. She was the one who'd gotten him to stare into his own eyes in a mirror and ask himself, "How is it I'm alive?" over and over until some invisible barrier broke inside him, and he felt the rush at the heart of the question.

He'd watched for any sign the arm put her off. If so, she'd never let it slip.

Jillian, Jill.

Why had he backed off? He'd gotten to third base in the backseat of a Chevy Nova, and home runs in the Starlite Motel off campus, but not with Jill.

Who'd meant far more to him.

Ed felt a pang of annoyance. He was letting his mind wander when he had a job, serious worries—a man gone, and the important thing was what Andrea Deluca had said,

if only he could make sense of it. A fang—fresh, not fossilized, and from a long-extinct predator. What in hell was
he supposed to do with that?

Rapping on his passenger window startled him; the
prosthesis nearly jerked the car into gear before he could
relax the hand inside. Dr. Deluca circled a finger at him
and he rolled down the window. Crouching down, she
studied him through the opening, head cocked, a parenthe-
sis of black hair draping one elegant cheekbone. "You by
any chance waiting for me?"

"For what you said to make sense."

"Oh. Yeah. I'm just coming out of shock myself." She
brushed back the runaway strand of hair, holding it in place
with her palm as if pondering some inner question. Whatever it was, she shook it off and said, "Anyway, I'm glad I
caught you before you left. You said you have to find
someone brave enough to go where a rottweiler won't.
Look no farther."

It brought back the jungle fantasy, Dr. Andrea Deluca in
a pith helmet, crouching into the hole in the Pentagon subbasement wall, a very big gun strapped to her shoulder.
Bravery wouldn't begin to describe it. "Thank you, Doctor.
The Pentagon has SWAT teams."

"Trained for going into holes in the ground?"

"You're going to tell me you are?"

"I've explored more caves than I can name and made at
least a thousand river and lake dives on both scuba tanks
and rebreathers, going after amphibians in their habitats."

"We're not dealing with an amphibian, you said so
yourself."

"What I said was, labyrinthodonts are extinct. But you
have a fresh tooth from one. Both can't be true, and we
have the tooth."

"Only a tooth."

"Mr. Jeffers, paleontologists write treatises off teeth.

The environment you described—subterranean channels carved out by groundwater—would be ideal for an amphibian, dark and damp, with access above to plenty of rats to feed on. If there's any chance, however slim, that a descendant of the labyrinthodonts has survived all this time undetected, living and propagating in underground caverns, I've got to know. And the only way I can do that is go after it."

Ed felt a smile trying to surface—incredulity, not disdain, but he knew to smother it. Dr. Deluca had not been in that dark place, heard that wet sigh; even so, she'd just told him more about herself than he could have learned in a year of small talk, and she deserved a respectful reply. "I appreciate the offer. I'll think it over."

"What's to think over?"

"Doctor, a few minutes ago, you said there couldn't be a big, predator amphibian down there, and now you seem to be saying there could."

"I'm saying you believe an animal may have carried off one of your workers, the tooth is amphibian, I'm a herpetologist, ergo let's go."

"It's just not practical. You need clearance even to go inside the building."

"Come on, 'Mayor' Jeffers, you can arrange that."

"Are you trained in search and rescue work?"

"No, but the title kind of says it all, doesn't it? I stay in shape and I've climbed more than one rope to get where I needed to be."

"The missing worker is big enough to hold a jackhammer sideways into a wall for hours on end. Probably at least two hundred pounds. If he's down there—"

"I'll tie a rope around him and a bunch of big strong musclemen of your choosing can pull him up."

"Look, it's just too dangerous, all right?"

"Mr. Jeffers, if I wasn't down with danger, I wouldn't

be here to lean on your car. I've survived a rattlesnake bite miles from nowhere. In the African scrub, all alone, I had a close brush with what is arguably the most vicious predator on earth."

"Even so . . . What predator?"

"Leopard. I was in Tanzania, looking for montane squeakers, a little frog, when a *ju/hoan*—that's what the bushmen call leopards—got above me in a tree. Bushmen are tough customers but they fear *ju/hoan* more than any other animal. It's the only big cat that kills when it isn't hungry. Smart, stealthy, and it loves to spring on you from above, but its one weakness is it forgets to hide its tail. From the corner of my eye I saw this humongous tail hanging down from the branch, a big male, for sure."

She's sucking me in, Ed thought. She can't go in that hole; just stay on message. "That's . . . you . . . what did you do?"

"I kept cool. If you act like you haven't seen it, a leopard might let you walk. Tense up like prey and you're meat. I knew that, and here I am. I've been in other spots almost as bad and I've never panicked. So forget that."

I'm in love, Ed thought.

But I can't be, not so soon—hell, not ever, or I'll have nothing with her, not even friendship.

"I believe you, Doctor, but it's not just a question of keeping your cool. The dirt around the sinkhole is nothing but a thin shelf. The next one to go out on it may find the ground dropping out from under him—"

"All the better to send in someone who doesn't weigh two hundred pounds."

"Right, but it must be one of our own people. Our security people are paid to take risks protecting federal workers. If I were to send a curator from our beloved National Zoo down in that hole and any harm came to her, it would be front page for weeks."

"Same as if that curator tells the *Post* you're hiding the disappearance of a worker inside the Pentagon."

He tried to stare her down; failed. "You agreed to say nothing about this."

"If it wasn't something people should know. I'm not convinced of that."

"But you would be if I sent you down in that hole?"

"I won't know until I get a closer look, will I? How about this: Just let me inspect the site where you found the tooth. I won't go any farther than you did. Then you can send in the marines. I can be there as an advisor, or—what do you Pentagon guys call it?—a consultant. I've got to do this. Come on, Mr. Jeffers."

"Given that you just blackmailed me, I think you can call me Ed."

"Some office," she said, inspecting his desk and the computer station behind, picking up the Tensor lamp on his blotter and switching the brilliant halogen bulb on and off.

Make yourself at home, he thought, a bit thrown by her casual impertinence with his things, but charmed by it, too.

She eyed the long conference table in the center of the room, then gazed around the walls at the potted scheffleras and corn plants that separated the dark oak armchairs found everywhere in the Pentagon. Still not done, she gazed up, inspecting the ceiling. "That's got to be twelve feet, at least. Are all the offices this tall?"

"On the lower floors," he said, admiring the smooth curve of her throat, "less so on the fourth and fifth."

"Pretty big windows for a view of a brick wall."

"Sandstone. And there wouldn't be much point to having light courts between the rings if you didn't have windows."

"Light courts—I like that. And a wall outside your window has its good points, I'm sure. If you looked out on, say, a gorilla habitat, you'd probably never get any work done."

Teasing him, revved up at this chance to hunt for what would be a huge prize to anyone in her profession. She toured the walls, looking at his photos of himself with coworkers, his mola from Panama, his two Rousseau prints—the monkeys in the jungle with back scratchers, the woman sleeping on the desert as a lion stands over her.

When she got to his photos from Tortola, her face lit. "A rock iguana. They were almost extinct at one point. Big for a female. She looks at least four feet."

"Her name is Cheepa. It means Pork Chop. She waddles up to the resort every morning and the caretaker—that guy whose leg she's crawling up—feeds her melon balls."

"On a long stick, I hope."

"Yes."

"And you have a Beanie Baby frog on your computer monitor. I do believe there's hope for you, Ed."

"How do you know it's a frog? It could be a toad."

"Herpetologists pretty much blow off that distinction."

That surprised him, most professionals being sticklers on their specialized nomenclature. He'd already cautioned himself not to mix the two up should the subject arise, toads more on land, frogs more in the water being about all he knew, and not sure about that. With luck she wouldn't find out he had the usual aversion to actual, non–Beanie-Baby reptiles and amphibians; that he'd shot the photo of Cheepa with a telephoto lens and a hollow stomach.

No doubt he had as much to learn about herpetology as Dr. Andrea Deluca did about the Pentagon. He'd like to get her talking about it again, maybe over dinner and wine— he could do that much without worrying what she thought of his arm.

But he shouldn't be thinking about it, not until he'd found Herb Bodine.

Andrea ended her tour at his pair of stuffed-leather chairs, dropping into one, arms splayed. "What's next?"

"I touch base with Captain Hardison, head of the Defense Protective Service, which takes care of Pentagon security. When I left to show you the tooth, he was arranging to have another search dog brought in—"

His beeper went off. Slipping it from his belt, he read the number. "That's him now."

He dialed his desk phone.

Hardison picked up at once. "Mr. Jeffers?"

"Right. Did you get another dog?"

"Couple of bloodhounds from Baltimore County near the bay, supposed to be able to smell bodies underwater. They wouldn't go in either. But listen, Mr. Jeffers, we have another problem."

"What's up?"

"A military deputy in Acquisition has gone missing."

"What?" Ed heard a sharp snapping sound and realized the hand had squeezed a hairline crack into the phone receiver. The servomotors weren't supposed to pack that much force.

"A Colonel Sheffield," Hardison said. "The director he works for, Dr. Wells, had her people working late to get a read-ahead to the undersecretary for a briefing early tomorrow morning. They finished the package and Dr. Wells sent Sheffield to hand-carry it to the undersecretary. About fifteen minutes later the undersecretary's colonel called her office asking where the package was. Her office is across the light court and a few down from yours in the E ring, concourse. She walked the route, no sign of her colonel."

"The undersecretary's office is near the River Entrance guard station. Any of your people there notice anything?"

"No one heard a thing. Colonel Sheffield didn't leave the building through the River Entrance and they'd seen only the usual traffic in and out all day, nothing to catch their eye or ear."

Because, Ed thought, who or whatever took Herb Bodine yesterday has been in here at least that long. "You were down in the basement while this was happening?"

"Watching the handler try and coax his bloodhounds into the hole."

So nothing came out that way, Ed thought.

Could it get up through the walls? He felt sweat prickling at his hairline. Andrea Deluca had sat forward in the chair; she arched a dark, questioning eyebrow at him. He held up a hand.

"Did you talk to Dr. Wells about this guy? Personal problems, so on."

"She says he's very conscientious. Nothing would stop him from taking that package straight to the undersecretary."

"Bloodhounds still here?"

"We let them sniff the colonel's hat. They followed his scent to the E ring junction between concourse and river then started sniffing the wall. There's a utility closet with a metal plate covering one of the plumbing and wiring stacks. The plate made the dogs extremely nervous."

"Call in one of your SWAT teams. Tell them to meet us there in ten minutes with their night-vision scopes and rapelling gear."

"Right."

"What?" Dr. Deluca said as he hung up.

He filled her in.

"Damn. A *vertical* crawl space."

"Stacks, yeah. It's how you run wiring and plumbing up and down between floors."

"Which means all floors are connected inside the walls to that sinkhole."

"With some acrobatic crawling, yes."

"It finds men tastier than rats." Her eyes shone with what might be either dread or excitement.

"Dr. Deluca—"

"Andrea, or I can't call you Ed."

"Andrea, we'll be meeting the captain of Pentagon security and a SWAT team in ten minutes. I do want you with me. I *don't* want you talking about any kind of 'it' making off with Herb Bodine and the colonel. You're a consultant, that's it. Stay in the background, observe, and if you have anything to say, say it to me alone. It won't hold up long, but maybe it won't have to."

"You're not going to tell the SWAT team they may be dealing with an animal?"

"They're trained to deal with the cleverest animal—terrorists, madmen, assassins."

"An assassin who kills a jackhammer operator?"

"Herb Bodine may have seen him tunneling in."

"And the tooth?"

"Doctor—Andrea—I don't know. The point is, we'll tell the SWAT team two men have disappeared, possibly from violence, and may be down in the sinkhole. Trust me, it will be enough to get the team as alert and ready as they can be. Like I was saying, human predators are the worst, in weapons, brains, and just plain capacity for evil."

"Then why not tell them all you know? Afraid of looking like a fool?"

"No, I love when that happens."

She studied him with faint disapproval. He felt himself flushing. What did she know? He'd worked long and hard to fit in, and they might call him the "mayor," but if he started sounding crazy, he'd revert to "man with the fake arm," and "shouldn't be surprised if his head's a little off, too."

Andrea said, "The only thing that would sound crazy is if we say it may be a big amphibian predator that's been extinct for two hundred million years. We needn't go into that. Just tell them I'm a biologist at the zoo, an expert on predators, and there's a long-shot chance it might be an alligator. The hunting tactics of an extinct labyrinthodont would likely be similar to the gators, who date back to that same period. It might save the SWAT team critical seconds of shock if something nonhuman comes at them underwater. And you'd know you'd informed them fully so that if—"

"You're right. That's how we'll do it."

Her look of surprise miffed him. Did she think he was too rigid to change his mind?

With a brisk clap of her hands, Andrea sprang up. "Let's go. I mean, I'm ready when you are."

As they approached the bend in the corridor, Ed saw a DPS sergeant and another man squatting with two bloodhounds—the guy from Baltimore Search and Rescue, trying to soothe his dogs. They had pulled back on their leashes to stay as far as possible from the utility closet. Their whipped postures unnerved Ed. All those stories about dogs risking their lives for the masters they adored, and yet two different breeds had now refused to track a man's scent, and it could only be because another smell terrified them, that chem/bio stink he'd noticed inside the wall.

An army captain walked by with a curious glance. Otherwise, the broad hall was empty, and Ed realized it was nearly nine P.M. Parts of the Pentagon were still busy in the various operations centers manned around the clock, but up here around the Secretary's office was a ghost town, the workday over.

Beyond the dogs, Ed saw Joshua Hardison hurrying up the concourse corridor of the E ring, a squad of black-uniformed men with him. The sight of them reassured Ed, even as it sent a twinge of envy through him. They looked invulnerable, ballistic helmets covering any receding hair-lines, armored entry vests bulking up their chests, black knights of the modern age, bigger than life, all hints of human frailty hidden.

Not that they had many frailties. Civilians with police backgrounds, they trained constantly, sweeping the halls of the Pentagon in response to bomb threats, deploying on its rooftops during security alerts, shadowy troops at the ramparts reassuring the folks pouring in from the huge parking lots in the mornings.

The entry specialists of the team slung Heckler & Koch MP-5 submachine guns on their shoulders, except for two who carried Bennelli M-1 twelve-gauge shotguns—full-length monsters that would throw an enemy against the wall and stick him there with his own blood. All the team carried Sig-Sauer .40-caliber pistols for close work, and LASH communicators with soft earplugs to keep them in touch at a whisper.

Ed nodded at the lieutenant who led the team, but he, his men, and Hardison were all staring at Andrea, no doubt trying to size her up. He saw her, suddenly, from their viewpoint—the lithe, youthful physique, the sweatshirt, dark slacks, and Nike Air Maxes, looking like she'd just come from a poetry slam.

Best to erase that impression as quickly as possible.

"This is Dr. Deluca from the National Zoo. A long shot we may be dealing with a large alligator here, and she's a specialist in reptiles. Let's hope we won't need her advice."

No one said anything. Hardison cleared his throat, and that was all.

Relieved, Ed said, "Captain, have you briefed the team on Mr. Bodine's disappearance and the sinkhole inside the basement wall?"

"Yes. Any questions for Mr. Jeffers, Lieutenant Size-more?"

The lieutenant turned, showing him a pale, freckled face with brows and lashes that looked almost white in the surround of dark helmet. "Captain Hardison says you told him the sinkhole was beyond a vertical piling about twenty yards inside the wall to the left."

"Correct."

"And you got right up to the sinkhole. Any idea how deep the water is?"

"Not just a puddle, at least where my stone landed. My impression was of some depth. It could be as little as a couple of feet, but not less, I'd say."

"Thank you."

"Anything else? Okay. Dr. Deluca, did you want to look at the closet?"

Andrea nodded. Keeping to the side of the doorway, she sidled into the small utility closet and crouched down, putting one cheek to the floor to sniff. To Lieutenant Size-more she said, "Can I borrow your night-vision scope?"

"Ma'am." He handed her a hunk of plastic resembling half a pair of binoculars.

"Would you get that light," she said, "and close the door." The lieutenant found the outside switch and flipped off the light, shutting her into the dark. Tension cranked Ed's neck muscles tight. What if the thing was still in there behind the access panel? In his mind, he heard Andrea scream, though a steady silence seeped under the door. The SWAT team and Hardison were all looking at him now, and he resisted an incongruous urge to grin.

Seconds later the door opened and Andrea emerged. She said, "The metal panel that covers the stack is wet in places; it's secured by only one screw, so it could be ro-tated up to get through and then drop back into place. The infrared scope registers some warmer damp spots on the floor that could be the remains of evaporated tracks. This is a garbage collection point?"

"Yes," Ed said. "The cleaning people empty it every evening."

"Still pretty ripe in there. Too many smells for me to be sure. Captain Hardison, did Dr. Wells or anyone else find that package Colonel Sheffield was carrying to the undersecretary?"

"Uh, no, Doctor."

I should have thought of that, Ed realized. If an animal grabbed the colonel, why would it take the papers, too? Could this be terrorists? Ed felt a chill. Water under the building was no longer the Pentagon's version of urban myth, it was fact, and it would now require some major rethinking. For starters, if the crack in the retaining wall that had let river water under the building was big enough to admit a man, a terrorist could slip into the Potomac, enter the underground channel below the waterline, and end up beneath the Pentagon with no risk of being seen at any point.

But first he'd have to know the underground channel existed, as well as the crack in the retaining wall—and, furthermore, that he could also find a stretch inside the wall where the floor was nothing but dirt. We didn't know about water under the building ourselves, Ed thought, until just now, because of Herb Bodine vanishing.

"Okay," Andrea said, "I'm done here."

"Let's get down to the subbasement," Ed said.

When they reached the stairs, Lieutenant Sizemore said, "Let's keep it quiet from here on. You folks should stay well back."

"I'll need to examine the site before you go in," Andrea said, "just a minute, and I'm out of your way. I won't make a sound."

The lieutenant glanced at Hardison, who nodded.

"Okay, Doctor."

The SWAT team took the lead, eerily quiet now, the coils of their rapelling lines doubled tight to silence the carabiners. In their cushioned black boots, the nine black-suited men floated down the flights, smooth as a vampire troupe. Descending behind them, Ed thought of the climb within the walls to get to that utility closet, navigating through the dark, avoiding electrical conduits stripped of insulation by the teeth of rats.

In the basement, the DPS had rigged floodlights around the hole in the wall, throwing a cone of yellow glare inside and heating the corridor up to eighty or more. Glancing at Andrea, Ed saw excitement in her eyes. How could she be feeling anything but dread? His gut was churning.

Sizemore gave her a nod and she slipped into the hole, dropping to her hands and knees, sniffing the ground and running a hand lightly over the dirt.

If someone or something jumps her, Ed thought, what do I do?

Andrea backed out of the hole. Sizemore gestured; two men ducked into the wall, entry specialists armed with a submachine gun and one of the two shotguns. The men with ropes followed, then Lieutenant Sizemore and two more. The remaining two stayed in the corridor, flanking the hole.

Ed looked a question at Andrea. She mouthed, *Later.*

Captain Hardison motioned them back down the hall toward him. Andrea didn't budge. Taking her arm, Ed managed to get her back a few yards before she set her heels.

He pictured what must be going down inside the wall. The goggles on the helmets had night-vision capability. They could be flipped up in favor of the ITT scope to get a long view down the inside of the wall. What would the scope show? An irregular slab on their left, glowing green, stretching away hundreds of yards, an unreal world riven at the top with pipes and conduits and over it all the huge ventilation ducts demanded by a building so large. The hole in the ground beyond the obstruction of the piling would be dark even in night vision until they got up to it.

They'd secure their rapelling lines to a steel bracket that held up the pipes and wiring and proceed on rope from there, in case the ground caved beneath them.

Ed's stomach swooped at the thought—falling through a shower of dirt, swinging down along a rope into . . . what?

One of the two men at the hole pressed a finger to his earpiece and looked at the other, giving his head a slight shake. Ed felt a cold spurt of alarm. Dear God, what right did he have to send anyone into such a place?

Two men missing, that was the right.

Captain Hardison came back to them, one of the LASH communicators in his hand, the other holding an earphone in. He said, "They got lines secured, and then a cave-in took one of them down. He's all right. The other rapelled after him. Away from the hole, the water gets deep fast— it's over their heads. They found a big cavern in there. . . ." Hardison trailed off, his gaze going distant as he listened. "Looks like a couple of tunnels lead out of the sinkhole chamber, but they can't get there unless they can find a shallower area to move across. They're circling around the edge of the chamber now, where it's more shallow."

"How many down there?"

"Two. The others are above to pull them up, but they're back farther than they like because of the cave-in."

Ed held out a hand for the communicator. Captain Hardison frowned, shook his head.

"I need to know what's down there," Ed said. "I need to hear it from them."

The captain took his earphone out and handed it to him, but kept hold of the transmitter. The first thing Ed heard was the slosh of water, the men wading. Then an urgent whisper. "Did you hear that, Kovac?"

"Yeah. Someone yelling help. Where's it coming from?"

"That tunnel there. What was the colonel's name again?"

"Sheffield."

"COLONEL SHEFFIELD!"

Ed ground the earphone against his head, but could hear no answer. His heart hammered, wild with hope.

"That's him," whispered the voice in the earphone. "He heard us. COLONEL, HANG IN, WE'RE COMING."

"Reggie, did you see that?"

"Where?"

"Three o'clock."

"I don't see it."

"The water moved over there, about twenty feet."

The sloshing sounds stopped, followed by silence. Ed pushed the earpiece so hard that pain spiked his eardrum. Nothing.

"Oh, God, shit, Kovac, KOVAC!"

A scream blared, distorted, in the earphone, then gargled away to silence. Ed jerked the earpiece free as gunshots sounded. His head rang with sound and shock. More shots came, muffled thumps leaking through the hole in the wall—the shotgun, judging by the spacing of it, then that died away, too.

"Give me that!" Hardison shouted, snatching the earpiece.

Ed ran toward the hole, dimly aware of Andrea dashing along beside him. The two men holding rear guard motioned them back, turning to train their submachine guns on the hole. Then one of them ducked inside the hole.

"What's happening?" Hardison shouted.

"Sir, get off the line, sir!" the remaining man shouted at

Hardison. A second later, he said, "Roger that," into his transmitter.

"Stay back. They've pulled them up. They're coming out."

Ed waited, frozen in dread. For what seemed an eternity, nothing happened. Then gunfire erupted again, the submachine guns this time, at least two of them, in long bursts. Then silence again and finally men stumbled from the hole, carrying a body, shoulders to feet, then another—

Oh, Christ!

Ed Jeffers turned against the wall, clenching his teeth to hold his gorge down. The second man they'd brought out was only half there, missing from the waist down. His helmet was off, his face the color of Ivory soap.

Blood poured onto the concrete as the man's teammates lowered what was left of his corpse to the floor. The other man wasn't whole either, but had lost an arm. The guys who had brought him out were working over him, tying off the bleeding stump with a length of the rapelling rope. Ed looked away, sickened anew, knowing too much about what lay ahead for the man.

Fury boiled up in him. He raced to Lieutenant Sizemore, grabbed him by his black shirt. Sizemore didn't resist or try to throw him off. His face was blank, white as the eyebrows.

"Did you get it?" Ed shouted. "Did you kill it?"

"So fast," Sizemore whispered.

A man with a shotgun came up to Jeffers, eyes wide, smoke still pouring from the barrel of his weapon. "Lieutenant? Lieutenant?"

"He can't hear you," Ed said. "Shock. What did you see?"

"Nothing. Not a goddamn fucking thing."

"Then what was all that shooting at the end?"

"We thought it might be following. Lantos and Elmendorf cut loose into the sinkhole. I was right behind them. Their flashes lit up the hole, but they weren't firing at anything I could see."

Panic, Ed thought. They didn't hit it. He wanted to swear at the man, then remembered how terrified he had been in there.

Turning to Andrea, he pointed at the half corpse on the floor. "Is that what the tooth does?" Incoherent, sounding like someone else yelling in his ear.

She nodded. "That's what the tooth does."

He felt cold, realized he was close to shock himself, babbling, unable to stop himself. "The colonel is in there, still alive. I have to send someone back in. But who? If a SWAT team can't save him, who can?"

CHAPTER 7

←————————————

Sudan
Wednesday, September 12

Lieutenant Terrill Hodge didn't mind the crocs.

The op either, though the briefing hadn't passed the sniff test.

What he minded was the fucked-up rules of engagement.

Terrill crouched on the bank of the Nile with his second-in-command, Master Chief Petty Officer Lincoln "Link" Washington, peering through the papyrus reeds at the river. Months of rain had washed tons of mud into the water, giving it a caramel flush. The color put him right at home, calling to mind the Chattahoochee branch that cut through the red clay back of the home place—those good summer days fishing and picking off moccasins with Dad's Remington .22.

But this wasn't Georgia, this was Jumhuriayat as-Sudan, biggest country in Africa, bigger than all Europe. For a thousand years before, during, and after Christ, it had gone by the name of Kush, a kingdom so mighty that, in its heyday, it had conquered even ancient Egypt.

Now it couldn't conquer itself, bloody civil war raging off and on—mostly on—ever since it had split from Egypt and the Brits in 1956. Two million dead and counting. Knowledge was power, and before you flew halfway around the world to night-drop into a fire zone, you'd best find out all you could that wasn't in the briefing.

"You'll be lucky to see ten feet in that silt." Link's soft smoker's rasp blended into the continuous gush of the river. Slapping at his forearm, he froze the blow a soundless hair's-breadth from his skin, then flicked the mashed skeeter off into the weeds. Terrill saw that sweat was running down Link's face, etching ebony lines through the camouflage paint. What must this feel like to Lincoln Washington—an African American, great-grandson of slaves, coming as a warrior to this land of ancient black glory, now lost?

I can't even imagine it, Terrill realized. We guys with yellow hair and sunburns have a different history.

"On the other hand," Link observed, "the water's up enough to move you right along."

Terrill nodded. Visibility was screwed, no question, but for the crocs, too, and the rainy season had swelled the Nile, speeding up the current even in backwater branches like this one. He calculated around five minutes beneath the surface, kick, stroke, and glide, to reach that bend sticking out into the river—where the rebel safehouse hid, if the intel on this op was sound.

No way to be sure from here.

Low scrub rose up the bank to a stand of baobab trees screening off any buildings that might lie beyond. From a military perspective, the point in the river was an ideal site to defend, protected on three sides by croc-infested water. On the inland approach, string some concertina wire and lay claymores and you could cover that way in with a single swivel-mounted M-50. Hell, might not even need the machine gun. The wire would blend into the jungle, and these SPLA guys had plenty of practice planting the surplus mines Uncle Sam had doled out with boatloads of other righteous ordnance back in the seventies, when the country had managed a brief spell of internal peace.

Seemed a bright idea at the time to arm the Sudan, with the Russkies pouring tanks and guns into Ethiopia next door. Way it worked out, the evil Soviet empire pancaked and all that Cold War weaponry turned to pushing up the body count of the poor bastards it was meant to protect.

God save us from the politicians, Terrill thought. More blood on their hands than any army's.

"'Course," Link said, "beating your way back upstream is another matter."

"A sawbuck says I swim the return leg in under fifteen."

The chief grunted.

Terrill glanced over his shoulder at the papyrus reeds upriver, but saw nothing of the rest of his squad hunkered down there, seven of the toughest sumbitches you'd never want to meet. John Wayne's great movie line came to him: *Son, if you saw them, they weren't Apaches.*

A mosquito whined around Terrill's ear, tempting him to pull on the headpiece of his wetsuit. The heat stopped him. Only ten A.M., the sun sealed away behind the hammered-lead sky of the rainy season, and still it had to be pushing ninety, sucking more out of him than a thousand bugs could manage. The wetsuit was billed as tropical weight, only a mil and a half, but it was sweating him like a fur coat.

Ditch the suit and go in naked?

Before the idea could progress, Terrill remembered

about the bilharzia, a nasty parasite the briefer had warned them to watch out for in the swamps. Watch out how? You'd need a microscope to see it. Get it on your skin and you'd have plenty of time, as you died, to wish the crocs had got you.

On the other hand, bilharzia was supposed to thrive only in stagnant water. . . .

Fuck it—it was the wrong way to die. Get in the water and the suit would cool off. Yeah, a nice day for a swim, hooyah.

"I've got a bad feeling about this," Link muttered.

"What's not to like?"

"The whole damn thing, Terror."

Terrill felt an uneasy surprise. Nicknames ruled in the bar, but on duty he was the lieutenant, the navy equivalent of an army captain. Best damn rank in any service, because you commanded the guys on the ground. On ops, Chief had always called him Lieutenant, or "Loo," until now.

"Terror?"

"Jesus, *what?*"

Terrill saw that Link was gazing at the opposite shore, a hundred feet away. The giant log covered with lichens had begun to move, sliding down the bank in a lazy, undulating motion. A shock rolled up Terrill's spine, sending a welcome wave of coolness through him. Look at that beast. Probably weighed over a ton—a monster Nile crocodile, survivor from the age of dinosaurs, hundreds of millions of years ago. His kind killed more people in Africa than any other animal. Had to be twenty feet, beady little eyes, huge jaw, smiling at him across the river, corners of that giant mouth turned up in a knowing way, as if the two of them were sharing a joke.

How could a creature so ancient still find the world amusing?

Link unslung the new sniper rifle he'd brought along

for this mission. A Finnish job, the Vaime SSR-1, a silencer built right into the barrel. Nice piece of work, matte black finish, compact, plastic parts wherever possible. At only nine pounds, it weighed a quarter of most older models, but the 7.62mm x 51 slug would make suitcases out of Dr. Croc, no problem.

Terrill pushed the barrel down before Link could aim.

"C'mon, Lieutenant, I can take him from here, no sweat. Less noise than a branch falling."

"And if he flops into the water and floats down around the bend where the rebels can see him?"

"Better than you being his Cheez Whiz."

"Let him go. He's too fat to want a piece of me." As he said it, Terrill felt a pleasant tightening in his gut. As always at moments like these, it struck him that he might be crazy, wanting the risk, needing it to pump him up and make him feel alive.

Couldn't remember ever being any other way, not since he was a kid in love with the river, jumping off that high bluff, feeling the air whistle past his face—a couple of seconds of free fall, and then he'd smash headfirst into the Chattahoochee, arrow down twenty feet to touch the bottom muck. Eyes open, staying down as long as he could to look for moccasins.

Then La Grange High School, captain of the swim team, breaking all the school records up to four hundred meters, and after that, Georgia Tech, where he'd set an even better record, his second year, out there off Savannah, pulling himself down the rope 240 feet deep into the Atlantic and back up on nothing but his own air. Made a single lungful last two and a half minutes, feasting on the hammering of his heart, the bright lights that spun around his head those last few feet back to the surface. A collegiate record free-dive for that time, it had gotten the attention of a navy recruiter on campus.

ROTC and then twenty-six weeks of BUD/S—the grueling initial training course you had to pass to make SEAL. Hardest thing he'd ever done, especially hell week—sitting in icy, pounding surf for hours, helping the other tadpoles hold a log overhead; running ten miles in the sand, boots laced tight, full pack on your back, five or six hours of sleep the whole week. Eighty-three percent of the class had rung the quitters' bell, but he'd made it, pushing his mind and body to the limit. And now SEAL Team 8, taking every op he could get. Team 8 was Africa, and the continent rocked, in terms of danger, natural and man-made. Only thing better would be Team 3, going after al-Qaeda, but this right here, swimming with crocs, was hard to beat. Stress, adrenaline, the pounding heart—if he didn't get it, he started to chafe, look for fights, anything to pump him up.

The next few minutes, after he got Link settled down, would be a down payment—get in the tub with Doc Croc, map out the route he'd follow tonight, and grab a quick sneak-and-peek at the rebel base to see what they'd be dealing with.

But tonight would be the big payoff. They'd brought infrared goggles along, but if the rebels had the right equipment, they could pick up the glow in the water, so he'd go in blind, feeling his way along in the dark water, nothing but proprioceptive memory from the first trip to guide him. The best op yet—enough to hold him a month.

Terrill saw that Link had set the rifle in the weeds rather than reslinging it. Chief watched, his face grim, as the croc slid into the river and disappeared with barely a ripple.

All of a sudden, Terrill could smell the beast, a sharp, carnivore scent.

"This is totally fucked, Lieutenant."

"Relax. The second I hit the water, I'm the meanest son of a bitch in the Nile, and that croc will know it."

"And what if he's as warped as you are, sir?"

"What's really bothering you, Chief?"

Link shook his head, looking pissed and frustrated. "Jesus, sir. Everything. For starters, you're the leader of this squad. What happens if you don't come back?"

"You take over. Look, my friend, it has to be me. With all due respect to you and those mean bastards back in the bushes there, none of you have been with crocs."

"And you have?"

"Gators, same difference."

"Bullshit. When?"

"Right after the Haiti op. I was TDY on R and R from SOCOM down in Tampa. Drove upstate one night to get me a look at the Everglades, and a civilian had a blowout right in front of me on that parkway runs through it."

"Route 75—Alligator Alley."

"That's it. Guy's car hit the swamp and sank like a stone, duckweed closing right over him. I grabbed my tire iron and dived. Found him, smashed the window, and got him out. Only eight feet deep along there, piece of cake, but a granddaddy gator moved in and I had to ram the tire iron through its head. The guy told everyone who'd listen, and it made the papers. The brass back at Norfolk put it in my personnel jacket. Didn't you wonder why the mission planners sent me instead of Ryker or Chillicothe, with all their Africa ops?"

"Okay, you're the bullfrog, sir, but why hog the glory? You could coach Doyle or me on staring down crocs and we could do the swim."

Terrill shook his head. "You've got balls, Link. You'd do it even though that croc scares the shit out of you. Trouble is, if the bastard smells fear, we *are* talking Cheez Whiz."

"You telling me you're not scared?"

Terrill said nothing. Being that screwed up wasn't something to brag about.

Link's head twitched as if to shake off a chill. "Before you go swimming with toothdaddy there, you need to think about the trade-offs, sir. We don't even know for sure the hostages are in danger."

"Aside from the SPLA threatening to kill them if Khartoum starts piping oil again?"

"Yeah, but see, that bothers me, too. Correct me if I'm wrong, but aren't the SPLA the good guys? The government up north are bad guys, that's for sure. They sell the south's oil out from under them and use the money to slaughter them. I hear they bought some Antonov bombers and are paying mercs—mostly ex-pilots from the Russian air force—to flatten towns down here."

So Link had done some reading, too, not looking at him now, staring at the water, his jaw set. Terrill hesitated, seeing claymores weren't the only land mines around here.

Couldn't blame Link. The National Islamic Front, who'd seized power over the Sudan in the early eighties, were Arabs from the north, who'd proceeded to fuck over the black Africans in the south ever since. Trouble was, the SPLA rebels weren't just blacks, but an unstable mix of disaffected military officers, communists, and even some Islamic factions shoved aside when the Front seized power.

Which was why Uncle's support of the rebels had been so half-assed.

"If it was women or kids," Link muttered, "but it isn't. It's three grown men. Oil company executives, for God's sake, and not even Americans."

"You sure about that?"

Link stared at him. "Canadians, man. The briefing— they're all executives from ShaleCom, big energy company in Canada, been pumping a fourth of all the oil for those murdering ragheads up north. Wouldn't surprise me if we're in this because ShaleCom's finding a way to get some of that oil to us, embargo or no embargo. Nobody goes through more crude than us. You going to risk your life for five cents less a gallon and three Canucks?"

"Last time I looked, Canada was a close friend and ally of ours."

"They've got their own special forces, some pretty bad dudes, I hear."

"Not like us, Chief. Ain't nobody else on the face of the earth like us. And I'm guessing at least one of those hostages is ours."

"CIA?"

"It would explain a lot."

"Shit. I'm supposed to bleed for some nonqual Ivy League spook motherfucker?" Link spat into the papyrus.

For a moment, nothing, just the rush of the river and the incessant whine of mosquitoes.

"I need you with me on this, Chief, a hundred percent."

"How we gonna rescue the hostages when we can't even shoot?"

"Unless they shoot first," Terrill reminded him.

Link didn't bother to respond.

Yeah, he'd put his finger on it, the screwed-up rules of engagement. Terrill could imagine the suit from State prepping the navy briefer: We don't want the SPLA to kill the hostages, but we don't want to piss them off, either, because default makes them our horse in this race. So no shooting unless they shoot first. Just have your men slip in there, grab one of them—the leader if you can—and put a gun to his head so they can't shoot when you signal the boat in. Load their leader into the boat as a hostage, get everyone away downriver, and let him out, simple as that.

What bullshit. The river approach would be watched the hardest, figuring any attack would come by boat—couple of mounted M-50s in those trees for sure, fully capable of sinking anything up to an MkV assault craft. No chance at all for a rubber raft, so they wanted him to swim up with nothing but a .45 and his dick in his hand.

Fuck .45s. You needed something that fired often and fast.

Terrill flexed his shoulders back, bringing the water-proof case hard against his chest so he could feel the reassuring heft of the Heckler and Koch MP-5 compact machine gun.

He said, "Chief, we start shirking ops, we're no better than a couple of nonquals ourselves. I'm getting damn hot in this suit. Let's just do it, all right?"

Link stared at the water a few more seconds, then tapped the fist Terror had held out with his own. "Whatever you say, Loo, but I see that croc going after you, I'm going to put lead up its ass."

"You will not. That's an order. I mean it, Chief."

"Sir, yes, sir."

Terrill hitched around so Link could check the Dräger LAR-V rebreather on his back and the canister of Nitrox beneath. Nifty device, the Dräger, no trail of bubbles to betray his passage along the river because every cc of air went round and round, rub-a-dub, through the box.

"You aren't back in forty-five," Link said, "me and the boys are coming in on the Zodiac."

"Better make that an hour, Chief."

"Aye, aye," Link said grudgingly.

Terrill pulled on his fins, then the hood and mask, feeling his heart thump as he slid forward into the river. Blessed coolness swallowed him up as the current tugged at him. Steep bottom, five backward steps and he was over his head, the weight coming off him as he turned into the flow, in his element now, the Nile cool and silky along his suit.

Most of the world feared water, even some of the bravest fighting men. To them it was a hazard, to be avoided. To a navy SEAL it was sanctuary. Night landing on a beach, you felt naked when you left the surf, safe when you burrowed back in. No croc worries in the ocean, true, but he'd swum with more sharks than he could count. Wasn't any predator big enough to kill a man that could match a great white for speed and grace in the water. On the other hand, sharks were stupid, whereas he'd seen an impressive animal cunning in the eyes of that croc across the river just now.

Which only made today that much better.

In the Everglades, seeing the gator come at him, yard-long jaws swinging open, flashing past him as he dodged left and drove the tire iron down—give that rush a seven out of ten. He'd never yet given anything an eight, but who knows, today might be the day.

The water parted over his mask, an endless golden veil. Keeping to the bottom, he followed a strip of sand swept clear of vegetation and weeds by the current, trailing his hand along it, concentrating on the pattern of undulations.

A sixth sense warned him to look up. A huge fish materialized from the silt ahead of him—had to be three hundred pounds, some kind of perch, maybe, its scaly side touching his shoulder as he swept past.

His heartbeat stayed slow, thudding in a steady beat against the waterproof gun pack. No scare value, but at least the fish had given him a read on visibility—about ten feet.

He stuck to the bottom, aware that the bank on his left was curving now, prodding him to the right. The curve sharpened, and he knew he was moving out along the promontory—that point of land sticking into the bend of the river. When it started to curve back again, he'd surface.

Where are you, Doc Croc? I need a fix. He felt himself grinning around the mouthpiece.

You are crazy, Hodge, fucking insane—

He almost collided with the wooden piling, swerving at the last second as it leapt at him through the swirling silt. Grabbing it in the crook of his arm, he let the current spin him around and past as he secured his grip. To his left he saw another piling in the murk, a hazy suggestion of two more beyond.

A dock—he had arrived.

Looking up, he made out a rectangle of shadow above him. He eased up the piling then pushed himself under the center of the shadow. Raising his head from the water, he slipped his mask up. Papyrus reeds lined the dock on both sides, giving him extra cover as he turned for a look at the shore. Through the thatch, he could see a cleared space leading up to a building—unpainted cinderblock under a tin roof. A guard in cammies lounged by the door, an M-14 on his shoulder. Good weapon, but no match in close quarters for the MP-5. Louvered windows on either side of the door showed deep shadow between the angled slats, yielding nothing on what was inside. But that had to be it, where they were keeping the hostages. You could count on more SPLA soldiers in there and in the trees that hugged up close to the building.

Where else?

Terrill felt the piling shiver against his hand; he eased back into the deeper shadow under the center of the dock. Looking up, he saw a boot settle on a crack between boards. At least one sentry up there, maybe another to keep him company. Most likely they'd mounted a machine gun on the dock, to spray any incoming boat that looked unfriendly.

"Likely" didn't cut it, he needed a look.

Slipping to the other side of the dock, Terrill inched out

through a break in the papyrus, keeping beneath the surface, turning in place and raising his head. Peering back through the weeds, he could see two soldiers with M-14s and, at the end of the dock, a tripod-mounted M-50.

Both guys smoking, a hamper between them, lunch probably.

All right. Time to go.

Terrill eased back under the dock, reseated his mask, and submerged. He worked his way from piling to piling out toward the end of the dock, wanting to go out deep to minimize any chance of the men seeing his darker shape in the water—

Damn!

Terrill stopped dead in the water, his hip holding him in place against the last piling, no more than six feet from the croc. It hung near the surface just off the end of the dock, side on to him, waving its mammoth tail like an oar to keep itself in place against the current.

The giant head turned toward him until its eyes stared into his.

His heart skipped a beat, then banged against his chest. He savored the rush, feeling the grin twist around the mouthpiece again. Look at him! The snout was thinner than a gator's. On the lower jaw, a mammoth fang protruded upward. The eyes, perched on top of the head, seemed filmy and Terrill remembered reading about the transparent nictitating membrane a croc slid across its eyes when it submerged. And, yeah, its nostrils were clamped shut, just like the book had said, a neat trick. No webbing on the front feet, just the rear ones.

Terrill eased his K-bar from his belt, knowing it was hopeless. The knife looked absurdly small. He was about to die, hooyah. Come on, big boy, come on.

The croc hung in the water, staring at him, and he stared back, thinking, *Go for its eye.*

He heard laughter above, dull and distorted through the water, then something splashed down close to the croc. The croc took its eyes off him and, with one sweep of its giant tail, lunged to snap up the sinking hunk of meat. Another splash—a dead chicken, Terrill saw. Another sweep of the tail and the croc had it.

Terrill pushed off against the current, feeling his legs power up in a smooth kick, then finishing the motion by pulling the water back with his arms, thinking of the Olympic-sized pool back at La Grange as he kicked and stroked away from the dock, back the way he had come.

He could hear the water boiling behind him as the croc went for another piece of meat. They feed it, he thought, but not too much. Just enough to keep it hanging around the dock. An extra line of defense. If they'd known I was there, they could have saved themselves some meat.

He pulled himself down along the bare bottom channel, swimming with deliberate, coordinated strokes, the way you must with sharks, conveying that he belonged here and was in no hurry. The back of his neck tingled, but he didn't look around, just kept going, working his way upstream, until he was back around the bend and could raise his head without being seen.

He spotted Link ahead where he'd left him.

Another minute and he was there.

Leaving the river for the bank, he felt let down. The fun was over, until tonight.

"Lieutenant, what happened?"

He realized the excitement must still show on his face. "Nothing," he said. "We're in the right place. Cinderblock hut, a wooden dock, one M-50, two sentries with their M-14s slung. I can take them and use them to get inside. It's going to work, Chief. Tonight."

"No, sir."

Terrill stared at him.

"Doyle got a call on the radio," Link said. "We've been ordered back to the drop point. They're pulling us out."

Terrill felt a rush of heat to his face. "The hell they are."

"Afraid so. Someone at the Pentagon wants us back there, ASAP."

"The *Pentagon*?"

"That's what Doyle said."

"It's got to be a mistake. The main threat there is a bomb or another hijacked airplane. Their SWAT teams are bomb experts and they've got F-16s and plenty of flyboys right there at Andrews. What do they want with U.S. Navy SEALs?"

"I guess we'll find out, sir."

CHAPTER 8

Armed Forces Institute of Pathology, Rockville Annex
Thursday morning

The morgue had no windows to let in the sun rising over Washington. Instead, fluorescent lights irradiated a cheerless, nearly square chamber, lending the white-tiled walls a bluish, skim-milk cast. The floor was a concrete slab, dark from a recent hosing. Formaldehyde gave the chill a prickly sting.

Be strong, Andrea told herself. Think of it as a big frog, like the hundreds you've examined in your lab.

The half man on the table.

Her eyes kept trying to complete him in jittery scans that crept around the back of her brain like a queasy fly. By adulthood, you have seen about every shape and pattern in nature, but not this. Exsanguination had left the chest, arms, and face pale as suet—Corporal Reginald Kovac of

Pentagon SWAT Team 2, blood loss so total that the water gurgling down the stainless steel table stayed clear. The waist ended in triangular flaps, as if he were a paper doll severed by pinking shears.

She was conscious of Lieutenant Colonel Herbert Anspach, eying her from the other side of the table, tall, crisp, and crinkly in his surgical greens, probably worrying was this woman going to pass out on him. Captain Hardison kept his distance against the wall, stroking his mustache, head cocked toward the giant exhaust fan droning beside him. Ed, standing at her shoulder, had gone nearly as pale as the corpse, his eyes watering, the determined set of his jaw warning her not to try and send him out.

Being here was what he'd meant by "my people."

She must help him. This half body was a cryptogram, offering badly needed clues to the beast they were hunting. No one on the SWAT team had gotten a good look at the animal—a big shape, incredibly fast in the water was the most anyone could dredge up. When she was done here, Ed would want to know everything she could tell him.

And a lot she couldn't.

Pulling on her latex gloves, she bent over the tattered waist and inspected the flaps, trying to match up the carnage with the tooth. A mastodonsaurus, with its huge jaws, could have bitten a man in half like this—if there had been any men two hundred million years ago.

Slipping the tooth Ed had found in the wall from the pocket of her lab coat, she fitted it into the serration at the severed waist.

A match, no question.

She examined the stump of spine. Lots of tooth marks, indicating it had been chewed through, not snapped in one bite. An image popped into her head of windup plastic teeth, like you get in a novelty shop, chattering away without pause.

Fast and powerful jaws. What else?

"Could you help me turn him on his side?" she said to Anspach.

The colonel took the corpse's shoulder and rolled it his way as Andrea lifted and pushed, the weight surprising for half a man. On the corporal's back, she found what she was looking for, a row of puncture marks below each shoulder blade from the animal's claws. Faint reddish bruises, slightly longer than a large man's hands, trailed away to the corpse's sides from each puncture. Bending close, Andrea could make out four such bruises on each side, the product of fierce pressure, left either by horny ridges in the animal's paws or by its "finger" bones themselves. Bruising from a blow or grip just before death was unusual, since the blood that discolors the flesh into a bruise stops flowing as soon as the heart stops beating. These marks indicated violent pressure from powerful forepaws, as the animal held the struggling body against its mouth. A crocodile or alligator might use its forelegs like that to keep prey from escaping until its jaws had made the kill, but no croc would inflict a hideous overkill like this.

Why such a frenzy?

A key question, and she could think of no answer.

She inspected the skin for any other bruises, taking her time, finding none.

Letting the corpse roll onto its back again, Andrea ran a swab along the flaps of flesh at the waist in case traces of the animal's DNA-bearing saliva might remain despite the immersion in water. She dropped the swab into a plastic bag and stepped back. "I'm done."

Anspach nodded. Hardison slipped out through the double steel doors as Ed released a breath beside her.

The waiting room was basic military—pine air freshener, spartan wood chairs with straight backs, round tables offering neatly fanned pathology and armed forces magazines. Both men settled into chairs, Hardison mopping his brow with a white handkerchief. Feeling a sudden tremor in her knees, Andrea sat, too.

Ed shook his head. "Let's not have another of those."

"No."

"So, Doctor?" Hardison's chair creaked as he leaned toward her.

"The animal that killed Corporal Kovac is no ordinary predator—"

He grunted. "We knew that already, from the fang."

"The tooth tells us it might resemble an extinct predator, Captain, but I'm not talking form now, I'm talking behavior. Most predators kill with cold efficiency. In the wild, survival is governed by an unforgiving equation: Energy expended must not exceed energy consumed. So predators do the minimum necessary to kill their prey."

"I guess you've never seen a cat play with a mouse."

Ed started to say something, but she cut him off. "I understand that you're upset right now, Captain, and I don't blame you, but try and listen. I said, 'in the wild.' Housecats are fed on a regular basis, which gives them the luxury of practicing their killing techniques in play. The animal under the Pentagon is not a pet guaranteed a regular supply of food, so the efficiency rule applies, and we must ask ourselves why this attack was not economical but profligately excessive. It's as if the animal were in a murderous frenzy. Animals, with the possible exception of apes and dolphins, do not murder as we think of it, so a key question for us is what could be provoking the animal to such hateful brutality?"

"How about if it was trying to defend itself or its territory?" Ed said.

"I don't think that alone could explain it. It's true that, when threatened, predators will expend energy in aggressive displays. But a display is usually all it is, the animal fighting only as a last resort if the posturing fails to drive its enemies off. This thing went straight for Kovac, no warning, no mercy, and kept after him long after any fight had gone out of him. Even a grizzly bear, one of the most irritable predators around, will usually break off an attack if you go limp."

"Doctor," Hardison said, "we don't need a lecture on how to survive a grizzly attack, we need to know what this beast is."

"Captain," Ed said in a low voice.

"Really, Mr. Jeffers, this is getting us nowhere."

"I disagree."

Hardison opened his mouth, closed it again. "I'm sorry. I've been rude."

"Forget it," Andrea said. "You lost a man."

"A damned good one. He and his wife had my family to dinner just last week. Potato salad, hot dogs, everybody happy. She's a schoolteacher. They have a three-year-old-daughter, Janey. . . ." Hardison looked away, blinking, and Andrea swallowed against a sudden lump in her throat.

"Why don't you head back to the Pentagon, Joshua," Ed said, "and see if Lieutenant Sizemore has remembered any more."

"He didn't see anything. We've asked him over and over."

"He was in shock. Could be he saw more than he realized, something you could tease out with careful prodding. I'll fill you in later on Dr. Deluca's assessment of the animal."

"All right." Hardison stood. "The SEAL squad is due in at Andrews within the hour. I've put the deputy secretary in the picture, as you requested, and he'll brief the team leader—a Lieutenant Terrill Hodge. You might want to be there, Mr. Jeffers."

"We'll be there."

Hardison walked out without looking at her.

"Sorry," Ed said.

"Don't worry about it." She couldn't decide whether his protectiveness annoyed or flattered her.

Maybe he hadn't been trying to protect her, but just to keep the discussion rational. That would have a high value for a man who probably spent half his waking hours in meetings. He'd never have made it in a place like the Pentagon if he couldn't handle conflict, but there were a lot of ways of doing that, some good and some bad, and you had to admire his—just three words, in a soft voice, braking Hardison without browbeating him.

Ed said, "I think you're right about the aggressiveness being important. Any more thoughts on that?"

"Not that fit with it being an amphibian, as the tooth suggests. The closest thing we've got today to labyrinthodontia are crocodiles and alligators, which are no more savage than they have to be to get a meal."

"Some people train their dogs to be vicious, to really go after people. Could that be done with, say, a crocodile?"

She thought about it. "Possible. Crocs are pretty smart, and even worms can be conditioned."

"Like Pavlov's dog?"

"Similar. The conditioning would be operant, not classical, but the same rules of association apply. We're talking behavior modification. The trainer would start with pain, teach the animal to fear and hate man, then reward him for attacking, shaping those attacks toward greater viciousness by giving greater rewards for more frenzy. But, Ed, I've never heard of such a thing being done with reptiles. A crocodile isn't easy to keep and it's even harder to transport—hardly an ideal attack animal."

"But our animal is a crocodile-plus," he said.

"That could make a difference," she conceded, "depending on what 'plus' is. Which brings us back to square one. What is this thing?" She felt an intense frustration, really wanting to help him. "I just wish one of the SWAT team had gotten a decent look. I had the same feeling you did about Lieutenant Sizemore. We should ask him to undergo hypnosis."

"I did. He refused. I spent half of Wednesday debriefing him—or trying to. If he did see something, he doesn't want to remember it."

"Maybe we'll get lucky and this SEAL squad can haul it out of there for us."

Ed only nodded, his expression grim.

What was he thinking? she wondered. That he'd ordered a man to his death, and now he'd asked for SEALs and what if they, too, came back in pieces?

She noticed that Ed's hands were in his lap, the left covering the right—the artificial one—and all at once she got the rest of it: Corporal Kovac was beyond pain, but his partner had lost an arm two nights ago. He'd have to learn to live with that, as Ed had.

Let it be, Deluca.

"It wasn't your fault, Ed. Guys join SWAT and SEAL teams because they want a shot at danger. That it can come down to 'kill or be killed' is a big part of what draws them."

"Is it?" His voice neutral, neither hot nor cool, but his eyes on hers now.

"My ex-husband, Mark, was a cop," she said. "That wasn't exciting enough for him, so now he goes around the world capping off burning oil wells."

"Ah."

His eyes lit with interest, and she realized he'd been wondering about her, as she had about him. The knowledge warmed her. She said, "The men who hire Mark will feel bad if he dies, but they'd be wrong to blame themselves."

"I'm sure you're right."

"You learned to live without your arm, so can Corporal Kovac's partner."

He continued to gaze at her, and she saw no reproach in his eyes, but no encouragement either, and then she realized what she was really seeing—a lifetime of concealing what he felt about the arm. Some bitterness and mistrust would be natural, but he let no trace show. If she was right about what hid up Ed Jeffers's right sleeve, he'd been dealing with it from before he learned to talk. And he'd gotten very good at it. He invited no pity, but he was considerate enough not to bristle at it either. Your arm wasn't something you thought about much if you had your quota, but he didn't, and that must have played a big part in forming him.

Maybe wondering what people thought of his arm was what had sensitized him to what people thought, period. Something had. He pays attention, Andrea thought. He listens, and that's so powerful it makes people forget his arm. So compelling, he's a leader of the biggest pack of humans under one roof in the world. He doesn't just listen, he gives a damn, or he'd never have set foot in that morgue. His caring is what draws me.

But can he let you care about him?

Ed stood. "The Pentagon's half an hour away," he said. "We don't want to miss that briefing."

CHAPTER 9

Pentagon

Terror sat in the E ring, in the outer office of the number two man in the Pentagon, wondering how in hell he'd ended up in the last place on earth he'd ever want to be.

"Coffee, Lieutenant Hodge?"

The woman behind the desk looked to have been a babe once, deep into her fifties now, her babehood sinking into cracks around her eyes and mouth. The granny glasses didn't help, nor the fifteen extra pounds her dark suit couldn't tuck away, but at least she had the manners to ignore the discomfort he must be flashing like neon off a strip joint. "Coffee would be fine, ma'am."

She winced. "Oh, please, call me Doris."

Leaving a desk bigger than the CO's back at Norfolk, she bustled to a little table with a silver tea service and poured him a cup, knowing not to ask about cream or sugar, give her another point for that. He stood to receive it, legs prickling from the starched whites.

"Thank you, Doris, you're a lifesaver."

Her smile melted some of the age away and he found himself wondering if a granny like her would look good to him in twenty years, when he'd be close to fifty, himself, assuming he kept on lucking out with bullets, mines, and crocs. He couldn't visualize it, didn't want to.

He sat down, pants crackling, and tipped back the dainty china cup with its gold rim, the coffee a bit weak but *très* smooth, strange on his tongue after all the slag he'd potted off sterno flames on ops. He'd take any caffeine he could get after flying all night. First the exfiltration by chopper, then hustling the squad aboard the lumbering C-130 Hercules in Ethiopia, twin props dragging them on to Germany where they'd finally caught something with speed, a C-17 jet for Andrews AFB.

Most times he could sleep anywhere he got the chance, but he'd been too jacked up on fury, losing none of it on the long, droning ride. Just a few more hours and he'd have had his night rematch with Doc Croc, and pulled the hostages out, whoever they might be.

What was so important the Pentagon couldn't wait half a day?

Whatever it was, chances were slim to none he'd like it.

No way would the suits and stiffs in this place define "important" the same as he would. To lay eyes on the Pentagon was to see a world of skewed perspectives. An enormous place, each of the five walls easily as long as three football fields. You couldn't see all of it without a lot of neck craning, even from way back in the south parking lot, which had to be forty or fifty acres.

Walking in, he'd damn near worn his arm out saluting, hardly a man or woman in uniform below the rank of commander or lieutenant colonel, officers who'd be kings out in the field, platoons of them swarming in from the sprawling lots to crowd themselves together, two to an office, or park themselves in anterooms like this one, carrying water for four-star generals and undersecretaries so their careers could advance. Right in this suite, a full-bird colonel sat in a cubbyhole down the hall, ready to play gofer to the suit in the big center office, the shadow-man haloed in bright morning light, flitting back and forth in there.

Sweat flushed from Terrill's forehead, not just the heat of the coffee but a squirming embarrassment at how small the place made him feel. Nine/eleven had changed how he thought about the Pentagon. Blood had been drawn here in the cowardly terrorist attack, and from all accounts everyone had acted bravely during and after. You had to honor that. It had been a terrible day precisely because the majority of the 188 who died in this place had been non-combatants. For every general or colonel in this place there had to be five civilians like Doris, here, who'd never held a gun, much less fired one. The fucking al-Qaeda hypocrites would scream bloody murder if an American shell landed on a mosque or school they'd been using to shield their own guns, but they thought nothing of killing a planeful of civilians and some harmless bureaucrats and military staffers who'd traded their swords in for not-so-mighty pens. Nine/eleven had given him a new respect for the Pentagon, but the bottom line was still that it was no place for a fighting man. If they ordered you to rotate through this monument to paperwork, you followed your orders, but no true soldier could ever feel at home here. Groping your way along the bottom of the Nile in the dark with a croc sliding in above you, that would be as unreal to these bureaucrats as the crock they put in their reports and position papers was to him. Twenty-foot monster, yeah, its mouth open so it could home on you with those pressure-sensitive nubs behind its fangs. That was real, that was where he belonged. There was nothing for him here—

Except maybe her —whoa, baby!

The woman who walked in past him was still juicy with babehood, dark hair swinging, dressed in jeans and a cream shirt with big, colorful stars sewn on, serving him a straight-up shot of her whiskey-brown gaze before Doris waved her—and the tall guy with her—through into the big office. Woman looked like she'd just rode her jeep in from a Texas ranch. Did she have anything to do with why he'd been called here?

Terrill was dreaming up possible connections when a uniform walked in. It took him a second to see the star on this guy's shirt—not there for decoration. Standing to attention, he located the patch on the general's shoulder, SOCOM—a flag officer in the Special Operations Command, highest-ranking brass of his own kind he'd ever seen.

"At ease, Lieutenant. I'm General Wallis, ranking SpecWar officer currently on loan to the Pentagon. I'll be your CO while you are here."

"Aye, aye, sir."

The man gave him a look, like he'd prefer the army "yes, sir." Forget that. Terror wasn't just navy, he wore the trident, and he wasn't acting otherwise for anyone.

For one thing, this guy might or might not truly be his own kind.

Terrill called to mind the talk he'd heard in bars from SEAL graybeards lamenting how much better it used to be. When the army green berets and rangers, air force commandos, and navy SEALs had been unified by Congress into a joint command back in '87, presto, a special forces bureaucracy was born. The army dominated it, since there were more green berets and rangers than anything else. Most of these new desk jockeys whipped their blotters at

Fort McGill down in Tampa where SOCOM headquar-
tered, but the command would need a constant Pentagon
presence as well, to stay in touch with what the mother of
all military bureaucracies was up to.

At the moment, Brigadier General Wallis, here, would
be that guy, a BG—"baby general"—temporarily marooned up here in papercut land, answering to the four-star
down in Tampa. Probably a staff bureaucrat who'd never
been a real CO in his life. I got pulled from swimming with
crocs for this? Terrill thought, and the anger that had been
simmering all night rose up to burn his throat.

"The deputy secretary is going to brief you," Wallis
said, "but after that you'll answer to me, is that clear?"

"I hear you, sir." Terrill noticed there were no scars on
the patrician face to talk to the litter on his own. Wallis's
gray hair was cut stubble short; he had the flagpole
straightness an actor might use to play a general.

Wallis was eyeballing Terrill's hair now. "There's a bar-
ber shop in the POAC, Lieutenant—the Pentagon Officers
Athletic Center over by north parking. Shop opens at oh
six hundred every weekday. I'm sure you'll get a chance to
use it before this is over. Ask for Sonya, she's as good with
scissors as you are with a knife. Tell her I sent you."

Terrill said nothing, returning Wallis's gaze. This isn't
going to work, he thought. He wants me to act scared of
him and I don't know how—not so I could fool him.

"Ah, there you are, General. And Lieutenant Hodge."

Terrill turned in relief. The man leaning from the door
to the inner office could be anywhere between fifty and
sixty. His slicked-back hair gleamed white at the temples,
a burnished red over the top, deeply grooved as if he'd
combed it through after hosing it with hairspray. He wore
a gray pinstripe suit as easily as if it were gym sweats.
Ruddy face, eyes the dense green of tinted contacts. The

XO of the Pentagon, saying, "Come in, gentlemen, we're ready for you."

Wallis marched into the office. Following through behind him, Terrill found his hand gripped by the deputy secretary, still at the door. A light vanilla smell came off the man. His hand was dry and narrow, the grip firm.

"Jarvis Keene. Welcome to the Pentagon, Lieutenant."

"Thank you, Mr. Keene."

The office stretched away on both sides, plenty of room for two separate couch-and-chair groupings. Red damask draped four huge windows that overlooked a parade ground and, beyond, the Potomac. The carpet color was the exact muted red of the drapes, seeming to flow out from them, soft as moss under Terrill's hard dress soles. Mostly landscapes and still lifes on the wall, all in muted colors—no danger they'd distract a desk jockey from his paper pushing. What these walls needed was a few Vargases, or if that was too brave, at least a Vallejo or two, those Amazon women old Boris painted for sci-fi book covers. Keene's desk was huge, must be the way they bragged about dick size in this place. It closed off an entire back corner of the room, diagonally connecting two bookcases that ran all the way up to a twelve-foot ceiling. An oak conference table big as Terrill's dining room back in the BOQ at Norfolk joined Keene's desk like the stem of a T.

The dark-haired babe Terrill had seen earlier sat on one side of the table, lounging back in her chair but looking keyed up all the same. On her left sat the tall guy in a suit who'd walked in with her, and next to him a pale, grim-faced man in the black uniform typical of SWAT teams. Alone on the other side of the table an older guy sporting the dark blues of Pentagon security fiddled with a pen. He had an overly neat mustache, the kind of guy who'd wear a bow tie with his civvies.

"General Wallis," Keene said, "you have already met these folks. Lieutenant Hodge, may I present Dr. Andrea Deluca, Mr. Ed Jeffers, Captain Joshua Hardison, chief of Pentagon security, and Lieutenant Jim Sizemore, head of one of our SWAT teams."

Everyone but Jim Sizemore returned Terrill's nod. The SWAT man's pale eyebrows went up when Keene mentioned his name, and he blinked as if he'd just wakened to find himself in a strange place. Where'd they get this zone trooper?

Never mind that, the babe was a doc—interesting. Take my temp anytime.

Terrill took the seat Keene indicated at the butt end of the table. General Wallis settled to his right next to Hardison. The doc, Andrea, was looking at him and he liked the interest in her eyes. A potential frog hog for sure. The guy next to her—Jeffers—seemed to be discreetly watching both Andrea and him, his face giving nothing away. Terrill realized he hadn't gotten a thing off the man since he'd walked in. One to watch, a smart-looking guy, broad shoulders and a mild expression that might or might not be a mask.

Deputy Secretary Keene sat down behind his desk and opened his mouth, but instead of speaking laid his palm to the top of his head and rubbed it back down to his collar. The hair sprang back, its grooves undisturbed.

"Boy, how to start this. Lieutenant, I'm sure you'd like to know why we'd pull you off a mission and rush you here when we have other SEALs closer at hand. And I imagine you're also wondering what kind of work we could drum up here at the Pentagon for you or anyone like you. I'll make it all as clear as I can as fast as I can, because we have a situation here, and the sooner we get you to work, the better. Before I say more, consider yourself under orders to keep what I'll tell you under close hold. No one but your squad is to know. Got it?"

"Got it."

Wallis cleared his throat, but Keene didn't seem upset at the lack of a "sir." He said, "Lieutenant, you may have noticed the renovation work as you came in. Big job, we're going to redo the whole building before it's over. Four days ago, on Monday morning, a work crew opened up a wall in our subbasement to get at some plumbing. While the rest of the crew was off at lunch, the man who'd jackhammered the hole disappeared. Couldn't be found anywhere outside the building, so Captain Hardison called in Ed Jeffers, here. As head of Washington Headquarters Service, Ed has ultimate responsibility for the renovation project.

"He went inside the basement wall and discovered a sinkhole. Dogs tracking the missing man's scent refused to go into the hole. Then another man—an army colonel— disappeared while inside the building, this time not from the subbasement but an upper floor. Captain Hardison sent a SWAT team, led by Lieutenant Sizemore, down into the sinkhole. Beneath the building they discovered partially submerged passages—channels carved out by an underground incursion of water from the Potomac. They heard the colonel shouting from back in one of the passages, but before they could do anything about it, they were attacked. One man was torn in half, dying instantly, and another lost an arm. According to Dr. Deluca, here, who is a herpetologist for the Smithsonian, a large fang Ed discovered inside the wall is of amphibian origin."

Terrill waited for the deputy secretary to smile. He'd smile now, and the others would smile, and everyone would laugh at how they'd led on this rough, tough navy SEAL.

No one smiled.

Sizemore, who'd closed his eyes when Keene had said, "torn in half," opened them again and darted a guilty glance at him.

This is real, Terrill thought. It happened. His pulse picked up.

"Yesterday, we broke another hole through the subbasement wall closer to the sinkhole," Keene said, "and stationed a squad of marines there. We've also lowered ultrasensitive mikes into the hole, but they've picked up no further sounds from the colonel. We don't know if he's alive or dead. Captain Hardison is reluctant to risk more of his men without being sure there is anyone to be rescued, and I concur. The SWAT teams here are brave and well trained, but not for underwater assaults. The Pentagon was built on landfill, and the subbasement dips below the level of the Potomac. Because the building is actually supported on huge pillars that go down to bedrock, the landfill stayed loose enough to be carved out by water. A retaining wall was built to keep groundwater from the river out, but the wall has apparently cracked over the years, possibly in several places, and we've got serious streams channeling between the support piers under the Pentagon. Water is SEAL territory, and your record makes you the best man for this mission."

"Are you telling me there is a crocodile beneath the Pentagon?"

"We considered that at one point, but no. Dr. Deluca?"

Andrea Deluca sat forward, fixing him with her big, dark eyes—which he'd better forget for now and just concentrate.

". . . fang resembles fossil teeth from a mastodonsaurus—a large, predatory amphibians extinct since the Triassic period. But the fang isn't a fossil, it's fresh. Crocodiles have survived since the dinosaurs, but certainly not in secret. It defies logic that an animal considered extinct could have survived undetected to the present time in an area that has become heavily populated. It couldn't be just one animal, after all—there'd need to be enough of them to keep breeding. Amphibians are comfortable underground and underwater, but for that many to stay out of sight, they'd be the world's masters at hiding."

"Were these mastodonsaurus . . . ses, sauri, smart enough to do that?"

Andrea did not smile at his fumbling and he decided he was definitely going to get next to her in a big way, this herpetologist lady. Convince her he was the original frog man and she ought to study him.

"Based on skull size," Andrea said, "and the fact that it was a predator, the mastodonsaurus was one of the brainier creatures of its time, but I see no way a viable breeding population could hide itself throughout human history. No reason for it to feel any need to, either. Until the past few centuries, a big predator would have had little to fear from man. And if an animal so striking had survived into the early days of the human race, we'd probably have found some mention in ancient records, a cave drawing, maybe, like we have of the woolly mammoth. We didn't know big amphibian predators existed until modern times, when we started finding fossilized remains."

"Okay, Doctor, if it isn't a mastodonsaurus, what *can* you tell me about the thing under the Pentagon?"

"Whatever sort of amphibian it may be, it *is* highly intelligent. The colonel was carrying papers when he was attacked, and he'd certainly have dropped them, but we didn't find so much as a Post-it note. Why take the papers, except to hide its trail? Think what that implies about the creature's sense of us, Lieutenant. I doubt even a gorilla or chimp who'd lived around humans all his life would be that smart."

"You're wrong, Doctor." Sizemore's voice was barely more than a whisper.

Andrea turned to him. "How so?"

"You said there are no writings from ancient times that describe this thing."

Silence pressed down, the air in the room taking on weight. Everyone looked at Sizemore, but he just went on staring down at the table, wouldn't lift his head.

The deputy secretary said, "Are you telling us you know what it looks like? That you *saw* it?"

Sizemore gave a fractional nod.

"Why in hell didn't you say something?" Hardison snapped. "You were thoroughly debriefed. You should have told us right away—"

Keene held up a hand, and Hardison braked himself.

Terrill found himself looking at Ed Jeffers, though the man hadn't moved a muscle. Jeffers didn't seem surprised, as if he'd suspected Sizemore was hiding something. Washington Headquarters Service, what was that? Sounded hopelessly bureaucratic.

Andrea Deluca put a hand on the SWAT lieutenant's arm, sending a stab of envy through Terrill. "What did you see?" she asked softly.

"The Devil."

Hardison snorted. "For God's sake, man."

Terrill said nothing, but he agreed—this guy was a mess, paler than his eyebrows now. Seeing your men torn up would be hard, but you had to suck it up, get a grip.

Sizemore stared at Hardison. "I knew no one would believe me. How could you? I'm having trouble believing myself. That's why I didn't say anything. I kept on telling myself it was only a glimpse, just a fraction of a second when it reared up from the water. I was scared, damn straight I was, I admit it, and fear can distort how you see things. Kept telling myself that's what it was, but now you're going to send this SEAL lieutenant down there, and I can't not tell you, even if you lock me away in St. Elizabeth's. I did see it, yeah, and I wish to Christ I hadn't." His hands started to tremble and he pressed them onto the tabletop. "It was about the size of a man, and it stood upright like a man, but it had a tail, a big muscular tail, and on its head were . . . horns. And it had . . . red eyes."

Hardison made another aggrieved noise.

In a reflective voice, Ed Jeffers said, "Haven't you ever wondered, Captain, where we got our image of Satan?"

"Frankly, no, I have not. But I would assume someone with a vivid imagination dreamed it up back in ancient times, when storytellers and artists were what TV and the movies are now. One thing I'm sure of: There's no way the Devil is down there under the Pentagon."

"I agree," Jeffers said mildly, "but what about an animal men have glimpsed on rare occasions over the ages? A manlike animal that has preferred, for whatever reason, to hide from us. Not Satan, but the reality behind our ancient images of him."

Andrea gave Jeffers an impressed look.

Time to nip this in the bud, Terrill thought. "That's interesting, Mr. Jeffers, but does it really matter at this point? The thing's smart, okay; it has a tail; it likes the water. I like the water, too. The sooner I and my men get down there after it, the sooner we'll know what the hell it is. If I'm that colonel down there and I'm still alive, I'm hoping 'soon' will be right now, this minute."

General Wallis shook his head. "We can't go off half-cocked, Lieutenant. We'll need a mission plan. I'll work that out with you before you go anywhere—"

"What plan, sir? We go down into that hole with breathing apparatus and night-vision equipment and spearguns with explosive-tipped darts for under the water and sub-

machine guns or shotguns for above it, and kill this thing
and drag it the hell out."

The general's face reddened, but before he could say
anything, Terrill turned to the deputy secretary. "Mr.
Keene, those marines in the halls with guns I saw coming
in—they're here on account of this?"

"Yes. As of yesterday, marine units from the downtown
barracks will remain posted in every hallway of the building, and as you can imagine, there are a lot of hallways.
They have been told it is a terrorist threat and to be ready
for anything, and I'm sure they will be. They'll be on
guard 24/7 until we find this thing, four-hour shifts to
make sure they're fresh at all times. The colonel vanished
from a floor several levels above the subbasement, which
means this thing can get up through the building inside the
walls. If it tries that again there will be soldiers with guns
and plenty of light to see by and a solid floor under their
feet."

"So I guess with the marines on duty, everyone in the
building knows what's going on."

Keene shot a guilty glance at Jeffers, who looked like
he wanted to say something but remained tight-lipped. The
deputy secretary said, "They've been told the same thing
as the marines, Lieutenant. We've put the Pentagon on
ThreatCon Alpha, as we've done before, when we had intelligence warning of possible terrorist attacks. I believe
it's the right course. Nine/eleven gave our workers experience with a terrorist attack. They did pretty well, and
they've had time to come to terms with the probability of
future attacks. This way we alert them to use extra caution
without scaring them beyond the point that's helpful, as
any talk of this beast would surely do. Avoiding a panic
that might clear the building and endanger national security is critical. So far we've been fortunate no one's
pressed us on this. Every member of our SWAT teams

swears a secrecy and nondisclosure oath. Their families are promised generous support in case of death or disability so long as they honor these oaths. Most family members need no incentive—they're as committed as their loved ones on the teams. The wife of the man who was killed is telling her three-year-old that Daddy died in an accident. She understands an accident is the story for anyone else who asks, as well. The man who lost his arm is also cooperating, as is his wife. The construction worker's buddies are assuming he fell into the hole and drowned, and they know we're looking for him. They've been given other jobs away from the basement site. Colonel Sheffield's grown sons are also both army officers, and you don't make it to colonel without a standup wife. His family has been assured we are doing all we can to find him, which is God's truth."

"That's a lot of people to keep quiet."

"Let us worry about that, Lieutenant. So far, we have a lid on, and I expect you to help us keep it there. You have any problem with that?"

"None." For the first time since Terrill had walked into the building, the air felt good, tingling in his lungs. Not only was this not a disaster, it was better than anything he could have imagined. An *underground* river, defended by no ordinary croc but a vicious man-eater with two confirmed kills and two possibles. The bullshit about it looking like the Devil was obvious hysteria. Crocs could stand up on their hind legs and their nubby little eyes on top could look like horns. A croc, yeah, somebody's pet, until it started getting too big and someone flushed it. It got out through the sewer into the river and grew up there. People had probably even seen it but assumed it was a log—first, because crocs were better at looking like logs than some logs, and second, because everyone knew there were no crocodiles in the Potomac. It ate fish and coons, or maybe deer from parks or the country outside of town. Now it had gotten under the Pentagon.

I'll get the bastard, Terrill thought, and pull it out for Dr. Deluca to study, and if that doesn't land me in bed with her, nothing will.

"One more thing, Lieutenant Hodge," Jarvis Keene said. "President Kuzmin of Russia and his defense minister, Constantin Arbatov, are due to tour the Pentagon tomorrow. I'm sure I don't have to tell you we don't want this thing leaping out of the wall and grabbing someone while they're here. There have been worries about Russia's stability since they lost the Cold War. Some of them might not mind slipping one or more of their stockpiled nukes to people like al-Qaeda. Arbatov is sensitive about the lost glory of his military, going back to his days as a colonel general in the Soviet army. The man still wears his uniform and goes by 'general,' not 'minister.' Let Kuzmin or Arbatov feel we exposed them to danger in the heart of the Pentagon, and you're talking a major incident that could escalate into something even uglier."

"Why not just cancel?"

From the corner of his eye, Terrill saw Wallis shake his head. A fantasy seized him, of putting his knuckles through the bridge of Wallis's nose.

"The Secretary would be very reluctant to do that," Keene said. "This is a gesture of friendship, meant to ease their paranoia about us being the world's only superpower. With terrorists on the make for nuclear material, we must do our best to keep Russia sweet right now. We'd be unable to give them a good excuse why we were canceling the tour, and it could do a lot of diplomatic damage."

"Understood."

"Good."

"Lieutenant," Sizemore said, "I know you're tough, but so are my men. We had big guns, too, and it didn't matter.

A man died and another is done with SWAT work forever.
I hope to Christ you go in there and kill that vicious son of
a bitch, but don't take it lightly."

"I don't," Terrill said.

That's why this is going to be so much fun.

Keene stood. "Lieutenant Hodge, thank you. I know
General Wallis has a meeting with the Joint Staff this
morning, but the others will go with you and your men to
the site. Mr. Jeffers and Captain Hardison can answer
questions about the building's layout, and Dr. Deluca and
Lieutenant Sizemore can help you get a picture of the animal's likely capabilities. I'll not delay you any longer.
Good luck, and we're counting on you."

"Thank you, sir."

Everyone stood and filed out through the outer office.
The corridor outside teemed with people hustling in both
directions. Military officers heavy with brass, men and
women in suits, and a few ladies in sexier clothes—
dresses and even some short skirts here and there, probably secretaries, who wouldn't have to act like guys to draw
a paycheck around here.

None of them could compare with Dr. Deluca.

She was walking on his left, Jeffers and the other two
beyond her, and his antennae told him she was about to say
something to him when General Wallis, on his right,
spoiled it. "Doctor, if you and the others will excuse the
lieutenant and me for a moment."

"Sure."

The general put a hand on his arm, holding him back as
the others moved ahead. Here it comes, Terrill thought.

"You were insolent in there, Lieutenant."

"Sorry, sir."

"Sorry doesn't cut it. Who do you think you are?"

Terrill was aware, suddenly, of the veins swelling in his
neck. *Easy, now.*

"I think I'm the guy who is going to bail out the deputy secretary of defense, and a whole big building full of other people, including yourself. I know you're a general, I appreciate that, but a general isn't what is called for here. Stay out of my way and we'll all look good, including you. I'll tell them it was your plan, and I only followed orders. You'll have what you want and I'll have what I want. Sir."

Wallis's jaws rippled and flexed. A dark flush had risen to his face. Terrill felt a clinical interest. Maybe he could get the asshole to pop a stroke.

"What exactly is it that you want, Lieutenant Hodge? A court-martial? Because you're headed straight for it."

"I want to go kill that thing down under your building, sir. That's what I want. You want to court-martial me afterward, fine."

"You think I can't?"

I *know* you can't, Terrill thought. Not if I get it. And if it gets me, it won't matter.

"I can reduce you back to ensign," Wallis said.

"That would be fine, because it'll keep me on the Teams. I start getting rank like you, they'll pull me out of ops and chain me to some desk, and I won't be a fighting man anymore and frankly, sir, I'd rather be dead."

From the corner of his eye, Terrill saw Ed Jeffers coming back to them. Civilians in this building had their own rank system, he knew, which paralleled the military. In the end, the Pentagon was a place where the civilians—led by the secretary of defense—ruled, and you could see it in both Jeffers's and Wallis's faces now.

"This isn't over," the general said in a low voice.

Jeffers looked at them both. "Problem?"

"No, sir." Terrill said it respectfully, knowing the "sir" would irritate the hell out of Wallis, and knowing, too, that he was being a fool. Screw it, who did Wallis think *he* was? Old fart, playing general with his Rolodex and Mr. Coffee.

"We all appreciate what you're about to do, Lieutenant," Jeffers said. "I'm sure the general is proud to have a man as brave as you in SOCOM."

Wallis gave a stiff nod.

That was a decent thing to say, Terrill thought. "Talk about brave, from what Secretary Keene said you were the first into that wall."

Jeffers looked embarrassed. "Only because I had no clue what was inside."

Andrea Deluca came up beside Jeffers, standing closer to him than Terrill liked. Relax, he thought. I haven't made my play yet. If I can't beat out a bureaucrat, I'll shave my head.

She said, "Any questions for me, Lieutenant?"

Something in her face warned him not to try and be cute. "No. Soon as I requisition the equipment we'll need, my men and I are good to go. Anything you want to tell me, aside from 'Be careful in there'?"

Shit. He'd been cute anyway, couldn't help himself.

The doctor gave him a ghost of a smile.

As Terrill led his squad past the first hole in the wall to the second, the marine sergeant snapped him a salute. A nice gesture, since normally, you didn't salute indoors. He touched his brow to the sergeant and his squad, five men in flak vests and helmets.

Some powerful lights blazed on the hole in the wall, fed by an independent power source—Terrill could hear the muffled hum of a generator in a side room off the hall. Beyond the marines, the impossibly long corridor— more a tunnel, really—stretched away into a murky distance.

Jeffers and the other men had gotten themselves out of the way, against the wall twenty feet back, but not Andrea.

"Lieutenant," she said, "I'll be monitoring you on the com. If you get a look at this thing, give me a description as soon as you can."

"You mean before it croaks me?"

"If possible. It could be pretty important."

"You've got it, Doc."

Terrill surveyed his squad, Link and the seven other navy enlisted men who had made themselves into so much more. Three white men, a Sioux, and three blacks, an equal opportunity bunch of maniacs. Seaman Doyle, getting old for ops, but still strong as a bull. Ratman Lucas, for whom no hole in the ground was too small. Steinholtz and Bearhill, Jew and Indian, the Brothers Grim, more in synch than any real brothers. Junior Abernathy from the Chicago streets, who had talked all the way back from the Sudan about getting him some tribal scars like the Dinkas. Dan "Bammer" Rizetti, who loved blowing things up and would be robbing safes if he were not a SEAL, and Calvin "Cool" Jones, the one you always thought of last, a guy who kept speech to the absolute minimum even when drunk, but was eloquent with any firearm. Master Chief Petty Officer Lincoln Washington mothered the seven the way Ma Barker had mothered her sons.

And I'm their old man, Terrill thought with pride. They trust me not to get them killed because whatever fucked-up situation I get them into, I lead with my own mug.

He looked at them, sculpted shadows in their black wetsuits, exotic gear hanging off them. They looked back, waiting for him to give the word.

Nodding at Link, he pointed out a length of rebar at the top of the hole in the wall, exposed when they'd jackhammered the concrete out. The chief rigged four rapelling lines to the iron strut and tossed them through the hole in the wall into the hole in the ground. The Brothers Grim lugged the heavy artillery, a couple of Pancor Jackhammers, nasty twelve-gauge shotguns with box magazines like assault rifles, no pumping necessary. They'd hang back, keeping their heads and the weapons above water, ready to blow the animal away if it broke the surface. The rest had spearguns, each dart tipped with a rounded charge of plastique that would blow a wicked crater in anything it hit. The swim masks were the latest toy from DARPA, the defense agency that lived to engineer high-tech gadgets for special operators. The night-vision goggles worked off FLIR—a built-in infrared broadcast beam that would light up even the darkest water. A three-volt lithium battery, good for forty hours, sealed behind a third broadcast lens centered above the goggles' viewing lenses, night into day, hooyah. Time to rock and roll.

Link started forward into the hole.

"Chief."

With a resigned expression, Link stepped back. Terrill turned to Andrea. "Sure you don't want to tell me to be careful?"

"Is that why you joined the SEALs?"

"No, ma'am, it wasn't."

"Call me ma'am again and I'll cut your rope while you're down there."

"Okay, Doc," Terrill said, baffled. Didn't she know "ma'am" was what you called a woman officer? That secretary, Doris, hadn't liked it either. Have to review his babe terminology, but now was not the time.

Turning, he leaned into the hole jackhammered through the wall. A couple of feet of ragged concrete brushed his shoulders and then he was gazing down into a gaping hole where the floor inside the wall should be. He withdrew from the wall to pull on his fins, check the slung speargun, and slide the mask on. Stepping through the hole, he grasped the line in both hands and swung down into the sinkhole, sliding firepole-style into the dark, then tightening his grip to slow his descent. The water below him looked dark as oil, with a crimson sheen from the goggles' infrared—or maybe an actual scum of blood from the SWAT team dead.

A slight surface ripple confirmed the water had a current—enough push, obviously, to have carved out channels over half a century. He smelled mildew and something sharper, like the whiff of crocodile he'd gotten from across the Nile.

"Colonel!" he shouted.

A smeared echo bounced back to him, like you might hear at the YMCA pool.

He eased his grip on the rope and the water rose to engulf his fins, then slid up his body, strangely warm through the suit. Choking off his descent once more, he panned the chamber from water level—a rounded cavern about twenty by thirty feet. Two tunnels exited through dark holes whose tops arched above the water. He eased himself on down until his fins found the bottom. His shoulders remained above water. Good—the Brothers Grim could take up station here.

Wading toward one of the tunnels, he stepped off a ledge and the water closed over his head. Softer bottom, depth maybe nine feet now, silt swirling around his face in infrared clouds, obscuring everything. Link splashed down beside him, and he counted off seven more splashes. When the water cleared again, he could see to the walls of the chamber.

The bottom slid away, bare as a gravel pit, no plant life, just a few rocks glowing red in the crisscrossing FLIR beams. The floor of the cavern sloped up as it reached the two tunnels. Terrill could feel his heart nudging his throat, the sweet adrenaline rush, his drug starting to pulse through him.

Tapping Link's arm, he pointed at the tunnel closer to the chief. Link nodded and motioned to Rat and Calvin to follow him. Terrill headed for the other tunnel, feeling Junior, Rizetti, and Doyle at his back.

With luck, this hole would be the one the colonel's shouts had come from.

The tunnel broadened, took a sweeping turn to the right, then grew shallow, forcing him to stand and slog backward, awkward in his fins, through knee-deep water. Terrill broke the seal of the mask to get a whiff. The air smelled close and fetid, too dense with odors to tease any one out. The water deepened again; with relief, he ducked back under and resumed swimming.

A tug on his fin stopped him, Doyle pointing down a branching tunnel.

Shit, he'd swum right past it.

He gave Doyle the nod, holding up five fingers—give it five minutes. Doyle vanished into the side tunnel.

Terrill motioned Rizetti after Doyle, keeping Junior with him.

The tunnel took a turn back to the left and Terrill added the change in direction to the map he was building in his head. The rounded floor of the channel continued to show nothing but stones along the floor.

Place was definitely spooky, like swimming through the arteries of some giant animal. He could just feel the current pushing at his back, maybe a couple miles an hour. What had they been thinking, to lay the Pentagon foundation below the level of a major river close by? Must have been the only place left in Washington by the '40s where they'd been able to find enough empty land.

One of the support piers Keene had mentioned emerged from the dirt wall of the tunnel, a mammoth concrete pedestal rising from the floor and disappearing above the water. He had to squeeze to get around it.

On the other side, the light from his mask flared off a large metal cylinder. It lay on the bottom, chrome bright, the size of an oil drum. Beside him, Junior shrugged a question. Terrill pointed to his goggled eyes, then ahead, and Junior nodded, taking up watch.

Terrill prodded the cylinder to roll it over. A word, etched into the metal, rose along its gleaming flank: *AB-WEHR*. Jesus and Moses. Hadn't Abwehr been Germany's military intelligence outfit during World War II? Nazi spies?

Junior tugged on his arm, pointing ahead. Terrill saw it, lying on the bottom, at the outer reach of the mask's infrared glow, something white and indistinct, stirring, lifting, and settling in the pulses of current. Terrill swam forward a few strokes, and the murky image resolved itself into a skeleton—white rib cage, gangling legs and arms, a grinning skull.

Terrill's scalp prickled under the wetsuit hood as he realized the bones weren't quite clean. A few scraps remained around the knees and elbows, bits of muscle meat, raw, red . . . *fresh*.

A freezing wave rolled up Terrill's spine. He was looking at all that remained of either the construction worker or the colonel.

Beyond the skeleton, the tunnel disappeared into murk.

You vicious fucker, Terrill thought. Are you back there? I'm going to put your lights out.

But first, they all needed to think again, because it probably wasn't a coincidence, finding the bones and the big canister together here. If it had just been the current, they'd have fetched up on the near side of the piling. The canister would be a tight enough fit to need help getting past that pillar. Which meant the animal had hidden it here behind the piling along with the skeleton.

The creature was connected to the can, to the Abwehr.

Whatever it was, it was damned well *not* a crocodile.

Terrill pointed to the canister, then back the way they had come. Junior grabbed the edge and started swimming, not panicked but jerky enough that Terrill knew he was unnerved. Terrill grabbed the trailing end of the canister and helped squeeze it past the piling. Turning back, he took the skeleton by the shoulders and towed it under him as he swam after Junior, back through the winding tunnel.

He saw Doyle and Rizetti ahead, turned around by Junior and heading back. When they got to the starting chamber, Link's team was already there, so their branching tunnel must have been shorter.

The ropes hung down in a cone of light. Terrill sent the others up first, man by man, hand over hand. Junior helped him wrap the trailing end of one line securely around the skeleton and a second around the can, then used one of the remaining two lines to shinny up into the light.

When Terrill climbed out of the wall, Andrea was waiting.

"Well?" she said.

Instead of answering, he pulled on the lines, finding the two that resisted. Junior helped him haul. A skull appeared, and Andrea gasped but did not flinch away, her hands gentle as she helped lay the skeleton out on the floor. By the time she turned, Terrill had the canister out.

The marine squad and Ed Jeffers and the other civilians edged in around the canister and the skeleton, staring, no one saying a thing. Lieutenant Sizemore groaned and turned away, a hand over his mouth, confirming what Terrill already knew: His days as a SWAT team leader were over.

Terrill rolled the canister away from the skeleton to expose the word on its side. The metal gleamed under the lights. Kneeling beside it, Andrea stared at the inscription.

The blood drained from her face.

"Scheisse," she whispered.

Terrill, who could swear in twelve languages, wondered why Dr. Andrea Deluca had just sworn in German.

CHAPTER 10

Ed was about to give up and ask Andrea himself when Terrill Hodge finally got the question out around a mouthful of cheese and pepperoni. "Wher'djyou learn German?"

She glanced around the huge Pentagon dining room, her face coloring as if he'd asked how many times a day she liked to have sex. "Who says I know German? I only know a few words."

And *Abwehr* is one of them? Ed thought.

He knew he should say it. Dr. Andrea Deluca was holding out. Why had she blanched when she'd spotted the inscription on the canister? He pushed people for answers every day, and time was too short for kid gloves now. While they used this forced delay to eat, only a few hundred feet from here, archivists from the Defense Intelligence Agency were hurriedly searching World War II documents filed away in a cell-like chamber with the door of a bank vault. The entire DIA records desk had been put

on the task, pressing to find any mention of a canister like
the one Terrill had pulled from the underwater tunnel. As
soon as they hit or came up blank, the SEALs now stealing an hour of rack time in the Pentagon infirmary beds
would shake off days of sleep deprivation and mission fatigue to follow their leader back under the building with or
without whatever Andrea knew and wouldn't say.

And if that scares either of them, Ed thought, they're
hiding it well.

He felt a grudging admiration. He hadn't yet been able
to force a bite past the worry that filled him like cold sand
from gut to gullet, and in that same ten minutes Andrea had
polished off a huge chef's salad while Terrill gobbled pizza
from his hand—not just pepperoni, but meatball, sausage,
and extra cheese. The guy had the same fear of heartburn
he'd shown going after the beast under the Pentagon.
Shoving the cholesterol in like he hadn't eaten in days—
which wouldn't be far from the truth. His squad had flown
all night after a grueling mission in the Sudan, then bussed
up from Andrews AFB straight to the deputy secretary's
office.

Ed made another effort to push his fork through the
crust of his mushroom and broccoli. Pizza was a star in the
Pentagon's big dining room, thousands of pieces sold
every day, but this particular actor must have dozed off
under the tanning lights.

"That word you used when you saw the canister," Terrill said. "Where'd you pick that one up?"

"Where did you?" Andrea countered.

"From a captain in the KSK—Kommando Spezial-
kräfte, a counterterrorist and assault outfit the Germans
formed four or five years ago, after the Berlin Wall fell and
the world decided it was kosher for Krauts to field crack
troops again. They sent a KSK platoon to our base down at
Norfolk for some cross-training in HAHO." Terrill picked

up his final slice of pizza and bit off the tip, chewing with the kind of pleasure Ed reserved for chateaubriand.

"You going to make me ask?" Andrea said.

"Sorry. HAHO is paratroopese for High Altitude High Opening, where you jump out of a plane at, say, thirty thousand feet and open your chute as soon as you're out. It's usually a night op; you're falling but also flying as you steer your chute. Up that high, you can see the curve of the world. You don't need a terrain map because the land is the map, spread out below your feet. You use that and your compass to navigate into your drop zone."

The way Terrill put it, Ed couldn't help but visualize it—floating like a god above the moonlit world. Sometimes, in dreams, he would find himself drifting over treetops looking down with a sense of wonder. Part of him would guess it was a dream, and he'd start to fall but then the slit eye of waking would close and he'd lift again, riding the dream winds, the ancient yearning we share in sleep. Terrill *lived* that dream, and many others. He couldn't be over twenty-seven or -eight, and yet what wonders he'd experienced.

Did he realize it?

". . . on oxygen the first couple miles down," Terrill was saying, "and it's so cold up there your goggles can freeze, so naturally—assuming you land without a serious case of dirt poisoning—you need some boilermakers to reheat the blood in your hands and feet. After a couple of beers and shots in the officers' club, Kapitän Horst Untermeyer unbent enough to tell me all the German swear words he knew. I gave him the English equivalents."

Andrea looked fascinated. "What does it buy you, tactically, to do a HAHO?"

"It's for when you can't land a plane or helicopter on your target and you don't want your jump plane detected. Way it works, your ride stays way up high in the commer-

cial air lanes of the target country. By opening early, you
get a long float down, which saves the plane having to fly
over your objective. You can bail out thirty or more miles
to one side or the other and navigate your way in, like
Rocky the Squirrel."

"That must take a lot of skill."

He shrugged. "Give Bullwinkle a Para-flight, Ram Air
free-fall rig and he could do it too."

"I think you're being modest."

She's not answering your question, Ed thought. She's
leading you away. Are you getting that, Terrill, or are those
brown eyes bewitching you?

As they have me.

Exasperation welled up in him. He was sitting here like
a lump, refusing to help Terrill push her, because he could
see she didn't want to talk about it, and he wanted too
much for her to like him.

Switching the fork to his artificial hand Ed severed the
crust in one stroke. He let the piece lie, his appetite fading
as he forced himself to think about where he'd end up if he
let what he felt for Andrea keep growing. About running
from Jill, back in college, and making the same U-turn on
Andrea, too much pain to end up with nothing.

Assuming it wasn't already moot.

The SEAL obviously had the hots for her, and she was
returning some of that heat, no question. Look at the
guy—Hollywood handsome with his soft Georgia drawl.
That square jaw, the blond hair, long as an actor's, no buzz
cuts for Terrill. Military, but at the same time a noncon-
formist—a fresh combination, and therefore interesting.
Heightwise, the guy was no Clint Eastwood, just an inch or
so above Andrea's five-eight, but if she liked muscle, Terrill Hodge had gone back for seconds. His shoulders
bulged, a neck and legs like oak trunks. Not merely show
muscles from some gym, either, or they'd have bound him

up like chain mail. He'd gone down that rapelling line hand over hand with the fluid grace of a gymnast, his forearms corded under the wetsuit—

Okay, enough.

Ed's baby arm twitched inside the prosthesis. The clock with the loud tick. People could forget the mechanical arm after they were in the room with you awhile, but every time they looked at it, clack, clack, clack. Had Terrill noticed? If so, he'd given no sign. He's so confident he can score with her, Ed thought, he's not even giving me a second look.

And since when do I want a second look?

"I got the idea you already knew the word *Abwehr,* too," Terrill said to Andrea.

"My college minor was history."

She's lying, Ed thought. With the truth.

"I guess I'm wondering why it shocked you."

"Didn't it you? You go under the Pentagon and find this—"

Ed gave her arm an urgent touch, the artificial hand closest, but it worked too well, shocking her still. She didn't even glance at the hand as he withdrew it but now Terrill *was* staring at it, giving it that second look.

A hot flush crawled up Ed's neck. He said, "We'd better save this discussion until we're out of here, don't you think?"

Terrill took his eyes off the hand to glance pointedly around at the armada of empty tables. At 2:10, the lunchtime crowd that typically topped a thousand during peak time had thinned down to a few hundred, scattered across the huge room. The closest other diners, a half dozen air force officers, sat at least fifty feet away.

Terrill said, "I think we're safe here."

"No," Andrea said. "Ed's right."

"The walls have ears, huh."

"Why don't you bring the rest of your pizza," Ed said, "and we'll go back to my office where we can be sure of our privacy. By now the archivists may have dug something up."

"The committee approach."

"I'll take all the input we can get."

Terrill gave his head a slight shake. "I hate to say this, Mr. Jeffers, but spoken like a bureaucrat."

Ed felt only a twinge of anger. If he wasn't used to the "B" word by now, he'd never be. And Lieutenant Terrill Hodge hadn't survived being a SEAL to this point by turning down any information he could get on his enemy. Without a doubt, he wanted everything Defense Intelligence or anyone else could scrape up before he went back into those tunnels. He was trying to sound superior in front of Andrea.

Whether he knows it or not, Ed thought, he does consider me competition.

Rising from the table, he felt his appetite returning.

Back in his office, with the door closed, he offered the couch to Terrill and Andrea, taking the armchair at right angles. Terrill had finished his pizza on the way over, rinsing his fingers in one of the Pentagon's 685 drinking fountains, and drying them on his navy whites. Andrea, seeing him do it, had smiled indulgently.

Beauty and the Bad Boy.

Ed said, "Before I check with DIA, does anyone have any theories of their own?" He gave Andrea a pointed look. *Come on.*

She shrugged. "Some assumptions, maybe. If Terrill's right, and the creature deliberately hid the canister and the human remains behind the piling, that would fit with it taking the colonel's papers. A number of animals will take steps to cover their trail, but this one keeps showing an uncanny understanding of what has meaning to us. That confirms it's pretty damn smart."

"So you're ready to assume the canister is part of the 'trail' the animal wants to cover—that it hid the can because it came from it."

"Isn't that obvious?" Terrill said.

"Far from proven."

"You're being too cautious, Mr. Jeffers."

"Call me Ed."

"Okay, Ed, look: the construction guy hammers through the wall, finds the can inside there, opens it up, and the thing pops out and kills him, then drags him down to the sinkhole. Simple as one-two-three."

Ed almost smiled. How did this live wire, this shoot-from-the-hip SEAL, manage to be so overbearing and at the same time oddly inoffensive? "Sizemore from the SWAT team said the thing he saw was the size of a big man. I don't think you could get much more than a child into that canister."

"So it's growing. It ate the construction worker, and probably the colonel, too. That's a lot of carbs, proteins, and essential amino acids."

Ed turned to Andrea. "Could an amphibian grow from child to man-sized in only a couple of days?"

Her brow furrowed. "Unlikely, but not impossible. Let's say we're talking about going from four feet tall to six, with the attendant growth in body volume—an increase of fifty percent. Cane toads from South America take around six months to grow from twelve millimeters to a hundred and twenty, an increase of a thousand percent. A thousand is twenty times fifty percent, so one twentieth of a hundred and eighty days means we'd expect our creature to take, let's see, nine days to grow the two feet.

"That's if it metabolizes like a cane toad and the food supply is average. If food is plentiful, amphibian growth can really accelerate, and like Terrill says, our creature has had a big meal, judging from how clean those bones were picked. The size of that skeleton, I'm guessing the forensic specialist will identify it as the construction worker."

"Herb Bodine."

"Right. Herb went missing first and according to Captain Hardison, the officer who disappeared—Colonel Sheffield?—was on the small side. Or is." She raised her hands, as if to apologize for the grisly assumption.

"But it would have been the size of a child," Ed said, "when it attacked the construction worker, like you say, a big strong guy."

"A leopard would be smaller than him, too, but could kill him easily."

Ed battled a sense of unreality. "You're saying this creature could have survived sealed up in a can buried inside poured concrete walls? We'd be talking nearly sixty years since those walls went up—and about that long since the Abwehr existed, assuming they went out with the Third Reich." He made it a question, aimed at Andrea.

She gave him an opaque return look.

"Help us out, here," he prompted. "You're the history minor."

She said, "The Abwehr was German military intelligence. It was permanently disbanded in 1944. Himmler, who had always distrusted it, did away with it and executed the man in charge for treason."

"I'm impressed," Terrill said. "I can't even remember what I minored in."

Ignoring him, she said, "Ed, exactly when was the Pentagon finished?"

"January 1943. They broke ground in October of '41. That's a hell of a thick wall down in that basement—concrete and rebar. It's a safe bet the canister could only have been put inside it sometime during that sixteen months."

Andrea rubbed at her forehead, clearly unhappy.

"Something wrong?"

"No," she said, too sharply.

Terrill said, "Back up, Ed. You're saying this monster rat maze went up in just sixteen months? Because I find that hard to believe."

"He ought to know," Andrea said. "It's his building."

Terrill gave him an assessing look. "So that's what Washington Headquarters Service means. The secretary of defense may run the military, but you're king of the Pentagon."

"Mayor," Andrea said. "They call him the mayor."

Terrill got up and paced to the conference table in the center of the room, plucking a Reese's Cup miniature from the candy dish Ed kept there for his staff. "So you deal out desks and office space, and like that."

"You looking for a desk, Lieutenant?"

He grinned. "Not hardly. But if you decided to move someone out of the Pentagon into, say, those overflow offices down by the railyard I passed coming in this morning, you could do it."

"Anyone in mind?" Ed asked, knowing he meant General Wallis.

"I might, depending how this goes. You got the clout to do that?"

"I don't think of it as clout."

"Bull. You're the king, not the mayor, and you know it."

"What was that?" Andrea said.

"I said he's—"

"No, I mean that sound. Like someone bent a piece of metal. It came from that big vent up there."

"It's the ductwork," Ed said. "It started out bolted tight, but a lot of fittings have corroded through over the years. That duct is an air return. It has a loud flex because it's so big—it circles the entire D ring. Whenever the A/C switches off, the metal expands and pops. I hear it all the time."

"Anyway," Terrill said, "why are we getting hung up on exactly which year the canister went into the wall?"

Ed waited for Andrea to answer, but she remained tight-lipped, so he said, "My point was, how could anything survive sealed away in a can for sixty years give or take?"

"Suspended animation," Terrill said, "don't you know anything about amphibians, man?"

Again, Ed found himself battling a smile. "Fortunately, we have an expert here who knows more than either of us."

Andrea rubbed a stray strand of dark hair back over her ear. "Well, amphibians can hibernate or estivate to escape extreme cold or heat. *Rana sylvatica*—a frog up in Canada and the northern U.S.—can freeze solid and stay that way for long periods. Its heart stops completely and no blood circulates. It stays alive through very slow body fermentation processes. It's not uncommon for some varieties of amphibian to maintain suspended animation for years."

"Sixty years?" Ed prompted.

"That would be way beyond anything we know of. But we're not talking amphibians we know of. And this isn't the animal going dormant in a hole in the ground or the bottom of a swamp, either. We're assuming a controlled environment inside a sealed cocoon, presumably filled with a nutrient life-support fluid."

"In the early 1940s? Were the biologists of that time up to something that sophisticated?"

"We know a lot more now, but we knew a fair amount back then, too. People tend to think most important scientific knowledge is recent, but that's wrong. TV was invented in 1928. The first computers were built in the 1940s off plans dating all the way back to 1839. Galileo's calculations from the sixteenth century still stand as pure genius. As for biology, in 1940 scientists were running the first clinical trials on penicillin, one of the greatest discoveries of any kind in history. Biologists knew plenty enough back then to have experimented with nutrient baths that might prolong hibernation in amphibians."

"There you go, hoss," Terrill said.

"But no way could they have made a new animal."

Terrill's triumphant look faded.

"If Sizemore's description is anywhere near accurate," Andrea said, "we *are* dealing with a new beast, with capabilities beyond any known amphibians, prehistoric or otherwise. To bioengineer such an animal, you'd have to know more about DNA than the most brilliant Nazi scientist could possibly have known."

"Why?" Terrill said. "Wasn't DNA discovered around then?"

"Ten years later," Andrea said. "Watson and Crick published their first paper in *Nature* in 1953. By then the Abwehr had been history for a decade."

"But say some Nazi genius got there a little sooner and kept it secret. That he figured out how to fool with DNA and—"

"The so-called scientists of the Third Reich weren't that bright, on the whole, Lieutenant Hodge. They, themselves, were more monster than scientist. And no one got to DNA before Watson and Crick, or the world would have heard about it, believe me. Being the first to publish a major breakthrough is something every serious scientist lives for. I can't imagine anyone discovering something as momentous as the structure of DNA and then keeping quiet about it for a decade, letting the glory go to someone else. Watson and Crick have been canonized by other scientists for what they did, and they deserve it. Could you pass up such a stellar place in history for any reason?"

Starting to answer, Terrill stood there with his mouth open.

"You couldn't, and neither could I. And the other thing is, even if you were right, and a Nazi scientist discovered the structure of DNA ten years earlier than Watson and Crick and hushed it up all that time, there's no way he could go straight from that to bioengineering a new, man-sized amphibian with the strength of a gorilla, similar brain power, and ten times the ferocity. We couldn't do that now, fifty years after Watson and Crick."

"And there's another part to this we haven't even considered," Ed said. "The 'why.' If the Nazis could smuggle a killer animal into the heart of their enemy's military, why put it in a coma and seal it away behind a three-foot wall?"

"Good point," Andrea said.

Terrill made an exasperated sound. "You know what your problem is—both of you? You think too much. In another minute, you'll talk yourselves into it being impossible to have a murdering beast loose under the Pentagon."

"He's got us there," Andrea said.

The office door opened and Emerson Wallis strode in. Dixie hurried after him, crying, "General, just a minute, General—"

"So here you are." Wallis glared at Terrill Hodge, who had come to a poor semblance of attention.

"I told him you weren't to be disturbed," Dixie said.

"It's all right," Ed said, waving her out.

"What the hell are you doing, Lieutenant?"

"General," Ed said, "have a seat. I was just about to call you."

"Is that so. Stand at attention, Lieutenant."

Hodge shifted the nonalignment of his body to the other side.

"General," Ed repeated more firmly, "let's all sit down here at the table."

After an obvious internal struggle, Wallis sat. "At ease,

Lieutenant," he said sarcastically, though Terrill had already sat, too.

I should have said no, Ed thought, when Terrill asked me if I could throw Wallis out of the Pentagon.

The general fixed him with a reproving look. "With all due respect, Mr. Jeffers, Lieutenant Hodge reports to me, not you."

"He called your office," Ed said, "as soon as we came up from the basement, over an hour ago. I believe your military aide told him you were in a meeting and, to coin a phrase, couldn't be disturbed. Is that correct, Lieutenant?"

"Yes, sir."

"I was with the Joint Chiefs," Wallis said importantly. "Lord help you, Lieutenant, if you ever get near them."

"I'm hoping to avoid that, General."

Wallis shook his head, as if Terrill had just confessed to being a moron. "Would it be too much to ask for a report now?"

Terrill filled him in with quick, concise skill—the kind of briefing Wallis would appreciate if he had any command experience. Instead, he said, "So you're sitting here going through endless conjecture instead of hunting down this thing and killing it like you boasted you'd do."

Terrill lowered his head a fraction, making Ed think of a bull about to charge. He felt his legs tense, ready to spring up and restrain Terrill, but then the lieutenant settled back.

"My men hadn't eaten a square meal in twenty-four hours, General, or slept in a bed for thirty-six. We looked for the creature, but it avoided contact. When we found the body and the can, I judged it best to take a rest and food break while we reevaluate tactics. Sir."

"*You* judged."

Ed said, "General, surely you agree it would help to give some more thought to what we're dealing with."

"That's a job for the command level, Mr. Jeffers, not the lieutenant, here."

"He's had some very good ideas," Andrea said.

Wallis blinked, perhaps taken aback that a civilian woman, just a consultant who didn't even work at the Pentagon, would dare butt into this. "Look, Miss—"

"Dr. Deluca. Unless you'd prefer first names, Mr. Wallis."

The general reddened.

With an effort, Ed kept his face straight.

Terrill didn't bother.

Wallis drummed his fingers on the table. "Good ideas, eh. Tell me, *Doctor,* whatever else this thing may be, it is basically an amphibian, right?"

"Given the tooth and where it's choosing to operate, there's not much doubt."

"Well, I'm not a *doctor* of herpes or amphibians, or whatever you call them. All I've done is watch the occasional nature show, but isn't it true—correct me if I'm wrong—that amphibians have delicate, sensitive skins?"

"Yes."

"Aren't they dying out in some places because of toxins in the water? Why not just poison the water down there?"

Terrill looked disgusted, as if Wallis had just suggested executing enemy women and children. Andrea's jaw dropped open, but no words came out.

"Or is that too simple?" Wallis said scornfully.

Ed felt the blood in his neck come to a sudden boil. He kept his voice calm. "General Wallis, remind me, when this is over, that we need to talk about office space."

Wallis flinched as though someone had pinched him awake in class with the teacher standing over him. "But I'm perfectly happy with my location."

"The renovation is making a fifth of our normal space unusable right now, putting the squeeze on what's left. I've got some higher-ups who need more room. We'll talk about it later."

The general looked nonplussed, and Ed felt a grim satisfaction. Wallis depended on ready access within the Pentagon to know what the military services were up to, so he could warn his special forces superiors down in Tampa as they maneuvered for any edge in the annual budget wars. He was basically SOCOM's spy, which meant the service chiefs on the Joint Staff would be happy to see him tossed out of the building. *Think you can push me around in my own office, General? We'll see who's got the push around here. . . .*

And then his anger drained away. Stupid. He wasn't pissed at Wallis pushing him, it was Wallis being rude to Andrea.

Who'd already shown she could stick it right back.

"General," Andrea said, "you can't be serious."

"Why not, Dr. Deluca?" Polite now—message received.

She said, "That water under the building comes from the Potomac and backflows into it. If we poison the water under the Pentagon we poison the Potomac as well, killing off a lot of river life."

Wallis gave a judicious nod. "Doctor, I don't make the suggestion lightly. I'm sure, as a curator at the Smithsonian, you must devote a lot of time and energy to fighting environmental toxins that threaten the animals you love and, believe me, I'd feel bad, too, if we harmed river life. But a lot of *human* life could be at stake, here, if Lieutenant Hodge continues to scr . . . to have trouble finding and killing this thing. I'm not suggesting we throw just anything into the water under the building. The Defense Department has some expertise in this area. Because of the threat of biological and chemical weapons, we've made a careful study of waterborne toxins over the years. I'm betting we could come up with an agent that would kill this animal with only a very limited risk to wildlife—which we'd do all we could to minimize."

"It's a bad bet, a gamble."

Wallis sighed. "I meant 'bet' as a figure of speech, Doctor. I'm in command of the military operation to get this animal, which at the least means I have to look into all options, including toxins. Surely you'd agree we must give the lives of humans more weight than a few fish or frogs? Who knows when this thing will strike again, grab someone else?"

"It isn't just animal life. The Potomac supplies drinking water for the region."

"Sure, after it's thoroughly filtered and screened at processing plants. All harmful elements are removed or reduced to safe levels. Any toxin used under the building would be diluted by the time it could reach the river. What difference would one more make?"

"General Wallis," Ed said, "would you like to be the one to explain to the greater Washington metropolitan area that the Pentagon poisoned the drinking water?"

"That's not accurate—"

"It's how the press would put it."

"They won't know, because no one is going to explain it. I'm sure I don't have to remind you that national security is potentially at stake here, which is why the deputy secretary ordered us all to keep this under the closest hold."

"Secrets leak, in Washington faster than anywhere."

"Not all of them." The general's voice was neutral but his meaning was clear—that he and his SpecWar brothers kept secrets worse than a little poison in the Potomac. Ed felt a chill.

"I have to think of my men, too," Wallis added a bit too fervently, as if to make up for it being an afterthought.

"You were there when that SWAT corporal got torn in half. My SEALs are risking disfigurement or death every time they go in. Poison would certainly be safer for them."

"*My* men didn't become SEALs to stay safe, General," Terrill said in a tight voice. "We'll go back in and find it, I promise you. We'll kill it, quick and clean."

"I'd like to believe that, Lieutenant. But time is running short."

"What about Colonel Sheffield?" Ed said.

Wallis turned to him. "I haven't forgotten him, Mr. Jeffers."

"I'm glad to hear it. I'm sure I don't have to remind *you* that the colonel may still be alive down there. If so, by now, he'll be drinking the water to survive."

"If," Wallis said.

"The DIA should report back any minute," Terrill said. "As soon as they do, we'll go back in. We'll find the colonel, or his bones."

Wallis stared at him. "I meant what I said about time running short. In case you've forgotten, tomorrow the secretary of defense will be hosting President Kuzmin and Defense Minister Arbatov of Russia on the goodwill tour, and that animal *will* be dead before then, do I make myself clear?" Without giving Terrill a chance to answer, he stood, looking at his watch. "I have another meeting. Lieutenant, I'll expect your briefing as soon as you've tried again."

"Yes, sir."

Terrill managed to get up before the general got out the door, but only just. He pointed at Ed. "You da man, Mayor Jeffers. You kicked his brass ass with that office space threat."

Ed shook his head. "Don't thank me. I shouldn't have done it. He'll remember I humiliated him in front of a junior officer. There's not a damn thing he can do to me. Which leaves you."

"I'm not afraid of him."

"You should be. Don't count on being untouchable if you kill that animal. They'll do all they can to hush it up, which means Wallis won't have to fight public opinion to screw you."

"Let me worry about that. I've been in fixes the general could not imagine, and I'm still here."

"But you're in his world now."

"That thing under the building has made this my world."

"Gentlemen—guys," Andrea said, "forget whose world it is. We can't let Wallis poison that water."

"Don't worry about it," Terrill said. "I'll kill it before he has a chance."

"Wallis won't drop the idea, will he?" Andrea said to Ed.

"I doubt it."

"Can you stop him?"

"I can make life at the Pentagon hard for him. But as it stands, he *is* in command of the military operation to kill the animal. We can try going over his head, but he'll give his side. He'll have his own military experts on toxins, and if there's a way he can make it seem safe enough, you can bet he'll find it. Is there a way?"

"There might be." She looked miserable. "Dissolving a poison, per se, into the water table would be far too dangerous, but there are some particulate toxins that might work and still be safe enough that he could make the case for them. Particulates work on contact with the skin and if you use one that settles out of water rather than dissolves in it, you can use water as the carrier—not the vehicle but the road, so to speak. There's always some uptake, but at levels far below that of a water-soluble poison. The Pentagon *is* far enough from the river that most of a particulate toxin released under the center of the building would probably settle out before it got to the Potomac."

"Probably?"

"I know. But you heard Wallis. He's got the trade-off argument, too. It *would* be safer for his men."

"They're damn well not his men," Terrill said. "They're mine, and I'll take care of them. I wish someone would show a little trust."

Andrea turned to him. "I know you'll do everything you can. But, as we're finding out, this is no ordinary predator. It isn't just inexplicably vicious, it's smart as hell, and Wallis isn't giving you much time. I've spent my professional life fighting the pollution that kills amphibians—"

Terrill raised a palm, cutting her off. "Stay still," he murmured. "Both of you." He turned his head slowly to one side, then the other.

The nape of Ed's neck prickled. What was he doing, listening?

No, sniffing the air.

In the next instant, he smelled it himself—a faint reptile scent.

It's here.

CHAPTER 11

Andrea's stomach knotted as the faint, fishy smell made it across the room to her. It's in the duct! she thought—what I heard before, that pop from back inside—

There!

She stared through the grating at the darker mass in the shadows. The creature had crept right up to the grille, the return of air to the duct keeping it upwind, holding back its smell. One push and it could spring down on them. From the corner of her eye she saw Terrill flow against the wall beneath the duct. Her legs trembled with adrenaline but she held still. This was like Africa—that leopard watching her from the tree. Panic and die, stay cool and they had a chance.

But position would be everything, and hers sucked, stuck here in the back corner, too far from the door, easy to see against the tall windows of the light court. She could feel the predator gaze assessing her: danger or prey?

Ed—he won't know what to do!

Andrea saw him a few steps from his chair—stopped in his tracks, good. "Easy, Ed," she advised in a low voice. "No sudden moves."

"I need him over here," Terrill murmured, "to give me a boost up."

"You don't have a gun," Ed said, "it'll kill you."

Andrea felt a small relief—he might be white as chalk, but his voice was relaxed, as if he were chatting on the phone.

"Andrea," he said, "you go out first, then Terrill and I will follow you, nice and easy. We'll find a marine—"

"Fuck that," Terrill hissed. "Andrea goes now, then you—after you get the fuck over here and give me a fucking boost."

Her mind clicked into gear: *Light!*

She got up, but did not walk out, instead picking up the lamp on the couch's end table—

No. The bulb wouldn't be bright enough, and the cord would not reach.

"Andrea?" Ed said.

"Stay still—both of you. If it has to keep an eye on more than one of us, it will attack."

There, that light on Ed's desk—a superbright halogen bulb, and the conical shade to focus the light if she could get close enough to the grille. Heart pounding, she strolled to the desk and tracked the lamp's plug to an extension cord beneath. She crouched and unloaded the other plugs, hearing the computer monitor crackle with static as it died. Now only the lamp was plugged in. Following the extension cord back to the wall, she found what she'd hoped for—extra length bound up in a flexible tie. Damn, she was twisting it tighter, a lefty must have wound this—*or a man with a sham right hand.* Working it back the other way, she forced her fingers to relax as she listened. Quiet

now, but if that grille crashed down, she'd have a second
or less before those teeth started tearing—

Got it!

The cord loops sprang fee, unfolding as she picked the
lamp up. Edging past Ed to the conference table, she saw
that Terrill had moved a wooden armchair under the duct
and was stepping up on it. If he yanked the grille out, nothing could save them.

"Terrill, stop."

Ignoring her, he reached for the grille.

"You'll kill us all," she said, "you fucking maniac."

The curse word did it, his head coming around, eyes
startled, and she used the moment to spring onto the table,
aim the lamp toward the grille, and flick it on. The squares
of blackness behind the grating bleached away and, for a
second, two red, slitted eyes stared back at her, then she
saw a flash of mottled green as it lurched back.

Thumps in the ductwork faded.

Her hand began to shake, and she dropped the lamp.

"Goddamn!" Terrill yelled. "It's getting away." He
grabbed at the grille, and at the same instant, Ed Jeffers
lunged into him, knocking him off the chair and sprawling
on top to pin him to the floor.

"Get off me, damn you."

"Don't be crazy," both of them shouting, and then the
door opened and Ed's secretary, Dixie, stared in at the two
men wallowing on the floor.

And me, up here doing a table dance. Andrea heard
laughter, then realized it was her own.

"Okay-y-y-y-y," Dixie said.

The two men scrambled up together.

"It's all right," Ed said. "Just a big rat in the ventilation
duct."

"I quit!" Dixie squealed. She backed out, slamming the
door.

Terrill set the capsized chair under the grille again.

"Forget it," Andrea said. "It's gone."

"Where does that duct go?"

"Everywhere," Ed said. "It circles the D ring and branches up and down between floors, too."

Terrill's shoulders slumped. "Fuck."

"What was it doing here?" Ed asked.

"Looking for carryout, I'd guess," Andrea said.

"But why here? The building has thousands of offices. Does it know our smell from the basement—did it hunt us down?"

"Why would it give a rat's ass about our smell?" Terrill asked. "This place is full of happy meals for that thing. You saying we're filet mignon and everyone else is hamburger?"

"I don't know. Andrea?"

She shook her head. Good question—amphibians had a far keener sense of smell than humans. The monster could well have tracked one or more of them here, but like Terrill said: *why?*

Clambering down from the table, she leaned on the edge, gripping it to stop the tremor in her hands. "I saw it for a second."

Terrill and Ed stared at her.

"The last time I saw eyes that red were on a *Hyperolius marmoratus,* but—"

"English," Terrill said.

"A frog from Africa, but these eyes were much bigger than any frog's, of course, and they weren't set on the sides of the head but in front—"

"You saw its head?"

"Just a glimpse. Big as a gorilla's."

"Horns?"

She shook her head. "I don't know. It took off so fast."

"What the hell were you doing?" Terrill said.

"Trying to keep us alive. Amphibians and reptiles have sensitive eyes and some have no eyelids—no way to blink. I figured a sudden, bright beam might temporarily blind it, drive it off."

"You did good," Ed said.

"Yeah, great," Terrill groused. "Now all we have to do is find the bastard again."

Andrea resisted an urge to throw the light at him.

He said, "Okay, expert, what'll it do next?"

"The ducts would be too dry for it to stay any longer than it had to. Probably it would head back to the water."

He started for the door. "I've got to cut it off."

"How?" Ed asked. "It has any number of ways down through the walls. It may not even be operating out of the original site anymore, which is why you and your men didn't find it there."

"You're a big help."

"Sorry."

Terrill blew out a breath. "Why am I chewing on you two? I'm who's supposed to get that thing. I wasn't ready, and I should have been."

Andrea could not stop thinking about the eyes. Front rather than sides confirmed a completely new species, never imagined by any herpetologist. If only there were some way to save it.

Impossible, she knew. The animal had killed at least two men and eaten one, and her own arm might be halfway to its stomach if the light hadn't worked. While it lived under the Pentagon, no one would be safe in the place charged with making everyone safe. She would fight Wallis on poisoning it, but a creature so fierce wouldn't let itself be taken alive.

At least, if they could get it, she'd be the first to study it—

Or rather, the first in sixty years. If they were right

about it coming from the can, there had been another lab six decades ago, an Abwehr doctor in a white coat examining this same creature.

Dad?

Her throat closed. No, she couldn't believe that.

"From now on, I'm packing." Terrill's voice startled her, as if both men had gone from the room, then popped back.

"I don't think that's a good idea," Ed said.

"The marines in the halls have got guns, what's one more?"

"The workers here know the terrorist alert drill, and a navy lieutenant walking around with a gun isn't part of it. People are already on edge; it could start the kind of rumors we don't want."

"I'll keep it out of sight, but Christ, man, I've got to have it. I could have nailed that sucker and had this over with."

Ed rubbed at his forehead. "I'll arrange it with Captain Hardison."

"Good." Terrill started for the door.

"Where are you going?" Ed asked.

"After it. With General Wallis talking poison, we can't wait for DIA. I'll get my guys and go back in, see if we can catch it coming down, or at least find the colonel or his body."

"Go," Ed said. "I'll walk over to the DIA vault, push them for whatever they've got and bring it down to you."

Turning, he gave Andrea a questioning look.

"If anything develops," she said, "call me. I need to go home for a few hours." He held her gaze and she felt a twinge of guilt. It's not a lie, she told herself.

Just less than he needs to know.

•　•　•

Andrea found him in his bedroom at the window that over-looked Rock Creek Park, a shawl wrapped around his shoulders, though it had to be eighty degrees in the room. The dull look on his face summoned a familiar ache in the back of her throat. A book had dropped from his fingers to the floor, one of his herpetology texts from years ago, still valuable for its vivid illustrations of toad species now gone.

She forced cheer into her voice. "Hey, Dad. Can I come in?"

His head lifted, eyes brightening. "Emera?"

She felt herself stiffen. Who was Emera? He would never say, and when his mind cleared, he'd deny using the name. Part of her wanted to know and part wished he'd never say it again.

"It's me, Andrea. Your daughter?"

"Of course. I know you're my daughter."

A crumb of Heidi's potato dumplings clung to the cor-ner of his mouth. Andrea cleaned it away with a tissue while he fussed. He had that musty smell again, and his clothes were rumpled. She spied an edge of his laundry bag sticking out from under his bed.

"Did you change your clothes?"

He shook his head.

"Dad, Heidi gave you a clean shirt and pants this morn-ing. Why dig into your laundry bag?"

"Didn't."

Okay, she thought. Okay.

"Where's Mark tonight?" he asked.

"I don't know."

"Don't know? Your own husband?"

"We're divorced, remember? Ten years ago."

Raising a trembling hand to his mouth, he stared through her, then focused again. "Yes, of course, how fool-ish of me. Ten years. Has it been that long?"

"Dad—"

"I hope he doesn't get shot tonight."

"He won't. He left the police, remember?" Taking his hand, she stopped its tremor with a gentle pressure. So thin. No matter how Heidi packed his favorite foods into him, he kept dwindling.

"Dad, I need to ask you something."

"Your hand is warm."

She smiled, containing her impatience. One of those in and out nights, happening more and more. Too soon it would be mostly out, then all out. How long before he couldn't walk anymore, until he never recognized her, then lost his ability even to speak?

Her heart shivered. No. No.

She felt herself rebelling against what she must do. The memories she would try to drag from him now might change her view of him forever.

But lives were at stake; she had to try.

She reviewed the timing: Dad had escaped Germany in early 1941, and it had taken almost a year for "Uncle" Luther to get him from France to Switzerland to the States. If they started building the Pentagon in October of '41, like Ed had said, Uncle Luther and Dad would have arrived with perfect timing to bury that canister inside the wall as it was going up.

The canister with *Abwehr* on the side.

"Go ahead," Dad said. "Ask."

"Who is Emera?" Someone else taking over her mouth, not the question she'd intended.

His eyes flooded. "I loved her, in spite of how it started. I really did."

"Was she before Mom or after?"

He gave her a reproving look.

Let it lie, she thought.

But today might be her last chance for this, too.

"Before," he said at last. "Years before."

Bands on her chest loosened. She'd gotten more than he'd given up before, the answer she wanted—that the mystery woman was not the reason a mother she'd never known had gone away and not come back. "Was Emera back in Germany?"

He turned away from her to look out the window, black treetops edged in silver from the half moon. *"Im Deutschland, ja."*

"Were you married?"

"Emera and me?" The dry wrench of his mouth was only technically a smile. "No, we never married. Must we discuss this?"

"No, *Vater.* Actually, I wanted to ask you about the early part of the war, that year or two you worked for the Abwehr."

"I thought we weren't going to talk about it anymore," he said petulantly.

Still on Emera. Strange—had she worked for the Abwehr, too—maybe part of his research team, an assistant he'd fallen in love with? "I'm not asking about her, now, just about your work at the labs, okay?"

He squirmed in his chair. "The clothes are too stiff. Heidi puts starch in them—she denies it, but I know she does. So I pull the ones I've been wearing back out of the bag, because they're softer."

And you can't smell them and you've stopped caring how you look, or if it bothers anyone. "That's fine, Dad."

He looked away, his jaw set.

She was being too frontal, she saw. Better to try sliding up on it. "Dad, let's talk about frogs. When did you first get interested in them?"

His expression changed subtly, the slackness leaving his face. "At the time I was working on my doctorate, geneticists were obsessed with plant inheritance. I wanted to know how heredity played out in something with a brain, and I chose to study frogs because I'd liked them since I was a kid."

The change in his voice was remarkable, as if a pilot flame in his mind had brightened on a sudden access of oxygen. She hardly dared move for fear it would topple him back.

"I was so young," he said, "only twenty-two when the call came. My article on the new species got his attention."

"Whose attention?"

"Canaris."

"Admiral Canaris of the Abwehr." Keeping her voice casual as her pulse tripped in her throat.

"Yes, of course. He gave me a lot of responsibility, and that went to my head, I guess. He was a good man, like a second father to me. He knew there were risks, but he didn't really comprehend how bad it could get, or he'd never have started."

"How bad what could get?"

Dad blinked, looked at her again. "I've been rambling."

"Not at all."

He sighed. "Yes."

"You were talking about Admiral Canaris—that he didn't realize how badly it would turn out."

"Well, I have no idea what I could have meant by that."

"And Emera?"

"Who?"

His eyes held no guile. Could he really be such a smooth liar?

Would he?

She put her hands to her head, feeling half mad with frustration. "Dad—"

"Andrea, dear, now that I have this disease, you mustn't keep trying to make sense of all my tangents. I still have a vivid imagination. All my life, I've always daydreamed a lot, but lately, everything gets all jumbled together—no, just listen, please. I've read up on Alzheimer's. As the disease progresses, its victims can become hurtful. If I do that, just remember it's not really your father talking anymore."

"Dad, you don't have to worry about—"

"Please, Andrea." He leaned toward her, his expression urgent. "I need to get this out while I still can. Everything we know of each other, even those we love, is what we put out to one other—conversation, smiles or frowns, a hug or a touch. Though we are *known* by these, they are not the mind itself—not *us*. They are all acts of the body. Alzheimer's unique cruelty is that it allows the body to go on acting and speaking until near the end, while eating away the mind behind the deeds and words. How, then, can we know whether the part we can't directly experience is still in there? Even though you are a scientist and you know all this, your heart will try to make you believe this body is me after, in fact, I'm gone from it. So you must test me every day. A day will come when I can't tell you your name or that you are my daughter. When seven of those days have gone by in a row, move this body out to a clinic, do you hear? Not a day longer, I beg you. I've written a will which forbids life support—feeding tubes, oxygen, so on. When this time comes, honor the father I was by doing for him what he can no longer ensure on his own. Don't let the clinic or nursing home prolong this body's life after I am gone from it. Promise me."

A hot coal had lodged in her throat, blocking speech.

"It's not just for your own sake but for Teddy's. I couldn't bear to think of this body being cruel to my grandson in my name. Seeing me as a vegetable day after day would hurt him worst of all. He's suffered enough, being left by his father. Now, promise me, dear Andrea."

Blinking back tears, she nodded.

A timid knock came at the door. "Mom? Grandpa?"

"Are you all right?" Dad whispered.

She patted her eyes with the soft, unbuttoned cuff of his shirt. Nodded.

"Come," Dad said.

The door opened and Teddy leaned in. "Hey, Gramps." His voice cracked low, bringing her an echo of Mark's mellow bass. "Mom, there's a guy here to see you."

"A guy," Gramps said approvingly. "No kidding?"

"Come on, Grandpa."

Andrea said, "Did this man give you his name?"

"Ed Jeffers."

"Ed," Dad repeated. "A good, concise name, always liked it. Is he handsome?"

"Forget it, Gramps, Mom don't need no stinking guy." Flashing the grin he'd inherited from his grandfather, maybe not even knowing he wasn't joking.

He might have reason to worry, the way Ed Jeffers kept growing on her. His slowness to anger—the way he'd weathered Terrill's little digs today without holding them against him, seeing them for what they were, being big enough to like the man anyway. His kindness, defending Sizemore's wild idea when Hardison was hot to ridicule it. Not the Devil, but the animal behind the image—that had really impressed her, both the kindness and what it said about his mind. He couldn't have made a remark like that, right off the cuff, unless he'd thought deeply about the world—explored that gap Dad had just talked about, between what we see and believe, and what *is*.

The arm, though. Could he let anyone past it?

It wasn't an injury or amputation. The only way the hand could move so well was if there was another, smaller hand—a real one—working it from inside the artificial arm. He was the right age to have been a thalidomide baby. The drug's signature deformity was stunted limbs with vestigial fingers or toes. Despite his skill at seeming un-affected by the arm, it had to be why he was alone.

He likes me, Andrea thought. More than likes—I'm not wrong about that. But he's not making any moves—

She realized with a start that Teddy and Dad were both watching her face as if it were playing an episode of *Jerry Springer*. "Ed and I work together," she said. "He's the guy I told you about, from the Pentagon."

Teddy frowned. "He should leave you alone at home. I'll tell him you're washing your hair." He started for the door.

"Teddy—"

"How about a game, Theodor?" Dad said quickly. "I'll spot you a bishop, since you don't know how to use yours anyway."

"I'll whip you with my eyes closed."

On her way out, Andrea ruffled her son's dark hair, making him twist away in a spastic-teen contortion. Her love for him stopped her breath for a moment, a giant hand squeezing down on her heart. Send your father away to spare your son—surely it wouldn't come to that.

Stopping in the hall, she stared at the ceiling and waited for the tears to sink back inside.

Marking time in the foyer, Ed thought about the boy—a surprise. He had assumed Andrea had no children, because she had told him she spent most evenings at her lab. On the whole, the boy didn't look that much like her, but there was no mistaking the brown eyes, the graceful arch of the brows.

She breezed into the foyer, dark hair swinging, exquisite in soft jeans and a rib-hugging cream sweater. "Hi, what's up?" a forced brightness in her voice.

"Just wanted to bring you up to date. Maybe we should talk outside?"

She glanced over her shoulder. "Sure. My truck's out front. That'll keep it private."

She led him down her front walk—not a follower, this woman, part of what drew him. A streetlight filtered through the maples on either side, dappling the ground with milky light. In the dark lacework of grass between, crickets sang their thanks for the summerlike warmth.

She said, "Where'd you find a place to park this late?"

"Two blocks down toward M. Someone pulled out after I'd circled for twenty minutes."

"That neighborhood's all permit parking for the home-owners. They have enough clout to keep the Georgetown cops after violators. You may get a ticket."

"Right now it's hard to care."

"True." Circling the rear of her pickup, she slid into the driver's seat. Waiting for her to unlock the passenger door, Ed imagined driving down through Rock Creek Park with her. Find a quiet spot by the stream and talk with her, ask her about the boy, why she'd gone into herpetology, what music did she like, had she ever stared into her own eyes in a mirror and asked herself how she came to be alive?

Enough.

But he couldn't stop so easily. He imagined the softness of her lips, their salty-sweet taste, how her ribs would feel through that fuzzy sweater against his palm.

The one that could feel.

His hand clutched inside the prosthesis, making the one below clench into a fist, the arm telling him he *must* stop, because Andrea was not Candace or Marianne or the oth-ers since Jillian—women he could care enough about, but not so much that, in bed with them, he'd be unable to get his mind off what they must be feeling as they tried to ig-nore the arm, the harness at his shoulder. He could remain friends with Candace and Marianne because the stakes stayed low, it wasn't love—for them or him. He could do that, get by, it worked, so stop thinking about Andrea. He'd never know how her arms would feel around him, so why torment himself imagining it?

She popped the lock on the passenger door. Opening it, he slid in, making himself focus on what he had to tell her, the two pieces of bad news.

"Did Terrill find the colonel?" she asked.

"His skeleton."

She looked away. He saw with surprise that her eyes were brimming.

"You knew the colonel?" he asked.

"No."

And then, before he could move, her arms *were* around him, her head on his shoulder, and she was crying as if her heart would break.

CHAPTER 12

Do something! Ed thought. She'd feel snubbed if he didn't respond — a comforting pat, something, anything — but she was crying on his good shoulder, blocking that arm, leaving only the prosthesis free. Free as in ten grand for microchips and clever plastic, so he could walk down the street looking normal.

A touch now would remind her he wasn't.

Or he could be really unfeeling.

Steering the hand across, he patted her shoulder, stubbed fingers tender inside the glove, as if it were her he was feeling, instead of the sensors in the VR glove.

She didn't recoil. But of course she wouldn't.

"What's wrong?" he asked.

"Nothing," she mumbled into his shoulder. "This is dumb, I barely know you."

Her cheek had dampened his shirt. Could she feel his heart thumping? Letting go of him, she pulled a tissue

from a box under the seat. In the dark it fluttered at her
face, a bantam ghost gorging on her tears. She leaned forward until her forehead came to rest on the steering wheel.
"What a wuss."

"I'll bet even Terrill cries."

She hiccuped a laugh. "That man wouldn't cry if you
pepper-sprayed him."

"You might have to."

She opened her mouth, closed it, and now he'd embarrassed himself, letting her know he'd seen them flirting—
that it had bothered him, because he wanted her, too, even
though he mustn't. Hard not to at the moment, her warmth
lingering in his side, this woman brave with leopards,
strong from hiking through jungles with heavy backpacks
and pulling herself up ropes, but still able to cry when she
hurt.

"Is it your father?"

She rounded on him, her shoulders rigid. "Why would
you say that?"

"When I first came to your office you mentioned him—
too old to be a Vietnam vet, but very antiwar, refusing to
chaperon your class when it toured the Pentagon. I guess
something in your voice or expression stuck in my mind.
Then, today, when Terrill pressed you on your reaction to
Abwehr, you seemed touchy about speaking German, and
on knowing arcane details about Third Reich intelligence
groups. I read once that kids of German war veterans often
have problems dealing with it."

"That's a hell of a lot of mental leaps."

"I'm sorry. I'm making you mad."

"No, explain. Tell me why you think my father could
have anything to do with the animal under the Pentagon."

"I didn't say that."

"You're implying it." Slipping her key into the ignition,

she turned on the dome light and searched his face, her eyes fearful.

He tried to gather his thoughts, not sure himself what he was driving at, because in one important sense, it did defy logic. "Today, you seemed anxious to nail down the time frame when the basement wall of the Pentagon last would have been open. If you learned German—and details of German war history—from your father, it would follow that he was probably born there, then came here. Did he by any chance leave Germany during the war, at the same time the Pentagon basement was built?"

She gave her head a quick shake, but it was not a "no." Turning away, she grabbed the wheel with both hands, as if she wanted to start the pickup and leave this discussion in the dust.

"I'm sorry," Ed said. "I want to help, but I'm only up-setting you more. Your father is none of my business."

"But he is. He worked for the Abwehr."

His pulse quickened even as foreboding pierced him. "What did he do for them?"

"He's never said. The war is painful for him. He proba-bly wouldn't have told me anything if he weren't so proud of having known Admiral Canaris personally—the head of the Abwehr. Dad was only twenty-two when the admi-ral himself recruited him. He just about worshipped the man, never got over Canaris's execution."

"Nuremberg?"

She gave him a chiding look, as though he'd just called the pope wicked. "Canaris was hanged, Ed, but not by the 'good guys' at Nuremberg. They'd have given him a medal. It was his own side, the bad guys, that executed him. He was in on the failed plot to kill Hitler. Heinrich Himmler found out and locked him away in the Gestapo's concentration camp at Flossenberg. In 1945, with the Al-lies closing in on Berlin and his hateful, filthy war lost,

Hitler ordered Canaris hanged, just days before G.I.s liberated the camp."

A chill went through Ed; he knew nothing about Canaris, but for a second he was inside the man's skin, sitting in a dank Gestapo cell, the approaching thump of bombs and artillery promising liberation—weeks of growing hope, and then the bitter futility of those last seconds of air before the rope stopped his breath.

"When I was a kid," Andrea said, "Dad would get into these dark moods, where he'd obsess over the admiral's downfall—how different Germany's fate might have been if the Abwehr had won out over Himmler's SS and the Gestapo." She jerked another Kleenex but didn't use it, instead wadding it in her hand. "Did you find out anything about the canister from those intelligence people?"

"DIA found no record of any biological experiments by the Abwehr. Isn't it likely your dad just did some spying for Canaris?"

"Then why not tell me? You did good at reading between my lines, Ed, but you missed on one count—I didn't learn Third Reich history from my father. I made my own study of the Abwehr over the years, trying to figure out what a man as good as my father might have done for them that he wouldn't want to talk about. I came up blank. Canaris wasn't like other Nazi leaders. In fact, he wasn't even a Nazi. He got away with never joining the party by making himself indispensable. Hitler loved hearing all the dirty gossip on Berlin's high society, which he both despised and envied, and Canaris kept him supplied with whatever tidbits his agents ran across. Knowing Himmler was his main rival for Hitler's ear, the admiral went to Himmler's house for parties, gave his kids candy, and lost no chance to butter him up. But as the war went on, Canaris went from mistrusting the Nazis to loathing them. He did something about it, putting himself with the good

Germans who truly did exist. Most people who saw
Schindler's List don't realize that Oskar Schindler, who
saved so many Jews, worked for Canaris. The admiral
himself, under the cover of his intelligence operations,
smuggled Jews out of Germany right under the Nazis'
noses."

"If Canaris was that principled, why are we worrying
about what your father might have done for him?"

She cocked her head, studying him. "You actually do
mean 'we,' don't you? You're worried right along with me,
even though it isn't your dad who might have done something awful—and in fact you urgently need to find someone who can tell you what this animal is."

"Guess I lost my head there, for a minute."

"Really? I had you down as never losing your head.
Can I count on you to do it again at some future date?"

Warmth flooded him, but he said, "Trouble with losing
your head is, you can't look for it until you find it."

"So you always take someone along."

"In case I can't stumble back over it myself."

"As you're trying to do right now."

Before he could think what to answer, she blew out a
breath. "Sorry. Look, Admiral Canaris clearly had a lot of
good in him, but he couldn't entirely avoid employing
Nazis. He was forced to accept a rigid party man as his
deputy, and we know that some Abwehr agents in the Soviet theater got into killing Russian Jews. My father would
never have had any part in that, but the Abwehr weren't all
angels, and Dad, for all his brains, has always been naïve
in some ways." She hit the wheel with the heel of her hand.
"Damn this. Damn it to hell."

He touched her shoulder again, the real hand this time,
and she gestured she was all right.

What she'd said rattled him. Would he really, for her
sake, rather have her father off the hook than able to help?

A quote from E. M. Forster popped into his head: "If I had to choose between betraying my friend and betraying my country, I hope I should have the guts to betray my country." Maybe, but Forster hadn't had twenty-five thousand people depending on him for their protection. If Andrea's father could help, he had to press, however much he hated to see her hurt.

But could it actually be? *Abwehr* on the canister, Abwehr in her father's past, her dad refusing to talk about it. Promising, no question, except for that one twist of illogic, and he was surprised Andrea hadn't thought of it.

"What are the odds," he said, "of me calling you in to consult on this beast, if your father was who walled it up in the first place?"

She gave a bitter laugh.

"What? I'm saying your father isn't involved—that it's too much of a coincidence."

"A coincidence is exactly what it's not. When you asked the Smithsonian for a herpetologist, you were asking for me because of Dad." Looking at him as if it were obvious, but it wasn't—or he was being dense.

"Could you untangle that a little for me?"

"First, it's not as if you had thousands of area herpetologists to choose from. There aren't that many of us altogether, and especially around here. Most are in Florida or out west, where the majority of amphibian and reptile species live. I was here for you to call on because this is where Dad came after the war and we've always depended on each other too much to live far apart. No area university has a big-time herpetology department, so the odds were high I'd end up at the Smithsonian."

"But you could have taken up any career—law, math. . . ." Then he realized he *was* being dense. Whoever had brought that animal into being was an expert on amphibians. His kids would be exposed to the field in a way most weren't. "Your father is also a herpetologist."

"A leading expert in amphibian genetics—or he was. All my life he's been my inspiration. From that first question you asked in my lab, you've been getting him along with me."

The misery in her voice erased any excitement he might have felt. "Andrea, we have to talk to him, press him hard, whatever it takes."

"That's what I was doing when you came, but it's not so simple. After decades of keeping me in the dark about what he did for the Abwehr, Dad's getting close to not knowing, himself. He has Alzheimer's, Ed."

"Damn," he said softly. So this was where the tears had come from, a pain deeper than he could have imagined. "I'm sorry."

"I said we depend on each other—he's lived with me ten years, ever since my divorce, always there for advice or help, or just to carry on about the animals we both love. I've kept him from being lonely and eating out of cans, and he's helped me raise my son, looking after him on the evenings I had to work. He's made my life better in a thousand ways. And now he's slipping away before my eyes. Tonight he . . . made me promise to put him in a home." Her lips quivered, then thinned into a firm line.

He took her hand, searching for words, but what could anyone say who had not gone through it? He thought of Mom, gone from a heart attack, after sixty years of a love beyond words. Her ration of torment over his arm must have been, in some ways, harder to swallow than his own, but swallow it she had, refusing ever to treat him or herself as anything but normal. Not until his thirties had he begun to fathom the endowment of her brave pretense. She'd shown him a third way between self-delusion and self-pity. You accepted your pain as part of life and looked away as much as you could. You pretended to be whole, and pretending worked better than the alternatives. Mom's life secret, which you'd never learn on an analyst's couch.

Andrea touched the back of his hand with a fingertip, running it over his knuckles, a soft circling that electrified him. "Let's talk about you," she said. "What do *you* think of me?"

He smiled. "That you're good, yourself, at reading between people's lines."

"You'd like to be able to lose your head."

"Part of me."

"What are you afraid of?"

"Cancer," he said.

"That's not what I—"

"And asbestos. A psycho creeping up the stairs while I sleep, someone outside my window at night staring in if I were to jerk the curtains open, viruses, rabies, tetanus, bacteria mutating to beat out penicillin, cholesterol, exercise, no exercise, other drivers suddenly veering across the median strip and crashing into me head-on, a meteor hitting the earth, winter, global warming, cat dander, the Pentagon renovation taking forever, a terrorist bringing a nuclear suitcase bomb onto a Metro train, my alarm clock going off, my alarm clock not going off, dentists, car salesmen, people who don't want public schools to teach evolution, the IRS, snakes—"

"Snakes!" She stopped laughing to slap the back of his hand. "Snakes are beautiful. They're shy and gentle. They eat insects and rodents."

He peered at her, sidelong. "I'd expect you to say that."

"You don't trust me?"

"Maybe I don't trust myself."

"Maybe I could help you with that."

He wanted to believe, wanted it with all his heart, and then he thought of Jillian, the night she'd come into the campus Ratskeller and seen him in a back booth French-kissing some girl he liked, but not too much. The pain on her face.

"Andrea," he said. "I want very much to know how this conversation will turn out, but right now, we have things to do, both of us, and there isn't time for this."

"Will there be later?"

"Unless a meteor slams into the earth."

But he knew exactly what she meant, and he was more afraid of her being right than of anything on his list.

"All right, Ed." She let go of his hand.

Pulling it away, he felt a loss so deep that, for a moment, he could not think.

With an effort, he forced his mind back onto her father. "Can you figure a way your dad might have gotten something—anything—inside the Pentagon walls?"

She gazed at him, as if trying to memorize the way his face looked right now. Then she turned out the dome light, and he felt both relief and regret.

"My godfather," she said. "Uncle Luther. In 1940 he was a captain in the U.S. Army, stationed overseas. By that time, having realized Hitler was a monster, Dad was looking to get out of Germany—or that's always been his story, such as it was. Dad got across the border and presented himself as a defector to Luther's unit. Luther had just been reassigned home, and he escorted Dad back with him. That's all either of them would ever say about it."

"Is Luther still alive?"

She shook her head. "Pneumonia, in a nursing home, just last year."

"Damn."

"But you'll like this: Luther's reassignment home was to the Pentagon construction project, as a logistical officer."

Ed felt his pulse pick up. "You're serious."

"Unfortunately."

"But why would an officer in the U.S. Army help a German defector put something inside the walls?"

"I've been thinking about that. Luther was always a dear to me, but on the subject of the war, he was as secretive as Dad. It's possible he was Abwehr. German spies inside the U.S. haven't been written about much, probably because it's embarrassing, but Canaris had a lot of agents working in the States. He had the foresight to get them in before America even joined the war, because he knew we'd end up enemies. He had agents in our aircraft factories and shipyards, passing along all our latest designs. And officers in our army and navy were reporting to him—probably more of them than we'll ever know.

"But, Ed, even if Luther was an Abwehr agent, why would he and Dad bring the animal here and bury it in the Pentagon? There's still so much about this that makes no sense. First, no way could 1940 scientists have bioengineered a new species. Second, even if they had, my father would have had no part in making an animal so deadly and vicious. And third, if someone else put such an animal into Dad's hands, he wouldn't take it across an ocean to hide it, he'd destroy it on the spot."

Ed didn't want to argue, so he nodded.

"I mean it. I can't have lived with him so long and be wrong about that."

"Okay."

"But, damn it, if I *am* wrong—if he does know anything about how this animal is made, we really need to get it out of him. Understand its biology and you'll know how best to disable or kill it, and that might save a lot of lives." She groaned, her hands clamped to her head, as if to keep it from exploding.

Then jerked toward him, as if startled. "You said Colonel Sheffield's body has been found."

"Yes."

"Then Wallis will think it's all right to poison the water."

"He's already ordered it."

"What? He's got a toxin this quickly?"

"SOCOM is trained in counterterrorism; they know about toxins from working with our chem/bio warfare experts. The anthrax letters —"

"When?"

"Tonight, as soon as Terrill and his men are ready to go back in."

"We've got to stop him."

"How?"

"We'll think of something." Starting the pickup, she slammed it into gear, froze for a second, then shifted back to neutral. "Wait here. I have to tell my son where I'll be."

He watched her run up the walk to the house, avid for every detail of her as she moved into the yellow light from the porch, and then she was inside, and he found himself breathing the cab in, winnowing for the scent of her hair, touching the wheel to find her sweat where her hands had gripped it.

Christ, he had it bad.

But how could it work, when it never had yet? Not just Jillian, but other women after her who might have gotten as close, ruled out as soon as he realized it?

He pushed a hand against his forehead. Stop this, damn it—he had other things to think about. This animal. If poison could work, maybe they ought to let Wallis go, because tomorrow would not be an ordinary day at the Pentagon, not with the Russians coming. He groaned, thinking of leading President Gregor Kuzmin, Defense Minister Constantin Arbatov, and the secretary of defense up and down the halls of the Pentagon, trying to seem calm and relaxed while he worried about a monster dropping from the ceiling. In his mind, he kept seeing the Russian president's severed head rolling along the Eisenhower Corridor, that deadpan expression of Kuzmin's still in place.

They still have their nuclear missiles—

He pushed it from his mind. We won't be able to stop General Wallis, he thought. He'll dump the poison tonight and kill the animal. Everything will work out.

Andrea slid back behind the wheel, and they were off, gunning it through the dark backstreets of Georgetown, narrowed to little more than lanes by the cars parked on both sides. Old homes, smallish and sedate, set back on narrow lots, wearing their ivy like the feather boas so popular when many of them had been built.

"What's he using?" Andrea asked. "Do you know?"

"Endosulfan—I think that's what he said."

"The bastard."

"Pretty bad?"

"Worse than bad, it's one of the few chemicals he can halfway defend."

"On what grounds?"

"It's a particulate."

"Meaning it won't dissolve in the water."

She darted a look at him. "You are a good listener, aren't you? It will dissolve in water, but slowly, and at any sane concentration, most of it would settle out before it could dissolve. Endosulfan is a contact insecticide, effective on a wide variety of insects and mites."

"And amphibians?"

"At doses above .03 milligrams per liter of water, it will kill a hundred percent of two-week-old tadpoles."

"This thing's a lot bigger than a tadpole."

"Which means it has a lot more skin available for contact. The ratio of surface area to biomass is what counts, and that will be roughly equivalent. If it does get into the river, it'll kill whatever amphibians it reaches and maybe a lot of fish, too, depending on concentration."

"Just by contact with the skin?"

"You better believe it." She sounded miserable.

"What about people? The Potomac does provide most of Washington's drinking water."

"The processing plants would remove most of whatever hadn't settled out by the time it got that far," she admitted grudgingly.

"Most?"

"Enough. You probably get a little in your system every time you eat an apple or potato. Farmers use it on tea, fruits, vegetables, and grain. Mammals seem able to degrade and eliminate small doses with very little absorption by the gastrointestinal tract."

"Then maybe we shouldn't fight it."

"I'm going to forget you said that."

"We really need to get this thing, Andrea."

"But how many innocent animals have to die? That bastard Wallis doesn't give a damn. He's never seen a frog gasping its life out because someone let toxic waste run into its pond. Frogs have beautiful eyes, Ed. I've watched them film over in death and thought, 'This is what used to sing us to sleep.' Wallis needs to imagine a poisoned environment with no frogs or crickets, no owls and kingfishers. He needs to think of a world where the summer nights of his grandkids—if they could survive on such a planet— will pass in barren silence. He thinks poison is just another weapon. It's evil, Ed."

"I agree."

"But?"

"No buts."

"All right then, you should understand something else: Endosulfan is tolerable to us humans only in small doses. If you took the amount Wallis will need to use tonight and dumped it into the purified end of a water processing plant, the pressure in the pipes would keep it moving right along, bringing convulsions, paralysis, and death all over this city. There wouldn't be enough room in the morgues."

"But we're not going to do that," Ed said.

Still, he felt a chill.

CHAPTER 13

←————————

"I'm green-lighting the op, Lieutenant."

General Wallis, getting over with his SEAL slang, telling them they had to poison the water. Terrill looked past him at who really mattered. Andrea's face was pale, her jaw set, shoulders hunched, black hair frizzed as if she'd taken an electric shock—to be honest, not beautiful when she was angry, but still the best sight the Pentagon basement would ever see. Beside her, closer than Terrill liked, Ed Jeffers crossed his arms, mech hand under, and studied the flasks at the general's feet with the stony fatalism of Cool Hand Luke.

Thirty minutes wasted, Terrill thought. Andrea and Ed upstairs trying to persuade the deputy secretary of defense that a man with stars on his shoulder could be dead wrong, while the guys who'd have to do the dirty work suited up, checked their loads, and marked time down here in the basement, tying Boy Scout knots in their own guts. Argument over, and right had not made might.

Big surprise.

Terrill fought a powerful urge to tell Wallis to go to hell. A disgrace to his uniform, ordering navy SEALs to poison water. Water was home, school, and church to SEALs. You'd arrange demolition, sure, to sink the enemy's ship or pin him in his harbor. With a limpet mine, water was still water when you were done. Wallis was about to perpetrate a mass poisoning, foul the water, sacrifice thousands of noncombatants, if that's how it worked out, to get one enemy. Even if it was only animals, that was not how SEALs worked.

"Lieutenant?" A glitter had come into Wallis's eyes, the man daring him to blow it now.

"Aye, aye, sir."

Wallis stared a second longer, in case anyone doubted he was the man and this lieutenant his flunkie. Terrill put it on account but showed nothing. The men at his back were looking to him. If he dissed a general in front of them—even a nonqual like Wallis, what would stop them from blowing off one of his own orders? To Ratman, Junior, Calvin, the others, *he* was the man, responsible for their lives when the shit hit the fan—all that really mattered, and he must do nothing to jeopardize it.

Turning to Andrea, Wallis said, "Dr. Deluca will now fill you in on the fine points of the op."

Bastard, Terrill thought. A control freak like Wallis surely would have vetted the plan with her, and knew it inside and out. He could have briefed them himself, but he was laying it off on her, knowing every word would burn her tongue. She'll do it, though, Terrill thought, because she wants me back in one piece a lot more than Wallis does.

Which wasn't saying as much as he'd have liked.

Stepping around the general, Andrea picked up one of the two flasks on the floor by its side-mounted handle. Each flask had a skull and crossbones on it, which ought to make pirates everywhere spin in their graves. "These will remain watertight," she said, "until you are ready to unload. You must sight the animal first. Then you pull this trigger inside the handle while pushing the button on top, to release the bottom seal. Both motions are needed together, in unison, as a failsafe against accidental dispersal."

Terrill glanced back at his squad to make sure they were listening. They'd scattered themselves around the narrow hall in a kind of antiformation, leaning or squatting, Doyle and Chief down on their butts, being older guys with the smarts to conserve energy. They all looked hot in their wetsuits, and more than a little irritated, staring at the flasks, the desecrations General Wallis was ordering them to take into their temple. Pissed, yeah, but on the other hand, to be a navy SEAL was to simmer along in a constant state of irritation, always a little mad about something. They were the good guys, and they were bad, no question.

Terrill turned back to Andrea. "Once we release, what if one of us accidentally ships water?"

"Don't. With your skin mostly covered up, contact shouldn't be a problem, but you sure as hell don't want to swallow any. You just want to get enough of it on the animal so it will die. I'd suggest going where you found the colonel's remains, using that as your starting point. How straight are the channels down there?"

"Not very. Water follows the path of least resistance. It's pretty much like aboveground rivers—straight in places, winding in others. And we're talking quite a few tunnels down there."

"Who is going to carry?" Andrea asked.

Terrill hesitated, reviewing the scheme he'd toyed with

from the moment Wallis had used the word "poison" in Ed's office. If I get close enough to see the animal, he thought, why not just shoot its ass dead? Okay, it's quick, but if it's far enough off, we get several shots at it, and if it's not far, the target's bigger. It goes under, we drop the poison; it doesn't, we shoot, I bring the poison back, and I'm Andrea's hero. The general lets it pass, knowing if fish were to go belly-up and the press found out he'd poisoned them, he'd go down as the Jim Jones of the Potomac.

So I'd best keep both hands free for shooting.

He said, "Link and Doyle will handle the toxin. Two tunnels branch from the access chamber, so I'm thinking half the squad for each, same as the first time we went in."

Andrea nodded. "That can work. There's enough endosulfan in each flask to provide a killing concentration if you can get within fifty yards or so. But never forget how aggressive this animal is. At all times, you want a man watching forward and back—both above and below the surface. It might try to ambush you from the bottom silt, so watch for that, too. Be aware of the flow. Ideally, you will see the animal a good ways off with the current at your back. If you're that lucky, just release and get the hell out as fast as you can."

"And if we see it with the current at our face?"

"How good are you at taunting?"

Terrill grinned at his men. "You bullfrogs follow that? We treat the bastard like a sugar cookie we just rolled in the sand in BUD/S training. We insult the hell out of it, make it so mad it has to come after us. When we're sure it's coming, we dump poison and it nukes itself swimming through after us."

"And if it won't come after us?" Chief said.

"It's a predator," Andrea said. "When you run from it, you'll be telling it you're prey. Given how belligerent it's been, that should be enough. If you can't find it, don't dump the poison—"

"Belay that," General Wallis said behind her. "I want that water poisoned whether you men can make contact with the animal or not. My experts tell me there's a fair to good chance of getting it even if you never spot it. We need a confirmed kill tonight, and we need it bad. Best case, you see it, get close, and dump. Only if you can't make contact and your air is so low you have to come back do you dump without being in sight of it."

Andrea's face reddened and Terrill felt his jaw clamping. Yeah, right—poison the water, risk killing a lot of river life, when it might not even get the animal. No way. He held Andrea's gaze, hoping she could see it in his eyes. To Wallis, he said, "What if it's not in the water, sir? What if it's up in the building?"

"Amphibians can't stay away from water for long. Shallow as it is down there in most places, your air will last several hours. It'll be there. Dump the poison then get back here. We'll hose you down here, seal your suits up for disposal, and send your equipment to decon. Any questions?"

No one said anything.

"Let's do it," General Wallis said.

Yes, *let's,* Terrill thought. You chickenshit son of a bitch.

He turned to his men, nodded at Doyle and Chief, who pushed up from the floor and retrieved the flasks. "Chief, Doyle, and I go first," he said to the squad, "Rizetti, you lower us the poison on my line, then the rest of you rope down."

"Aye, aye, sir."

Terrill checked each face, the men on the balls of their feet now, every eye on him.

"Lieutenant?"

He turned at Andrea's voice.

"Be careful down there."

He gave her a smile. "You've got it, Doctor."

He flipped the night-vision goggles down, grabbed his line, and swung through the hole. The black water seemed to rise into his feet. Letting himself slide all the way under, he savored the coolness washing through the suit as he looked around beneath the surface. Nothing in sight but the pebbled bottom of the chamber, sloping up toward the two tunnels. He detached his fins from the back of his belt and pulled them on as Chief and Doyle splashed down beside him and did their own pan of the chamber, the water enforcing that stately grace on their movements. In their peaked hoods, they looked like creatures from the black lagoon.

Terrill jerked a thumb up, and surfaced with the others in time to see the flasks descending on his line. He had to stop from taking one himself. Spreading poison was shit duty, and he didn't want his squad thinking he'd ask them to do what he wouldn't. But both men looked okay with it, and wasn't Chief always crying about him hogging all the dangerous parts of an op?

The rest of the squad rapelled down into the water, choking the rope to keep the splashing to a minimum. When they were all in place, Terrill motioned them close. In a low voice, he said, "Junior, you and Bammer go with Calvin, Rat, and Chief this time. Steinholtz and Bearhill, you're with Doyle and me. Now listen up. We see this thing, we don't dump."

"Sir?" Link said.

"I repeat, we do not dump—not first thing. You've got Calvin, Chief, best shot in the squad. He tries to shoot it first, and if Junior and Bammer have a clear field, y'all feel free to join in."

Calvin grinned beneath the goggles—you'd get no words from Cal unless you asked him a direct question.

"I'm the primary shooter in my group," Terrill said, "with Steinholtz and Bearhill backing me up. Doyle, be ready to dump, but not unless we miss and it's charging down our throats. Same with you, Chief."

"I like it," Chief said, "but you're putting your ass in a sling, sir. The general said—"

"The general's not down here. What he wants is this thing dead. We give him that, everything else will shake out. We're not dumping this shit unless there's no choice. I take full responsibility."

Chief and Seaman Doyle nodded.

Ratman Lucas cocked his head.

Terrill heard it, too, a faint sound coming from one of the tunnels.

"Was that a scream?" Rat whispered.

Terrill motioned for silence. Seconds later, it came again, louder now—a man calling for help, the sound smearing around inside the chamber, seeming to come from everywhere.

"Shit," Doyle whispered. "It's got someone else down here. It must have gone up through the walls again and grabbed some poor bastard."

"Hel-l-l-l-f." A man's voice, bouncing around the chamber, loud enough to be heard down here, but not up above.

Doyle pulled a lungful of air, but Terrill stopped him before he could yell back. "Which tunnel?" he asked Ratman, unable to pin down the sound.

"That one, sir." Ratman sounded positive, and he knew tunnels.

"Let's go—stay together."

"What about this?" Doyle asked, holding up his flask.

"Bring it. We may still have to use it. A man will survive it on his skin if we can get him under a shower quick. But what I just said still goes: Before you dump, if anyone can get a clear shot, take it."

"Hel-l-l-l-f," wailed the voice again, bouncing around the cavern, slapping off the surface.

Chief slipped under and took the lead. With a curse, Terror went after him, stroking hard across the glowing red bottom, rising to the base of the hole Chief had vanished into, feeling pressure bursts from behind him as the rest of the squad followed. Terrill sighted Chief's fins ahead, crimson smears churning the water in the infrared light. Foreboding gripped him. This tunnel was deeper than the other. Would he be able to stand clear enough of the water to shoot? Terrill pulled hard, watching the bottom, hoping it would slope up. The Glock was seconds away in its quick-release waterproof pack on his chest, but he'd need his shoulders above the surface to fire.

He was gaining on Link. Encouraged, he cranked it up another notch, determined to pull ahead. The tunnel entered a straightaway that angled back under the building toward the A ring. Breaking the surface, he looked ahead.

There—out at the limit of the infrared beam, had that been a man's head being jerked under?

Terrill dived under again, and saw that Link had used the interval to stretch his lead.

Damn it, I'm in command, I go in first, what the fuck is he doing?

Terrill put everything he had into catching up. When he was twenty feet from Link's flashing fins, Chief suddenly stopped swimming and his flippered feet reached for the bottom.

Terrill broke the surface and saw what Link was staring at:

Not a man, the beast itself, a terrible monster head, cleaving the water straight toward Chief, twenty yards and closing. A chill bubbled up Terrill's spine. He tried to find bottom, his fin barely scraping as the water lapped his chin. He fumbled at the waterproof pack, knowing the

Glock would shoot until the powder got wet, but the water slowed his arms, made his fingers slip on the seal—not enough time.

"Link!" he shouted. "Release! Release the toxin!"

Chief raised the flask, pushed it toward the head of the monster, ten yards off now, thrusting it toward him as if casting a spell, and Terrill realized what was happening: the poison wasn't dumping—in his panic, Chief had forgotten the failsafe.

"The top button too!" he yelled, tearing the pack open, fumbling the Glock out, then losing his grip, feeling it slip away, *Jesus!*

Link jerked and disappeared beneath the surface.

Terrill dived under, grappling for the speargun strapped to his leg—get a spear into it, yes, explode the mother-fucker.

A submerged, gargling yell reached him.

Terrill saw it under the surface, circling Link then rushing in to a second attack, incredibly fast, a giant head, ruby eyes, flexing its long body and tail like a dolphin. Terrill fought the straps on his thigh, tearing the speargun loose as the creature drove into Link's body again—too close; if he hit Link, the charge would blow his leg off; and then Link's leg *was* off, floating past Terrill's head, the poison flask sinking toward the bottom, still sealed, and he was trying to shout under water, furious, as blood began to cloud the channel around him.

In the spreading murk of hemorrhage, he caught glimpses of Link's body, jerking around, head down. Something bumped his goggles—Christ, Link's arm, and he realized it didn't matter so he fired the speargun, heard it detonate, but now the water was opaque with blood, the infrared refracting back in his face, and he couldn't see a damned thing near the surface.

On the bottom, he glimpsed the Glock. Diving under

the cloud of blood, he grabbed it and dodged to the wall, clawing at the dirt to pull his head up again, breaking the surface enough to aim the gun, but there was nothing to see, nothing to shoot.

Pieces of Link bobbed on the surface.

Behind him, Terrill heard shouts filling the tunnel, the rest of the squad catching up, and then he lost it, out of his mind crazy fucking mad, diving under to swim after the fucking bastard, catch it, kill it with his hands if he had to—

Something grabbed him from behind and he wheeled under, driving his hands up like blades, but the thing slapped them away and grabbed him around the waist. He struggled, waiting for the tearing pain, a distant part of him wondering if it would hurt or just go numb, and then he heard shouts above the surface and realized one of his men had hold of him. He spat out the mouthpiece and drove himself and the weight on him upward, breaking the surface to see Doyle's big scared face inches from him.

"Let me go, damn you."

"It'll kill you."

"Let me go, let me go."

"It's gone, Lieutenant, calm down—please, sir."

But he kept struggling while Doyle slipped around his back and squeezed his neck and everything went black.

He came around lying on his back in the middle of the basement hall, and they were laying out the parts of Link they'd brought back.

He could hear someone throwing up, saw it was Ed Jeffers.

He rolled to his side and got up, groggy, his body weighing a ton. His first coherent thought was to count off the squad. Everyone back but Link, who would never be back.

Fury gave Terrill new strength. Where was General Wallis, the fucking prick?

Must have left the basement after the squad went down. *Jesus, Link, not you.*

Andrea moved in, her face white, and grabbed his hands. Her lips were moving but nothing was coming out, and then his hearing clicked in.

"—the toxin?" she said.

He forced himself to focus, looking around the floor, not seeing either flask. "Doyle!" he shouted.

The big man lumbered over. His eyes were red, and Terrill saw that he was crying. "I'm sorry," Doyle said. "I'm sorry."

Terrill reached back in himself for the strength to be calm. "The poison," he said in a low, distinct voice. "Where is it?"

"Gone, sir." Doyle wiped at his eyes but the tears kept pouring.

"What do you mean, gone?"

"It took it."

"What?" Andrea said.

Terrill shook his head, not comprehending. "What took it?"

"The animal," Doyle said. "I had to drop my flask to help you, and it caught it on the way to the bottom, and then it was gone. While Rat and Bammer were getting you out, I looked for Chief's flask but it was gone, too, along with his goggles."

"Dear God," Andrea murmured. "It's got the poison."

"Why?" Terrill said. "Why would it do that?"

Andrea, the closest thing they had to an expert on whatever the fuck this thing was, shook her head.

CHAPTER 14

Friday

Just let us get through this, Ed prayed.

He stood in the innermost, A ring of the Pentagon, on the second floor, between Corridors 6 and 7, the hallowed alcove where glowing walls herald our most honored names. Standing with the top man in Russia, Gregor Kuzmin, the gray apparatchik whose expressionless, fox-like face made you think of a hit man or maybe a nightclub comedian.

And beside him, Defense Minister Constantin Arbatov, a hefty slab of Slav who preferred his old title of General and the uniform that went with it—a bolt of olive drab straining to contain him, his collar pinching his face red, making his crowning snow fort of hair look even whiter.

And their host, John McCarver Hastings III, United States secretary of defense, on the big side himself, trademark colorful suspenders hidden by a dark suit coat un-characteristically buttoned—"Torpedo Mack" Hastings, formerly a submarine admiral and still a dark-haired bear of a man with eyes too observant for some people's comfort.

Arguably three of the more important people on earth, and it now fell to Ed to make this tour of the Pentagon a diplomatic success, if he could only shut his mind's eye to a basement floor awash in blood. A veteran navy SEAL, a master chief petty officer, eighteen years defending his country, not just dead, but in pieces, like the SWAT corporal before him. What must not happen again, had.

Could I have prevented it?

According to Terrill, the mission had been knocked off course almost at once by a man shouting for help under there. No one had been reported missing from any Pentagon office before the squad went down, which left construction workers. But this morning, Hardison's investigators had been unable to find any renovation foremen with absent laborers.

Ed heard himself saying that the Medal of Honor is America's highest award for valor, given by the president in the name of Congress, and that over 3,400 people have received it since the first in 1861, that nineteen people won the medal twice, and that the Civil War occasioned more awards than any other.

Why had the beast taken the poison—both flasks?

You needn't be Jane Goodall to know that chimps, monkeys—and some lower animals, too—sometimes made off with shiny objects. The flasks were dull black except for the white skull and crossbones, but maybe that had caught its eye. Maybe next it would accidentally push the button while pulling the trigger and poison itself.

Or maybe, somehow, it knew exactly what it had taken.

Ed tasted a queasy burn in his throat, though he'd eaten

no breakfast. The next step in this logic was too awful to imagine. No, he couldn't even think about it now. For the next fifteen minutes, all that mattered was that the creature—whatever it was, whatever it knew—stay under the building.

Ed glanced down the corridor at the marines. Full dress uniforms, each soldier bracing to attention as the dignitaries strolled past, just as a ceremonial honor guard would do. If Arbatov or Kuzmin wondered about the semiautomatic rifles, they'd shown no sign. No one had mentioned ThreatCon Alpha to them, and guarding the route of such important visitors would be sensible.

But if any of those marines had to start shooting, it would be a disaster. No clear field of fire, people everywhere, a milling crowd that included the entourages of all three VIPs, their military assistants, interpreters, national and local press, and the videocamera crew from the historian's office. Everyone smiling, eager to treat the Russians as esteemed guests, no mention that this huge temple of stone was where the Cold War had been won, or that the esteemed guests had lost it.

Andrea, Ed thought, out of the blue, and his heart lifted. He remembered her warmth against his side, her finger tracing the back of his hand—

"Mr. Jeffers," the interpreter said, "the defense minister asks how many of these medals were awarded to your soldiers for action against Russian soldiers."

"None, I'm glad to say."

After the translation, the red-faced Russian in the bemedaled uniform spoke again, his guttural voice cold. The interpreter, a striking blonde who might have come straight from the anchor desk at CNN, said, "The defense minister asks if you are aware how many Russian soldiers died in the Great Patriotic War."

Ed shot a glance at the Secretary, who returned a bland

nod of encouragement. *Thanks a lot.* "I believe the number was over thirteen million."

The Russian general spoke again, staring at Ed.

"Do you also know how many Russian civilians died in the war?"

"Over seven million."

Torpedo Mack gave him another paternal nod. The defense minister cleared his throat and fell silent. Ed realized Gregor Kuzmin was now looking him in the eye, the first time he had done so. Kuzmin began speaking, and the interpreter translated, her voice warmer now. "It is good to be in the presence of an American with the respect to know how tragically the Russian people suffered to rid the world of Adolf Hitler and his fascism. I would assume he is also aware how many of his own countrymen gave their lives in that war."

"Almost three hundred thousand soldiers."

"Two hundred ninety," Kuzmin corrected him through the interpreter. "And how many civilians?"

"None."

"Ah, but only to be expected, since the war was fought not in your homeland, but in ours."

Ed realized why Secretary Hastings wasn't stepping in. While scoring their points, the Russians would also carry one away — that an ordinary American could know enough about them to understand their point of view and sympathize.

What they would not know was that he hadn't slept last night, because every time he closed his eyes he saw the severed pieces of men slaughtered by what might be the last combatant of the Third Reich, a vicious animal created by those same fascists Kuzmin had just mentioned. Trying to drive out the bloody images, he'd sat at his computer monitor, trolling the internet for facts about the men he'd be escorting tomorrow. As a young lieutenant, Arbatov had seen his commanding general, Marshall Zhukov, send 250,000 Russian soldiers to their deaths in the Kursk campaign alone. If Arbatov asked, Ed could break down the World War II casualty numbers even further and note that the Russian army had lost more platoon commanders than the total combined casualties of the British and Americans.

Bureaucrats might not jump out of planes, Ed thought, but we do plan ahead.

Kuzmin was speaking again. The interpreter said, "So, Mr. Jeffers, is it true you keep a section of the Berlin Wall here in your defense ministry as a trophy?"

"As a reminder," Secretary Hastings cut in at last, "of how mutual mistrust can prevent two great nations from achieving the deep friendship that should rightfully be theirs."

Kuzmin shot the Secretary a fleeting smile.

Saved, Ed thought. Now let's move this along and get these men out of here.

"I would next like to see your Berlin Wall exhibit," Kuzmin said through the interpreter.

Ed suppressed a groan.

"Lieutenant Hodge, the blood of your master chief petty officer is on your hands." General Wallis was leaning into Terrill's face now. Terrill's eyes made Andrea's arms prickle, like that time with the diamondback—seeing it beneath her reaching hand the instant before it struck.

Did Wallis have any idea the danger he was in?

Turning away, he talked over his shoulder as he paced to the wall behind his desk and surveyed the photos there. "All you had to do, Lieutenant Hodge, was pull a trigger while pushing a button. But you handed the job off, and your men panicked, and the enemy, a mere *animal,* killed a man and took the goddamned poison away from you." Wallis straightened a picture of himself and Deputy Secre-

tary Keene so it squared up with the frame next to it—
Wallis and a couple of three-star generals. The big wall
was full of photos; Ed had given the general plenty of
space along with the outside view he'd denied himself—
green parade grounds and, beyond, the city of Washington,
shimmering in the late-September warmth. But the wall
would be Wallis's favorite view, Andrea knew. With these
pictures backing him up, he felt in control, comfortable,
confident.

Too confident.

So far, Terrill had kept his cool, staring through the general and taking his abuse, as his duty required, but that
could end any second. Maybe that's what Wallis wanted, to
provoke Terrill into throwing a punch, then use her as a
witness to end his career. But the lieutenant was no regular navy officer, rotating through the Pentagon to earn his
next promotion. The United States military had, with society's tacit approval, stripped Terrill of our deepest taboo
and remade him a killer—not just a few weeks of basic
training learning to do pushups and shoot guns and stab
stuffed dummies with a bayonet, but the most brutal in-
doctrination any military had ever devised. If Terrill attacked a senior officer, it would be because he had lost
control to the programming in his nerves and muscles—
not barroom punches but quick and efficient death.

Wallis turned from his photos back to Terrill. "Your
mission was to get that thing before Kuzmin and Arbatov
came near the building. Well, Lieutenant, they're in it now,
and if that animal shows itself, or takes another life, you'll
have dealt a major embarrassment to your country. You've
had your chance. I'm relieving you of command."

No! Andrea thought.

But Terrill seemed not to have heard, eyes distant, body
remaining still.

Wallis gave an irritated cough. "I've arranged with your

commander at Norfolk to send the other squad of your platoon here. They'll be reporting within the hour and Lieutenant J. G. Mark Rowalski will assume command of the full platoon."

"General," Andrea said, "when you called, you told me you wanted me here at this meeting for my expert advice on the animal. I know amphibians and reptiles, but this creature goes way beyond any I've seen in size, intelligence, speed, and aggressiveness. Lieutenant Hodge *has* seen it, which makes him the closest thing you've got to an expert. He knows how fast it is in the water and its tactics for getting in close. He's now seen an attack from a few feet away, watched its moves. I'm sure he'd rather have died himself than lose a man, but that loss is now part of his experience. Put a green commander in cold and your risk of losing more men goes up not down."

Wallis shook his head. "I need a man who will follow my orders to the letter. Lieutenant Rowalski's file suggests he is that man."

"General," Andrea said, "I know I'm here to talk about animals, not people, but we're not that different in some respects. Our sociobiologic tendencies come from our evolutionary history as animals, and often we're not aware of them operating. You and Lieutenant Hodge rub each other the wrong way—I've noticed that from the beginning. If a young wolf refuses the respect a pack leader demands, there's trouble. Of course, the advantage of our bigger human brains is that we've reached the point in our evolution where we can suspend our primitive animal responses when the situation demands. It demands it now. I mean neither you nor Lieutenant Hodge any disrespect when I tell you that you're reacting to each other on a primitive level that's all about dominance—"

"Doctor, you're here to be an expert on that animal, not me. And this isn't about dominance, it's about responsibility, the part of his duty Lieutenant Macho, here, never learned. He thinks he's entitled to despise me because I never carried logs for ten miles or sat in cold surf. I'm just a no-nuts staff officer, totally useless. He never stops to think where the Zodiac boat that hauled his ass down the Nile came from. It, and his guns, and his fancy rebreather, and his infrared goggles, and everything else on his back and under his feet came from officers like me fighting the budget wars in order to get enough funding for special forces. Every day I go up against the army, the navy, and the air force, not to mention the civilian budget people who lord it over SOCOM and all the services. I did not ask for some goddamned animal to get loose under the Pentagon—in water, no less, where no one but a SEAL can get at it—but I've got it. I am the senior SOCOM officer on the scene of engagement. My record may be staff, but I *am* in command, which makes the ultimate responsibility mine, whether I want it or not."

Andrea said, "I'm sure your work is important, General, and I'm confident Lieutenant Hodge could learn to respect your budget prowess. What's important right now, if you really want to stop this animal, is that you respect what Lieutenant Hodge does best. You wouldn't send him in to argue for more funding, so please have the sense not to think you're better at *his* game, just because he's a lieutenant and you're a general. You say this is about responsibility, not dominance; prove it. With lives in the balance, you have the responsibility to set aside your feelings and use the most experienced commander available."

"Are you through?"

Andrea saw Terrill, beyond the general, giving her an urgent nod, then wagging his head twice to one side. He wants this over, she realized with surprise, and us out of here, even though he's just been put out of action.

"Dr. Deluca, you've said your piece. I have to prepare

for a budget meeting with the assistant secretary of defense
for Special Operations and Low-Intensity Conflict. I hope
to persuade him that our special forces need their own air-
lift support. If I had won this argument last year, Lieutenant, you'd have been able to get here before sunrise
yesterday, which would have given you six extra hours to
get this animal. Who knows, with the extra time, you
might have gotten lucky. You are dismissed."

Terrill headed for the door. Andrea hesitated. She'd said
her piece, yes, but Wallis hadn't listened.

And nothing she could do would make him.

The broad corridor outside Wallis's office was full of
men and women in uniforms and business suits heading in
both directions with purposeful expressions, spared—for
better or worse—having to fear the real danger behind this
particular TheatCon Alpha alert.

"Let's get some air," Terrill said.

She followed his weaving course through the crowd
down to the mall entrance, midway along the corridor. Six
DPS guards manned the entry, triple the number she'd seen
up to now, giving everyone who entered a close look as
they swiped their badges at the turnstiles. One guard
watched them exit.

Outside, Terrill veered over to the sandstone pier that
flanked the steps. Hopping up on it, he stared out at the distant city as Andrea climbed up beside him. On the broad
green, men in Revolutionary War uniforms and powdered
wigs stood in perfect ranks, faces gleaming in the sun, an
unmoving formation that might have stepped straight from
a history book. They must be waiting to entertain the Russians, still inside with Ed.

"Look at all the toy soldiers," Terrill said.

Andrea put a hand on his arm. "Wallis had no right to
talk to you like that."

"Sure he did, and I have the right to go back at him when this is over."

"It is over—for you."

"No way."

She looked at him, alarmed. Had Terrill been so zoned out he hadn't even heard Wallis? "He relieved you."

"Of command. Did you hear him order me out of the platoon?"

"No, but—"

"So I'm still in the platoon, you're my witness. That's all that matters. So far, Wallis has spent about ten minutes total down at the entry site. It's not his favorite place, so with luck he won't be there to see me going in with Rowalski. Row and I are like brothers. He will give me a shot at that fucking beast—he's got to."

"Terrill—"

"I'm getting that thing, Andrea, whatever it is. It killed my best man, my best friend, right in front of me." He'd gone pale again. "I told them to hold back with the poison. I said let's shoot it, and that may have cost Chief his life."

"You aren't why Chief died, Terrill. From what you said, the animal had gotten too close. Even if Chief had been able to release the poison, it would have had plenty of time to kill him before it died."

Terrill tried to say something, then clamped his jaw, staring out at the soldiers on the green. Finally, he said, "I couldn't get my gun out. I dropped it. Then I was slow on the speargun."

"You weren't slow."

"You weren't there."

"No, but you need to get it through your head, Terrill—that animal is in its element in a way you can never be, good in water as you are. You weren't slow, it was fast. And it's going to go on being fast, so you've got to stop thinking you're going to go in there, draw a bead on it, and pump it full of lead."

He gave her an angry look, then snapped his head away. "Then what's the answer, Andrea, God damn it?"

"I don't know. Maybe it will break open the containers it stole and poison itself."

"You don't believe that."

"No."

"What do you believe?"

"Terrill, I don't know. I'm the expert and I'm the one who's failing."

"Fuck that. You've been a big help, Andrea. Don't wimp out now. Talk to me. Why did it take that poison?"

"Why do you think?"

"What I think is it came from a canister with *Abwehr* on the side. I know you're sure the Nazis couldn't have made it, but however it came to be, they had it and now it's here, and we have to ask ourselves what they had in mind for a real smart animal at home in the water. I'm just a dumb sailor, but if I had to guess, I'd say underwater sabotage."

"It's an animal, Terrill."

"Yeah, but dogs can be trained to attack suspects or sniff out bombs or drugs, and the U.S. Navy has worked with dolphins, training them to attach mines to ships. Monkeys are trained to be the hands and feet for quadriplegics, bringing them food, turning lights on and off, and like that."

Andrea felt a strange irritation at him, wanting him to stop, but she said, "Go on."

"My guess is poison containers have been marked with skull and crossbones for a long time. What if it knew what it was taking and what to do with it? The basic layout and architecture of water treatment facilities is another thing that hasn't changed much in sixty years."

"You're forgetting, it's penned up under the Pentagon."

Terrill sighed, rubbed at his eyes. "No, I'm not. That's the one thing about this we have going for us."

She stared out at the tableau on the mall, the sunny vision of soldiers from a war long past, and thought about the retaining wall built to keep the river out from under the building. Clearly, it had cracked in one or more places, but what if it had more than cracked? What if a chunk had crumbled away, and one of those wide passages under the building stayed wide right out to the river?

Then the creature could get out.

But could an animal—even a highly intelligent one— be trained to carry out such a complex and purposeful task as poisoning a city's water supply?

"Terrill, the animals you talked about being trained—in every case, they do what they do in response to cues from human controllers. They don't chain it all together and act on their own."

"No?" He sounded hopeful.

"No."

"Well, if my theory is bullshit, no one is happier than me. The fact remains, the sooner we kill this bastard the sooner we'll all start sleeping at night again."

"Yes, but don't throw away your career. Let Rowalski and the full platoon do it."

"It killed Chief, right in front of me. Now I kill it, Andrea, or I die trying. That's how it is."

She felt both admiration and a familiar exasperation. Mark had been like this. Sometimes it had seemed admirable, and others tiresomely macho. Why did life keep putting such men in front of her?

Terrill's face softened. "You were beautiful in there. Wallis doesn't give a damn about your expertise, he wanted you at the meeting to increase my humiliation. He was an idiot to think he could use you that way. No one uses you, I knew that the minute I laid eyes on you. That's why I'm so crazy about you."

He gazed at her with such desire that she felt an answering heat low in her stomach. So handsome, that square jaw and golden hair, the poignant vulnerability of the scars. A body that looked good even in the shapeless khakis with which he'd replaced his dress uniform—

Annoyed at herself, she tried to cut off the response of her body. This was exactly how she'd fallen for Mark. He'd been handsome and fearless, too—and a terrific lover. His tenderness in bed had so addled her emotionally that it was years and a child before she could understand they did not love each other and never could.

Mark's one and only true love had been excitement and she'd seen nothing in Terrill to say he was different. Neither of them were bad or shallow men; it was just how they'd been born. Hungry for sensations, experiences— banging into the outside world all the time to get it; neither of them stupid, either, just unable to focus on what was inside them or someone else for any length of time, because they were blind in those inner wavelengths, with no goggles to cure it. For them, it was too dark and soft and silent in there, a cruel form of sensory deprivation.

Next time she fell, she wanted it to be in love—with a guy who didn't just want to come inside you in bed, but to be inside *with* you at the dinner table or the swing on the back porch.

A guy like Ed.

Later, he'd promised—unless a meteor smashed into the earth.

She remembered his hilarious litany of fears pouring forth in a nonstop stream. Doing it to make her laugh, sure, but also to give her a piece of him most men would refuse to see in themselves, much less confide. He does want me, she thought, I felt it even when he touched me with the artificial hand. But he holds back. Why? He's calm and confident as a top executive. He's not Terrill but he's good looking—big, not an ounce of fat, great hair, and the bluest eyes I've ever seen. He may not be hot, but warm can be better. Women must have thrown themselves at him a lot harder than I did, and unless I'm all wrong about him, he's taken some of them up on it.

What is it about *me* that scares him?

What he said was that maybe he didn't trust himself, but what does that mean?

She remembered Terrill's accusation, tossed at both of them: *You think too much.* Was that it—Ed, because of his arm, worrying about what she'd think when the clothes came off? That would be a first in her experience with men. What decent-looking woman at the beach hadn't had fat guys with hair on their backs ogle her without a trace of self-consciousness? She thought of some of the men who'd flirted with her since she'd split with Mark—guys with bad breath; guys with grimy shirt collars; Smithsonian board members old enough to be her father, with potbellies their thousand-dollar suits couldn't hide; that Belgian curator of apes at the international zoologic conference who looked like he'd never washed his hair; all coming on to her without a thought of what they were offering her, looking to score and thinking only how great it would be for them. The reason it was absurd, the reason they had no chance, was not the age or the potbellies or the hair on the back, but something men just didn't understand.

Maybe Ed, in his completely opposite way, didn't get it either.

She realized there was no "maybe" about it. He *did* care how it would be for her, but he cared too much.

She shook her head at the irony. If that was it, she could fix it—if he'd give her a chance and just listen.

"Andrea?" Terrill said.

He looked indignant, and she realized with dismay that she'd left him hanging. He'd just told her he had the hots for her, a stud navy SEAL, and she'd gone off into a reverie about a bureaucrat with one arm. She felt herself blushing. God, Terrill, what do I tell you?

Before she could say anything, the doors beside them burst open and two women and a man hurried out. Others followed on the run; the woman in front stumbled and fell to one knee, and as one of the men with her tried to shield her, more people poured out the doors, trying to dodge around but tripping over her as the panicked crowd behind pushed them straight forward, spilling them down the steps. Andrea heard glass breaking down the long outside wall of the Pentagon, saw people tumbling out a window. It seemed not quite real, somehow, and then a siren started up inside the building, and through it, she heard the screams.

"The president would like to know what is the size of this building?" the interpreter was saying.

"Just under nine-tenths of a mile in circumference," Ed answered, looking ahead to the Berlin Wall alcove, feeling like he was plodding up a down escalator. The tour had been planned to take half an hour, but this unscheduled stop would add at least fifteen minutes. All he wanted was to usher these men out to the parade ground, where the army's Old Guard from nearby Fort Myer were waiting to march to their fifes and drums for the visiting dignitaries. Get them out of here so he could find Andrea and see if she'd figured out what an animal could want with two flasks of poison.

He said, "Five U.S. capitol buildings, wings included, could be set down inside the Pentagon's outer walls. Its total floor space is 6,500,000 square feet. To help you visualize that space, imagine your beautiful and spacious Red Square multiplied by thirteen."

As the blonde translated, Kuzmin gave a blasé nod. If impressed, he hid it well. They reached the alcove where a section of the Berlin Wall, toppled by jubilant East and West Germans over a decade ago, had been set back up. The west exposure faced them, pitted by hammers and axe blades, scrawled with graffiti, mostly in German, messages of disgust and contempt that would be painful indeed to any Russian who longed for the "glory" days of his nation.

Dear God, what was he going to say about this?

Not a damned thing, unless he had to.

Facing the wall, Kuzmin rested an elbow on one palm and put a contemplative finger to his chin. General Arbatov cleared his throat. He seemed unsure what to do with his hands, finally lacing them behind his own back and staring through the wall as though it weren't there.

"Malyenkey," Kuzmin murmured.

The interpreter said nothing, giving a nervous smile.

"It does seem small in here," Torpedo Mack said, "but out there it was far too big. May all the walls the great Russian and American people have put up between ourselves suffer the same fate."

Someone laughed down the hall, a shrill bleat, and then Ed realized it wasn't laughter but a scream.

He felt as if a cold stone had dropped into his stomach—*please, God, no*—stepping back from the Secretary and the two Russians to look down the hall. In that instant, he heard more screams, saw people spinning away to both sides of the hall, as though a frenzied gavotte had started up. He realized they were leaping out of the way of something, scattering like grass from a mower blade.

He saw it before it could quite come clear in his mind, well over seven feet, now, powerful legs, long tail, a big head—Christ, a dinosaur except for the head. A marine guard stepped into the creature's path, bringing up his rifle, but before he could fire, it was on him, striking with an arm far more powerful than the wizened forelegs of *T. rex*. The marine's head flew off in a spray of blood as his knees buckled, the creature past him now.

In a thawing part of his brain, Ed realized it was coming for them, its eyes on the man beside him.

"Bozhyestvo!" exclaimed the Russian defense minister.

The blond interpreter gave a yelp and ran into the Berlin Wall, bouncing off to fall into a motionless heap.

Kuzmin stared, pop-eyed, at the creature.

The secretary of defense yelled, "Holy shit," grabbed Kuzmin, and pulled him back behind the wall, as Ed tried to move his legs, do something, the creature bounding straight at him and General Arbatov.

Shots sounded down the hall, then someone screamed, "Hold your fire!" as one of the newsmen fell over. A mist of blood from the man's shoulder rained down on him. A siren began to wail, the creature only ten yards away now, its ghastly red eyes fixed on the Russian general, who had not moved, either, but now put out his hands, as if they could stop the charge.

Ed glimpsed the muscular tail swaying behind the animal with each leap as it closed the last few yards, and then he found himself shoving Arbatov aside—

Putting himself directly in the creature's path.

It slashed at his right arm, fangs bared, and the prosthesis tore away and spun, clanking, across the floor, taking his coat sleeve with it. In a distant part of his brain, Ed realized his baby arm now hung out exposed for everyone to see.

The monster froze, staring at the stunted arm, and then into his eyes. Ed's vocal cords strained, but no sound came out.

And then the beast grabbed him, and he was jolting along the corridor, head down, his baby arm dangling out to the side, numb with fear. In the next instant, the creature ducked into a utility room, and Ed glimpsed the dangling cover of the access panel, a dark maw behind, and then he was inside the Pentagon walls, and his head banged a jutting edge and the darkness faded to nothing.

CHAPTER 15

Command this, General, Terrill thought. A chill swept through him as he watched screaming workers continue to pour from the Pentagon. The human stampede tore one of the huge wooden doors from its hinges to cant and spin before crashing down to the side. Terrill felt Andrea clutching his arm. His helplessness galled him—not a chance in hell of forcing his way back inside through that solid mass of people running for their lives.

The siren kept pumping, then cutting off for a canned loudspeaker announcement: *"There has been an emergency situation. Please cease your activities and exit the building."*

Bureaucratese for "Run like hell."

Terrill boiled with frustration. It's in there, he thought, loose in the halls—a hell of a lot of people must have seen it to start a panic like this—and I can't get at it.

Too bad for Wallis he relieved me; who can he scape-goat now?

Terrill watched, hoping to see the prick running in ter-ror, but he'd either missed him or the general had hauled ass out some other door.

Or maybe hurled himself out a window, like people were doing all up and down the wall on the second floor. It made Terrill's gut clench to watch them fall, with about the same impact you'd feel landing in a parachute, but if you hadn't trained for it, you could snap your ankles or worse. People leapt, legs clawing the air, hitting hard, then rolling or crawling down the bank in their desperation to get away from the building. Many of those who managed to land all right were helping their hurt or shaken cowork-ers. Impressive—he'd never felt panic, but from what he'd seen, it could turn smaller mobs than this into mind-less animals who'd trample their own grandmas. In their terror, a lot of these bureaucrats were showing humanity at its finest. How horrible it must be for them—barely a year since the flaming airliner had sent them running from the building, and now this. They had done better than anyone had a right to expect last time; pray to God they would again.

Metal crashed in the distance, drawing his head around. The orderly rows of vehicles in the vast north lot had scrambled into chaos, cars crashing into each other, steel crumpling in a rash of fender benders as thousands of peo-ple tried to hit the road at once. The Old Guard from Fort Myer, dressed in their Revolutionary War uniforms, had broken ranks now, some heading for the parking lots, oth-ers swarming up to the building to help people injured in the stampede—men in powdered wigs bending over fallen workers.

This was fucking insane.

Trying to fathom the fear, Terrill remembered what the

burned-out SWAT guy—Sizemore—had said of the monster: *It looked like the Devil.*

He heard gunfire, faint shots inside the building. Was it *still* in the halls, out in the open? That would sure explain everyone running for their lives.

He felt a surge of nerve in his legs. He *had* to get in there.

Turning to Andrea, he said, "I'm going in through one of those broken windows. You should get away from the building."

"I'm sticking with you."

"I don't suppose there's any way I can talk you out of it."

"Let's call Ed, see if he can tell us where the monster is." She whipped out her tiny cell phone and dialed.

I should have thought of that.

Holding the midget phone to her ear, she frowned. "No answer."

"He probably can't hear it ring in there, with all the screaming and sirens."

"The animal came to his office that time," she said. "What if it went looking for him while he was leading the Russians around?"

"Let's hope not. We think the Russians are paranoid now—if they actually saw the thing they'll be screaming bloody murder at the UN tomorrow."

She stared at him. "Is that all you can say?"

Yeah, right, it wasn't world peace she was worried about right now, it was Ed. Did she think he wasn't? "Let's go," he said.

She jumped down from the pier before he could move, leaving him to follow her, skirting the side of the building, away from the mob that continued to pour through the smashed doors, twenty-five thousand people in there, as many as the town where he grew up—

"Here!" Andrea yelled. She was staring up at the nearest broken window, and when he reached her, he saw it wouldn't work, too far up, even if she was strong enough to boost him over her head. The first-floor window was within reach, but not broken.

We can fix that.

Terrill stooped to find a rock, a brick, anything, then saw that Andrea already had hold of a fallen limb from an oak tree near the windows. Raising it over her head, she rammed it through the glass, then used it to whack out remaining shards.

"Okay," he said, "but next time I get to do it." A manic exhilaration pumped through him. It was in there, the thing that had killed Link, and now he'd get it.

Fumbling open the bottom buttons of his uniform shirt, he pulled the Glock from his belt and stuck it back in outside of his shirt, so he could get at it faster. He crouched and leapt, falling just short of the sill. Putting all his strength into the next jump, he got it this time, pulling himself up and over the sill.

He scanned the room—metal shelving stacked with reams of Xerox paper, staples, paper clips, and file folders.

"Hey!"

Andrea, shouting outside—she couldn't reach the sill. For a second, he thought of leaving her, but no, she'd hate him for that, and he'd deserve it, so he bellied down over the sill, dangled his hand, and grabbed her wrists, hauling her up and in. As she brushed past him, he saw the fire in her eye, smelled her sweat, and wondered if he might actually be falling in love with this one. At once he suppressed the thought.

"Come on!" she shouted.

Following her down a narrow hallway off the supply room, he squeezed past file cabinets and computer printers, glancing in the door of each office he passed. No one in any of them—everyone in here had "ceased" and "exited." As he reached the suite's open central door, he saw people running past in the main hall. A watercooler inside the door roused a dry spasm in his throat. Stooping, he sucked straight from the spigot.

"Raised with wolves?"

He gave her a dripping grin. "Doc, it's Armageddon. We're after Satan and fuck the rules."

In the main hall, he took a second to orient himself. This was the mall corridor of the E ring, first floor. The bigwigs lived up on two and three, and that's where all the windows had been breaking so the next thing he needed was a stairway.

"There!" Andrea shouted.

A marine corporal in a dress uniform was beating feet toward them, an M-14 rifle gripped in both hands. Be nice to have it. Pull rank?

No, you didn't take a man's weapon. "Corporal."

The marine nearly ran past him, then skidded to a stop. "Sir."

"Where is it?"

"We don't know."

"God damn it, man, report!"

The corporal snapped to attention. "Sir. It attacked some people in the E ring, concourse, then circled around to the mall side. I heard it took the head off a marine, sir, and there was shooting. They say it went straight for the Russians, but some civilian stepped in front. It tore his arm off, sir, and took him into the wall with it."

Andrea grabbed his sleeve. "Do you know which man?"

"Someone taking the VIPs on tour, that's all I know."

Andrea's face paled. "It got Ed."

"We don't know that," Terrill said with a sinking feeling. "Corporal, where did this happen?"

"Over by the Berlin Wall exhibit, sir. It's not in the A

ring anymore; they moved it out to E to use that space for offices during the construction. Follow me."

Terrill ran up the broad staircase after him, holding the Glock out front now, hearing Andrea just behind him. Down the second-floor corridor, a SWAT team had deployed across from the Berlin exhibit. A headless body lay in the hall, the tiles around it black with blood.

"Jesus," the marine groaned, kneeling beside the corpse.

Terrill hurried to the SWAT team, grabbing the arm of a guy with sergeant's stripes. The man who rounded on him chilled when he saw the navy uniform. "Lieutenant, you have to evacuate."

Terrill pointed to the trident on his chest. "I'm Hodge."

"Oh—the SEAL."

"Did it go in there?"

"Yeah. It took Mr. Jeffers. I've got guys inside now in radio contact. It's pretty tight in there but not tight enough to stop it. Lot of different ways to go—you want in, I can spot you a light."

"Damn straight." He snatched the flashlight the man offered, an Underwater Kinetics—good gear: barely bigger than a Magic Marker but brighter than most big flashlights.

"You twist the front ring left to turn it on," the sergeant said.

"Terrill."

Something in Andrea's voice made him turn. She was kneeling in the hall, holding an arm. It still wore the sleeve of the blue pinstriped suit Ed Jeffers had been sporting this morning. A whole fucking arm, no blood, just some wires trailing out. He'd figured just the hand was artificial. How the hell had the guy moved those fingers?

Didn't matter. Unless he caught up to the thing, Ed wouldn't be moving any more fingers on either hand.

"We've got to save him, Terrill," Andrea said. "We can't let it have him."

"I know." He ducked through the opening in the back of the utility closet, into the wall, forced to his knees by pipes and vents. Behind him, he heard the SWAT sergeant say, "My men went right. That's the nearest stack."

So he turned left, crawling on hands and knees, the walls pressing in on both sides. The light in his hand gave a jerking view of rat droppings, thick along the floor, and before he could be grossed out, he realized a lot of the little turds had been smashed—recently, by the smell—which meant something big had come through here not long before him.

Trying to screen away the rat and mold smells, he sniffed for any hint of carnivore but, with a world of stink in here, he could pick up nothing.

He pushed ahead, trying to move faster, hanging his shirt up on a pipe stub. Cursing, he tore free, then realized he *was* smelling it now, that meaty scent he'd gotten off the gator in Florida and the croc across the Nile, and again in Ed Jeffers's office. His scalp drew tight.

Hang on, Jeffers.

What the marine had said came back—*He stepped in front of the Russian.*

You crazy civilian, what were you thinking? Should have let it take the Russkies.

But Terrill knew that wasn't true. Civilian or not, Ed had acted like a man, and now he had to get him out so he wouldn't end up in the kind of pieces that bled.

Thinking of the arm again, Terrill was surprised to feel a grin. What must the monster have thought when Ed's arm went *clank* instead of thud and no blood sprayed out? Probably the first time Ed had been glad he had a tearaway arm—

Fuck!

Terrill banged his chin as his hand plunged down into a hole in the floor, all the way to his shoulder, nearly knocking the Glock from his grip. He'd found a "stack"—one of those chimney spaces inside the wall to allow ductwork, pipes, and wiring to pass up and down between floors.

A two-foot gap gave him room to squirm between the vertical duct and the edge of the hole. He stuck the Glock back into his belt. Dropping down through the hole, he hung by one hand, shining the light down.

Through swirling dust motes, he saw that the duct beside him continued to descend through another hole, next floor down.

Wrapping an arm around the duct, he let go of the ledge above him and half fell, half slid down the column of metal, feeling his shirt tear again, keeping hold and squeezing against the duct to pass himself through the square-cut hole in the first floor and on down toward the mezzanine—the upper of the two basement levels.

As he descended, the air thickened with swirling dust and the gator smell intensified. Arm-locking the duct, he stopped his descent. In the abrupt silence, he heard a bang below him—sheet metal flexing. He stuck the butt of the flashlight into his mouth and drew the Glock from his belt again, thinking, *I'm close.*

A wet sigh drifted up to him, sending a buzz across the nape of his neck.

"Ed?"

Another faint sigh, but the flashlight showed only dust floating over stippled concrete below. He remembered what Andrea had done with the Tensor lamp—the thing must be sensitive to light, maybe not able to blink. It took him back to BUD/S training, the stuff about night vision. After a few moments in darkness, the visual pigment on the rods of the human retina would power up to sharp night vision, but a sudden, bright light would flash-bleach that

pigment, damn near blinding a man for the next twenty
seconds. This motherfucker wasn't a man, but Dr. D had
proved its eyes were even more sensitive—had to be, or it
couldn't navigate in here without visible light. So the thing
was down there below him now, making those wet sighs.
It had to be getting some of his light, so turn it off, let the
beast dark-adapt again, then—pow, blind it long enough
to shoot it dead.

Worth a try.

Freeing a thumb and forefinger from the Glock, Terrill
managed to twist the light off without dropping the gun.
Darkness, complete and suffocating, closed in around him,
amplifying the silence until he heard his heart thumping in
his eardrums. Was this really such a great idea? Now it
could see and he couldn't.

But he could hear, and no way was it going to shinny up
this duct without making a sound.

Terrill waited through another slow, bubbling sigh
below him.

Soft thumps, then nothing.

Then he felt the duct tremble against his side.

Okay, you shit, come on up.

The duct flexed against his side, popping loud in the
dark, and he could feel it through the metal, *knew* it was
creeping up, that it could see him, the gun pointing down
in his hand, and he couldn't see a damn thing, his eyes
wide and straining in the dark.

How close was it?

The raw meat smell was strong now, filling his head,
but he made himself wait, his mind serving up an image of
it climbing to him, red eyes intent, fanged mouth grinning,
maybe only a few feet from him now, its tail wrapped
around the duct to stabilize it, able to spring the last few
yards when it got close enough—

Fuck this!

He twisted the light on.

It was there just below him, red eyes blazing in the sudden brilliance, and he brought the Glock around, but before he could fire, he saw something below over its knotted, green shoulder, *Ed!* and then it let go of the duct, dwindling as it dropped down. Landing astride of Ed, it brought him up, limp as a rag doll, using him as a shield.

Terrill's teeth ground the butt of the flashlight. Shouldn't have hesitated, damn it. Now the monster was lumbering in a circle, averting its eyes from the light, keeping Ed's body in the line of fire.

It's still too blind even to run, Terrill thought. *Take your shot!*

But no, it kept moving, circling in place beneath him, Ed dangling over its brawny shoulders like a rag doll. Where Ed's right arm should have been was . . .

God, a tiny right arm, like a baby's.

Terrill felt an involuntary disgust. *He's probably dead anyway, shoot the beast, he killed Link, may not be another chance.*

Terrill tracked the rotation of the thing's shoulders, waiting for a head shot, his other arm starting to ache from its grip on the duct. Do it, do it now—

Ed groaned and opened his eyes, blinking up at him.

"Hang on, buddy. It's me, Terrill."

No recognition in his eyes. Concussion, Terrill thought. I can still get a shot. His finger squeezed the trigger, but the beast moved back the other way; sweat popped out on Terrill's face as he straightened the finger a hair short of firing—the bullet would have gone into Ed's brain.

Ed and the creature vanished down the crease of the wall.

Go, GO!

Terrill released his aching grip on the duct, falling too fast, hitting hard on his heels. The impact jarred the light from his mouth, and it spun away, disappearing into the stack to drop to the subbasement below.

"Fucking goddamn shit!" he yelled.

The light was still on below, sturdy enough to survive the fall. He had to have it, go down for it, no way could he fight the monster blind when it could see in the dark. "I'm coming, Ed!"

Squeezing into the gap left for the ductwork, he slid through the floor and down to the subbasement level, grabbed the flashlight and gripped it in his teeth again. He shoved the gun into the back of his belt to free up both arms. Grabbing the duct he started up, feeling pain sizzle along his right hand as it sliced open on one of the jagged metal hangers that girdled the sections of ductwork together. Blood spurted and he felt himself slipping, sliding back down.

With a curse, he tried again, his hand greased with blood now, slipping, slipping, as his mind served up an agonized vision of the creature scuttling away and gone on the level above him.

Come on, come ON!

Useless—he couldn't get a grip.

Terrill realized he was hearing voices.

Turning away from the stack, he saw a cone of light entering the wall about twenty yards down. What the hell?

A hole in the wall, which meant he could get out, run back up a floor, find a way back into the wall.

As he thought it, he knew it would be useless, the thing would have Ed far away in God knew what direction before he could get back up there and in. But his body was already in motion, carrying him forward on hands and knees over the dirt, and now he could see another hole beyond the first.

Voices outside the wall broke off as he scrambled out

into the light, blinking at a ring of U.S. Navy SEALs pointing shotguns and Glocks at him.

"Don't shoot," he croaked.

"It's Terror!" Doyle's bass rumble.

Squinting into the light, Terrill saw Lieutenant J. G.
Mark Rowalski's round, freckled face and rusty Vitalis
Pompadour. Rowalski straightened from his two-handed
shooting crouch and lowered his Glock. "Jesus, Lieutenant, you look like hell."

He realized he was so covered with dirt, sweat, blood,
and rat droppings that he halfway looked like a monster
himself.

"You better thank your lucky stars you don't have a
tail," Rowalski added.

Terrill was about to tell him to go fuck himself when he
remembered Rowalski was now in command.

He told him anyway.

CHAPTER 16

Wake up.

The subway platform remained solid under Andrea's feet, the scared mob around her real. Her throat ached.

Ed, please don't be dead.

If only she could trade with Terrill Hodge, be the SEAL, but she was the "expert," and her job now was to get back to her father, force him to talk this time, pry loose anything that might give them an edge.

If she could just. Get. Out. Of. *HERE*.

Two hours she'd been trying, slipping and sliding, like running in the deep end of a pool. According to Ed, back when the Pentagon first went up, thirty miles of new highway interchanges had been built to ease flow in and out of the huge parking lots.

In a panic, it wasn't enough.

Multicar pileups caused by fleeing workers had blocked all feeder roads and ramps, backing them up to the lots.

Nothing, including cabs, buses, and emergency vehicles, could get in or out. So she'd given up on her pickup in north parking and found her way to the subway platform downhill from the concourse entrance, at the foot of a towering, roofed escalator.

But thousands had gotten here ahead of her, workers whose panic had eased enough to let them go near the building again for a chance to get home. They had massed on the tracks, scary because of their fear. Just one shout—"There it is, behind us!"—and the stampede would shove everyone in front down onto the tracks. Seven hundred fifty volts would flash-fry anyone in contact with the power rail and everyone on top. If there was an attack, it *would* come from behind. The mammoth escalator back there, along with the elevators for wheelchair traffic, gave the only direct access from inside the building straight to this platform. Some military police and a couple of armed DPS guards had stationed themselves up there at the entrance. Coming from inside, the creature would have to get past them, then descend the escalator while they shot at its back. But she knew from firing tranquilizer darts from rifles that shooting down a steep slope was tricky, and if the creature had hold of Ed or another hostage, forget it.

The round warning lights along the platform edge began to blink, and Andrea heard another train rumbling in the distance. Finally she was close enough to the front of the pack to have a good view as the train roared into the station with a screech of brakes, pushing a gritty bow wave of air that stank of burned rubber. The crowd controlled its surge forward, as it had with each train, but you could feel the dread crackling around you, ready to ignite into panic again.

As the train pulled out again, a draft rose up from the tracks around her ankles, and she realized the escalator might not be the animal's only approach. Under the far platform, she could see a square of darkness—an access tunnel. The rail bed was almost as low as the subbasement, and who knew where the streams beneath the Pentagon might reach?

It won't come, she thought. It's got Ed.

Blinking back tears, she became aware of the weight of the plastic bag. She'd scavenged it from the utility room where the monster had taken Ed into the wall. His arm, doubled up to fit into the bag, weighed less than she'd have expected.

Would she have a chance to give it back to him?

The packed train rumbled away and at once the crowd pressed her forward, sliding her toes over the platform's edge. She gasped, tottering, and then an army captain grabbed her arm and shouted, "Back up, folks!"

The crowd loosened away behind them.

Thanking the man, Andrea felt her heart pounding. Every minute she spent stuck here lowered the odds Ed could be brought back alive. The marquee on the last train had been blue, so the next should be orange, and she'd make it on board this one. The Georgetown city fathers had spurned a station when the subway was built, but the Orange Line would take her to Rosslyn, upriver along the Potomac's Virginia bank. From there, she could hike across Key Bridge into lower Georgetown, then uphill into her neighborhood.

And then she would do whatever she must to find out what Dr. Johannes Witte had done for the Abwehr.

This time he wasn't in his room but in the paneled part of the basement with his grandson, watching the big-screen TV, Teddy five feet from the set, his head cocked forward in rapt attention. Dad had cringed to the side in the big easy chair, his bony hands gripping the arms. ABC had preempted their afternoon soaps with "Breaking News,"

Peter Jennings squared up to the camera, looking stunned and perplexed, as if he could not believe the lines he was reading from his TelePrompTer:

". . . the Pentosaur, as someone has dubbed it, because it looks like a compact version of a prehistoric tyrannosaur or perhaps a velociraptor, is still on the loose. President Gregor Kuzmin of Russia, while declining to be interviewed, has issued a statement that he is reserving judgment on whether the creature is, as Secretary of Defense Hastings insists, a mystery to his Pentagon hosts, or if it is, in fact, the result of an experiment by the U.S. Defense Department to genetically engineer a biological weapon of war—an attack animal so monstrous it would terrify opposing forces into submission. Kuzmin is asking for an investigation by the UN Security Council. General Constantin Arbatov, Russia's defense minister, while echoing Kuzmin's views, did express concern for the man he says saved him from the Pentosaur's attack. According to Arbatov, Mr. Edward Jeffers, the Pentagon senior executive leading the tour, pushed him out of the way and took the creature's charge himself. Other sources confirm this, saying the animal slashed off Jeffers's arm, then carried him inside the walls of the Pentagon through an access panel in a utility room. Mr. Jeffers, informally known as the 'mayor' of the Pentagon because he oversees the physical building itself, is still missing, despite an extensive search by SWAT teams and military personnel, who are bravely hunting the creature and its prey in the crawl spaces and narrow cavities within the miles of wall in the Pentagon. It is possible Jeffers survived the attack, because the arm the monster slashed from his body was prosthetic. In another bizarre note, the arm is missing from where it fell in the E-ring hallway—"

Andrea dropped Ed's arm on the chair beside her father.

Teddy jumped. "Mom! Cripes, you scared me. I didn't hear you come in."

Dad did not turn, his gaze still frozen on the screen.

"We have a statement from a General Emerson Wallis," Peter Jennings was saying, "taken by ABC's Erin Hayes, who was on the scene to interview the president of Russia after his tour." Jennings and the studio vanished, replaced by Hayes and Wallis, standing on the parade ground with the river entrance in the background.

Andrea snatched the remote from the arm of Dad's chair, pointed it at Wallis, then decided she'd better hear this.

"General Wallis," Hayes said, "I understand you are the senior special forces officer in the Pentagon at this time."

"That's right. And I want to assure you, Erin, and the American people, we are responding vigorously to this unfortunate incident." Wallis stared straight into the camera, his handsome, buzz-cut head looking every inch the seasoned combat officer he was not.

"What steps have you taken?" Hayes asked.

"I've brought in a platoon of U.S. Navy SEALs, all veterans of combat, and they are hunting down this animal as we speak. If possible, they will rescue Mr. Jeffers, and we pray he's all right, but in any case, they will find and kill the beast."

"The Pentagon is a big place, General. How long do you anticipate the search to take?"

"It should be possible to kill the animal before morning. My men won't rest until they do, and they are the best fighting men in the world." Again, Wallis looked straight at the camera. "Let me be crystal clear to any enemies of our country who may be watching. All vital weekend personnel are now back inside the building, under the protection of U.S. Marines. All essential offices manned around the clock will stay fully manned. And by Monday morning, this animal will be dead and the rest of the Pentagon workforce will be safely back at their posts, performing their duties in support of the defense of this nation. Now if you'll excuse me, Erin, I must see to my men."

"Thank you, General Wallis."

Andrea muted the set, feeling like she'd just eaten something greasy.

"Grandpa, look. She's got it—Mom's got the arm." Teddy had noticed the bag on the chair—the realistic hand protruding from it. "Holy shit, Mom, how did you get it?"

"Language!" At once, she felt foolish. All hell was breaking loose and she could still worry about Teddy swearing?

Dad's head inched around until he was looking at the bag. Ed Jeffers's hand stuck out, so realistic it even had a neat mat of fine dark hair on the back, above the knuckles.

"Lieber Gott," he whispered. Slowly, his gaze rose to hers.

"Teddy, would you excuse your grandpa and me."

"Mom-m-m—"

"Use the TV in the kitchen. Get up there quick, I may want to ask you about the reports later."

He started to protest again; she flicked off the TV.

Moaning, Teddy bounded up the basement steps. When she heard the door slam, she said, "Dad, we have to talk."

"I can't."

"You can and will."

Picking up the bag, he drew the arm from it with trembling hands, turned it over, inspecting it with a glimmer of interest despite his obvious dread. "How did you get this?"

"I was there. Dad, that animal they're talking about came from a canister marked *Abwehr.* It was found when the wall of the subbasement was opened to get at plumbing and ductwork for the Pentagon renovation. That wall was last open at the very time Uncle Luther brought you to

Washington and took up his duties on the Pentagon building project. The creature is either reptile or amphibian,
maybe some of both. I think you know how it came to be.
I think you made it, though I can't imagine how."

"No." His voice a whisper.

"Dad."

"You don't understand."

"Because you've lied to me—"

"Never."

"Kept it hidden, then, all these years. Refusing to tell
me anything about how you left Berlin or what you did for
Admiral Canaris. You made this animal for him somehow,
I don't now how. . . ."

Weakness rolled through her knees. She grabbed the
straight chair Mark had contritely glued back together after
kicking it apart that long-ago Sunday after the Redskins
lost in overtime. Sagging into it, she felt as if she'd been
whipped, the adrenaline gone now, the inevitable fatigue
reaction flooding in behind it.

Dad offered her Ed's arm.

"You hold it. Think about the man it belongs to. He's in
terrible danger because of you."

"You care for this man?"

"I think I might have fallen in love with him." Hearing
the words from her own mouth added weight to the idea.
How could she have fallen in love with Ed Jeffers in so little time? Never mind—whether she had or hadn't, it was
the right thing to say to Dad, she could see it in his eyes.

"I love him, and my only chance to save him might be
knowing enough about this animal to stop it. Dad, if you
care for me at all—"

He gave a pained cry. "How can you say that? I didn't
tell you because it would only have hurt you. I knew I had
no hope of making you understand, and it would be painful
for both of us. Not all must be spoken, even when you love

someone with all your heart, as I do you. Sometimes love is why something must *not* be said."

"Say it now, for all love, while you still can. Whatever it is you fear I'll think, I'll forgive you. But I must know now. What is this animal? How did it come to be?"

"Andrea, there's nothing I can say that will help you."

"It has two flasks of poison."

The breath seemed to leave his body. His face went gray, sending a jolt of alarm through her. Heart attack?

As she started for him, he pulled himself straighter in the chair, waved her off. "Poison," he whispered.

"Yes. It took two flasks of endosulfan from the SEALs."

He shook his head drunkenly, his eyes pinched shut. "Andrea, can it get out from under the Pentagon?"

"I don't know."

"You must find out, at once." He pressed his hands to his face.

"Then it is a saboteur."

"It was supposed to be."

Goose bumps stood up on her arms. "Dad, talk to me. How did you make it?"

He dropped his hands, stared at her. "I didn't."

"Then who—"

"A druid chieftain discovered how to do it, two thousand years ago."

Andrea's heart sank. The Alzheimer's. *Please, God, keep him with me.*

"Not the . . . creature in the Pentagon, of course," he went on, "but the original one."

"Impossible," she said.

"Why?" He gave her a sharp look. "Have you forgotten what I taught you? Do you think we have all wisdom now—that nothing mankind has learned has ever been lost? Pharaonic mummies have flesh on their bones after three thousand years. We couldn't do that now, preserve human cells that long."

"Dad, there is no way that druids could have bioengineered an animal with what little science they had in that time and place."

"Who said they bioengineered it?"

"What else is there?"

"Come on, daughter, think. Break out of your box."

Trying to teach her, even now, but her mind was blank.

"Teratology," he said. He held Ed's arm up like a pointer to some mad equation on a blackboard.

A tremor passed through her: teratology—from the Greek words for "monster" and "study of." Before approving any new drug to be used by women, the FDA, badly burned by the thalidomide babies, required lab studies not merely of efficacy and primary side effects but also of the drug's potential to cause birth defects. Mice, rats, rabbits would be dosed and their offspring monitored for deformities.

Birth defects.

No, please God no. "Dad, teratologic studies are done to prevent monsters, not create them."

"Now, yes. We're talking ancient druids. They practiced herbal medicine, you know. Historical records on this fact are sparse, but at least one druid, named Chyndonnax, was every bit as observant as modern-day scientists in cataloguing the effects—and side effects—of various pharmacologic agents he derived from plants. In early 1940, shortly before Canaris recruited me, agents of the Sicherheitsdienst—a rival intelligence branch in Himmler's Gestapo—learned of an ancient inscribed stone found by a Nazi sympathizer in northern Scotland. Himmler took an immediate interest, fascinated as he was by anything ancient or occult—"

Appalled, she hugged her arms to her, wanting him to stop but knowing she must hear it all now.

"Of course, the SD and the Abwehr spied on each other constantly, and Canaris got a look at the Gestapo report on the stone's message. It interested him for a reason that had nothing to do with the occult. That's how a highly secret joint mission of the Abwehr and Gestapo came to be— something that would have been unthinkable even three years later. Canaris recruited me and sent me on a U-boat to retrieve the stone. The Gestapo sent a Major Grau." He shuddered as he said the name, and his face paled. After a moment, he went on: "We retrieved the stone. It recounted how Phoenician traders had supplied Chyndonnax with plants from the Amazon rain forest to test for medicinal effects. One of these plants turned out to be what we would now call teratogenic."

Controlling her horror, she made herself listen as he told her the rest of it.

Ed felt consciousness drifting back toward him, coming closer, and this time he knew what it was and that he wanted it.

He lay still, eyes closed, feeling his mind knit back together.

First came hearing—the constant slap-slap of water, echoing as if in a tunnel. Then pain welled into a vicious throb at his temples. Gritting his teeth, he probed his head with a finger, found a lump behind his ear. Blow to the head—a concussion. How long had he been out? No way to know. He tried to pull together what he knew about concussion—something about keeping the victim awake for twenty-four hours to avoid coma? He felt a stroke of pain down inside one ear, cold as an axe blade. Lying still, he waited for it to subside. His throat grated as he tried to swallow. Thirsty—he'd been out longer than it seemed.

Where am I?

He opened his eyes.

Nothing, total darkness.

Were his eyes really open? Inching a fingertip over one, he felt the lashes. Open, yes, he could feel his lids straining but still could not see.

Blind.

Panic surged through him, making his heart hammer. Staring up, too frightened to think, he made himself breathe deeply, focus on his other senses. He became aware of damp earth under his back, and then he understood. Water—damp earth, he was under the building.

The monster got me.

He wasn't blind; there just wasn't any light down here, but if he didn't find a way out, he'd never see again because he'd be dead. He lay there, heart thumping, panic rolling through him.

I should be dead already. Why hasn't it killed me?

He struggled to rise, the stubby right arm pushing as he did when he rolled out of bed mornings, but his small, stunted hand slipped on the wet dirt. He tried a slow sit-up, the kind he used evenings to pump himself awake enough for a couple more hours of work. He was able to rise into a sitting position without bumping his head. Pain drove down through him from his head, flaming behind his shoulder blades, making his stomach shrink. He held still and it faded.

He flinched back from a cool touch on his arm. Something bumped his left hand, a piece of plastic dangling against his palm. Taking it, he felt its contours.

Goggles.

He remembered the SEAL telling Terrill that the animal had taken the poison and Chief's goggles. A chill shook him, making his teeth chatter. For an insane second, he wanted to fling the goggles away. Conquering his squeamishness, he held them against his eyes and nose with the short arm and used his good one to pull them on. The world leapt into crimson life.

The monster sat a few feet from him.

A chill skated up his spine. *God, get me out of here.*

Pulling a deep breath, he stared at the monster. It stared back, sitting with its knees to one side, the great tail curled around them. It had planted one brawny arm in the dirt beside it; the other rested on its lap.

It *is* the Devil, Ed thought.

He wanted to turn away, but he made himself go on looking, getting it into memory for Andrea, in case he could make it out alive. Its eyes were a vivid red, the pupillary slits almost round—no doubt because of the darkness. Not much of a nose, just two vertical vents below the eyes. The lower part of its face bulged out into a rounded shelf forming the mouth—a crease with the barest suggestion of lips that wrapped around far back on either side of its face. The protuberances on top of its head were not horns, Ed realized, but the ends of a mantle of greenish skin that ran back from where the nose ought to be, terminating in spikes that resembled horns.

Like a horned toad, yes, just a cousin of the frogs he used to listen to on his cousin's farm at night, bullfrogs singing love songs on their lily pads.

His mind flashed on Link, severed into pieces on the basement floor, and then he cut the thought off.

How was the animal able to see him? A faint bioluminescence from the water? Or maybe it could detect wavelengths of energy other than the spectrum visible to humans.

Ed swallowed, his throat parched.

The creature reached out slowly, one hand, turning its body away from him in an unmistakable effort to calm him. He held himself still as the hand closed on his vestigial arm, feeling it up and down, from where it joined his shoulder down to the stubby fingers. Its touch was gentle, but he could not stop from cringing. He never let anyone touch that arm, hated to touch it himself when he had to wash it. Now this monster was fondling it almost lovingly.

"Okay, that's enough," he said, pulling away with a shudder.

The creature gazed at him and he realized that, though it was only an animal, he was seeing what looked like an expression—pity and amusement, mixed. The monster's mouth opened, revealing wicked fangs. Terror spurted through Ed. He prepared himself to die, and then it said, *"Wir sind derselbe."*

He stared at it, stunned. A deep, raspy monotone, almost a machine voice, but this was no machine.

Suddenly he was able to comprehend what he was seeing—that long-waisted torso, the legs, the opposable thumbs, the positioning of the red, amphibian eyes, not on the sides of the head like a frog, but in the center of its face, like a primate.

A man.

The creature said the words again—*"Wir sind derselbe."*

"I'm sorry," Ed heard himself say. "I don't know German."

The monster pointed first at itself and then at him, then repeated the sequence, with slower, more exaggerated movements, until Ed grasped what it must be trying to say: *Wir sind derselbe*—We are the same.

We are both monsters.

CHAPTER 17

←—————

"What will the baby look like?" Emera asked.

Johannes Witte glanced around, a nerve jumping in his stomach, but no one sat near enough to have overheard her. At three in the afternoon, the Café Stutzflügel had attracted far fewer patrons than he remembered from his visit here only a year ago. Just a few old burghers smoking while their fraus sipped *Kaffee* at tables along the opposite wall, and that young man with the newspaper at the window, gray as a ghost in the tobacco haze.

Abundant potted greenery cushioned whatever sound did not erase itself in the dark rafters overhead. The grand piano of the café's name sat between them and the other patrons, a Victrola on its shuttered lid sealing them away behind a crooning curtain of Liebeslieder.

The only danger in answering Emera would be to her.

Sipping his thick Turkish coffee, Johannes eyed her over the top of the cup to see if she really wanted an answer. Yes, she looked quite serious, her elegant jaw set, causing her lips to purse out in the slightest of pouts—that lush, exquisite mouth, so maddeningly inviting—

"What's wrong, Herr Doktor? You're blushing."

He had the mad urge to confess he'd just envisioned her naked body—smooth and pale as cream, the sinewy strength of her thighs, the Danube blue of her eyes. A tender warmth spread through him. He wanted to reach over and stroke her honey gold hair, caress her cheek.

Instead, he said, "I think those two at the second table might be trouble."

She followed his gaze with a nervous jerk of her head that fanned his own smoldering anxiety. Major Grau had warned them about going outside the villa grounds, though he'd refused to be specific. Berlin was on edge about rumors of a coming air attack from the British, but surely if it happened, the villa would be as vulnerable as this café.

The major had no right to be so pushy. Emera had endured without complaint six weeks cooped up in the villa, and she needed to get out. From today on, it would not be so easy.

"It's probably nothing," Johannes soothed. "The old man has been giving me pointed looks, but he's probably just wondering why I'm not in uniform."

"Let him look. Your work is important. The Führer himself sent me a letter, commending me for taking this assignment." Her eyes shone.

Johannes wouldn't dream of telling her that Hitler's name had probably been forged by the Himmler aide who had selected Emera from the Hitler Youth's Bund Deutsche Mädels branch because of her open adoration

of her Führer. She'd do anything for him, even give her
body to the Fatherland.

Johannes felt a twinge of pain in his lip and realized
he'd bitten it again, as he was doing more and more. She
has not given her body, he told himself, only loaned it.
When this is over, she'll go back and finish out her service on a farm or helping raise the children of good German matrons whose husbands have marched off to war.

Or maybe I shall ask her to marry me.

The thought made his pulse race. Would she have
him? Her signals of admiration might be nothing more
than crumbs falling from the table of her true hero, the
Führer.

Probing his sore lip with his tongue, Johannes wished
he were more sophisticated about romance. At twenty-
two, he had only two years on Emera, and women grew
up faster in ways of the heart—or so Mother told him
whenever he went back to Stuttgart to visit: "My poor
Johannes, all you've done is go to school. How will you
know whom to marry?"

To which his father would say, "Leave the boy alone,
Mutti. He'll find a nice fräulein when the time is right,
just as I did."

But I didn't find Emera, Johannes thought. Fate itself
has thrown us together. I was as embarrassed and self-
conscious as she—even more so. Who would imagine
under such circumstances we could have any affection
for each other?

Emera said, "That nosy old *Geschaftelhuber* should
stare at the man by the window. He's almost as young as
you."

"He has a cane," Johannes said, "see it there, hooked
onto his chair, and if you also notice, his left shoe is built
up."

As Emera peered to see if it was true, he admired her profile, the perfect straight nose, the exquisite chin.

"You're so observant, Herr Doktor."

Her praise gratified him. Most people thought him obtuse, but hadn't he been the one, while still a grad student, to notice the fine differences in pigmentation that defined an entirely new species of tree frog? The resulting article in the *Journal of Animal Ecology* was what had won him the notice of the most observant man in all Germany, the reason he was sitting here now with this beautiful young woman, a true heroine.

He felt a touch of awe as he thought of this morning—how Emera had taken the powder without hesitation, drunk it down in a glass of water, then handed the glass back to him with a breezy "There," as if it were no more than an aspirin. Until now, Johannes thought, the villa has been our fantasy world. Medieval tapestries, Persian carpets, a spotless, well-equipped lab for me, a nice suite of rooms for her, every need tended to.

But now it really begins. She has been pregnant six weeks, we have followed the stone's instructions on dosage to the letter. Now we will see how brave we really are.

"Maybe you ought to tell Major Grau to get you a uniform for when we go out," Emera said. "You'd look dashing as a captain in the Gestapo."

He hid his distaste, reminding himself that she had not seen Grau break an old man's neck or shoot helpless, fallen Indians in the back of the head in the rain forest. "We'll be all right," he said, but he was far from sure. Tension hung in the air, thicker than the tobacco smoke. Something wasn't right in this place, even if he couldn't put his finger on it.

"Are you going to answer my question, Herr Doktor?"

"We've discussed this. The less you think about the . . . child, the better."

"But it's not fair. If I'm not to see the baby, you ought at least give me some little hints."

"It will not be a baby at all, really."

"But how is that possible?"

What could he say? She had no scientific training that could help her appreciate what might, today, have begun to take place in her body. If the stone had been accurate about the plant, the timing, and the dosage level, the minute the drug had crossed through Emera's placenta, the fetus in her womb had begun to diverge from normal human development. Those who thought only a standard baby should result from a pregnancy would call the results birth defects, but if that were truly the case here, he'd never have taken part in this. The promise of the ancient stone and the skeleton found with it was not a defective human but a phylogenic combination of the best features of humanity and one or more of its aquatic ancestors. Amphibian structures and functions that normally showed up only briefly during human intrauterine development would, instead, persist. The skeletal structure of the fetus would be heavily influenced by developmental forces dominant in earlier human evolution. For example, amphibian bones developed no terminal epiphyses to limit growth and neither would those of the fetus. Its skin and respiratory system would also include amphibian characteristics. The tail invisibly vestigial in most humans would express itself in full, muscular grandeur. Photographs taken by the old Scot of the outsized skeleton in the cave could not settle whether the fingers had been webbed, but such details, while fascinating, didn't really matter. What mattered was that, according to the stone, the "water man" had been born with a near human level of intelligence that had proceeded to develop on the far speedier maturation schedule of amphibians.

Johannes's heart quickened as he thought of it. From his point of view, a magnificent new life-form, but how could Emera find it anything but shocking?

"I wouldn't have to see it right away," she said. "You could take it away and clean it and let me recover from the delivery. Then, a few days later, I could have a look at it, just so I wouldn't wonder the rest of my life."

Johannes wished she'd let it be. Within a few days of birth, Emera's "child" would be too large for her to believe it could have come from her body.

And neither the Abwehr nor the Gestapo would want her able to describe it. The water man was meant to become a devastating secret weapon against the naval might of the Fatherland's enemies. If Emera learned enough to endanger that secret, the men behind this experiment might coop her up for the remainder of the war, just to be sure she could not let something slip without meaning to.

"Look, Emera, not seeing it is for your own protection. Pride yourself that you will bring an entirely new life-form into the world to serve your Führer."

Closing her eyes, for a moment she said nothing. Then: "Yes, Herr Doktor."

His heart went out to her. This couldn't be easy, but she was trying her best to be brave. Could she see it through? I'll be with her all the way, he thought. I'll help her in every way I can. And then, maybe, when it's all over, we can even have a normal life together.

He took her hand, and she returned his squeeze, sending a thrill through him.

He saw her attention shift as a shadow flickered at the corner of his vision. Turning, he saw a man in uniform silhouetted in the door of the café—a tall figure exalted

at the thighs and head by the dashing curves of an officer's breeches and cap. The man passed from the brilliant rectangle into the softer light of the coffeehouse
and Johannes saw that his uniform was gray—that of a
colonel of the Wehrmacht. A captain stepped through behind him, along with a couple of privates.

The colonel glanced at the crippled man, who returned his look without interest and went back to his
newspaper. The colonel scanned the café, drawing nods
and smiles from the old people. Johannes felt a tremor as
the man's gaze settled on their table behind the piano. In
a few brisk steps, the colonel stood beside them, gazing
down at their joined hands.

"Good afternoon," he said.

"Good afternoon, Colonel," Emera answered brightly.

Johannes confined himself to a nod, hoping he would
take the hint and go away.

"May I see your papers, please." A handsome man of
about fifty, his blond hair streaked with white, the impe-
rial chill of his voice negating the polite wording.

"Certainly," Johannes said. Fishing in his coat, he
pulled them out, handed them to the colonel. Emera was
nudging his knee under the table, probably hinting that
he should stand up, but he'd be damned if he would. I'm
doing as much or more for the Fatherland than this man
could ever hope to do, Johannes thought. He should
salute and leave me and my woman the hell alone.

The colonel studied the papers, a sneer lifting the corner of his mouth. "It says here that you are a doctor."

"That's right."

"And that you are twenty-two."

"Also right."

"Do you think we are fools?"

"I haven't made up my mind yet."

The colonel's face reddened, and Johannes realized, a trifle late, that he might be in trouble.

He could say the address on his papers was a private lab developing new medicines for the war effort, but no more than that, and if the colonel didn't believe he was a doctor, he wouldn't believe that, either.

What if the man turned him over to the Gestapo, and they also refused to believe him? The project was so secret that his only hope of rescue would be to insist they call Admiral Canaris or Heinrich Himmler, and what Gestapo underling would risk that on the say-so of one so young, an obvious coward evading conscription?

"Stand up." No "please" this time.

Johannes stood.

"You will come with us."

He tried to protest, but his mouth had gone dry.

"But it's true," Emera said. "He's a doctor who works at—"

Johannes cut her off with a warning look.

The colonel tipped his hat to Emera. "Don't let this pup stifle you, fräulein. What were you going to tell us?"

"Only that he is who he says. You're making a mistake."

"Thank you. I'm sure you are sincere, but I have experience in these matters. The captain will be happy to escort you home, but this man is coming with me. No good German can have any use for those who would evade service to our Führer."

All at once, Johannes realized how odd this was. After all, Emera was in street clothes, too. Since March of '39, service in the uniformed Hitler Youth had become compulsory for all young men and women. Her papers identified her as Bund Deutsche Mädels, but the colonel hadn't even asked for them.

They didn't just happen in here, Johannes thought. They came for me.

His heart turned to ice. He must keep Emera out of this.

She gave him a pleading, do-something look.

"Go with the captain. It will be all right. He can take you to your mother's place. I'll call you after this is straightened out."

She stood. The captain offered his arm but she ignored it. "If you take him in," she said in a firm voice, "you must take me also."

"No," Johannes protested. *How brave she was!*

The colonel cleared his throat. "I'm sure you are a patriotic girl, but believe me, fräulein, you don't want to go where we are taking this man."

"And where might that be?" said a mild voice behind him.

The colonel wheeled around on one booted heel, his mouth opening, then snapping shut again. Beyond him stood a small man in the black uniform of the Kriegsmarine, an admiral—*Canaris!*

Johannes's knees went weak with relief.

The colonel snapped to attention, as did the captain and two privates. "Sir, I have determined that this young man is evading conscription."

"He has no papers?"

"Fake ones. They say he is a doctor, and that is clearly impossible."

Canaris held out a hand. The colonel handed over the papers and the admiral made a show of studying them. He eyed Johannes. "Dr. Witte . . . *the* Dr. Witte, who was written up in all the papers for being the youngest man ever to take a doctorate at Universität Stuttgart?"

"Yes, sir."

"What an honor and a pleasure to meet you." Canaris thrust out his hand and Johannes shook it.

The colonel's face had gone stony. He's not fooled, Johannes thought. He realizes this must be Canaris and that the admiral already knows me.

"I think you owe Dr. Witte an apology," Canaris said to the colonel.

The man's face reddened. "Of course, Admiral . . . ?" Canaris said nothing.

The colonel clicked his heels together, gave a stiff bow, and said, "I apologize, Herr Doktor."

"I accept your apology, Colonel."

The officer turned back to Canaris, but before he could say anything, the admiral said, "You are dismissed. I suggest you return to your unit and reflect on your inexcusable behavior, so as not to insult any other good German citizens. In return, I will not take your name with a complaint to your commanding general."

"Yes, sir. Thank you, sir."

In seconds, all four Wehrmacht men were gone.

"Thank you, Admiral," Johannes said.

Canaris nodded. He looked weary, frail even, his smart black uniform hanging loose on him. He probably hadn't worn it since taking over the Abwehr five years ago, a job demanding enough to shrink any man, physically. Even in military dress designed to intimidate, he looked kind, grandfatherly. Hard to imagine a threatening look on that mild face, with its generous nose and ears. His white hair dodged straight over from a neat part to end in an incongruously boyish tuft on the right side. He suffered a bit of a stoop, his head riding forward on the small body.

"My car's outside," he said. "May I offer you and your young lady a ride?"

An offer Johannes would never refuse even if he

could. How uncanny—Canaris, coming personally to his rescue, only the third or fourth time he'd seen the great man.

And he must go on acting as though it was the first. The less Emera knew about who was behind the project, the better for her.

"A ride would be very nice, sir," Johannes said.

A large black staff car waited in the street—a Mercedes? Johannes could not be sure, never having picked up the passion for cars that baffled him in other young men. Canaris motioned him into a backseat of plush gray leather. Emera slid in next, and Canaris settled himself on her other side. "Where to?"

Johannes gave the address, just as if they were strangers. The driver, dressed in a petty officer's uniform, nodded and a pane of glass slid up, sealing off the backseat.

Emera's face had flushed, Johannes saw, and her usual serene poise had deserted her, leaving her hands unsure what to do with themselves. Folding them on her lap, she said, "Is that the Iron Cross, sir?"

"Yes, my dear."

Canaris gave her an indulgent smile as she touched it reverently. Johannes wished he could tell Emera that it was an Iron Cross *first class*, awarded Canaris by the great Kaiser Wilhelm himself, along with a promotion from lieutenant all the way to naval captain, for his daring solo escape from a British prison camp back in the last war. Or that he'd made his slight frame into an asset by commanding a U-boat of that war. That he had taken over the venerable Abwehr five years ago and turned it from second rate to the sharpest intelligence service in the world. Next to Hitler, Wilhelm Franz Canaris was arguably the most important man in all Germany—the master of secrets.

But his service to Germany went far beyond spying.

Canaris had formed a new, ultracovert group in the Abwehr—Section II, an elite cadre of saboteurs, trained to inflict devastating damage on the enemy. In the past two years, fires and explosions had taken out or damaged a number of French and British factories and shipping companies, as well as some cargo vessels. Merchant ships, and the warships that attacked and defended them, were playing an increasing role in the conflict, sure to intensify as vital supplies had to be replaced.

Strategically, the best point of attack against these ships came when they were in port. Once they made the open sea, huge effort and resources must go first into hunting them down and then into the demands of attacking moving targets, free to zig and zag, while their destroyer escorts lashed the depths all around them with sonar. It would require far less in resources and manpower to attack them massed together, sitting still, landbound on two or three sides.

But this was far easier said than done. From the moment Günther Prien had sunk the *Royal Oak* at its moorings in Scapa Flow, harbor security against U-boats had gone from lax to vigilant. All ships of any importance were heavily guarded in port now, men on watch at the rails at all times, not a scrap of cover for anything approaching on the surface. It would now be exceedingly difficult for a U-boat to slip all the way into an enemy port without being detected, as Prien had done, and if one did manage it, the moment a torpedo exploded, the surface would crawl with small, deadly ships brandishing first asdic, then depth charges. Effective attack from the air was possible only if the harbor was undefended by its own fighters; the British had beefed up RAF presence around all their ports.

Unless an enemy could be caught off guard, a ship in

his harbor was well protected. Once on the open sea it was catch as catch can. No one had found a way to neutralize these factors.

Until now.

Johannes longed to tell Emera that she might now carry inside her the ultimate naval saboteur. That if all went well, her offspring would be only the first of a cadre of underwater warriors who could mine every vessel in a harbor, then swim out to sea without being detected. Not even a mammoth battleship or carrier could have any real defense against such a master of the water—no metal tanks to be detected by sonar, able to swim for many hours without tiring, going farther and faster than any mere man, leaving no trail of bubbles. If enough such saboteurs could be brought into action, no enemy ship would be safe where every ship must go. Their stealth attacks could increase tenfold the tonnage of critical war supplies sent to the bottom. At the same time, they could destroy at their piers the enemy subs that could strangle Germany's supply lines. They could, if necessary, force surrender in an arduous siege by slipping into a city's water treatment plants through its river and sabotaging the filtration equipment.

The life inside you, Johannes thought, could lead the way to winning the war, and save tens of thousands of German lives.

"What ship do you command?" Emera asked the admiral.

He gave a pained shrug. "I'm afraid I've grown too old for that. Commanding a ship is a job for men with stronger legs and straighter backs."

"The Führer's brave young captains," she said in a worshipful voice.

"Quite."

The car slowed, and Johannes realized it had pulled

into the long drive of the villa, an estate of several acres near the Tiergarten, Berlin's vast answer to New York City's Central Park. The stone front of the villa's house looked more inviting than he'd have dreamed an hour ago.

As he started to open his door, Canaris motioned him to stay then turned to Emera. "My dear, would you be good enough to bring me a glass of water? In all the excitement at the café, I neglected to get the drink I went in for, and now I'm exceedingly dry."

"A pleasure, Admiral."

"And if you, young man, would be good enough to keep me company while I wait, I'd love to know how anyone could earn a doctorate at such a young age."

The driver opened the door on Canaris's side and he slid out to free Emera. Back inside, he watched her go with a wistful expression. "A beautiful young woman."

"Yes," Johannes said.

"She must be protected. Promise me you won't go out again."

"Of course. I'm sorry. That colonel—"

"Sent by the Gestapo to harass you. No doubt Major Grau alerted his people you were leaving. They decided to throw a scare into you so you wouldn't go out again. They used a Wehrmacht officer so you wouldn't suspect them." Canaris sighed. "My fault, really. In my haste to recruit you, I neglected to teach you tradecraft. That young man in the front of the café was Gestapo. The elevated shoe is not to cure his limp but to produce one."

"How did *you* know I was at the Stutzflügel?"

"The old man at the second table is one of mine."

Johannes did not know whether to laugh or groan.

"You are watched at all times by the Gestapo and the Abwehr, you know that now. You are a very important young man to both Himmler and me." Canaris turned on

the seat to face him. "Be wary, my young friend. Here—
I want you to carry this with you at all times when you
are at the villa." Reaching inside his uniform jacket, he
pulled out a pistol.

Johannes's stomach went hollow. "I don't want a
gun."

"Then I'm afraid I must order you, Doctor. Look here,
it's just a vest-pocket pistol, easily concealed—the new
Mauser. Most of them are 6.35 millimeter but I got you
the 7.65 because it has more stopping power."

"But I've never shot a gun."

Canaris sighed. "Point and pull the trigger. Here's the
safety lever and its release button. You take the safety off
like so and you're ready to shoot. Now I've put the
safety back on, you see? The clip is fully loaded, nine
shots."

Reluctantly, Johannes accepted the pistol. The metal
had a browned finish with smooth wooden grips on
either side of the handle. Men who found guns beautiful
would no doubt like this one, but he detested all guns.
The Mauser felt cold and greasy in his hand. I won't
shoot anyone, he told himself. He stuck it down inside
his shirt, into the waistband of his trousers.

Canaris gave a grim nod. "Good. Let's hope you don't
need it, but if you do I couldn't live with myself to have
left you unarmed. All might be well, but we can't depend
on that. One must never trust the Gestapo. They have
their own agenda. If it truly coincides with mine here,
fine, but it might be quite different."

"Why do you say that?"

Canaris rubbed at his eyelids. "In your last report to
me, you mentioned that Major Grau has you working on
a nutrient medium in which our water man could be co-
cooned for an indefinite period."

"Yes."

"Have you thought why they should want that?"

"I was told it was to enable sea transport over long distances in a supportive environment—for example, to attack ports in California, if the United States comes into the war."

"They will, I'm sure of it. I only wish I could convince Hitler." Canaris sat for a moment, apparently lost in thought, then said, "I suppose it would be difficult to keep our water man wet throughout a U-boat voyage that could take several weeks, water being such a scarce commodity on board. As the U-boat approached the U.S. coast, it would have to stay submerged more. Yes. But why is the Gestapo concerning themselves with such scenarios? They are neither scientists nor marine experts. What are they up to?"

"Maybe nothing."

Canaris gave him a dry, half-lidded look, clearly finding the idea absurd. "Dr. Witte, if all goes as we hope, our water man will not be a mere outsized frog who can sink without a thought to the bottom of a pond to hibernate for the winter. He will be like us in many ways, with an active life of the mind. He might well balk at going into suspended animation."

"Do you want me to stop working on the fluid medium?"

Canaris hesitated. "No. It could well be useful. But you must learn to think as a spy, Doctor. Major Grau is not your friend, and the man behind him even less so. Heinrich Himmler plays his own game, always. He's a dark one, that man, and his use for what we are doing here may turn out different from ours in ways neither of us would like."

Johannes felt a chill.

"Think of the photos of that skeleton. The being we are trying to create will not only be a natural aquatic saboteur far superior to any mere human, it will be very powerful. It may look quite frightening. That was its value to the man who first stumbled across the way to cause such a birth—this fellow Chyndonnax who left the stone. The power to terrify and intimidate are qualities the Gestapo prize even more than the destruction of ships far from Berlin and their own concerns of power. I take a chance when I tell you this, Johannes, but I have believed for some time that Himmler is not a patriot at all, that he's more than simply dark, an evil man, possibly even psychotic. We must be ready in case he tries to subvert this being to an inhuman and inhumane use, not against our military enemies but against his own perceived foes."

Johannes felt shaken. He did not like Grau, but what Canaris was saying about the Gestapo as a whole was unnerving.

The admiral eyed him. "You're a good man, Doctor. I can see that you're fond of Emera, supportive, and I'm glad for that. But have you thought also about how the birth will hit you?"

"What do you mean?"

"What did you think when Grau told you who he wanted the father to be?"

"It seemed logical," Johannes said. "It limits the people who know."

"Logical, yes. But Johannes, don't you see they might also be trying to co-opt you? We must be ready to turn that to our advantage. We have our people at the villa, as many as we could place in this joint operation, but Himmler knows who they are, of course, and has picked his own people with equal care. If they plan to subvert this creature, the first move will be theirs, and they'll make it against those I've put there to stop them. Major Grau has good reason to believe he has neutralized you

as a threat, Doctor, and in any case, they need you on the
project, as much as I do. Which means stopping them
could come down to you."

"I'd do all I could to save it, sir."

"I'm sure of that, Doctor, but what if the only way to
save it is to destroy it?"

Johannes's stomach knotted. He became aware of the
gun under his belt, hard as a tumor.

Canaris put a hand on his shoulder. "Could you kill
your own son?"

CHAPTER 18

←

I have to steal the poison.

Ed's injured head throbbed from the effort of squeezing out the thought. His arm and legs felt distant, numb. Before he tried stealing anything, better make sure he could still move. Faking a yawn, he stretched his spine and left arm, his suit crackling with dried mud, the floor of the cave firming up painfully against his back.

The monster, a motionless smear at his feet, did not move.

Ed tried to blink some moisture into his eyes, parched despite the protection of the goggles. His lids felt layered with sand, sticking painfully, then sliding, until finally his vision cleared. How had he gotten so damned weak? The concussion must have been worse than he'd thought—still woozy every time he moved, and the monster headache showed no signs of abating. Dehydration was probably starting to weigh in, too. He was thirsty all the time now, no longer able to screen out the enticing gurgle of water just a few feet away.

The sound had other, more ominous meanings: The current here was far swifter than anything Terrill had reported. He couldn't have forgotten to mention something so significant. Which meant that, despite extensive searches under the building, the SEALs had never found this passage.

He could not hope for rescue.

Worse, the current's speed and strength indicated that the foundation retaining wall of the Pentagon was close by—with a sizable hole in it. A gap big enough for the monster to escape to the river whenever it pleased.

Which was why he must get the poison away from it.

Ed flexed one leg, then the other, the monster continuing to gaze at him with its unnerving red eyes, as if trying to read his thoughts. Not a word since *Wir sind derselbe.* Sitting there, still as stone, drawn-up knees clutched in a brawny arm, the massive tail curled forward around the webbed feet.

The *other* monster, so deformed that only speech could prove it human.

Clearly it, and not the current, had dug this indentation in the channel wall just above water level. Only a man's eye and hand could have made the floor so flat and level, the walls so well shaped and symmetric. The niche was about ten feet long and six deep, the back wall curving up and over to a height of around five feet. It reeked of the monster's raw, fishy smell. This was its den, a place beyond the SEALs' reach for the monster to eat its kills and sleep—and now to guard its prisoner.

Until it tired of staring at his deformed arm and wondering about him.

A tremor passed through Ed, making his teeth chatter. Even if he didn't try for the poison, he couldn't have long to live. He didn't want to die, he wanted to see Andrea again and say, "Let's talk about us right now—let's more than talk."

Too late. He'd had his last glimpse of her. He'd never know what they might have had with each other if he'd been braver.

Panic scooped at his gut, and he trembled again, though the passage was warm. Damn it, Jeffers, get a grip. Never too late to be brave, or at least pretend. He could do it, even with the cold fire burning along his nerves. No one lived forever, and at least there would be no more headache and thirst, no more galling regret about Andrea. All it took was concentration—put his senior exec brain back to work one last time: The monster had the two flasks of endosulfan in a protected position behind it, against the wall. He must wait until it took another dip in the channel to wet itself down. Every hour or so, it plunged into the water, then back out in seconds to settle into the same position as before, greenish skin glistening in the infrared light of the goggles. Next time it slipped from the shelf into the water, he must grab the flasks, trigger open the seals, and throw the powder into the water, getting as much of the insecticide as possible on the monster.

Ed had the panicky sensation of falling. Pinching his eyes shut behind the goggles, he felt his heart pounding as if it would explode. Could he do it—give his life for a city of strangers? The monster's victims up to now had died on his turf, in the building he was supposed to make safe. How many victims now? He remembered nothing past the Russians asking to see the Berlin Wall exhibit, but at least four people had died, starting with Herb Bodine, the construction worker.

Or five—if there really had been an unknown captive under here when Chief was killed.

But, now that the creature had poison, it could make the death toll soar, because it wasn't a mere monster. It was part human, however vicious and grotesquely deformed. It *had* known the meaning of the skull and crossbones warning on the flasks and what the poison inside could do. A deliberate "monster" birth, brought about by the Nazis, aggressive and murderous, and now it had armed itself for chemical warfare.

When it had crept up to the ventilation grille in his office, it would have heard them talking. Even with no English, if either "poison" or "toxin" sounded similar in German, it could have grasped General Wallis's plan right at that moment. There probably hadn't been a fifth victim. The monster had heard its earlier prey scream for help and would know that all it had to do was imitate the pleading cry and SEALs would rush to the rescue.

Whether aware of Wallis's poisoning plan ahead of time or not, it had lured Terrill's squad into its ambush, then taken both flasks of endosulfan, and all it need do now was follow this channel back through the earth to the river. Staying submerged, it could swim to a water treatment plant. The closest was on the District side of the river, only a mile west of the Pentagon. It could slaughter the plant's security guards and employees before they could react, and by the time an alarm was raised, thousands of Washingtonians, men, women, and kids, waitresses and tourists and museum guides, people who'd done nothing more than drink water from a fountain or their faucets, would be dead or dying.

I'm not *their* mayor, Ed told himself. They're not my responsibility.

It didn't help.

Stopping the animal was up to him. No way could he get what he knew back to Andrea and the others. The concussion had made him too weak to escape, even if he could swim with one arm, which he'd never been able to manage in his life—

Abruptly, the animal leaned toward him, and he flinched back, but all it did was give his wizened right arm a gentle touch.

"Warum haben Sie dieser Arm?" Shrugging to show it was a question.

"Thalidomide," Ed said. *And what in the name of all that's unholy did they give your mother?*

The creature pointed to the arm again and repeated the shrug.

Ed felt a feverish irritation. Why keep asking, when it couldn't understand? It hurt to talk, like spitting up ground glass.

On the other hand, while it was listening, it wasn't killing him.

"A drug to ease morning sickness," he rasped, "marketed between 1956 and 1961. I was born in '59, well before anyone caught on to what else the drug was doing, so Mom had no way of knowing."

The monster nodded. Maybe it had picked up meanings in his voice that he could not hear, himself. Ed's eyes welled with a sudden, welcome moisture. Despite the raw pain in his throat, it felt strangely good to say these words he had put away for so long.

"Most of the mothers who took it gave birth to normal kids. Then there were my kind, and much more severe— I'm only phocomelic on one side, and a lot of us don't have fingers at all, or elbows even. Just stubby, flipperlike appendages. The critical factor was the timing of when the mothers took it—you know, at precisely what point during pregnancy. I presume that was the same for you."

The human monster gazed at him. Its lips lifted an inch from the wedge-shaped teeth, reminding him of the fang that had fallen out. No gap in the front, there, so it must be from the back or side, a bad tooth working loose during all those years in the can, or maybe tearing out when it at-

tacked Herb Bodine. All it had needed was a big meal to
tighten its gums and get it growing again.

Was it hungry now?

Ed cast around for something more to say. "I understand
the FDA is thinking of letting thalidomide out again,
strictly to treat leprosy."

Staring, staring. Had he seen it blink yet? No. Andrea
was right—no eyelids.

Despite himself, he felt pity for it.

But he must not.

It *will* kill you, he told himself. The endosulfan won't
finish it off right away, even if you can get most of the
powder on it while it's in the water. It'll have plenty of
time before it dies to tear you to pieces.

The monster pointed to its chest and said, *"Scheusal."*

For a second Ed was too startled to respond. "Scheusal?
That's your name?"

The creature pointed to him and he realized it was now
asking his name.

"Ed."

The human monster tipped its head back and gazed
down at him over the shelf of its mouth, teeth showing
again—dear God, a smile? "Ed," it repeated.

Then it offered him its hand, big but well formed, the
fingers webbed at the base, with wicked claws in place of
fingernails.

Swallowing, Ed held his own hand out. Scheusal was
careful to keep the claws off him as it closed gently. The
softness of the hand surprised him, and then he reminded
himself of the vulnerability of amphibian skin—the weakness that would bring about both their deaths.

Gravely, the monster shook his hand. *"Freundin?"* it
asked.

Freundin—friends? Was it asking him if they were
friends?

A sense of unreality gripped Ed. It had identified with him because of the arm, and now it was trying to bond?

No, he thought. We are not friends. You are worse than a predator, you're a man, which makes it murder.

But if it will help me stop you, I can say it. "Friends."

The monster smiled its ghastly smile again. *"Sind Sie hungrig? Möchten Sie etwas zu essen?"*

Ed hesitated. *Hungrig*—hungry? In fact, though he had no appetite, the hollow feeling in his stomach had to be from fasting as well as fear. Food, with its water content, would make him stronger for what he had to do, but what could this murderous creature possibly have to give him, aside from a piece of human meat?

"Actually, I'm more thirsty—"

"Durstig?" The monster pointed at the water.

Longing surged in him. He imagined the cool wetness on his tongue, its soothing passage down his throat. If he could just be sure it was safe. Vomiting and diarrhea would finish him quicker than thirst, making him too feeble to do what he must.

Scheusal pointed at the water again.

Ed shook his head, bringing on a wave of dizziness that sent his fingers digging into the dirt.

The monster leaned out over the channel and dipped water up to its mouth, slurping it down then patting its belly to show it was fine, safe to drink. *"Gutes Wasser."* Scheusal pointed at him and then itself, then to the water, the meaning clear: I'm not an animal. I'm a man like you.

Ed nodded, afraid to offend. Scheusal might have started out a man but he'd been changed into a beast before he could take his first breath. His amphibian genes were adapted to the bacteria in swamp water just as a squirrel could lap away at a birdbath starlings had used as a toilet all day. A man crazy enough to think he could do the same would double over in minutes.

Just go rinse off again, so I can end this for both of us.

With a slow, reproving shake of its massive head, the monster settled back. Ed's parched eyes stung with frustration, too dry for tears. If Scheusal didn't get back in the water soon, he'd be too weak to act.

Scheusal began to talk in a low voice, rambling along in what could only be German, watching him as if he could know how to respond. He shrugged, then shook his head, but Scheusal went on talking. What could the creature be saying to him, in this new and different voice, low and mournful?

Didn't matter.

Andrea's face shimmered in his mind, those full lips turned up at the corners, the elegant, arched eyebrows, and the thick, dark hair that could come either from her German father or the mother she'd never mentioned—Italian, Jewish, Native American? She was saying something to him—*Maybe I could help you*—and he wanted to say yes, help me, please, but his throat was too dry.

He jerked awake with a start. Scheusal was still talking.

How long had he been out of it? The monster's skin didn't seem wet, so he hadn't missed the plunge, but he dare not zone out again. Must keep his mind working, hold himself awake just a little longer.

So. How long had he been down here?

Seemed an eternity.

His watch was gone, probably torn off while he was out cold, being dragged through the walls. He missed it terribly. Being marooned here drove home how important the clock had become to him. For most of his adult life, he had checked his watch or glanced up at some dial or digital display probably forty or fifty times a day, not even realizing he was doing it. At night, he'd roll over in bed, squint at the red numerals to see how long he had left to sleep. He'd let time become the air he breathed, his boss of bosses, overseeing all he did, marking his way, subdividing each day and night.

And now, at the end, the hours and minutes had deserted him. No idea how long he'd been here, whether it was night or day. His only clue was the thirst, but the concussion could make that seem worse than it was—nothing to measure it against because he'd never tried to go without drinking before. The craving for water he felt now could be anything from a bearable nuisance to severe dehydration, giving him a final warning before he lapsed into a coma and death—

Scheusal rose to a crouch and plunged into the water.

Ed stared, blinking. Had he hallucinated it? No, there were the two flasks of endosulfan against the end wall, unprotected.

Quickly!

For a horrifying moment, he could not make his muscles work, and then he lurched up, crawled forward on hands and knees, his arms trembling with effort. He saw the monster, facedown in the channel, its head toward the current, the powerful arms stroking from above to the sides like a man's, while the massive tail waved back and forth to help keep it in place.

You may be a monster, Ed thought, but at least you've got both arms.

He grabbed the two flasks by their side handles, then realized he'd need a hand free to depress the top button. One at a time—*hurry!* He crawled to the edge and rose to his knees, holding the flask out over the channel above the monster's head. When the bottom seal broke open, the powder would drop and the current would wash it along the length of the monster.

Scheusal started to surface.

Pushing the button on top of the flask down, Ed groped for the trigger in the handle.

Christ, where was it?

There was no trigger in the handle.

Grabbing desperately for the other flask, Ed saw two small, crescent-shaped pieces of plastic lying in the dirt. The triggers, both of them.

Scheusal had snapped them off!

The monster's head broke the surface, the red eyes finding him, seeing what he was doing.

"Nein!" Scheusal roared. An arm swung up from the water, throwing Ed against the back wall of the niche. Before he could move, the monster had lunged up onto the shelf of dirt. He tried to dodge away, but his strength left him and he collapsed. Too weak to dodge, he saw the blow coming at his head and knew it would kill him, but Scheusal did not strike him, plucking the goggles away instead, plunging him into absolute darkness.

Terror surged through him. "No, please—"

"Halt den Mund."

The soft hand closed over his mouth. The monster screamed other things in its dreadful voice, shouting, wailing, raging at him. He couldn't breathe. Struggling against the smothering hand, he gasped as it released him.

He lay on his side, dragging air into his lungs, his mind blank with fear.

He realized Scheusal had stopped raging. There was no sound except the splash of current. He had to be close by, only a few feet away, that red gaze able to see him while he remained blind. Ed's skin crawled. He stared around him, afraid to reach a hand out, imagining he could see the big, deformed man, a darker blackness on his blind retinas.

"Scheusal?"

No answer.

"I thought you planned to use the poison. I didn't realize you'd broken off the triggers."

Silence.

Ed sat up cross-legged and closed his eyes against the suffocating darkness. "You had no intention of using the poison, I see that. You didn't want anyone to. Forgive me. I want to be friends."

What was the word Scheusal had used? *"Freundin,"* Ed repeated.

He heard a soft grunt in the darkness.

Pointing to his eyes, he said, "May I please have the goggles back?"

After a moment, they nudged his hand.

Terrill felt so tired he could barely haul himself back up the rope into the light. Not so much weariness as disappointment, deep in his bones, as if someone had kicked him up and down. Damn it, searching for twelve hours, the full platoon this time, with no luck. Every tunnel had been combed through.

No monster, no Ed.

Terrill burned with frustration. He had to save Ed Jeffers and kill the beast that had ripped Link apart, and so far he'd done dick.

Stepping through the basement wall, Terrill realized something was out of whack, the platoon standing around tense and quiet, looking awkward as Catholic boys at their first dance.

His heart sank when he saw General Emerson Wallis in the hall with some guy in dark pants, blue shirt, a wild tie, and suspenders with a pattern of cigars stitched on them. A big guy with black hair, a deeply tanned face, and shrewd eyes, standing off to the general's side, like some civilian brother-in-law Wallis was taking on a tour of the Pentagon.

Forget the civilian. I'm fucked.

Wallis's eyes narrowed. "Lieutenant Hodge. What are you doing here? I relieved you."

"Of command."

"He put himself under my orders, sir."

"As you were, Lieutenant Rowalski."

"He's worked his ass off, wouldn't even take a break, and I needed every—"

"*As you were, Lieutenant.* What now, Hodge? You think you are a JAG lawyer? Relieved means you're out—"

"Hold on." The civilian speaking up. "General, what is this?"

Wallis turned to him. "I relieved Lieutenant Hodge for dereliction of duty and insubordination."

"Before or after that reptilicus thing killed a bunch of people and made the whole world even more paranoid than it already was about the United States military?"

Good question, Terrill thought. Who is this guy?

Wallis hesitated. "Before."

"What was the dereliction of duty?"

"Failing in his mission to kill the animal. Allowing the beast to take the poison away from his squad and to kill a man under his command."

"And the insubordination?"

"He has been insolent from the start. If he'd executed my orders to poison the water, the animal would be dead, and there'd have been no disaster with the Russians."

"So the dereliction and insubordination were the same thing. Failing to get the son of a bitch."

"Well, technically—"

"Same thing."

Terrill got a faint whiff of cigars that had to come from the man, not his suspenders. Wearing civvies, but he talked like brass. Some bigwig up from SOCOM Tampa?

"So by extension," the civilian went on, "you, General Wallis, as the top SpecWar officer at the Pentagon, are also insubordinate and derelict in your duty."

Terrill fought a smile—Wallis was starting to look boxed in.

"Derelict if I fail to get this animal, I am, yes."

"If you fail? You're giving yourself more time than you gave Lieutenant Hodge, even though you're doing nothing except saying, 'Get it,' and he's the one going down in the hole?"

"The ultimate responsibility remains with me however long it takes. Whereas the proximate responsibility—"

"Okay, that's enough. As secretary of defense, I pardon you both. I've read Lieutenant Hodge's file, and if anyone can get this bastard, it's him, so let's let him do his job and keep the hell out of his way."

"Yes, sir." Wallis flushed red.

Terrill felt like a vise had just let go of his chest. The secretary of defense, the legendary Torpedo Mack Hastings. Thank you, Mr. Secretary, he thought. You just squared Wallis and me up, saving me ten years in the brig for what I'd have had to do to him after this is over.

"Okay," Hastings said, looking around at the platoon. "Listen up and then the general and I are out of your hair. Most of our essential people have gone to their posts in the building this evening, even though they know that murdering son of a bitch is still down here. Our 24/7 types are especially high on motivation, thank God, or they wouldn't be pulling duty in our safes and secured areas at all hours to begin with. We've put squads of marines with them for protection and, thank God, none of them have needed it yet.

"But the longer this evil bastard hangs on under here, the more risk, and come Monday morning, we've got serious trouble. Even if half our workforce is brave enough to risk having their heads torn off and they can actually do some work while their knees are knocking, half ain't critical mass. The Cold War's over, but 9/11 proves we've still got plenty of enemies out there who'd love to catch us with our pants down. We're under siege here, and that has to end. I know you're tired, but Ed Jeffers is a damn good man. God willing, let's see him alive again. As for this crazed lizard that took him, find it and kill it. Tonight would be better than tomorrow. Lieutenant Hodge, coming out last, you missed Lieutenant Rowalski's report. He says you've pretty well covered the tunnels. I'd like your take."

"Sir, no disrespect to Rowalski, but it's got to be in there somewhere. Dr. Deluca, our biological expert, says it has to immerse itself in water on a regular basis, and we've had guys in every tunnel in rotating shifts since just after it took Mr. Jeffers. No way can it stay up in the walls that long."

General Wallis said, "Our chem/bio people have supplied more poison. I think it's time we used it."

Torpedo Mack's black eyebrows shot up. "With Ed Jeffers and maybe someone else in there, possibly alive?"

"Unlikely, Mr. Secretary. Lieutenant Hodge, did you or anyone else hear any shouting, any cries for help?" His tone courteous now, as if there'd never been any bad blood between them.

"No, sir, none of us have heard anything." Hated saying it, but there it was.

Where are you, Andrea? I need you.

Wallis said, "Surely, Mr. Secretary, if Mr. Jeffers or anyone else were down there alive, which is to say with his head above water, we'd have heard him yelling. As the lieutenant says, it must be in there, because it needs to stay wet. Somehow, it's evading by hiding under the surface. Our expert assured us the toxin is far more dangerous to amphibians than humans. Assuming it hasn't yet killed Mr. Jeffers, he could survive the toxin."

"Not if he has to drink the water," Terrill said. "And the only way he can stay alive is to do that."

"We have to accept that Mr. Jeffers is dead," Wallis said, "probably the minute this beast got him back to the water. Poison the animal and it's all over. We can bring the workforce back in."

The secretary of defense tugged at his earlobe.

He's considering it, Terrill realized.

"Mr. Secretary," he said, "let us go in once more. Maybe we missed a tunnel."

Wallis turned to Rowalski. "What do you think? Is that possible?"

Rowalski looked miserable. "I'd have to say no, sir."

"Then—"

"It's more than possible. It's likely."

Andrea! Terrill felt light with relief as he saw her push around Wallis and square up on Hastings, out of breath, like she'd run up the hall. Jesus, woman, where have you been?

Never mind, you're here now.

"Sir, I'm Andrea Deluca, curator of herpetology for the Smithsonian. I've been helping out with your effort to get this creature. I've chased after all sorts of amphibians, including diving in the Amazon as well as high mountain rivers in the cloud preserve in Costa Rica. To find amphibians you've got to know the rivers, ponds, and lakes they live in. I do. Burrowing lizards and caecilians are hardwired at birth to find underground streams and tunnel into and between them, and all amphibians share these abilities to varying extents. If these men have charted all the tunnels they can see and not found the creature, it means there are more tunnels."

"How, Doctor?"

"If the Potomac can wear through a crack in the retaining wall in one place, it can do so in another. There could be two or even more separate incursions, resulting in water channels running alongside the ones we can get to from this starting point. This creature, as an amphibian, could

hear or otherwise sense such parallel channels and easily
burrow between them."

"Did any of you men find such holes?" Wallis asked in
a skeptical voice.

"They wouldn't. This is no ordinary amphibian. Remember, when it took Colonel Sheffield, it also took his
papers along to cover its trail. It's far brighter than any
known amphibian, easily smart enough to fill the hole behind him—itself. Which means Ed Jeffers could still be
alive, and you might not hear him shouting."

Terrill realized there was something different about Andrea, a new grimness. Until now, she'd managed to keep
up a game front, even when the monster took Ed. Not now.
Something had shaken her.

"Come on, Doctor," Wallis said, "isn't this a stretch?
You're fond of Ed Jeffers, we all are, but—"

"General," Secretary Hastings said, "are you a herpetologist?"

"No, but—"

"Hodge, it's your platoon. What do you think?"

My platoon! "What she said, sir."

"Agreed. What should they be looking for, Doctor?"

"It's hard to describe. I'll know it when I see it."

"Excuse me?"

"I'm going in, Mr. Secretary. It's the only way."

CHAPTER 19

Dr. Johannes Witte suffered a bad moment as he turned from his view of the park. What room was this? The marble floor seemed to have turned to wood. The tall kid who'd spoken to him held out a chessboard, apparently wanting to play. Crooked grin, lots of dark hair, probably thirteen or fourteen—reminded him of himself at that age.

But why did he call me Gramps?

Something told Johannes to contain his annoyance at the interruption. "No, thanks."

"C'mon. You're staring out the window again. It's dark, there is nothing to see. And even if there was, you've seen that exact view of Rock Creek Park a thousand times, just a bunch of treetops. Aren't you bored with it?"

"It's pretty. So peaceful. I've been watching the bats in the moonlight. They're diving around the trees for insects."

The kid rolled his eyes. "Come on, it's Friday night,

Mom's gone, and Heidi's gone to bed already. We're in charge. We can eat junk food and watch bad movies if we want. I rented *Scream 4*."

"Where did your mom go?"

"The Pentagon, where else? CNN just said they're still looking for that guy the monster took down in the wall. They showed some marines escorting Mom into the building—it was cool. I just wish she'd take me, but she said I'd need a special pass and no way would they give it to a thirteen-year-old. It's discrimination, that's what it is."

Johannes tried to follow what the kid was saying, but his mind lingered on the Pentagon. He caught a whiff of damp earth and fresh cement, or maybe only a memory.

The kid sighed. "Sure you don't want to watch *Scream* with me?"

Johannes turned back to the window. The door closed behind him, jarring him for a second, and then the treetops transported him back to the park view from the villa off the Tiergarten. Back to where everything was so much clearer, more vivid and real, as few things seemed anymore.

"I want to see him," Emera was saying, over and over, no matter how he tried to calm her.

"It's just not possible." Evening sunlight streamed into his sitting room, flaming off the cushions of the Louis Quinze chairs, giving the marble floor a buttery sheen. Dust motes winked in the slanting rays, bathing the room in a tranquility he could not feel. He needed to get back to the urgent, coded report he was composing for Canaris. The situation was deteriorating fast. He'd been unable to find Karl, his lab tech, all day, and no one seemed to know where he'd gone. Alarming because Karl was Abwehr— big and tough, a background in the Kriegsmarine, probably the most capable fighter Canaris had in here. Johannes's mind kept serving up images of Karl lying bound and gagged in some closet. Were the Gestapo betraying their

Abwehr "partners," as Canaris had feared? Let the admiral decide, Johannes thought. All I need is five more minutes to finish coding the message.

But he couldn't just send Emera back to her rooms in her agitated state. Who knew what she'd do, demand to see Major Grau, perhaps—dangerous if Grau was making a move. Normally, she'd be too frightened of the man to approach him, but she'd reached a new depth of desperation, that was clear. Her hair, untouched by a brush or comb, stood out from her head, gleaming like a Pharaoh's gold in the sunset. His heart compressed as he saw the red rims under her eyes. Sobbing in her room again, still in her bathrobe, hadn't even dressed today.

Guilt scalded him. This was his fault. If only he could have found work to distract her, but what could an outdoor girl do here, shut up in the villa? Major Grau hadn't even allowed her to walk in the gardens without one of his goons dogging her every step.

Raised on a farm, she'd had no taste for the filing jobs Johannes had persuaded the Hitler Jugend records office to send over. Seeing the work reports of other young people only made her long to be serving her own *Landjahr* on some absent soldier's farm, as she'd been about to do when Himmler had pulled her from the HJ assignment pool and sent her over to Grau.

I haven't found enough time to be with her, Johannes thought. And how could I, working day and night on the support fluid, ten o'clock or later by the time I've gotten free, leaving her alone all day and most of the evening— too much time to think. The fluid's ready, finally, but it's too late, she can't take any more of this place. I have to get her out. If they insist on holding her, I'll demand it be somewhere else, far from Berlin.

A lump swelled in his throat. He'd miss Emera more

than he dared imagine, but to hell with that. Her welfare mattered more than his own fears of loneliness.

And if he was right about the Gestapo, she might not be safe here much longer.

"I want to see Meersohn," she said.

Son of the Sea, her name for the creature she had never seen, even on the day he'd pulled it from her womb.

And thank God for that.

Johannes felt a queasy ripple in his gullet. He'd be happy to wipe that day from his mind: standing at the foot of the birthing table, his heart banging as the head began to emerge.

At first it had looked like a baby's, except for the greenish color, but then, as he'd tried to get a proper grip, his fingers had encountered the mantle that had since lifted into hornlike points. The shock had nearly made him let go. Gritting his teeth, he'd pulled at the head.

As the red eyes had slid into view, he'd stifled a gasp, afraid Emera might hear it. The sodium pentothal would start wearing off soon. Major Grau had wanted her totally under, relenting only when he'd insisted it might jeopardize the birth.

As the head came free, the next shock was the thick muscularity of the neck, slit on both sides by gills. Then the long slash of its mouth opened, revealing triangular fangs already in place. It didn't scream or cry, thank God. As he continued to pull, the scarlet eyes gazed at him with unnerving sentience. The shoulders were nearly too wide, even with the episiotomy, but he got them through, and the slender lower body slid out easily, revealing its tail, dear God, long as a snake.

"Wunderbar!" Major Grau had exclaimed over his shoulder.

His own face had drawn tight over the bones. He'd had a good idea what to expect, but there was no way to prepare for this. Fortunately, he hadn't eaten for fourteen hours, fretting that a caesarean would be necessary. So when Karl took the newborn human/amphibian from him, and he leaned his bloody hands on his knees to retch, nothing came up. Everyone in the delivery room—Abwehr and Gestapo alike—had hurried out after Karl to inspect the infant. Staggering back to Emera, he'd stroked her peaceful, dozing face and wept.

And wondered what was wrong with him.

The Fatherland would have its perfect saboteur. Thousands upon thousands of German lives would be saved.

"Are you listening to me, Johannes? I've waited six months. I want to see my baby. I demand to see him."

"He isn't a baby anymore. He's almost four feet long, big as an eight-year-old. He's talking." Or was, Johannes amended silently. Until a month ago, when he began to turn savage. Canaris hadn't seen him since the change. The admiral was still hoping to begin Meersohn's training soon, but in this state it would be impossible. I must get Canaris in here to show him, Johannes thought. Bring him in at two A.M., like last time. Tonight, if possible—I'll put it in my message.

"Emera, can we discuss this in an hour? I'm writing a report to my superiors. I must finish it."

She took his hands. "Johannes, do you care for me?"

"Of course I do. Haven't I said so many times?"

"Do you love me?"

Oh dear. What to say? "I think I may. You are the first woman I've ever cared for so deeply. I have nothing to compare it to."

It seemed to satisfy her. She said, "If you do not get me in to see my baby right away, I will kill myself."

He stared at her, shocked. "You mustn't even think such a thing."

"I mean it."

"Emera, the lab is under guard at all times. If I take you there, Major Grau will be told. If his superiors know you've seen it, they may keep you here for the entire war—which might be years."

"I don't care. They're keeping me here anyway, aren't they? So I want to see it. I must."

Pulling free of her grip, he paced to his window and rubbed at his face, shaken. Would she really kill herself? If he refused her, and she did it, how could he live with himself?

"All right."

Her face brightened. "Oh, Johannes, thank you. I won't make you sorry, no matter what. I promise."

"It will be a shock. You must prepare yourself."

"I've been preparing for months, since the day he was born. Before he came into this world, I thought I could live without seeing him, but once I knew he was here, only a little distance away from me, impossible. I know it won't be easy, but I'm ready."

You're a wreck, is what you are, he thought with another spasm of guilt. And who can blame you, poor Emera? He thought of taking her into his bathroom, rinsing her eyes with cold water, or combing her hair, then decided against it.

Let the guard see her as she was, feel the urgency. Maybe it would be one of the Abwehr men tonight, though lately the guards had been mostly Major Grau's—another warning sign he must put in his report.

He led Emera down the carpeted hall that smelled always of wax and polish, between the huge paintings of glowering German dukes and princes, to the broad central stairway of the villa. A baroque wonder of varnished oak, it squared its way down from a glorious chandelier in the ceiling of the third floor to the tiled warrens of the basement, where the labs were. He could hear Emera breathing in small, excited gasps as they descended. Despite the runner of burgundy carpet, each step seemed to creak louder than the last. The dining hall, where most of the project staff would be this time of day, was at the end of the west wing, well away from here, but all it would take was one straggler to spot the two of them heading down together, and Grau would know within minutes.

They reached the bottom of the stairwell without encountering anyone, and Johannes felt a small relief. He glanced at Emera to see if she was all right. She managed a little smile, tight with foreboding.

He was glad for her fear. It would arm her against shock.

The guard at the door was Joachim Schwarz, one of Grau's, a stolid fellow, none too bright—a member of Hitler's Brownshirts a few years back. Not the worst, but not the best, either, which would have been one of Canaris's men. Now, even if they could talk their way in, Major Grau would certainly hear of it.

"Good evening, Doctor. Fräulein."

"Miss Bettendorf would like to see her son."

Schwarz frowned. "But Major Grau said it would be best if she did not see it—him."

"It has become necessary. I'm in charge of the project and I authorize it."

"The *medical* part of the project," Schwarz corrected him. "Major Grau is in charge of security."

"Schwarz, you can't be thinking Miss Bettendorf would harm her own son. She just wants to see him. She understands it will be a shock."

"Still. . . ."

The man seemed to be waiting for something. A bribe? Johannes fished in his pocket, pulled out a wad of deutsche marks. Schwarz eyed the bills, but still hesitated.

Johannes said, "Of course, neither Miss Bettendorf nor I will ever say anything to anyone about this."

"I could get in a lot of trouble."

"If you don't tell anyone, who's to know?"

"What if Major Grau comes along while you're in there?"

"I will take full responsibility."

Schwarz snatched the money and stood aside. "Remember what you just said, Herr Doktor. And please be quick."

Johannes went through the door first, nagged by a sense of wrongness. That was too easy, he thought.

Or had Canaris's habitual paranoia finally worn off on him?

When Emera was in the small security anteroom, the outer door locked behind her, Johannes used his key to unlock the door to the main lab. The large room was dim, as usual. Meersohn had no eyelids to shield his retinas from light, just the extra, transparent membranes that commonly protected the eyes of snakes by repelling minor debris and keeping the moisture in.

Johannes looked around, first at the pool and then at the low enclosure filled with fragrant, black earth from the Tiergarten. The shower nozzles in the ceiling above the enclosure sprayed suddenly, making Emera cry out.

"It's all right," he told her. "They're on timers. They keep the earth damp, the way Meersohn likes it."

A gleaming row of canisters along the side of the lab caught Johannes's eye. They must have arrived in the week since he'd been in here. It looked like Major Grau had gotten his specifications for the various sizes right. Johannes could not resist straying over to inspect one. The lid seal looked good—a ring of vulcanized rubber which fit precisely into a groove around the canister head so the side handles could lock down tightly.

The *Abwehr* stamp on the side of each canister surprised him. Wouldn't Grau have preferred *Gestapo*? And then he understood: No one in all of Germany with half a brain would be stupid enough to open a canister marked by either intelligence service, and if something did go wrong, the *Abwehr* stamp would point the blame at Canaris rather than Himmler.

"Where is he? I don't see him." Emera's voice shook.

"I don't know. He should be either in the pool or the enclosure."

"But he was in here when you came earlier today?"

"I . . ."

"Johannes?"

"I've been terribly busy, Emera."

"How long since you've seen him?"

"Perhaps a week."

"You promised me you'd look in on him every day."

Her dismay shamed him. "I'm sorry. I was working under a deadline, but you're right, that's no excuse—"

A growl right at his elbow sent a cold shock through him. Emera let out a yelp. *What the hell?* Johannes stepped back from what he'd assumed was the shipping container the canisters had come in. It was too big to be much else— up to his shoulder and perhaps three meters wide by two deep.

Lifting the tarp that draped it, he jumped back as something rushed from the dark at him. He saw first the red eyes, then the bars of the cage, as Meersohn banged against them.

Johannes's jaw dropped in horror. "What . . . ?"

Emera gripped his arm. "Jo . . . han . . . nes."

Meersohn glared out at them, rubbing his shoulder. A cage, a barred cage like in a zoo, except it had a toilet stool in the corner and a pallet on the floor.

"What have they done to you?" Johannes whispered, appalled.

Meersohn bared his teeth.

"Johannes, you must get him out of there, now."

"How? The cage is locked and I don't have the key. I knew nothing about this, Emera, I swear it."

Meersohn was looking at her now, the long slash of mouth rippling in a snarl. Two months ago he had been talking, the accelerated development of amphibians matching up with the powerful brain and vocal physiology of a man. And then, a month ago, he'd fallen silent, at least whenever Johannes checked him over. Angry, agitated, but until a week ago, he'd still had free run of the lab. Not this, not caged up like an animal.

Meersohn wasn't an animal, he . . .

He *was* an animal.

We're all animals, Johannes thought, his mind reeling. Humans are just animals with big brains. "Why have they caged you?" he asked.

"Warum? Ich bin ein Scheusal. Scheusal!" It spat the last word.

Scheusal—monster. What cruel bastard had told him his name was Monster?

Emera stood frozen, her hands pressed to her mouth.

What was that on Meersohn's arms? Edging closer to the bars, Johannes made out dark, round circles up and down both biceps and forearms. An emerging pigment? The markings had not been there a week ago.

"What are they doing to you?"

"Pein!"

"Lieber Gott!" Emera whispered.

Pain. They've tormented him, Johannes thought with revulsion. They put these wounds on him.

But why?

Horrified, he said, "I will get you out of here, understand? Tonight. No more. No more."

Slowly, the lips closed over the terrible fangs. Meersohn turned away, leaning his head into a corner of the cage and going still. Had he understood?

I did this, Johannes thought, anguished. I helped them.

Turning, he took Emera's arm. She followed him into the anteroom, her legs stiff, feet not working right. He locked the lab door then hugged her to him, bringing her head around with his hand, feeling a deathly coldness in her cheeks.

"Listen to me," he said. "When we step through this door, there can be no hysterics in front of the guard. Just go to your room and get dressed. Put anything you want to take with you into your little suitcase and wait for me. I have a radio in my room. I will radio a coded call to my superior and he will send someone to pick us up."

"I won't leave Meersohn."

"We're not leaving him. You saw those canisters. We'll seal him inside one with a nutrient bath."

"But if you seal him in, how will he breathe?"

"If he's in there long enough for the air to run out, he'll go into hibernation and take oxygen through his skin from the fluid, which also has nutrients to support all vital functions. He'd be asleep, Emera. The fluid could support him for years, but he'll be in there only until we can get him away somewhere safe and try to undo what's been done. No more discussion. We must hurry. Can you do it?"

She gave a jerky nod, her eyes glazed with unshed tears.

Taking her other shoulder, he gave her a shake. She swallowed, blinked rapidly to clear her eyes. "All right. I'm all right."

"Good. You might have to wait awhile in your room, but don't worry. I'll come for you as soon as I've radioed and received confirmation we'll be picked up."

"How will you get Major Grau to let us go?"

"We're not alone here, Emera. We have friends who will act with us—"

"Johannes, are you sure? The past few days, I haven't seen as many people around. Mostly just the ones who act friendly with the major."

His heart skipped a beat. Could this be true? Not just Karl but all of them gone? He'd been in a fog, working on the formula for the life-support fluid, testing it on frogs, spending twelve hours a day in the lab, even taking his meals at his bench. Today, when Karl hadn't shown up, had been his first clue anything was wrong, but it might be far worse than he'd thought.

"We have to try," he said. "If they stop us, the people my superior will send will come in and get us out. All right?"

She nodded.

He wished he could feel as positive as he'd just sounded.

As they left the anteroom, Schwarz eyed Emera. "Are you all right, miss?"

She pushed past him, and Johannes wished she had said something to reassure the guard, but maybe no comment was best, because, by the look on her face, she'd come within an inch of clawing Schwarz's eyes out.

Johannes checked all the radio's tubes again to make sure they were glowing, then nudged the case around until it was perfectly square with the desk. The underside of his lip panged him distantly.

Come on, Admiral, come on, come on.

Over an hour since he'd transmitted. Canaris had promised to be accessible night and day. Maybe he was wondering if his young protégé had lost his nerve.

I fought Indians in the jungle, Johannes thought. I

stayed calm while a deadly poisonous snake crawled up me. Just because I'm young—

The radio chattered, the sign-on burst of clicks from Canaris himself. Grabbing a pad, Johannes wrote down the short groups of letters. The message ended and he grabbed his copy of *The Street Guide to Berlin,* the key for this date, and found the page the first grouping indicated, working through the substitutions: Canaris was brief: *Extraction confirmed for two and canister. Twenty-two hundred hours, front drive.*

Ten o'clock, one hour from now.

Johannes started for the door. Emera must be half crazy with worry by now. He'd go to her, let her know the plan, then find whomever he could of Canaris's people to help him in the lab. No one but the guard should be down there this time of night. If he could find even one Abwehr man, that should be enough—

At the door, he stopped, remembering the gun Canaris had given him. He hated guns, but maybe tonight he should make an exception. Returning to his bed, he reached between the mattress and box springs, pulled the Mauser out, and slid it into his pants pocket. It made him feel heavy on one side as he walked. Surely if he ran into anyone in the halls, they'd see the outline in his pocket and know everything.

But he met no one. At Emera's door, he knocked softly, then louder. No answer. Maybe she was in the bathroom.

Stepping into her parlor, he found the lights off. A hollow feeling expanded in his gut. She kept the bathroom light on even when she slept. Flicking the switch by the door, he blinked in the sudden brilliance of the chandelier, then his breath left him.

Emera hung from the chandelier, her feet circling the crimson rosette in the center of her carpet. A chair lay kicked over, a meter from her feet.

He lunged to her side, grabbing her around the thighs and lifting to take her weight off the cord, praying to hear her cough or gasp. Nothing. He had to let her down again to grab the chair. His breath came in sobs as he stood on the chair and grabbed her around the waist, lifting with his hip and one arm so he could work at the knot with his other hand, dimly aware it was the cord of her bathrobe. His fingernail broke in a spark of pain and then the knot came loose, and he sprawled to the floor with her.

Scrambling to hands and knees, he pressed his head against her chest. No heartbeat. Her tongue protruded and her eyes stared into infinity.

Still, he rolled her over and pulled at her arms, trying artificial respiration, feeling his own breaths tear his throat as he begged God not to let this be, to back up an hour, let him bring her to his room and keep her with him.

Dead, she was dead.

On the floor beneath the chandelier, he saw the note:

Dear Johannes. I'm sorry. It's more than I can bear. I do love you. Emera.

No, he thought. She did not write this. He felt a bulging pressure in his head. For a moment, he knew nothing, then came to himself striding around her room. The Mauser was in his hand, and he tasted metal on the roof of his mouth.

Grau did this, he thought. Grau.

You filthy bastard, I'll kill *you.*

Grabbing up the note, he stuffed it in his pocket. He closed Emera's bathrobe over her, tears stinging his eyes.

Pain.

A terrible clarity lit his mind. They've been working on Meersohn at night, he thought. They wouldn't risk it during the day, when I might catch them and report it to Canaris. Torturing him, tormenting him, they are probably down there hurting him right now.

And then he was at the bottom of the central staircase,

with no memory of having gotten there, striding toward the
lab door, where Schwarz was still on guard. As the big man
turned, Johannes held the Mauser out at him. Schwarz's
eyes widened, and he reached for the Schmeisser machine
pistol he'd propped by the door.

"Touch it and you die." The voice that came out of Johannes was not his own.

Schwarz raised his hands above his head. "Whatever
you say, Herr Doktor. But you—"

"Shut up." He realized he'd forgotten to take the safety
off the pistol. "Get down on the floor," he said, and
Schwarz complied, stretching out facedown. Picking up
the Schmeisser, Johannes slammed the wooden stock into
the back of Schwarz's head, as hard as he could.

"Gah—" Schwarz said as his nose broke against the
floor. He lay still.

Johannes looked at the Schmeisser, the clear spot in his
brain calculating whether he'd be able to shoot it. He could
not find the safety. It might kick too hard. No.

He put it back down, took the safety off the Mauser as
Canaris had shown him, and let himself into the anteroom.
He could hear voices through the inner door, not German,
English. And then something else . . . Russian? Easing his
key over, he opened the door a crack and looked in. What
he saw made him fear he had lost his mind.

Three men stood in front of Meersohn's cage. One wore
a Soviet military uniform, one a British army uniform, and
the third the attire of a U.S. Army captain. The one in the
American uniform was Major Reinhard Grau. The others
were his top two lieutenants.

"You disgust me, *Scheusal*," Grau said to Meersohn—
Scheusal the only German word, the rest in English.
"You're so ugly. We Americans kill and eat your kind."

Meersohn turned away. Poking a metal rod through the

bars, Grau touched the tip to Meersohn's shoulder. Meersohn screamed and jumped away.

Electric shock, Johannes thought, sickened. *Pain.*

Grau shocked him again and this time Meersohn leapt at him, raging, trying to get at him through the bars.

"Good!" Grau said in German. "Very good." A box inside the cage opened, and a piece of raw meat dropped down. Turning away, Meersohn scrambled for it, ripping and tearing with his teeth. With horror, Johannes saw that it was a human arm, tattooed with a prison camp number.

The bulging pressure filled his head again.

He stepped through the door and into the room, unaware of his feet touching the ground. He was almost to Grau before the major turned. "Dr. Witte! What is that? A little pistol?"

Johannes pushed the barrel of the Mauser into the center of Grau's chest and pulled the trigger. Grau looked astonished at the loud bang. Blood spurted from the tie of the American uniform. His knees thrust forward and he leaned back, smacking the floor with his head before settling with a rattle in his throat.

His two lieutenants were still frozen in shock.

Johannes pointed the pistol at the one in a Soviet uniform and pulled the trigger twice more, two loud bangs ringing through the lab as the man spun away, dancing as if on hot coals, then sprawled facedown into the dirt of Meersohn's enclosure.

The Gestapo man in the British uniform tried to edge past him, his face a distorted mask of fear, saying something Johannes could not hear.

He shot this man, too, pulling the trigger three times and watching him fall and kick himself around in a circle on the floor before going still.

Johannes sat down and leaned against the bars of Meer-

sohn's cage, staring at the blood now spreading around
Grau's body. After a moment, he felt a hand on his shoulder, and in a dim part of his mind realized it was Meersohn,
but he was too tired to acknowledge it.

Some time later, a man was leaning over him, and he
realized it was Canaris.

All of a sudden he could move and speak again. "About
time," he said.

"Dr. Witte," the admiral said in a disbelieving voice.
"What have you done?"

"You were right about them. Too bad neither of us has
been right about himself. You have the stone and the formula. If you want to make another, I can't stop you. But
my son and I are finished with this."

Canaris looked past him into the cage. Johannes realized Meersohn's hand was still on his shoulder.

The admiral passed a hand over his eyes. "You can't
stay in Germany. We must get you far away as soon as possible, tonight—now. The Abwehr has a man in the U.S.
Army. He's in France right now. I'll get you to the border
and he can take you to America, where you'll be safe from
the Gestapo and Himmler. Fräulein Bettendorf can go with
you."

"Grau hanged her in her room."

The admiral's face blanched. "The swine."

"I won't go without my son," Johannes said.

"I can't let the Americans have him."

"That's not going to happen."

"They are going to join the war against us, Dr. Witte.
It's only a matter of time."

"Not with my son."

"I know you mean that, but tonight proves we can't always control even what we are determined to control."

"That's a chance you'll have to take."

Canaris looked exasperated. "Why must I take that chance, Doctor? Tell me."

"For the same reason you'll destroy the stone. When you see what is right, you do it, no matter the danger. It's the way you are, or I'd never have followed you."

CHAPTER 20

⬅

"We need to talk," Andrea said.

"Go ahead, I'm listening." Terrill adjusted the water-proof pack on his chest where he stowed his Glock, letting out straps to bring it lower. She glanced down the hallway. Secretary Hastings had left, towing General Wallis in his wake, but the marine support unit remained on watch, and most of the full platoon of SEALs were within earshot, sixteen men securing their rebreathers, doing final checks of their gear and weapons.

Taking Terrill by the arm, she led him back behind the stand of arc lights, where the glare and noise from the generator would give them some privacy.

"I didn't look," he said, "if that's what you think. And I made sure none of my swabs did either."

She realized he meant when she'd stepped back here to strip down and pull on her wetsuit. She choked back a laugh. Right now, she could care less if he'd seen her in her bra and panties. When Terrill died, would his last thought be about sex?

Are we about to die?

Her stomach thrummed; she felt jacked up, like she'd slammed five cups of coffee. *We have a chance. I know who he is, if he'll just let me talk.*

She said, "I've found out what we're dealing with."

"Then everyone should hear it."

"No."

He stared at her. "Andrea, I won't endanger my men by keeping them in the dark—"

"Your men couldn't be in any more danger whether they know what I'm going to say or not." She summarized what her father had told her about how the creature came to be.

Terrill leaned against the concrete wall of the Pentagon's subbasement, rubbing his blond hair back flat along his scalp. "Christ, Andrea, if you seriously believe this vicious bastard is your half brother, I can see why you don't want that to get out. But you *can't* be serious. I've seen the murdering son of a bitch, and if it's a deformed human being, the elephant man was Ben Affleck. We're not talking bearded ladies or nine-foot-tall men, here. Line up every circus freak in history and none would come close."

"People in sideshows were not deformed on purpose, Terrill. This baby was. The reason you're having trouble believing it is because we don't even want to think about it. Birth defects—just the words make our minds recoil, but we can't afford that now. Is Ed Jeffers a freak? He was born with only one normal arm. Other people are born with six fingers on each hand. Maybe someday a composer will write a piano concerto just for one of them, and then the rest of us will be the freaks."

"Come on, Andrea—"

"You had gills starting out, and you've probably got a tail too small to see."

"No fucking way."

"Way, Terrill. Don't feel bad, most of us have vestigial tails hidden away at the ends of our spines. Genes are a code, billions of switches flipping up or down, mostly before we're born. When we're in the womb and everything's flashing like it never will again, moments come and go when a dose of the wrong stuff could alter enough ones and zeros to bring us out half chimp, or give us gills or webbed feet. You won't find that in any book because we've never put it to the test, thank God. We're too civilized to imagine purposely drugging mothers during pregnancy to produce abnormal babies. Except, maybe, if our backs were against the wall, and we thought a new kind of human might save us." Her throat ached suddenly. *My own father.*

Maybe you had to be there.

Terrill glanced back into the light, where his men now stood around waiting. Andrea's nerves twanged with urgency. Time was short. Getting Terrill on her side was a long shot, but she had to try.

"This thing can actually talk?" he asked.

"German."

"And you can, too. You were coy about that before, but you speak it, don't you?"

"Terrill, we've got to get moving. Tell your platoon they're looking for a circular plug of dirt around two feet across that looks smoother than the earth around it. The plug will probably be a foot or less above the waterline. Whoever finds it is *not* to dig through. They are to report to me. There will be no digging until I'm there. And once we've broken through, I will go in alone."

"Like hell."

"I'm serious."

"So am I, Andrea. I'm not going to let it get you, too."

"He *is* my half brother. I can tell him that—in his own language. I can talk to him, maybe end this without any more blood in the water, but not if you're pointing a gun at him."

Terrill's expression hardened. "Dr. Deluca, this beast having some of your genes doesn't cut any ice with me— and it damn well shouldn't with you. You never spent five minutes with the bastard so it is not your brother any way but technically. It *is* a vicious fuck that killed my best friend and took Ed Jeffers—"

"But Ed may still be alive. My brother saw that he was deformed, too, and that may be the reason he took him, not to kill him but to . . . to *be* with him."

Terrill spat on the floor. The violent heat of it sent a shock crackling around her heart. "If it has kept Ed Jeffers alive," he said, biting off each word, "and you can negotiate to get him back, great. But the only way I keep my men on the other side of the wall is if I go in with you."

A sense of futility weighed her down. *You'd keep your men out whether I asked it or not, because you have to be who kills him.*

Arguing was useless, she knew. She must think of Ed now. He'd suffered a head injury, knocked out cold when Terrill had seen him inside the wall. Assuming he'd come to, he'd be hungry and dehydrated by now—a man with his list of near phobias would not drink filthy water until he was half mad with thirst. Even if he was alive, he might be dying, whether her half brother wanted it or not. If they found the hidden tunnel, she'd just have to do her best to keep Terrill from shooting. For Ed, time was wasting.

"I go in with you," Terrill repeated. "That's it."

"All right," she said.

• • •

In the water she had trouble calming her breath, jerking air like there wouldn't be enough. She'd told Torpedo Mack she'd dived plenty of rivers, and she had, but never like this, in light no human brain was meant to see. Swimming underground in a Styx not mythical but real, a shoreless river of death, carrying blood and body parts under a pentagram of earth with the power to decide the fate of all Earth—

Forcing air from her overinflated lungs, she searched for calm. The concrete mountain above her had another reality, too, different from what she'd imagined—a place with pizza and Beanie Babies and pictures of families on the desks, where normal folks named Dixie and Joshua and Ed prayed for peace while keeping the nation's powder dry.

Dear God, please soak Terrill's bullets now.

His fins sent bursts of pressure against her mask, swiping up and down a few feet from her face, and then he veered to the left wall of the tunnel—time for another spot check. His fins stopped thrashing and sank to a foothold where the bottom curved up. Surfacing with him, she stared at the walls on either side, studying every inch for a sign of burrowing.

Nothing.

Glancing at Terrill, she could not be sorry he'd insisted on sticking with her. The black suit molded his corded muscles, giving them an inhuman sheen, a powerful frogman with a talent for killing. She'd thought of Terrill when Dad had told her how Meersohn had been brutally trained and conditioned to kill. The founding job of SEALs was underwater demolition and sabotage. Did Terrill realize he was an inferior prototype of the being he hunted? That brutality had been systematically applied to him, too, to condition him to take life? Did he get that the monster he now yearned to kill was actually one of his own, raised to perfection, the ultimate frogman?

"Lieutenant! Doctor!"

The shout echoed up and down the tunnel. Andrea's skin prickled against the suit. She sent up another quick prayer: *God, help me save them both.*

As soon as she saw it, Andrea knew it was what they were looking for—a rounded plug of dirt a foot above the waterline. Four of the platoon held Terrill and Mark Rowalski up the curving wall so they could dig. Clay-rich dirt splattered down into the water, the only sound, everyone keeping a disciplined quiet.

And then the dirt stopped coming.

Rowalski gave a thumbs-up, and the two men straining to hold him aloft on the wall let him slide back down into the water.

With alarm, Andrea saw that Terrill wasn't backing out but wiggling through, his waist disappearing, then his hips.

Lunging, she caught his ankle.

Rowalski put a hand on her arm, then let her slap it away.

Terrill, you bastard, you promised, squeezing her fury into his ankle.

He stopped wiggling and backed out of the hole, smeared with dirt. Keeping a hold on the bottom edge, he held a hand out to her. Other men put their hands on her rump and knees, shoving her up. As she wormed, head and shoulders, into the hole, she felt a crushing claustrophobia, all the building's weight on her back now. She forced herself to keep breathing, just another specimen dive, yeah.

Her head emerged into the parallel tunnel.

She looked left: nothing.

Her half brother was there on her right, ten yards away, glaring at her with his beautiful red eyes; crouched in a shallow cave he'd dug into the side of the tunnel, his tail coiled behind him, hands and feet both down, ready to spring. She could also see a pair of legs in a filthy suit.

They weren't moving.

The weight on her chest increased.

She said, *"Ich heisse Andrea—"*

"Andrea?" Ed's voice.

Joy swept her. But he sounded so weak. "Are you all right?"

"I just got a lot better." His head emerged from the back edge of the cave into the tunnel, his goggled face filthy, except for a spotless ring around his mouth that gave him a clownish look. Where had he gotten goggles?

Never mind.

With shaky movements, he turned his body away from her, to hide the wizened arm. His shame pained her, but she could not think about that now.

In German, she said to Meersohn, "I have no weapons. I'm your sister. I'm here to help you."

He stared at her, the massive shoulder muscles quivering. The tunnel was rank with his fishy smell.

"Please," she said. "We can end this."

"Schwester," he said.

She felt Terrill squeezing her ankle back on the other side. She tried to kick his hand loose, but he wouldn't let go, of course not. She'd never keep him out of here, and he'd pull her back unless she continued through.

"I'm coming through," she said to Meersohn. "A man will follow. He wants to shoot you but I can stop him if you'll stay still."

Meersohn's long mouth twitched up at the corner in what might be a bitter smile, but he said nothing.

She wormed forward, showing her brother her empty hands, letting Terrill push at her feet until her weight took her and she slid on her belly down into the water. The current here was much stronger than on the other side of the wall, sweeping her toward the cave. She realized what it meant—they were near the retaining wall in the earth, and there was a big hole in it. Before she could complete the thought, the big arm struck down at her. Fear stopped her breath but she did not resist as his fingers intertwined in her hair. With effortless ease, he pulled her up from the water into the cave. On her hands and knees facing Ed, she held herself still, waiting for the hand to let go of her hair.

"He won't hurt you," Ed said.

"It's okay, I'm all right."

He settled back with a groan. Crusted blood covered one side of his head, over his left ear.

"His head is hurt," her brother said into her ear.

She felt the big face nuzzling the back of her head, and then her cheek, his foul, snuffling breath nearly choking her. What was he doing?

"Vater?" he inquired.

Smelling me—his father's DNA.

I'm why he crawled through the ductwork to Ed's office, she thought. His animal sense of smell told him he and I were the same litter, and his humanity made that mean something to him. He got wind of me in the sub-basement that first night, then tracked me to Ed's office.

Where I attacked him with the bright light.

Meersohn let go of her hair.

Down the tunnel, Terrill's head emerged from the hole. She did not like the set of his mouth. "Don't be afraid, brother," she said in German. "He's with me."

"I have seen him before. You're right, he wants to kill me."

"Show him your hands, Terrill."

He held his empty hands out, spreading his fingers, wiggling them in what Andrea knew was suppressed fury.

"Come on through," she said, "but stay down there."

"How? The current looks too fast." His voice was deathly calm; impossible, with the goggles, to tell where he was looking, but she knew he was staring at her brother, and that murder was in his eyes.

"Just keep an arm hooked in the hole," she told him, "and wait there for me. Ed's here. He's alive. I'm sure I can get him out if you just stay the hell back, Terrill."

"Whatever you say."

He slithered through into the water, hooking one arm back into the hole, just as she'd instructed, to hold himself in place.

Was this actually going to work?

Litter on the dirt between her and Ed registered—cellophane wrappers, and an empty Pellegrino bottle. Suddenly the clean space around Ed's lips made sense. "You brought this man food and water?" she asked her brother.

"From his place upstairs."

"I think he knocked over a vending machine for the Twinkies," Ed said. "I never tasted anything so good."

"Did you hear that, Terrill? He's been feeding Ed, bringing him water."

Down the tunnel, Terrill said nothing. The arm hidden away inside the hole worried her. Its hand had been empty a moment ago, but the whole platoon was probably on the other side of the wall by now, all of them packing, all itching to avenge their slain chief petty officer. There was no way on God's earth if the hand came out of that hole it would still be empty. The only thing keeping Terrill from shooting her brother right now was that she was in his line of fire.

Making sure she remained there, she turned back to Meersohn. "We have the same father."

He gazed at her. "The father of a monster."

"Is Ed a monster?" she asked.

"Hey," Ed said.

"Rest," she said over her shoulder, "and let me get you out of here."

"Ed is a *Mensch*," her brother said.

"Thank you," Ed said. "We're friends," he added. *"Freundin."*

She would have smiled if she weren't so afraid of Terrill. "You are a *Mensch*, too," she said to Meersohn. "What happened to Ed's mother before he was born was also done to yours. That's why you were born as you are. But you're as much a man as Ed."

"No. I'm a killer."

"Remember the men who caged you, hurt you if you wouldn't attack and gave you food when you did—men in uniforms?"

"I have been remembering." His head twisted away, and she saw his throat constrict.

She did not want to ask, but she had to, because Herb Bodine had not been wearing a uniform. "Why did you kill the first man, who was not a soldier?"

"He jumped on me. I was afraid."

And hungry, she thought, ravenous. At that first, confused moment of waking, your conditioning took over. Herb Bodine was food because the men who shocked you always rewarded you with raw, human meat for fighting back. That's what Dad said—reward and punishment, like Pavlov's dog. She said, "Those men hurt you to make you kill. You don't have to anymore. They're dead. You're free of them."

The broad, green chest heaved; he looked away from her, then down. "Too late."

"No," she said, "not if you leave here and never come back."

"Will you come with me?"

"I have to stay here and make the men you have angered believe you are dead."

"Like that one?" He nodded toward Terrill.

"No. He sees us. He'll have to know."

"He won't help you. I killed his man."

"He's my friend."

The misshapen head cocked. "As my mother was our father's friend?"

"No."

"What happened to our father?"

"Alive. But old. You were asleep a long time. His mind has weakened."

"He saved me."

"Yes."

"He should have killed me."

She wanted to protest, but what right did she have? How could she know what it was to be this cruelly morphed man, alone in all the world?

"Could you love me?" her brother said.

"I've loved life like yours since I was a child. But you have to get away. The water moves fast here. Is this a way out?"

"To the river. Around that bend, it drains back through a big hole in the wall. It's the best way in and out."

The sudden burst of fluency surprised her, a more adult phrase than he'd yet spoken. Those who had made him a monster had given him language so he could follow their commands. The thoughts that came with it, he'd found on his own.

She visualized the Potomac, remembering a remote place where she and Dad once searched out salamanders on a Sunday afternoon in the cloudy, leaf-scented coolness of autumn.

The father she'd thought she knew.

She said, "If you follow the river west for twenty kilometers, you'll come to an island in the middle. It starts with a rock as tall as me that looks like a man's face. The island has plenty of trees. There should be small animals to eat, or fish from the river. No people live there. You can be safe if you stay out of sight from the shores. The next time the moon is full, I'll come there to see you." *And by that time, I'll have figured out a way to get you where you can really be safe.*

"I should die." Her brother looked past her. "Your friend will shoot me now."

Turning, she saw with a shock that Terrill had let go of the hole and was nearly across from them, his right hand dug into the wall ahead to hold him against the current. The left pointed the Glock. Her brother had made no move to escape. With him sitting at the edge of the cave, no way could she get between him and Terrill.

"Don't," she said. "I'm begging you."

"I have to," Terrill said.

"He killed Link because you were coming after him."

"How about the colonel, those SWAT guys, the marine he killed in the hall, and that construction guy?"

"The worker attacked him; so did the SWAT team, and the others were all wearing the uniforms of his enemies. That's why he charged the Russian general. The last time he was awake, the world was at war. They made him a warrior, like you, but he'll never kill again. He understands his battle is over."

"Not quite."

"He could have killed you, Terrill."

"His mistake."

"It wasn't a mistake, and you know it. He could have kept me between us, until he was on you, then torn your head off."

"Let him kill me," Meersohn rasped. "I want to go back in the dark."

"No, you don't have to," she said in German. "If you give it time, the pain and the fury will be less."

"What did he say?" Terrill asked.

"Nothing." Her throat burned.

"Let him shoot me. I want to die."

A terrible urgency filled her. Meersohn didn't mean it. But no way was Terrill going to let him swim out of here.

Plan B, then. In English, she said, "I think he would let us take him back to the zoo. Confined, he'd pose no danger. We'd build him a habitat. . . ."

"Andrea."

"You can't kill him."

"Is that what he wants—to be a prisoner in a cage? Let you and your friends prod him and study him? Somewhere along the line, Andrea, one of you scientists will figure out how to make more of him. Once something like that is known, it will be done. There are people in the Pentagon who'd want you to do that for them."

"Bullshit," Ed said, his voice ragged with feeling.

"All right, if not our generals, someone else's. Can you imagine what al-Qaeda, with all the money they've managed to hide from us, would pay for a terrorist like this? This . . . whatever he is, he's a killing machine. He'd be worth an entire SEAL team. . . ." Terrill stopped, licked his lips, as if they'd gone dry.

It's dawning on him, Andrea thought with a sudden, cautious hope. If Terrill could see Meersohn not as a monster but as himself taken to the tenth power, maybe he wouldn't shoot.

Terrill aimed the Glock at her brother's forehead.

"Don't," Ed said.

"Turn your head, buddy." Terrill's finger started to squeeze the trigger.

"They programmed him to kill," Ed said, "just like we did you. You have to break that programming now."

"It isn't that easy," Terrill whispered. "He knows it. He wants to die, or he'd have killed me. Andrea's right. All he had to do was keep her in front until he got close to me. Link never had a chance up close, and neither would I. And I was not fucking programmed. I chose it."

"He didn't. They started on him before he was born."

Meersohn said, "I want to go back in the can, but the can is too small. There's nothing for me out here. Sleep was better. I want to sleep."

"Nein," Andrea whispered.

Meersohn put a hand on her shoulder, gentle at first, then gave her a rough shove. He started for Terrill, a clumsy, sluggish movement, far beneath his skills. The Glock was deafening in the confines of the tunnel. Terrill fired until the clip was empty.

EPİLOGUE

The Potomac River
October 2

The full moon rolled Andrea's shadow along the bottom of the boat to Ed's feet in the prow. The warm night, perfumed by cedar and weeping willow, had inspired a congregation of crickets in the woods on either shore. The river flowed wide and tranquil here, the lazy current moving with her. In the moonglow, the boat gleamed like a pearl on velvet.

"I do wish you'd let me row," Ed said. "It's not so bad, going in circles."

Smiling, she felt her tension ease. He'd begun showing a sense of humor about his arm, working to get them past it. Might just have a future with the man—if they could get through the next few weeks. Follow-up stories on the "Pentosauer" had faded back to page A22 in the *Post*. The

congressional hearings were running out of steam, thanks
to Secretary Hastings. As the House and Senate Armed
Services Committees had grilled them from their high
chairs, he'd beat back their demagoguery with—of all
things—candor:

"Mr. Secretary, if you did not create this monster in a
'black' project run without Congress's knowledge, where
did it come from?"

"The river, I presume. It was an amphibian."

"You say 'was,' but how can we be assured it's dead,
when no body has been found?"

"Senator, you have the sworn testimony of three people
whose integrity is beyond question. Lieutenant Terrill
Hodge, the U.S. Navy SEAL sent after the monster, testified that its head was nearly severed by a full clip from his
Glock before the current carried it away. Mr. Ed Jeffers,
who was abducted by the animal, saw and confirmed this.
Dr. Andrea Deluca, esteemed curator of herpetology for
the Smithsonian, also witnessed the shooting and confirmed in no uncertain terms to this committee that there is
zero possibility it survived."

"You don't seem to understand where I'm coming from,
Mr. Secretary. The world is already paranoid about us. What
must they think when day after day passes with military
divers combing the river and failing to find this animal?"

"That the current carried it away. By now, it is either
being eaten by crabs in the bay or currents have carried it
into the Atlantic."

"I wish I shared your confidence. Some say it's just too
convenient that the flow in the tunnel whisked the corpse
off before anyone could grab it."

"Convenient to whom, Senator? What motive could any
of those who testified have for not bringing the corpse
back with them?"

Andrea stopped rowing and gazed at the island ahead,

the dark silhouette of trees, the outcropping where she and Dad had once hunted salamanders. Irrational, to have thought she could spirit Meersohn here—she could see that now. The Secretary had asked the senator what motive they might have for not bringing back the body, and the Secretary had given a good answer, unaware as he was that Meersohn was buried deep beneath the Pentagon, the biggest building in the world for his tombstone.

She wondered, was there any difference between the sleep Meersohn had gone to and the soft embrace of earth the golden toads had chosen in the cloud forest of Monteverde? They hadn't come out, and neither would Meersohn. No one would study his corpse, no one would take his cells and implant them in a hollowed-out frog egg to make another of him. He would be a mystery, like the golden toads.

Like them, he would rest.

Maybe Terrill had been right, and it was the most merciful option available—to let Meersohn leave a world bound to exploit or destroy him. If death was sleep, awake had been the nightmare, men in blue and tan and olive drab uniforms, monsters who shocked him with a metal stick. Then awake again, hunted through tunnels by men bound to kill him.

Dad couldn't end him, she thought, and neither could I. It had to be Terrill.

She knew it was right.

And also that she'd never forgive Terrill.

For me, Alzheimer's is the enemy, Andrea thought. But maybe not for Dad.

"Land ho," Ed murmured.

Andrea backed on the oars, and the prow of the rowboat edged onto a narrow beach. Ed jumped out and pulled the boat up farther. Moonbeams slanted down between the trees, rippling through a waist-high bank of mist.

The place still had magic.

"Is the Amazon like this?" Ed asked.

"Not far different."

"I can see why you like it."

"So will you come on a field trip with me next summer?"

"Sure," he said at once, but she could hear the reservation in his voice.

"Guess who I saw yesterday," he said. "Terrill Hodge. He came up on leave from Norfolk and dropped by my office. Want to know if he asked about you?"

She took his hands, both of them. "Ed, listen carefully. I'm going to tell you the secret of women."

He cleared his throat. "Okay."

"We like to look at great male bodies, and we fantasize sex with Brad Pitt, but when it comes to hairy backs or potbellies or one arm being shorter than the other, it is the great good luck of men that we love who we love."

Leaning forward, she kissed him on the lips. For a moment, he was stiff, and then he melted, and both arms went around her. After a moment, he stepped back. He said, "Want me to tell you the secret of men?"

She laughed. "You don't have any secrets. Not from us."

"Then you tell me. Why did Terrill shave his head?"

in memoriam

◀━━━━━━━━━━━━━━━━━━━━━━━━━━━━━━━━━━━━▶

The author notes with sadness the passing, on June 22, 2002, of the incomparable David O. "Doc" Cooke, Mayor of the Pentagon. In 1958, having served in World War II, Doc retired from the U.S. Navy at the rank of captain. He was just getting started. For the next forty-four years, he served under and advised fifteen secretaries of defense as the department's top career professional, responsible for the Pentagon and everyone in it. In a position of great power, Doc showed even greater humility, avoiding the spotlight while loving and caring for his people. As the massive Pentagon renovation project got under way, Doc insisted on the Kevlar curtains, the steel walls, and the blast-resistant windows, which would save thousands of lives when the Pentagon was attacked. Afterward, he said, "We'll rebuild it," and he did. On the job at age eighty-two, he died from injuries suffered in a car crash, after living to see the smashed and gutted section of the building seamlessly restored to life. Doc was buried with full military honors in Arlington Cemetery, on a gentle slope where his spirit can continue to watch over the building and people he loved. In the words of Vice President Dick Cheney, one of the fifteen secretaries of defense who depended on Doc, "He represented the very best of the career men and women who serve this nation."

CLEAN

A NOVEL

CUT

THERESA

MONSOUR

PUTNAM